little black dress
· IT'S A GIRL THING ·

Dear Little Black Dress Reader,

Thanks for picking up this Little Black Dress book, one
of the great new titles from our series of fun, page-turning
romance novels. Lucky you — you're about to have a fantastic
romantic read that we know you won't be able to put down!

Why don't you make your Little Black Dress experience
even better by logging on to

www.littleblackdressbooks.com

where you can:

- ♥ Enter our **monthly competitions** to win
  gorgeous prizes
- ♥ Get **hot-off-the-press** news about our latest titles
- ♥ Read **exclusive** preview chapters both from
  your **favourite** authors and from brilliant new
  writing talent
- ♥ Buy **up-and-coming** books online
- ♥ Sign up for an essential slice of romance via
  our **fortnightly email** newsletter

We love nothing more than to curl up and indulge in an
addictive romance, and so we're delighted to welcome you
into the Little Black Dress club!

With love from,

The *little black dress* team

Five interesting things about Kate Lace:

1. When I left school I joined the army instead of going to university – there were 500 men to every woman when I joined up – yesss.

2. While I was there I discovered that there were more sports than hockey and lacrosse and learnt to glide, rock climb, pot hole, sail and ski. I also discovered that I wasn't much good at any of them but I had a lot of fun.

3. I met my husband in the army. We've been married for donkey's years. (I was a child bride.)

4. Since I got married I have moved house 17 times. We now live in our own house and have done for quite a while so we know what is growing in the garden. Also, our children can remember what their address is.

5. I captained the Romantic Novelists' Association team on University Challenge the Professionals in 2005. We got to the grand finals so I got to meet Jeremy Paxman three times.

By Kate Lace

The Chalet Girl
The Movie Girl
The Trophy Girl
The Love Boat
Moonlighting
A Class Act

A Class Act

Kate Lace

little
black
dress

First published in 2010 by
LITTLE BLACK DRESS
An imprint of HEADLINE PUBLISHING GROUP

A LITTLE BLACK DRESS paperback

1

Cataloguing in Publication Data is available from the British Library

ISBN 978 0 7553 4794 0

Typeset in Transit511BT by Avon DataSet Ltd,
Bidford-on-Avon, Warwickshire

Printed and bound in Great Britain by
Clays Ltd, St Ives plc

Headline's policy is to use papers that are natural, renewable and
recyclable products and made from wood grown in sustainable forests.
The logging and manufacturing processes are expected to conform to the
environmental regulations of the country of origin.

HEADLINE PUBLISHING GROUP
An Hachette UK Company
338 Euston Road
London NW1 3BH

www.littleblackdressbooks.com
www.headline.co.uk
www.hachette.co.uk

This book is for the RNA in recognition of fifty years of excellence in promoting and supporting romantic fiction as a genre. Here's to the next fifty!

And it is also for Ian, my hero. For everything.

Acknowledgements

I owe thanks to Ned Kingdon who made sure I used the correct terminology for the skateboarding bits. He was very patient with me – clearly recognising that I didn't have a clue about any of it. I think it's something to do with my age, Ned.

I owe my great friend Annie Ashurst a big thank you and possibly a very large drink for the 'mouse story'. It really happened (a poor little mouse got stuck to the floor in her garage) and she gifted it to me as a perfect way for two characters to meet. Now that's what I call friendship!

I must also thank Leah Woodburn for her great editorial input. She has a brilliant eye for the parts that need tweaking or clarifying and is incredibly tactful when she makes her suggestions. It's almost a pleasure doing the line edits.

And last but not least I want to thank Craig Fraser for my wonderful covers. I have loved every single one I've had for my books – they are just fabulous. So fab, in fact, I've had them all framed. And very classy they look, hanging side-by-side.

Tilly could hear Judith guiding a group of tourists through the great hall towards the main stairs, just as she was about to nip down them to the estate office and the only working computer in the place with internet access. Shit, it was Tuesday and she'd completely forgotten. And because it was Tuesday, it meant that she was supposed to be helping out with the visitors by standing guard in the long gallery and making sure none of them were demented enough to try and make off with any of the decrepit family heirlooms on display. As if they would; even the dumbest of their visitors would surely have more sense than to clutter up their own houses with the rubbish her family had accumulated over the centuries. She did acknowledge that the Gainsborough might be the exception, but it was the *only* thing in the entire house worth nicking. The last thing she wanted was to be stuck indoors answering inane questions from some ghastly coach party of Women's Institute stalwarts, or worse, family groups with kids her own age who would look at her as if she was something out of a freak show. Stuff the computer and downloading some music; that could wait. And stuff doing the job her father had specifically asked her to do; she couldn't face it, not again, and she was sure the long gallery would be fine without her. Escape was what was called for, and right now.

She dodged back up to the top floor while Judith

continued to inform her audience about the first owner of
the house, Guy de Liege, 'pronounced de Lee nowadays',
who had got it in 1080 by sucking up to William the
Conqueror. Only she didn't phrase the last bit quite like
that. But it amounted to the same thing, thought Tilly, as
she walked along the third-floor landing towards the back
stairs. Shame that sucking up to royalty these days didn't
cut any ice. If it did, she might have had a go at throwing
herself at William or Harry. Not that she wanted to marry
either of them – shit, no. But she wouldn't mind being a
casual shag if it got her a bank account with some cash in
it, a nice weatherproof house and a wardrobe full of
decent clothes.

She was halfway along the corridor when the heel of
her shoe caught in the worn carpet and she almost went
flying.

'Is there nothing in this crummy house that isn't
falling to bits?' she muttered angrily as she spun round to
glare at the offending hole. Like a lot of the soft furnishings, and even more of the structure of the house, it
was way past its 'best before' date. She made a note to
bring the defective carpet to the housekeeper's attention
– maybe Mrs Thompson could patch it up, as there
certainly wasn't the money to replace it.

She turned into the narrow passage that took her to
the back stairs. At least there were some bits of the house
that the bloody tourists never got to see, well away from
the prying eyes of the trippers, and which provided a
haven for her, her sisters and her dad. Of course the
bits not on show were the bits in the worst shape; the bits
with the damp patches, the threadbare carpets, the
pale rectangles on the walls where some painting or other
had had to be sold to pay to mend the vast expanse of roof,
most of which seemed to leak. And of course, as the
family's private rooms were all on the top floor, they got
the full benefit of the pails and old hip baths that had

been strategically placed to catch the worst of the drips in the winter when the roof's shortcomings were at their most obvious.

If the tourists only knew how slummy this place really was, thought Tilly savagely. If this were a council house, the tenants would have been moved out years ago and the whole place flattened. Dry rot, wet rot, damp, mould and mildew were just a few of the endless things that they had to wage a perpetual war against, to say nothing of mice, woodworm and death-watch beetle. Unfit for human habitation was probably putting the crumbling wreck in a flattering light. She thought there were rats that lived in better holes than this place, because rats were about the only vermin she could think of that they *didn't* have a problem with. A place too crappy even for rats to live in – that must be a first!

She ran down the narrow, uneven back stairs, her feet instinctively making adjustments for the variety of depths of the risers of the six-hundred-year-old steps – the back stairs being a relatively modern addition to the original fabric of the house. She reached the bottom and peered round the partially open oak door to check that the visitors had vacated the great hall and had been swept onwards into the kitchens by Judith.

The kitchens had been made over when Henry VIII was king and had once been the last word in design. They were now one of the main draws for the trippers who came to see over the place. The copper pans around the wall gleamed, a roaring (faux) log fire, complete with a spit big enough to take a whole pig, burned in the gargantuan grate, the huge table groaned with (plastic) produce, and (realistically stuffed, long-dead and preserved) pheasants, hares and deer lay artfully draped over another table as the (waxwork) cook brandished her knife ready to skin and gut them for a feast. Along one wall was a dresser laden with antique glasses, dishes, tureens and bowls, which the family never now used as they couldn't afford to entertain, despite the fact that the paying visitors were given the impression that the residents still lived in the luxury and style of their ancestors and ate like princes every night.

The reality was that the family cooking was done in a 1960s Formica and quarry-tiled kitchen – which now was more of a health hazard than a leper with plague wandering through IKEA on a crowded Saturday – up on the third floor, which had been installed originally for the maids before the last-but-one round of death duties had stripped the family of every last bit of spare cash. Furthermore, they lived mostly on a diet of mince, fish fingers and tins from the reduced bin at the local supermarket and frequently ate in front of the ancient TV in the tatty sitting room, which, with a portable Calor Gas fire, low ceiling and thick curtains, was the one room in the house they could guarantee to be warm all year round, especially as the dining room radiators didn't seem to be able to compete with the through-draughts. If only the trippers knew, thought Tilly as she slipped into the great hall and then out of the side door hidden behind a screen, which had primarily been placed there to hide the woodworm in the panelling rather than anything else.

Once outside, she made her way through the pretty but overgrown garden – their one remaining gardener, Thompson, who had to cope with fifteen acres single-handedly, was fighting a permanently losing battle with every weed known to mankind – round to the main entrance.

'Boo,' said Daisy, popping up from behind the lavender hedge, her blonde curls dancing and her blue eyes glinting with mischief.

Tilly jumped, her guilty conscience at escaping from her allotted task making her nervous. 'What the fuck do you think you're playing at?' she snapped at her ten-year-old sister. Besides, having escaped from the awfulness of the guided tour, she was in no mood to play stupid games with her siblings.

'Christ, you're such a pain when you're in a mood,' said Flora, Daisy's identical twin, appearing from behind the hedge on the other side of the path.

'It's Tuesday,' said Tilly bleakly by way of explanation.

The twins sighed. They'd forgotten what day it was too. 'It's always bloody Tuesday,' grumbled Flora.

'Except when it's Thursday, Friday or Saturday. How would the trippers like it if we tramped round their poxy houses?' asked Daisy.

'I expect they'd love it; being visited by "wan of the oldest femilees in the countree",' said Tilly, doing a perfect impression of Judith's rather strangled vowel sounds. Her sisters giggled. None of them liked Judith, the senior guide, who gave them grief for not taking more of an interest in their family history and heritage and sprang questions about long-dead relations on them at every opportunity and then looked smug and superior when they couldn't answer.

'Aren't all families old?' asked Flora. 'I mean, don't we all have the same number of ancestors? Aren't all humans descended from apes or Neanderthals?'

'Well, you two certainly are,' said Tilly, although she conceded to herself that her sister had a valid point, not that she'd give the twins the satisfaction of admitting it. Little sisters had to be kept in their place, especially as the twins had a nasty habit of ganging up against her that had to be discouraged at every opportunity. Give them an inch and they'd take a mile. 'The only reason Judith bangs on about our family is that it's better documented than most.'

'And Judith knows *all* the names.'

Tilly sighed. Didn't she just. And their nicknames, and their mistresses' names, and probably the names of their dogs and cats. And their favourite colours. But stuff Judith. Thinking about her and talking to her sisters was just delaying her and making it more likely that she would be caught by her father and forced to help out with the tourists.

'Still, on the plus side, the house'll be closed to the public after this week. And thank fuck for that.' Like a lot of visitor attractions and stately homes, the 'open' season stopped at the autumn half-term, before resuming again around Easter. 'Anyway, sod the visitors, I'm off,' she said as she moved on down the path.

'Where are you going?' the twins shouted in unison at her departing back view.

'Out.'

'Where?'

But Tilly didn't answer. She didn't want the girls following her. She shoved her hand in the pocket of her skirt to make sure the fags she'd nicked from her father's packet were still safely there. And the box of matches she'd pinched from the kitchen. And the fiver she'd liberated from the housekeeping. She made her way out of the gardens and on to the vast expanse of gravel at the front of the mansion that lay like a lake between it and the gatehouse. She scrunched her way over it, head down, hoping none of the staff would see her go. Her father would be livid if he found out, because he wanted her on hand as free labour. Well he could shove that, thought Tilly rebelliously. If he wanted her to be there, he ought to pay her. His argument that it was her heritage he was trying to preserve cut no ice with her. She hadn't asked to be conceived. It was his idea to have kids.

She stood to the side of the kiosk in the gatehouse, out of sight of the cashier's window, choosing her moment to make her bid for freedom. After a couple of minutes half a dozen punters pitched up wanting to visit and she used the opportunity to fly past.

'Matilda,' bawled her father, who was the duty ticket-seller. Shit – that was all she needed. No pretending she'd just forgotten her duty now. He would know from the way she'd deliberately ignored him that she was skiving. But sod it. She'd face the music another time. She raced away, her long, tanned limbs effortlessly covering the yards, over the moat and down the tree-lined avenue that led to the main road and the town.

A few minutes later she leaned, puffing slightly, against the pillar of the huge stone entrance ('erected by William de Liege in 1783', as Judith would tell the punters if they enquired – and often even if they didn't) till her breathing steadied. At least, she thought, there was one advantage to always being utterly broke and not being able to afford designer labels; like almost everyone else in the country she shopped at Primark so was able to blend in with the locals pretty seamlessly. And because there was never the money to allow her to go to the sort of society junkets she saw featured in *Tatler* or *OK!*, society junkets that the daughters of her father's friends and most of her peers at school seemed to go to, she never got her picture taken by the press either. She didn't think there was anyone in Haybridge who would be able to pick her out as the local posh totty.

She strolled along the road to the bridge over the river and then up the hill and on to the main shopping street that crossed at right angles. Like most towns Haybridge had all the major chain stores, interspersed with occasional boutiques, an independent bookseller, a couple of antique dealers who over the last few years (when the tax man had made threats they hadn't been able to ignore) had fleeced their dad when he'd been forced to sell the family silver to pay the bills, plus the usual range of fast-food franchises, small supermarket outlets and a bookie.

She slipped in the door of the betting shop, filled out

a slip and handed it over to the cashier along with the pinched fiver.

'Gentrified to win in the three thirty-five at Haydock Park,' checked the woman behind the counter, barely giving Tilly a look.

'Yeah.' She tried to sound bored but was really bricking it that the old bag would ask to see ID to prove she was over eighteen, ID that she didn't have because she wasn't. Well, not quite.

The woman entered the bet into the system and handed Tilly her receipt, still hardly glancing at her customer. Relieved, Tilly took it and tucked it carefully back in her pocket along with the matches and the fags. If the nag came in first, she'd get over fifty quid back. On paper it bloody well should, but that was the problem with the gee-gees: predicted form and reality didn't always match up. At least her family had been good for one thing: her dad and her uncle both knew a lot about horse flesh and had taken her to the races at Haybridge racecourse for as long as she could remember. They'd taught her how to read the form books, and while most of the lessons she'd endured at school had made almost no impression on her brain, every word about blood lines, trainers, form, the going and jockeys had stuck with her. She didn't always win when she placed a bet, but she made more than she lost. And hopefully this bet wouldn't be an exception. Not that there was anything she could do now except keep her fingers crossed.

Glancing at her watch, she saw she still had a couple of hours before the horse ran. Skint and bored, she wandered idly along the high street, staring at the enticing things in the shop windows, none of which she could even dream of buying. Even if her horse won, she had other demands on the money – her mobile phone bill for a start. Wouldn't it be wonderful, she wished for the umpteenth time in her life, not to have to worry about money? Wouldn't it be wonderful to be rich? Fat chance of that, though.

She got to the end of the street, at the point where the shops ran out and the rows of terraced houses started, and considered her options. She could go back the way she'd come and do more pointless and frustrating window-shopping, or she could go to the rec and hang out there. The rec seemed marginally the less shit option. And anyway, she still had the fags burning a metaphorical hole in her pocket, and if she hung out there she could have a smoke in peace and quiet. The rec it was then.

Ashley stood at the top of the half-pipe, his skateboard balanced on his left toe, as he contemplated the drop. It wasn't extreme and he'd seen other, younger kids tip themselves down the vertiginous slide, swoop up the other side and land safely on the opposite platform. Of course it could be done. He just needed to go for it. The trouble was, unlike the kids he'd seen whizzing up, down and over the ramps and pipes of the skate park or grinding along the rails, he hadn't been a skateboarder since he was old enough to stand. In fact he hadn't been a skateboarder until a couple of weeks ago, when a mate of his had bet him a tenner that he wouldn't be able to stay upright on a board for more than a few minutes. Ashley had retorted to Darren that if a ming-mong like him could do it then anyone could. At which point Darren had raised both the stakes and the ante.

The bet was now for twenty quid, and Ashley had to complete a one-eighty and land it.

He glanced nervously around. Unusually for the half-term holiday, the rec was almost deserted, which was why he was going to have a go now. He didn't want to make a complete fool of himself in front of an audience; certainly not an audience of younger kids. That really would be uncool. There were a couple of young mums pushing their kids on the swings, nattering as they swung the toddlers, ciggies hanging off their lower lips, and a few children of primary-school age playing on the round-about. Their shrieks and screams as they whirled round reached him over the constant thrum of the traffic on the ring road that ran along one side of the park, but they were too engrossed in their own fun to give him a second glance. This was probably one of the last weeks of the year they'd get the chance to play out, and they were making the most of it. Signs of encroaching winter were all around. The trees that flanked the park were shades of russet, yellow and ochre and the ground beneath was already spotted with fallen leaves. A couple from a nearby sycamore had drifted on to the metal of the ramps and were stuck there like stranded starfish on a beach.

Ashley pulled his attention back to the half-pipe. He took a breath and geed himself up.

'You going to do it then?'

Ashley whipped round to see who'd spoken.

'You scared or something?'

Looking up at him was a girl about his age, casually smoking a cigarette. At least she looked about eighteen but you couldn't really tell these days. There were some kids in Year 9 at school who looked eighteen – and who smoked to make themselves look older still – so he knew it was dead difficult to guess about girls' ages. But no matter if this girl was eighteen or not, she was a stunner. Really lush. For a moment Ashley just stared at her huge, round blue eyes set wide apart in her delicate face, her mouth pouting seductively around the filter tip of her fag, her neat nose and the whole framed by short, spiky blonde hair. He was so taken aback by her presence and her beauty that he let go of his skateboard, which dropped and slid down the ramp.

The girl giggled and smirked. Ashley jumped down the ramp after the board, his trainers squeaking against the metal. He gathered it up, his mind made up. He'd show her. Back on top of the half-pipe, before he had time to think about it, he balanced his board on the edge of the platform, and then kicked off. There was a split-second whoosh of fear and elation before he knew he was completely out of control and the elation vanished. He saw his board arcing through the air without him as he and it parted company, and then he was plummeting on to the ramp. The thud as he connected with the metal was bone-jarring, and then the screaming pain he felt in his arm and head was subsumed by blackness.

'It's all right, son, you'll be fine. Can you tell me your name?'

Ashley couldn't get a handle on what the fuck was happening. One minute he'd been trying to impress this fit bird, and now . . .

'What's your name, son?'

Shit, what *was* his name? God, why did grown-ups always want to know stuff? And what did it matter what his name was? Couldn't they just leave him alone? It was at that point that he became aware of the pain. Jeez. He wanted to scream out, but somehow he was incapable of anything. A wave of nausea flowed through him, but he felt too weak to even turn his head to one side. He hoped to goodness he wasn't going to hurl. That was the last thing he needed.

He felt something being put over his face. Having a mask clamped over his nose made him feel even more panicky, but then, oh the relief, the crushing, hideous stabbing in his arm mushed into a dull throb as the gas and air mix took effect. He breathed deeply. Man, this was good shit.

'We're going to lift you now, son.'

So? What did these guys want, a medal? But then he realised it was a warning as the pain exploded again and he sank back into unconsciousness.

*

He woke up feeling groggy and sore and then, almost immediately, befuddled. Where the hell was he? He shut his eyes again while he tried to make sense of the images he'd just seen. He managed to link them with a memory of pain and a vague recollection of hearing two-tones. After about five seconds he reopened his eyes to see if his suspicion that he was in hospital could be confirmed. A vision of utter beauty was bending over him.

'Hello,' she said.

'Hnnnn,' he managed to groan back.

'How are you feeling?'

Ashley made an enormous effort, licked his lips and said, 'Rough.'

'Can I get you anything?'

Ashley thought a stiff drink, painkillers and an explanation would be good but he didn't have the strength or the energy to articulate any of his desires. 'Na,' he croaked.

'Would you like some water?'

'Ya.'

'It's all right. They've set your arm. You're allowed fluids now,' said the beauty.

'Huh?'

'You broke your arm. Skateboarding.'

Ashley remembered. And the beauty had been there. She'd seen him make a prat of himself. 'Oh.' He became aware of a hideous stabbing ache in his left arm. He reached over with his right hand and felt it – it was encased in plaster.

'That plaster cast is only temporary. They're going to give you something lighter in a few days,' she offered helpfully. She held out an appointment card for the fracture clinic with the date for his next consultation already marked on it. Ashley just looked at it, so she laid it on the bed. Then, 'I'll get your water.'

The girl disappeared and reappeared about thirty

seconds later with a paper cone of cold water. She slipped her arm under Ashley's neck and lifted his head up very gently. Any discomfort Ashley felt was completely negated by the feeling of euphoria at being nestled against the girl's chest. He drank gratefully, draining the cup quickly. He hadn't realised how thirsty he was.

'More?'

Ashley nodded. Actually, the worst of his thirst had been slaked, but he wanted to rest his cheek against her tits just one more time. Almost worth breaking his arm for.

She returned again, and once more Ashley was tucked against her breasts as he sipped the water as slowly as he could. But there was only so long he could drag out the moment. He sighed as he drained the last drop.

'What time is it?' he asked as the girl laid him gently back down.

'Half six.'

'Half six? Bugger.'

'Sorry,' she replied, like it was her fault it was getting late. 'Problem?'

'My mum'll be worrying. I told her I was only going out for a while. Said I'd be back in time for her to go out.'

'I can ring her if you like.' The girl produced her mobile.

'My phone's in my trouser pocket,' he said. 'Assuming I didn't land on it and break that too. And,' he added looking into her amazing blue eyes, 'if you want to take a chance and find it.'

The girl raised an eyebrow. 'You must be feeling a whole lot better. That's a chat-up line I've not heard before.'

Ashley grinned weakly. 'I don't even know your name.'

'Tilly.'

'Nice name.'

Tilly shrugged. ' 'S all right.' She forbore to tell him

that it was short for Matilda, a name she loathed and abhorred with a vengeance. She didn't care that there had been Matildas in her family since before the ink on the Dead Sea Scrolls had dried; it was still a pants name.

'Ashley. I'd shake hands but . . .'

'But you're a cripple.'

Tilly reached forward and slowly slipped her hand into Ashley's pocket.

'It's the other one,' he said, after she'd felt around in it.

Tilly withdrew her hand and stood up. 'Want a slap?'

'You wouldn't. I'm an invalid.'

'You're a randy invalid,' she said. She walked around the trolley in the cubicle and delved in and out of his other pocket in a second, finding the phone almost instantly. 'What's your mum under? "M" for Mum or "H" for home?'

'Mum.'

Tilly pressed the buttons and then put the phone into Ashley's good hand. Ashley in turn expressed as succinctly as he could the facts – he'd had a fall, broken his arm, was in hospital, was still alive and hoped to be going home shortly. Even Tilly, standing at the end of his bed, could hear the shrieks and exclamations from his mother, followed by anger that he'd only just thought to phone her.

'I'm sorry, Mum. Yes, I know I promised. No, Mum. I'm fine and I can walk home from here. No, you don't need to come and pick me up. Honest. Look, I've got a friend with me . . . No, no one you know. I'll ask her to walk with me so she can pick me up if I pass out. No, Mum, that was a joke. I'll let you know when I'm leaving. Yeah, yeah . . .' Ashley held the phone away from his ear and pulled a face at Tilly. She grinned back. Shit, she was so pretty when she smiled. Ashley said goodbye and disconnected. 'She was cool.'

'Yeah, right.' The sarcasm in her voice was obvious. 'And yes, I'll walk you back.'

'No. No need. I just said that to get my mum off my back.'

'' 'S OK.'

'Nah. Honest.' Ashley really didn't want Tilly to see his house. He wasn't exactly ashamed of it. His mum kept it pretty well, considering what a dump the council had put them in, but the estate it was on was rank, and there was something about Tilly that made him feel she really wouldn't be happy in such a place. She had class – that was obvious. She didn't speak like most of the kids he knew. She wasn't off his council estate, he was certain.

'So where do you live?' she asked.

'Just around the corner. You?'

'Other side of town.'

Where the smart houses were. 'I've not seen you at school.'

Tilly shrugged. 'No, you wouldn't have.'

'Don't you go to King John's?'

'King John's?'

Ashley was confused. All the kids in the town went to King John's. Everyone knew King John's. 'The local comp. You know, the only school in town,' he added helpfully.

But from the look on her face, she didn't.

'Your family new to the area or something?' he asked.

Tilly barely missed a beat as she looked him in the eye and said they were.

A nurse bustled up and checked Ashley over. 'Your lady friend can wait outside.' She hustled Tilly out and swished the cubicle curtains shut. Tilly went to the waiting room, where she flipped through antique and well-thumbed mags and wondered how she could find out if Gentrified had won the three thirty-five.

By the time Ashley was discharged half an hour later, she was almost catatonic with boredom.

'You waited.' He was surprised.

'Just wanted to make sure you're OK to get home.'

'I said no need.' His discomfort made him snappy. Besides, he'd hoped his mother might have come along to see how he was. He knew it would be tricky having to tow the little 'uns along too, and he had told her she needn't bother, but even so . . . He'd broken his arm, hadn't he, and she was his mum after all. His disappointment hurt almost as much as his arm, which throbbed like buggery. He'd been prescribed some industrial-strength painkillers but they hadn't kicked in yet, and, although the nurse said she didn't think he was suffering from concussion, his head hurt almost as much as his arm.

'Text me later. To tell me you're all right.'

'OK.' He fished his mobile out and pressed some buttons. 'Give us your number.'

Tilly reeled hers off and Ashley tapped it in, then he pranked her. 'And now you've got mine.'

'Bye then,' said Tilly, checking her screen.

'And thanks,' said Ashley.

'It was nothing.' Tilly stood on tiptoe and planted a kiss on his cheek. Then she ran off, leaving him feeling dazed.

You get home ok
    Yes
    How r u
    Shit ☹
    Poor u. Want to meet tmrw
    Sk8 park. 3?
    Gr8 nite
    Nite xx

Ashley wondered if he'd got a bit heavy putting the kisses on the end of his last text. But then, he thought, rubbing his cheek, she'd kissed him first. Despite the painful dull ache in his arm, he went to sleep and dreamed of Tilly.

*

Tilly lay in bed and stared at the lit screen on her phone until it switched off automatically. Then she pressed a button to recall it again. Nite xx

Two kisses, was that significant? Or was it an automatic sign-off? She had mates at school who always added lol or some emoticon at the end of a text. She wished she knew. She wanted it to be something that he'd thought about, that he'd meant, not something that he'd just added mindlessly.

She flipped her phone shut and put it under her pillow. She shut her eyes and pictured him standing at the top of the ramp, his jaw set in concentration as he stared down at the half-pipe. Oh God, he's so gorgeous, she thought. Such a hunk. That dark hair, and eyes even bluer than hers. And those eyelashes. So unfair for a bloke to have them. She'd kill for eyelashes as long and as black as that. That was the trouble with being a natural blonde – blonde eyelashes. Without mascara she looked like a skinned rabbit. Well, she'd just have to make sure that Ashley never saw her without her slap on. She snuggled down under her duvet and imagined her and Ashley on a date until sleep overwhelmed her and her imaginings morphed into a dream.

'What's up with Tilly?' Flora asked her twin. 'She was actually nice to me today.' The twins were sitting on their beds, staring at each other across the faded Turkish carpet that covered a small square in the middle of the expanse of oak boards in their large shabby bedroom.

'You too? I asked if I could borrow her hairbrush this morning and she just passed it to me. No hissy fit, no snidey comment, nothing.'

'Weird.'

Daisy nodded. 'Maybe she's sickening for something.'

'Hopefully something serious.'

'No.' Daisy shook her head vehemently. 'That'd be bad.'

'Why?'

'Because she wouldn't have to go back to school on Sunday, dummy.'

'Shit, you're right.'

The twins stared at each other glumly. 'Better hope she's all right then. But it still doesn't explain why she's being so nice.'

Flora flopped back on her bed and stared at the ceiling of their shared bedroom, mottled with yellow damp patches and peeling paint, the effort of thinking about her older sister having proved too much for her. She changed the subject. 'Daisy?'

'Yes.'

'If Fa runs out of money—'

'Fa's always running out of money.'

'Yes, but I mean really, *really* runs out.'

'Goes bankrupt, you mean.'

'Yes. If he does, we won't be able to go to Heathercliffe like Tilly, will we?'

'I suppose not,' said Daisy thoughtfully.

'That school costs a shedload of dosh every term, doesn't it?'

'Thousands.'

'And there's two of us. So that's two shedloads.' A worried frown creased Flora's high forehead. 'I mean St Bede's must be bad enough but it's not boarding. How much more does boarding cost than day?'

Daisy shook her head. 'Heaps I should think. All those extra meals for a start.'

'Shit, we might have to go to the comp.'

'It's a dump.'

'We don't know that.'

'Huh.' Daisy obviously knew better – or thought she did.

'Do you think Daddy would let us stay at St Bede's till we're thirteen?'

'If he decides we've got to go to a state school I expect he'll make us go at eleven.'

'That's next year.'

'Double shit.'

The pair stared at each other in horror.

'It's so unfair. Tilly always gets the best deal because she's oldest and there's only one of her—'

'Thank God.'

'But it's still unfair, though.'

'What's unfair?' said Tilly, breezing into the kids' room without knocking.

'Nothing,' they said in unison.

She fixed them with a disbelieving stare but didn't contradict them. 'I need a favour.'

'What sort of favour?' said Flora warily.

'I'll pay you.' Tilly waved a ten-pound note at them. 'A fiver each.'

'Where did you get that?' said Daisy, her voice shrill at the injustice of her sister's wealth.

'The nags,' said Tilly airily.

'That's so unfair,' said Flora.

'God, *everything's* unfair where you two are concerned. Just because I often win money doesn't make it unfair.'

'It's unfair that you're old enough to get away with it,' snapped Daisy.

'Never mind that.' Tilly was already bored by the company of her sisters. 'Are you or aren't you going to do me this favour?'

'What is it?' There was a lot Flora could do with a fiver, but she wasn't so desperate for the money that she'd take it on any terms. Tilly's favours could be *very* demanding.

'Fa wants me to help stock the souvenir shop.'

'So? It's your turn. We did it last week.'

'So that's why I'm offering you this.' She shoved the money in Flora's face. 'Try not to be thicker than you can help.'

Flora and Daisy exchanged a look. They knew what the other was thinking: although it was hideously attractive to piss Tilly off by refusing to co-operate, the money was even more of a draw.

'Why can't you do the shop?' asked Daisy.

'Because I've got better things to do.'

'Like what?'

'None of your business.'

'Well, we can't help, then. We've got things to do too.'

Tilly's eyes narrowed dangerously, but she didn't dare

push the twins too far. She needed them if she was going to be able to bunk off and meet Ashley again. 'I've got a date,' she admitted sulkily.

'Oo-ooh,' shrieked the twins in unison in an irritatingly camp way.

'So will you – help me out?' There was a pause. 'Please.'

The twins exchanged a quick glance. 'OK,' said Daisy. 'What's he like?' asked Flora.

The twins saw Tilly's face soften and glow just for an instant before she threw the money on the bed and shot back out of the room. 'None of your business,' she said over her shoulder as she whirled away.

'I reckon she's in lurve,' said Flora as the pair convulsed into giggles and rolled around on their beds, hooting with laughter.

Free from the constraint of chores, Tilly fled the house once again, joyful anticipation of another meeting with Ashley giving her step a carefree lightness. Her date with him on Wednesday had been everything she'd dared hope for. They'd met at the rec and then drifted off into town, where they'd hung about in Starbucks for an hour or so making a couple of coffees last for over an hour. They'd discussed music and films and she'd discovered he could play the guitar, and she'd told him that she had twin sisters and in return he'd told her about his two younger half-brothers, but in the time they'd spent together she knew that they hadn't really talked. Not properly. It was chat. Nice chat but just chat all the same.

Perhaps this time she'd get to find out what really made him tick. Perhaps they'd get to the stage when they'd become more than just friends; a boy and a girl who'd met by accident and who happened to live in the same town. Maybe he'd be someone she could really look forward to meeting, to being with the next time she came home from school. Maybe this time they'd snog. Oh God, just the thought of it made her weak. She felt her innards go all fluttery at the idea. She wanted to be with him so much, to have him as a boyfriend, it almost hurt.

Actually, even if they didn't become proper boyfriend and girlfriend she still wanted him as a friend. She couldn't admit it to anyone, certainly not to her sisters, but she was agonisingly lonely. Other girls from her school went to stay with friends, but as Tilly could never bring herself to invite anyone back to the dump where she lived, no one invited her to their places either. And as she was too proud to admit she was ashamed of her shabby home, the other girls at her school just thought she was a prissy snob. Lonely at school, unhappy at home, life for Tilly was far from the privileged idyll outsiders might have thought she led, given the stunning beauty of Haybridge Manor, her ancestry, her looks and her connections. The reality was really rather different.

She hurtled over the gravel, through the gatehouse and down the avenue. As she raced, she glanced at her watch and then increased her pace from a lope to a run. Ashley's appointment at the fracture clinic was at two thirty, and unless she shifted she'd be late.

At the hospital she stared at the plethora of different-coloured signs directing visitors to Outpatients, X-Ray, A&E, Maternity, Paediatrics, ENT and all the other multitude of departments and specialties. But no fracture clinic. For a panicky second Tilly wondered if she'd got the right hospital – perhaps the fracture clinic was held somewhere else – but then reason kicked in. There *was* no other hospital, well, not for a twenty-mile radius; this had to be the right one. Then she saw a woman on crutches with her leg in plaster heading, painfully slowly, towards Outpatients. Tilly decided she was probably there for the fracture clinic too and followed her. She waited patiently while the woman handed in her appointment card and was directed down the corridor, then followed at a discreet distance until the woman finally stopped at a side room with orange and grey moulded plastic chairs, one intermittently flickering neon strip light and a couple of dusty pot plants that looked as if they ought to be either sent to an intensive care unit or bunged on the compost heap; either way they seemed to be enduring some sort of near-death experience. The woman sank gratefully on to one of the chairs, tired after her exertions with her crutches. Tilly hung about the vending machine, conscious that she had no valid reason to be there, trying to look inconspicuous.

After a bit she realised that no one cared who sat in the waiting room or why, so she found a vacant seat. She looked at her watch. Where was Ashley? She was sure his card had said he was due here at two thirty, and now it was nearer to two forty-five. Maybe she'd missed him. Bugger. She decided to give it ten more minutes and then she'd sack the whole idea. She'd lose the will to live if she stayed in this shit-hole much longer.

She was just about to give up on the whole stupid idea and get the hell out of the place when she saw Ashley walk in through the door. She felt her heart give a little jump. For a few seconds he didn't see her – he was casting around for a free chair – but then his eye lit on her and a smile transformed his face. Eagerly he hurried over to the corner where she was sitting.

'Tilly! What the f . . . I mean, what are you doing here?'

Despite her thundering pulse she put on a cool façade. 'Just thought I'd see where loser skateboarders spend Friday afternoons.'

Ashley laughed and looked pointedly at the other patients in the room. There were several middle-aged women, a man in a business suit, himself and a couple of primary-school kids. 'Not many skateboarders that I can see.'

'I said *loser* skateboarders.'

'Well I suppose that narrows it down to me, then.' Ashley grinned.

'Correct. Anyway, how's the arm now? Still sore?'

'No, just itchy. Awful. Drives me nuts. And it's worst at night. I just want to rip the cast off and scratch.'

A nurse appeared with a sheet of paper and called a name. One of the middle-aged women got up and followed her to a consulting room.

'You were late,' said Tilly as they watched her leave. 'I thought you were supposed to be here at two thirty. You might have missed your appointment.'

'Places like this always run late.' Tilly conceded that he had a point. 'But I couldn't help it. Got held up at home. You know how it is.'

'Yeah. I had to bribe my sisters to do a job for me, otherwise I wouldn't have been able to come. What about you?'

'I was babysitting the little 'uns. Had to wait for Mum to get back before I could leave.'

'And she got held up?'

'She forgot,' said Ashley in the sort of tone that even Tilly understood meant he didn't want to talk about it.

'What you going to do after?' she said, carefully changing the subject.

'Dunno. Better get back, I suppose.'

'Oh.' Tilly felt a stab of disappointment – and then annoyance. If she was only going to get to see Ashley in this poxy waiting room with all the other cripples listening in to every word they said, it was a rotten waste of a tenner. 'You got to do more babysitting, then?'

Ashley nodded morosely.

'I could come back with you and do it with you.'

Ashley shook his head. 'No. Kind of you to offer and all that, but I don't think so.'

'Why not?' she persisted.

'It'd be tricky.'

Tilly shrugged. 'Come on, it's only babysitting. I do it for my sisters.'

'It's not that.' He looked really uncomfortable.

Another nurse appeared and called out Ashley's name. With a look of relief he fled from Tilly, leaving her wondering just how tricky his home life might be.

It took an hour and a half for Ashley to reappear, this time with a light, moulded plastic form bonded to his bandaged arm by Velcro strips instead of the heavy cast.

'This is the bizz,' he enthused. 'I can take it off to have a shower – as long as I'm really careful – and it means I can have a good scratch when my arm itches. And it weighs about ten tons less. And look,' he wiggled his fingers, 'I might even be able to play my guitar in a week or so.'

'Neat. So are you free to go now?'

'Just got to make another appointment for a couple of weeks' time and that's it. Thanks for waiting. You must have been bored stupid.'

Tilly shrugged. 'Yeah, well, it beat being at home.' Which was true but she'd still been bored out of her skull, although knowing that Ashley was only a few metres away in a nearby consulting room had helped, as did the anticipation of seeing him again when he emerged.

'Your home not good neither?' asked Ashley quietly.

Tilly glanced across at him as they ambled through the long, stark hospital corridors. 'It's OK – just . . . you know . . . Dad's a pain, my sisters are worse, there's never any money to do anything, the place is a tip.' She sighed. 'I know I shouldn't complain. There's lots worse off than me; we've got enough to eat, running water, but . . .' She stopped. 'Listen to me, I sound like an Oxfam appeal.'

Ashley laughed. 'No you don't. Being poor sucks, doesn't it?'

Tilly nodded. 'It's the pits.'

She waited beside him while he made his next appointment and then accompanied him out of the automatic doors and into the cooler air outside the overheated hospital.

'Phew, that's better. I was sweating in there,' said Ashley. He turned to face her. 'I really appreciate you giving up your afternoon for me like this. It would have been dead boring with no one to talk to. But you shouldn't have hung about all that time waiting for me to come out again.'

'No worries,' said Tilly. 'I didn't mind. You don't have to go straight back this instant, do you?'

Ashley shuffled his feet. 'I should.'

'But no one at home will know how long the appointment took. You could still be waiting to be seen for all they know.'

'Yeah, but . . .'

'Oh, come on. Can't we go for a coffee or something? I've still got a few quid.' Actually, now that she'd paid her phone bill, bribed her sisters, replaced the money she'd nicked from the housekeeping and bought a couple of packets of smokes, a few quid was almost an exaggeration.

'I'd love to, but . . .'

Tilly knew this was going to be a no. 'Tomorrow?' she offered instead.

'Got work – at the garage. Valeting cars.'

'Saturday evening.' Now she was beginning to sound needy and desperate.

'Dunno. I'll have to let you know. Probably not.' But she could tell from the anguished look in Ashley's eyes that his rejection of her wasn't anything personal. 'It's not that I don't want to,' he added quickly. 'It's just me mum and the little 'uns . . .' Tilly nodded in understanding. 'What about Sunday?' he said.

Tilly's heart sank. Half-term was over on Sunday and

her dad would drive her back to school in the morning so he'd be back home before dark.

She shook her head sadly. 'Can't.'

'Well it'll have to be next week then.'

'Still can't.'

'What? None of it?'

'I won't be here.'

Ashley looked bewildered. 'All week? What about school?'

Tilly felt sick. How could she explain to Ashley that she went to boarding school? Boarding school was for rich toffs, everyone knew that – except in her case it was for a poor toff with a dad selling bits and pieces to pay the fees. Ashley'd think she'd been lying to him all this time about her circumstances and her family. So she bottled it.

She turned and fled.

Ashley stared after her rapidly retreating back and wondered what on earth it was he'd said. He felt totally gutted. He thought the world of Tilly; she was a stunner, she was kind, she was bright and funny . . . In fact as far as Ashley was concerned she was the best thing that had ever happened to him. Not, he thought, that his life so far had had much that was worth shouting about. His father was unknown – at least to him; his mum must have been introduced to him at some stage and had him on a short list of possibilities when she'd discovered she was up the duff – and then, when he was five, she'd shacked up with his step-dad. Ashley supposed that as step-dads went, Dave probably wasn't so bad: no actual abuse, no violence, nothing to make him want to have Childline on speed-dial, nothing that made his teachers take him to one side and ask, in that concerned way they had, if there was anything he'd like to talk about. Like he'd *ever* tell teachers anything, anything personal, that is. No, there wasn't *that* much wrong with his step-dad, but there was nothing right either.

For a start, Dave mostly ignored him. *Really* ignored him, like he didn't exist. Most of the time Ashley half wondered if he had some sort of invisibility cloak on as far as Dave was concerned – unless of course he got between Dave and the TV, when it was 'fuck off out of the way, you stupid bleeder.' Then there was the business with his half-brothers, Craig and Kieran. For kids, they weren't too bad, but Dave never told them off, so they got away with murder. And because Ashley had to share a bedroom with them, he never had anywhere to go on his own – unless he went out. And there was nowhere quiet in the house where he could go to do his homework, mostly because Dave didn't see the point of homework and resented the fact that Ashley was still at school when at eighteen he could be out earning his keep: could have been for two years. So if the kids mucked up his school work or scribbled on a project or made a racket while he was trying to revise, Dave didn't give a toss.

And if Ashley got angry with the kids, if he told them to lay off or asked them to be quiet, Dave would shout at him and storm round the house and then his mum would get upset and it was horrible. And then there was the way his mum cowered and flinched when Dave was in a strop and throwing his weight around, which made Ashley wonder, even though Dave didn't hit him, if he hit his mum. But it's not the sort of thing you can ask your mum.

His thoughts about his troubled home life didn't answer his worries about Tilly, though. Why had she run off like that? Was it something he'd said? Ashley kicked at a bit of gravel on the pavement and slowly meandered home. Then he had a thought: maybe her parents had split up and she was on an access visit. Yeah, that was probably it; that would explain why she didn't seem to know the area that well, like she didn't know about the local school. And it explained why she thought home life was shitty. And why she wouldn't be around the following week. And – and this was important – why she hadn't ever mentioned her mum. Maybe she had a step-parent like him. Or maybe she was in care and only allowed to see her natural dad at weekends. Whatever it was, they seemed to have a lot more in common than he would have thought at first – given her classy accent and looks. No wonder they seemed to hit it off.

'And where the fuck have you been?' was his greeting from his mum when he opened the front door. No *hello, love, how did you get on at the hospital?* Or, *how's your arm?* Ashley sighed. 'You're late. I was getting worried, wondering if they'd found something else wrong or you'd gone under a bus.'

'No, just the hospital running late,' he said.

'Oh, that's all right then, except you've made me late now.' She was putting on her coat as she spoke. 'The kids have had their tea. I'm off down the bingo. Dave'll be back later. There's a steak pie to heat up for him and you'll have to do some chips to go with it. There's probably enough for you to have some too. Don't overcook them this time. I don't want you upsetting him.' She shot him a meaningful glance and, picking up her handbag, swept out.

'Bye, Mum,' said Ashley to the closed front door, wondering what it was she was escaping from: the drudgery of living on the estate, Dave or her kids. Whatever it was, she took any excuse to get away from all of them. And what about his tea if there wasn't enough for him and Dave to share? He supposed there'd be some bread in the bread-bin if all else failed. Thanks, Mum. He knew, deep down, that she loved him really, but sometimes she made it hard for him to keep believing it.

He glanced through the living room door at Craig and Kieran, who were slumped on the sofa watching children's TV.

'Hi, boys,' he said. They weren't bad kids really; it was just Dave never seemed to say no to them. And they knew that if it ever came to a choice between them and Ashley, Dave would always side with them. The pair ignored him. Not that Ashley cared that much – situation normal. He had a good half-hour before Dave was due back, which gave him a few precious moments, assuming the boys stayed glued to the TV, to finish off his A level coursework. He made his way up to the room he shared with the two boys and then stopped in horror at the door. The files containing over a year of school work towards his exams were lying on the floor, papers, work sheets and notes spilling out of them, some torn and crumpled where they had been trampled and trodden on, and the whole lot smeared with a sheen of some gelatinous gloop. Hair gel. He could see the empty tube lying oozing on the carpet.

Feeling beaten and defeated, Ashley stared speechless at the sight. The top papers, representing half a term's work, and due in on Monday, had taken the brunt of the assault and as far as he could determine were wrecked. He felt like crying. As if he didn't have enough to contend with already, and now this. How the fuck was he going to get a decent education and find an escape route off this crappy estate if he didn't get his A levels?

He was too dejected to get angry. What was the point? What did it matter whether the mess had been caused deliberately or by accident? The outcome was the same. Wearily, hampered by his bad arm, he gathered up the papers and files, trying to keep the stuff with the worst of the hair gel on it away from those assignments that had missed it. The half-hour he'd thought he had free to finish his work was entirely taken up with sorting out the mess.

The damage wasn't quite as bad as he'd feared at first, although his coursework would need copying out in its entirety before he could hand it in – half a day's work in itself. He had a couple of free periods at school on Monday; maybe if he asked Miss Edwards, his tutor, for an extension till the end of the school day, if he explained the circumstances and showed her the wrecked papers, she'd allow him to hand it in a little late. And of course he did have the excuse of a broken arm. That would probably swing it. He could only hope. Maybe it was a good thing he wasn't going to be able to see Tilly on Sunday, as it gave him a chance to finish his work and get the rest copied out before the deadline. A chance only available if he could find somewhere quiet to work.

'Oi, Ashley, where the bleedin' 'ell are you 'iding?'

Great, that was Dave home. Could life get any worse? No – life wasn't that bad any more; meeting Tilly had improved things out of all recognition, which meant he had to make sure that he saw her again. He didn't care how long he had to wait till she came back to Haybridge; he'd be there for her when she did. She was the best thing that'd ever happened to him and he wasn't going to lose her.

Tilly ran from the hospital and only stopped at the rec to catch her breath. The place was deserted as the weather, although still dry, was now distinctly chilly at the dying end of the afternoon. On Saturday night the clocks would go back, the afternoons would be suddenly dark by tea time, and any idea that winter was still some way off would be blown away by the long nights. She sat on the bench where she'd first caught sight of Ashley, lit a cigarette and slumped against the uncomfortable metal back of the seat.

She had fallen for Ashley, she was almost over-whelmed by her feelings for him, but she wasn't going to see him again for weeks now – and that was assuming that he wanted to see her again. Given the way she'd just run off, he mightn't bother to hang around to see if she ever turned up again. Oh God, supposing he didn't? That was a devastating thought. How was she going to cope? Why was life so shitty? Why couldn't she live in a normal house with a normal family and go to a normal school? Why couldn't she go to school with Ashley? How cool would that be? How much better to go to a school with boys instead of all those pathetic girls she was stuck with. She let her gaze rest on the trees skirting the acres of grass and reconstituted rubber tyres that formed the safety surface of the play park and drew again on her fag, but she didn't see the foliage in all its Technicolor autumn glory; she was visualising Ashley: Ashley with his amazing blue eyes, Ashley with his gorgeous dark hair, Ashley who she ached for, lost sleep for, longed for.

Did he long for her as much as she did for him? He obviously fancied her – she was sure. From the look in his eyes and his tone of voice to his body language, it was all positive. It wasn't as if she hadn't had boyfriends before and was mistaking the signs through wishful thinking. She wasn't completely naïve; she knew if a boy liked her or not. But the way she felt about him . . . This was a first. Just thinking about him caused her heart rate to soar, her temperature to rise and her insides to go all squishy. She thought about him in every spare minute; she even had a picture of him on her mobile (one she'd taken when he wasn't looking) that she could gaze at, although it really wasn't necessary as she'd totally memorised his features. But was it reciprocated?

The more she thought about him, the more she realised she knew surprisingly little about him. He played the guitar but he couldn't skateboard, he had a step-dad, he lived and went to school locally . . . But what was so bad about his home? That was a big issue and she had no clue what the answer was. But the way he dodged the subject of his personal life was nearly as obvious as the way she dodged his questions about hers.

She knew, like for her, that money was an issue, but his problems probably didn't stem from trying to keep a massive ancient house from falling down. The more she thought about it, the more she came to the same conclusion: Ashley was skint because there was no money in his family. Maybe they existed on benefits and handouts. Shit! She'd been bitching about being broke, but her idea of being broke and his were continents apart. With a jolt of guilt, Tilly realised that she didn't have a clue how the other half lived. She might complain about never having any money and the fabric of Haybridge Manor falling down around her ears, but if push really came to shove and the family sold everything, neither she nor her sisters would ever have to work for a living. And probably their children wouldn't have to either. It was the effort of trying to keep the sodding house in the family that drained every last penny they possessed. Ashley's family probably didn't have much in the way of pennies to start with – which was why he worked and why he went to the local comp.

Tilly took a last drag on her cigarette and ground it out under her heel. It was now getting really chilly. The sky was turning apricot and magenta and pink as the sun sank towards the horizon, the breeze was lifting, and much as she'd like to carry on dreaming about Ashley and trying to piece together everything she knew about him to get a clearer picture, she knew she ought to be getting home; not least because she had a mountain of homework that she hadn't even thought about tackling yet and most of it had to be in on Monday. Bugger.

Tilly managed to get in the side door and make it up the back stairs without being detected, but as she was tiptoeing past their third-floor sitting room she heard her father call her name.

'Matilda,' he bawled. The fact that he was calling her Matilda was always a bad sign. He'd once said that he only used her full name when he was cross because you could get a lot of venom into three syllables. Which was exactly what he'd just done.

'Yes, Fa,' she answered meekly. She slunk into the sitting room and stood in front of her father, who was dressed as he always was in Harris tweed jacket, corduroy trousers, checked shirt and tie – the very epitome of the landed gentry at leisure. 'You wanted me?'

He eyed her with a hard stare. 'And where have you been?'

'Out.' He might be cross with her, but she wasn't going to give him the satisfaction of seeing she was worried or had a guilty conscience.

'That doesn't answer my question.'

'In town.' More false bravado.

'Doing what?'

'This and that. Hanging out.'

'Answer the question, dammit.'

Tilly jumped. Her father rarely raised his voice, but when he did, it meant the shit you were in was deep. He'd spent years in the military before he'd inherited the house and he expected orders and commands to be obeyed. 'I went to meet a friend.'

'Who?'

'A boy. Ashley.'

Edward de Liege's cold blue eyes narrowed and he fingered his regimental tie. 'Ashley.' He paused, contemplating the name. 'Ashley,' he repeated, the disdain this time more obvious. 'A local boy?'

'Yes.' Tilly felt her act crumble.

'I don't beggar this family to send you to a decent school to have you "hang out" with the local oiks. You have duties and you have responsibilities – firstly to the family and secondly to yourself. You seem to have totally abrogated any sort of sense of duty to your family – from failing to help with the visitors to bribing your sisters into doing your jobs. . .' Tilly opened her mouth to protest about the twins sneaking on her. 'And before you blame them for telling tales, I got the information out of them when I saw you weren't working in the shop *as I had explicitly asked you to*.' He thundered the last words of the sentence out so loud Tilly had to brace herself from rocking back at the force of them.

'Yes, Father,' she whispered.

'So I have decided that as you appear to wish to disassociate yourself from this family then you should have your wish granted. Bearing this in mind, I have rung the school and made arrangements to take you back tomorrow instead of Sunday, and furthermore I have told them to cancel your next exeat. You obviously don't want to spend time with us – so be it.'

'No!' Tilly couldn't help letting a wail of horror escape.

'That will give you six clear weeks away from me and you sisters, enough time, I think, for you to decide where your loyalties lie.'

'But I know where they lie, Father. I do. Honestly. Please don't send me away till the end of term with no exeat.'

'You should have thought of this before, Matilda. I only asked for your assistance twice this week and both times you decided that you were above helping out with the visitors. I'm sure I don't have to remind you that the entrance fee these people pay is one of the few ways this house makes any money. Money that puts clothes on your back and food on the table.'

'I'm sorry, Father.'

'Too late for that now. My mind is made up. Best you go to your room and start packing.'

'But Daddy . . .'

'Go.'

When Tilly stood her ground, Edward rose from his chair and swept past her, leaving her white, shaking and then crying. 'Daddy,' she screamed after him, but her plea was answered by the sound of a door slamming.

Tilly raced along the corridor to her room and flung herself on her bed, quaking with sobs. Huge gulping wails that racked her slim body. She cried until her ribs ached and she became so exhausted that the sobs were reduced to little more than hiccoughs. She'd never dreamed it was possible to feel so miserable and cry so much. This was what was meant by 'heartbreaking'; she was sure she could feel it cracking and falling to pieces. But slowly, eventually, with stuttering breaths, she cried herself out.

Feeling drained and numb, she sat up on her bed, the room now in darkness, and groped for her phone. She had to tell Ashley the awful news that she wouldn't be able to see him till Christmas. A lifetime away. With trembling thumbs she jabbed in the text message, telling him that she had family problems and that because of them she wouldn't be around. Given the fact that Ashley seemed to suffer from tricky family circumstances too, she thought he'd believe that and probably not ask too many questions. She hit send and then wearily flopped back against her pillows as she waited for his response.

She wouldn't blame him if he decided that she wasn't worth waiting for. Six weeks! That was for ever. No one could be that patient. But if he didn't wait, if he decided she wasn't worth it, she'd die. She knew she would.

Slowly her feelings of loss and despair were replaced

by a hatred of her father. What right had he to send her away like this? Didn't he know he was ruining her life? She hated him. If her mother were here she'd stop him being so beastly. But her mother wasn't and hadn't been for ten years.

Tilly wondered where she was these days. LA? Monaco? New York? Paris? Apart from wonderfully extravagant Christmas and birthday presents they hardly ever heard from her. Her public excuse was that her filming schedules were so hideous that she didn't have time for herself, let alone her estranged family. Frankly, thought Tilly, she didn't blame her mother; once she escaped herself – as soon as she turned eighteen and left school – she wouldn't come back either.

But Tilly did miss her terribly. And it was getting harder and harder to remember her. Not that visual memory had faded – far from it. When your mum was an international film star you saw her on the box quite often so it was tricky to forget, but Tilly could barely remember what it was like to have her as a mother; her touch, her laugh, the quiet, cuddly moments they'd shared. There were bits that came back: the way when she read bedtime stories she acted out all the parts, being the wolf, the granny and cute Little Red Riding Hood; the way the house smelt of her perfume; her exquisite clothes; the flowers in her room; the way her father used to smile at her; the way she lay in bed till almost midday before being wafted by car back up to London for the evening performance of some play or other. But all the stuff that had really mattered to Tilly, all the stuff that had just been her and her mum on their own, was now getting very blurry, because just after she produced the twins, her mother got her big break and went from being a West End actress with potential to a Hollywood star. So she left them to go to Hollywood.

Suddenly the name Susie Hutton was everywhere – as

was she, with interviews in the press, on national TV, on chat shows and all over the glossy mags. At first she told the family that she couldn't come back from LA because as one film finished she was contracted to make another and she was on a relentless treadmill. Tilly longed for her return and clung to the hope she would come back, but weeks turned to months which turned to years.

There was speculation in the press, but not for long. There was no scandal and no divorce so the public awareness that Susie Hutton was supposed to be the wife of Edward de Liege and mistress of Haybridge Manor dulled and faded. To help the process along, her portrait was removed from the public rooms and placed in the family apartment – well out of public sight. The official word was still that she was busy with her movie career, but Tilly knew that was a total lie, because she knew the real reason for her mother's defection.

About a year after her mother's departure, when the twins were still babies, she'd been in the sitting room playing with her dolls when the phone rang. Eager to be helpful, she'd jumped up to answer it, and she must have lifted the receiver at exactly the same time as her father, as he was completely unaware that she was listening in on the extension.

'Hello, Edward,' she heard her mother's breathy voice say, sounding so beautiful even over two thousand miles of transatlantic line.

Tilly was just about to shriek 'Hello, Mummy!' back when she heard her father say coolly, 'I imagine you're calling because you've heard from my lawyers.'

Tilly gripped the phone tighter. She knew that tone of voice. It was the one he used when he was telling her off, the one he used to put the staff in their place; it was his angry voice. Why was he angry with Mummy? she wondered.

'Oh darling, don't be like that.'

'You're my wife, Susie, and the mother of my children and I'm not going to divorce you.'

'But that's ridiculous.'

Tilly remembered listening to her parents argue, not really understanding the words they used, not understanding what it all meant. Now, nearly ten years on, her memory of what was said was fuzzy, but she did recall one thing.

'Bugger that, I need you at home, the children need you,' her father had said.

'The children barely saw me even when I lived there, and you know that. As for the twins . . . the nanny looks after them far better than I ever could, and you know that too. And you know how important the money that I make is. Even if you won't agree to divorce, I'm staying in America.'

So that was it. Her lovely beautiful mummy wanted money more than she wanted her children. She longed for her to come home again but it wasn't going to happen. Her mummy must have stopped loving her, for surely that could be the only reason why she wasn't coming back, and Tilly wondered what on earth she'd done that was so terrible. Shaking, she had put the phone down, still thinking it had to be all her fault. And even now, all these years later, she still wondered what she'd done to make her mum stop loving her.

When Edward drove his daughter back to Heathercliffe the next morning, she sat in the passenger seat in total, angry silence. One thing she'd learned at boarding school was that she wasn't alone in being the product of a broken home and that none of the other kids blamed themselves for being the cause of the divorce. Not that that stopped a residual guilt, but it was assuaged by the knowledge that it couldn't have been her fault alone. And given the way her father had just treated her, she thought angrily, if he'd treated her mother similarly, no wonder she'd buggered off.

What right had he to demand that she work for nothing at the Manor? It was his poxy house; she didn't want to live there. And what right had he to judge her friends? Calling Ashley an oik. He'd never met Ashley. He had no idea what he was like. He wasn't an oik. And sneaking round the Manor shop checking up on her – it was so unfair. Over and over she turned all of the things her father had done that were so outrageous, so out of order.

That was the one good thing about being sent back to school early: she didn't have to spend another minute under his crappy roof. She didn't have to risk being in the same room as him, eating at the same table. Not that she would – she'd have insisted on eating in her room, and if he hadn't allowed that she'd have starved. That would teach him, she thought, blackly.

But being back at school meant being a hundred miles away from Ashley. And for six whole weeks. She wasn't sure she was going to be able to bear that. His response to her text with the bleak news that she wouldn't be home again till Christmas had been sympathetic but puzzled, although thankfully he hadn't pried into the reasons. Obviously he'd accepted her excuse that it was family reasons at face value and respected her privacy. He'd told her to let him know as soon as she was back in Haybridge and they'd meet up. But it was still no guarantee that he'd wait for her. A fit bloke like him would have girls queuing up to date him. And she was out of sight, so out of mind.

Once at the school, Tilly dragged her case out of the boot of the tatty old Volvo and hauled it into the main hall. She didn't give her father a backward look; she didn't say goodbye; she even ignored the ten-pound note he held out to her. She wanted nothing to do with him. He was poison.

The one good thing about being back at school early was the fact that it was almost deserted. Apart from a couple of army brats whose parents lived in such far-flung places it was unfeasible for them to go home for the half-term holiday, and a few members of staff who lived on the premises, she had the place to herself. Lugging her case, she made her way up to her study bedroom, threw her bag on her bed and slammed the door.

She stared around at the four walls. She imagined an open prison must feel much like this – but without the restrictions. Feeling dejected, abandoned and pretty much unloved, she plonked down into the one comfy chair in the room and swung her feet up on to the bed. Life sucked.

There was a tentative knock at the door. If this was one of the fourth-form army brats she could get stuffed. There was a second knock.

'Come,' she said.

Miss Cunliffe, her house mistress, put her head round the door.

'Tilly. I heard you were coming back early.'

'Yes.'

'Nothing wrong at home, I trust.'

Tilly stared at her. Was this woman completely stupid? Of course things were *wrong* at home. Everything was *wrong* at home. For a start she had a shit for a father. If things were *right* at home she'd still be there.

'No, everything's fine.'

'Only if you want to talk to anyone . . .' Miss Cunliffe blinked her watery eyes nervously behind her large unfashionable glasses.

Like she was going to talk to her house mistress. She wasn't that much of a loser.

'Thank you, Miss Cunliffe, but my father just had to drop me back early.'

'But you're not going home for the exeat either.'

No, Sherlock, I'm not, thought Tilly venomously. 'It's tricky. Workmen,' she lied enigmatically with a smile she forced over her teeth.

'Ah.' Miss Cunliffe gave her a fleeting smile in return. 'As long as there isn't . . . Well, I'll leave you to your unpacking.'

'Thank you, Miss Cunliffe.' Now fuck off and shut the door.

Miss Cunliffe did.

The autumn slowly turned to winter; days of wild winds and driving rain becoming increasingly frequent as the daylight hours decreased and the temperature dropped little by little. The school heating struggled to cope with the draughts that whistled through the ill-fitting sash windows, and the girls trudged around the corridors, muffled in scarves over their uniform tunics and pullovers. The trees were stripped of their last remaining leaves, early-morning frosts rimed the grass, and Heathercliffe School geared up for Christmas with Advent hymns in morning assembly and endless rehearsals for the school carol concert.

Tilly, from her lofty position as a sixth-former, despised the excitement of the lower years over the pre-parations for the festive season, although she had a chart in her room on which she ticked off the days till the end of term. Not that she cared a toss about Christmas; her excitement was all driven by the steadily lessening number of days till she'd be reunited with Ashley. While the younger pupils at the school were working themselves into a lather about Christmas, she was getting herself into a state about whether or not it would be the same between her and Ashley after six whole weeks apart.

To judge from the tone of the texts they exchanged, all was well, but it was hardly a satisfactory or intimate means of communication. Besides, although she was sure she was still as crazy about him as she had been when they'd been together for those few brief days in October – she thought about him every waking minute, she dreamed about him over prep, she doodled his name all over her file covers and in the margins of her schoolwork – she didn't want to scare him off by texting I love u, and because he was a bloke, she was sure he'd never make the first move on that score. So their text exchanges were disappointingly banal. Caring and friendly – but banal.

Though Ashley always signed off lol xx. Did that *really* mean he was sending her lots of love followed by two kisses or was it just a reflex signature? She wished she knew, but she didn't dare text and ask him in case she got an answer she didn't want to hear.

Eventually the end of term arrived and her father came to pick her up in the old Volvo. Although he seemed to have forgotten the acrimony of their row, Tilly certainly hadn't. She wasn't going to forgive him for banishing her. If he thought that after six weeks and no exeat she was going to be all lovey-dovey, he was deeply deluded. Huh! She responded to his questions about the term with monosyllabic answers and then lapsed into a cold, sullen silence. The conversation faltered and petered out and it seemed a long journey back to Haybridge.

As soon as the car scrunched over the gravel and drew to a stop outside the front door to the Manor, Tilly leapt out and flew back the way the car had just come. She ignored the fact that she was quite unsuitably dressed for being out in the open at the end of December; she didn't care. She was going to see Ashley, and the knowledge warmed her more than any coat could have done.

Once she was out of sight of the house and, more

importantly, out of earshot of her father, who had been yelling at her to return *this instant*, she stopped and pulled her mobile out of her pocket.

Im back where shall we meet

She hit send and then raced over the bridge above the Hay river, which was in full spate, full of winter rain. Every few minutes she hauled her phone back out of her pocket to check that a message hadn't slipped past. She knew she was being irrational – of course she would hear the bing-bong of an incoming text – but she couldn't believe that Ashley was taking so long to reply.

Taking a guess at where he would suggest for a rendezvous, she made her way to the skate park. Maybe he was waiting there for her and hadn't replied so as to surprise her. Her heart thundered like the Hay at the thought. She felt quite weak with longing and excitement by the time she got there, but the park was empty and the bench deserted.

In disbelief she stared at the empty acres of grass around her. But he *knew* she was coming home today. He *knew* she planned to escape from home as soon as she got back to come and see him – she'd told him often enough in previous texts. Surely he'd been waiting for her text to say she was back. Surely he'd have rushed to meet her here as soon as he got it.

But he hadn't. Tilly felt torn apart. This wasn't the scenario she'd dreamed about all those weeks at her poxy school. In her imagination their meeting would be like something out of *Wuthering Heights*, with the pair of them spotting each other from a vast distance and then flying into each other's arms, followed by Ashley raining kisses on to her face. This empty park, this anticlimax just filled her with plummeting despair.

Blinking back tears of bitter disappointment, she made her way across the park towards the bench. Well, that was it then. He didn't want to see her. He'd been nice to her, answered her texts when she was dozens of miles away, but now she was back . . . So it was over. Text was OK, but a proper relationship? No chance.

Feeling weary with crushing misery, and with an awful empty, aching void forming around her heart, she wrapped her arms around herself for warmth and waited, trying to keep alive the fast-dying spark of hope. Maybe he wanted to come but had been held up. Maybe there'd been a problem with his phone. Maybe he'd turn up in a minute or two . . . Or in the next hour . . . But by the time the sky was turning dark, and the last amber and pink traces of the sun were fading in the west, she was shivering uncontrollably and numb with cold, and it was obvious he wasn't going to.

'You may have your mobile phone back now, Ashley,' said Miss Edwards, coming out of the staff room holding the offending object, which she had confiscated earlier that day. 'And if you must bring it to school, please switch it off in classes.'

'Yes, Miss Edwards,' responded Ashley contritely.

Miss Edwards sighed. 'You were just unlucky, Ashley; having said that the next phone to ring would be confiscated, I could hardly make an exception just because it was you.'

'No, Miss Edwards.'

She handed the phone over. 'Frankly, if it had been any other pupil in that tutorial, I'd probably have given out a detention too.'

Ashley shrugged. He knew Miss Edwards was trying to make amends and he did understand her position – she'd made a threat and felt obliged to carry it out – but he was the one pupil in the class who hadn't been mucking about. So it was just his tough shit. But then a lot of tough shit had come his way over the past eighteen years, so he ought to be used to it by now.

'Night, Miss Edwards.'

'Night, Ashley.' She watched him walk away. He was a nice kid, she thought, and he so deserved any success that might come his way in the future. He tried so hard, despite the fact that he obviously got absolutely no support from home; the family didn't even own a computer, so he often had to stay late at school or come in early to use the ones in the library. She really hoped he got his place at university, although how he'd cope if he got there, she wasn't sure. There patently wasn't going to be a snowball's chance of any financial help from his parents, and kids who had to earn money as well as study had a much higher chance of dropping out. She wished him well but feared the worst.

As soon as Ashley had turned away from his tutor, he flipped his phone open. *1 new message* appeared on the screen. Shit, it was from Tilly. She was going to meet him. He didn't even have to look at his watch; the message had been sent at two in the afternoon, and it was now dark. He slung his backpack on to his shoulder, and zipping up his jacket as he moved, he thundered out of the school. Dodging pedestrians on the pavements, weaving his way across roads without waiting for lights to change or cars to slow, ignoring the blaring horns that followed his progress, he raced through the centre of Haybridge to the park.

Nothing. Not a soul. He was too late.

Dejectedly he flung himself on to the bench, his chest heaving as he tried to suck air into his burning lungs. When he'd recovered enough to move, he hauled his backpack off his shoulder and reached inside for his phone.

Sorry problem at school can u meet l8er

He hit send. Would Tilly forgive him? He couldn't believe his bad luck. Of all the days to have his phone confiscated. If Miss Edwards hadn't taken it, he could have told Tilly he had a late tutorial and wouldn't be able to meet her till gone four o'clock. Shit. He picked up his bag and made his way wearily home. And he'd been so looking forward to seeing her again.

Feeling utterly miserable and rigid with cold, Tilly wandered into the grotty kitchen to see if there was a remote chance that there might be anything worth snacking on in the ancient fridge. Besides, it was also one of the few relatively cosy rooms in the house, and the vast antique boiler that lurked in one corner was guaranteed to warm her up if she snuggled up to it for a few minutes. Mrs Thompson, their cook-housekeeper, was standing by the sink peeling spuds.

'Hi, Mrs T,' said Tilly. She didn't mind being nice to Mrs T. She had no grouse with her – it was just her hideous family that pissed her off. Besides, Mrs T had looked after the family since she'd come into service at fifteen and was worth her weight in rubies. For Tilly and the twins she'd almost come to replace their mother: looking after them when they were ill, listening to their woes and troubles, giving them hugs and cuddles when they looked miserable and always being there for them. They couldn't really afford to keep her on, but getting rid of her was totally unthinkable, so somehow Fa managed to find the cash for her and Mr T's wages each month. Tilly thought they would rather have gone hungry than let her go. It would be as unthinkable as selling the twins to a white slaver – although, she pondered, if the price was right . . . She eyed Daisy, who was also there, waiting for the kettle to boil, two mugs on the counter, tea bags at the ready, and wondered what she might fetch on eBay. Nah – perhaps not. Fa would object and make a fuss.

'Make me a cup,' said Tilly, not bothering to greet her sibling, whom she hadn't seen for six weeks. She opened the fridge, took a look inside at the almost bare shelves, then slammed the door again in disgust and crossed the floor to the boiler.

'And hello to you too,' muttered Daisy. More loudly she said, 'It's "make me a cup, *please*".'

'Make me a cup *now* or I'll give you a Chinese burn.'

'You and whose army?' demanded Daisy, careful to keep her voice low enough for Tilly not to hear, but she got another mug out of the cupboard on the wall above the kettle anyway. 'Where have you been?'

'Out.'

'Where?'

'Nowhere.' Tilly really didn't want to talk about her abortive trip to the skate park. It was all too raw. As soon as she got her tea and thawed out a little, she was going to her room. She didn't want anything to do with anyone. The whole human race was hideous, her family was worse and she wished she was dead.

The kettle clicked off and Daisy poured water into the three mugs. 'Fa's organising a party over Christmas.'

'Bully for Fa,' replied Tilly tonelessly.

'Quite a big do.'

'Whoopee.'

'He said there's be quite a lot of people our age there.'

'He means people under sixty,' sneered Tilly.

Daisy plonked Tilly's tea on top of the boiler. 'Whatever, but it's got to be better than no party, hasn't it?'

'Doubt it.' Tilly wasn't in a mood to be cheered by anything.

Daisy left her to it; she couldn't be arsed to get enveloped by her sister's rubbish mood. Why was she so gloomy? It was the first day of the school hols, it was almost Christmas and there was the prospect of a party. Surely even Tilly could find something out of that lot to enjoy. But apparently not.

Tilly's phone bing-bonged. It couldn't be Ashley – he obviously wanted nothing to do with her. Maybe it was someone from school, although given that she was hardly Miss Popular with her peers, it was a long shot. So who on earth could it be? Desultorily she flipped open her mobile and saw the message. The twins heard her squeal of delight even through the shut door and over the music they were playing.

'**W**here are you going?'

Tilly stopped dead in her tracks. Not that she had much choice, as her father had appeared out of the family sitting room and was directly blocking her path to the main stairs.

'Out,' she said sullenly.

'I don't think so.'

Tilly stared at him. 'Why not?'

'Because Mrs Thompson is preparing a meal for all of us and I want to talk to you and your sisters over dinner. Besides, as this is your first day home for a while . . .'

And whose fault is that? thought Tilly angrily.

'. . . I thought it would be nice if we all ate together.'

'I'm not hungry.'

'Frankly, my dear, to coin a phrase, I don't give a damn. You can sit at the table and watch the rest of us eat for all I care, but you *will* sit at the table and you *will not* go out. Do I make myself clear?'

'But . . .'

'I am not interested in your objections, Tilly. You are not going out. Which bit of that sentence needs explaining?' Tilly, hyped up with longing for Ashley, combined with her natural teenage rebelliousness, was about to turn and head for the back stairs when her father added, 'And don't try going out the back way. I've had the side door locked.'

'But you can't . . . I've got to . . .'

'Tomorrow you can go where you like, but tonight I want you at home.'

The icy quiet of her father's voice left Tilly in no doubt that if she disobeyed, the consequences would be horrendous. She had no idea what sort of sanctions her father might impose on her, but she didn't think it would be worth her while to find out. The last time she'd pissed him off it had cost her an exeat and a weekend with Ashley. Maybe it would be better to sacrifice meeting him right now so as to be able to spend the majority of the Christmas holidays with him. But it was so UNFAIR. Her father was a TYRANT. A TOTAL SHIT! She let out a howl of frustration and disappointment and returned to her room, slamming the door with such force that several flakes of peeling paint floated down from the corridor ceiling.

Dinner was a miserable affair. Mrs Thompson had produced a shepherd's pie well up to her usual standard. And as her usual standard was always utterly delicious no matter how basic the ingredients, the four de Lieges should have tucked in with gusto. Sadly, Tilly's poisonous mood affected them all, and although she was the only one who actually just pushed her food around her plate, the others, tainted by the atmosphere she exuded like a black miasma, found their appetites lacking too. The conversation was sporadic at best, non-existent at worst: Tilly sulkily silent, the twins scared to open their mouths in case they upset either their father or Tilly, neither of which they felt would be advisable, and Edward – who found small talk difficult at the best of times – disinclined to make conversation just for the sake of it.

After twenty minutes Mrs Thompson returned to the dining room. She surveyed the remains of the meal littering the plates and sniffed.

'Do you want me to bring in the dessert, or should I tell Mr Thompson to put it straight on the compost heap?'

'Sorry, Mrs Thompson,' said Tilly as she handed over her almost full plate.

'And you've got no cause to be dieting – or is there another reason why you're not eating?'

'I'm fine,' she mumbled.

Mrs Thompson sniffed again. 'Looks like it, Miss Tilly.' She loaded the plates on to a trolley at the side of the dinning room and wheeled it out.

Edward placed his napkin on his side plate and looked at his three daughters. 'As the twins know, though it may be news to you, Tilly, I plan to throw a party for New Year.' Tilly glowered at him but Edward appeared not to notice and carried on. 'I thought that as we haven't done any sort of entertaining for some years . . .'

'Since Mum left, you mean,' said Tilly.

'. . . for some years,' said Edward, glowering back at her, 'it was about time we did.'

'So what have we flogged this time to pay for it?' Tilly was in no mood to cut her father any sort of slack. She was still livid at being grounded.

'For your information, young lady, this is being paid for out of an unexpected windfall; I've got an investment that is making a better than anticipated return.'

'So why aren't we getting the roof fixed?'

'My investment won't cover that too.'

Tilly shook her head in disgust. She could think of a dozen better things to do with some spare cash than a poxy party for her father's poxier friends. But as she wasn't being given a vote, she wasn't going to display the least bit of interest in the party or – if she could possibly avoid it – help with the preparations.

'I'll be getting caterers in to give Mrs T a hand and I imagine you girls would all like new dresses.'

Daisy and Flora instantly got quite excited at this prospect. They would, thought Tilly sourly. Easily pleased. There was no way she was going to admit to anyone, not even herself, that the prospect of a new dress for a special occasion was rather nice.

For the next few minutes, while Mrs Thompson dished up apple charlotte and cream, Edward went over his proposed arrangements – although Tilly couldn't see why he was bothering to share the information with his daughters. It seemed to her that everything from the guest list to the food to the proposed decorations to the accommodation for the guests – every last detail – had already been decided upon, so all the girls had to do was pitch up on the day in their new frocks.

'But why now?' she said.

'It just seems like a good idea,' said her father.

'So you get some money and you want to blow it on a party?' Tilly shook her head. 'Sorry, Fa, but this doesn't add up.'

'Whatever my reasons, they are no concern of yours. I thought you'd be grateful to see a bit of jollity in this house over the festive season. Sadly I see I was mistaken.' With a harrumph of annoyance and disappointment he threw down his napkin and left the table.

'I still don't see why,' insisted Tilly after he'd gone. 'Why spend precious cash on something like a party? Fa never does things like that, so what's his game?'

'Isn't New Year a good excuse?' said Flora.

Tilly gave an exasperated sigh. 'But why this New Year? Why not the last one, or the next one? And why a party at all? Why not spend the money on the wiring or the rot in the long gallery?'

'But why not a party?' said Flora, panicking in case Tilly managed to persuade her father to cancel. 'Why not? For heaven's sake, Tilly, a party is a party. Does there have to be a reason? I mean, Fa said at dinner that he had a lot of friends and colleagues he owed hospitality to. And he's got some spare cash.'

'I'd rather he spent it on us or the house than his mouldy mates.'

'But it'll be fun,' said Daisy.

'You think? Fa's stuffed-shirt friends, all as boring as fuck, standing around drinking Fa's booze, making polite conversation and telling lame jokes. Oh yeah, it'll be a riot.'

'It won't be that bad,' suggested Flora.

Tilly snorted. 'And seeing as how he's a total cheapskate, we're bound to be roped in as waitresses. In fact he probably wants us to go out and buy new dresses – little black dresses – so he can bundle us into white pinnies and caps.'

Daisy and Flora rolled their eyes at each other. 'He wouldn't do that,' they said.

'Huh. Personally I wouldn't put it past him. I had a letter from him while I was at school saying that now I'm nearly eighteen he expects me to do Christmas dinner this year. He said it was high time Mrs T was allowed to put her feet up and spend the whole day with Mr T.'

'You? You do Christmas?' The tone of horrified surprise in her sisters' voices wasn't lost on Tilly.

'Thanks for the vote of confidence.' She was hurt by their reaction, even though she was angry and very daunted at the prospect herself. But she wasn't going to give them the satisfaction of seeing that their comment had found its mark. 'See, even you think it's a crap idea,' she said airily. 'I told Fa as much but he won't listen. Which proves that as far as he's concerned, the three of us are here to provide cheap labour around the house. Let's face it, we already have to graft when the place is open to bloody trippers. And now he's expecting me to take over from Mrs T. I'd watch it if I were you – he'll have you doing the skivvying soon as well.' And having delivered her dark prophecy, she swept off to her room to text Ashley to arrange a meeting the next day.

How come ur already on hols I have another week 2 go, replied Ashley to Tilly's text. Cant meet till after school

Meet me tmrw @ sk8 park @ 4 C u then xx

Lol xx

Tilly looked at her watch. Eighteen hours to go. Ages. Oh God, how was she going to last that long? She knew she'd managed to live through the six weeks that she'd been stuck at her rank school, but she'd thought she'd be seeing Ashley today. And now she had to wait till tomorrow. The disappointment was so intense it hurt. She'd missed Ashley so much, with his lazy smile, his humour, his looks. Oh God, he was so lush! It wasn't as if she hadn't met other boys or had crushes on pop or film stars, but never, ever had she felt such an instant attraction as she had for Ashley. That had been why she'd spoken to him that day in the skate park. She never normally behaved like that, but she'd just had to do something to get him to notice her and to see if the attraction she'd felt for him was reciprocated in any way. And it was – the chemistry had been instant. But now her father seemed to be shoving every obstacle he could find in her path to ruin their friendship. He'd better not try to stop her from going out tomorrow, though, she thought grimly. If he did, she wouldn't be responsible for the consequences.

She put her phone on her bedside table and flopped back on to the bed. Quite apart from meeting Ashley and any hurdles she might have to negotiate to make it happen, she had another problem she needed to think about. The last thing she wanted to do at New Year was to spend it with her father's awful friends. She had planned on her and Ashley seeing it in together. So would it be an idea to invite Ashley to her father's planned party, or would she be better trying to bunk off? The party might be a whole lot more fun for her if Ashley were there, but on the other hand, her family at close quarters was enough to frighten anyone off. And apart from the awfulness of her sisters and her father, she had enough common sense to realise that Ashley might be a fish out of water amongst her father's friends. She knew what they were like, and she just couldn't see Ashley being able to cope with them. She'd met a few of them over the years, because although her father spent most of his time trying to keep the Manor afloat, he also had some business interests in London – he sat on a couple of boards as a director. She had no idea quite what that involved, but the people he associated with made occasional appearances at the Manor, where they brayed loudly at their own weak jokes, leered at her over their brandies and called her a 'filly'. Christ knows how they'd treat Ashley, and that was the worry. The thought of spending New Year's Eve with the collection of freaks her father called friends was a nightmare – and worse, she really didn't think it would be fair to inflict them on Ashley. She could just imagine the sort of patronising or just plain rude remarks they might be capable of.

No, putting Ashley in the same room would just be awful. But she so wanted to spend New Year with him. Maybe she could appear at the start of the evening and then disappear. If there was a big crowd, no one would notice her absence, surely. But – and this was the big problem – where could she disappear to? The end of December wasn't known for offering a chance of decent weather. She and Ashley could hardly hang out at the skate park if it was lashing with rain and blowing a gale. She supposed they could meet at a pub, but that took cash and neither of them had very much. They could always wander around town, but that was what losers with no mates did. Maybe Ashley had some friends locally who might offer them a house to go to for the midnight countdown, because she certainly didn't have any friends in town. That was the worst thing about boarding school – apart from the gross food, the teachers, compulsory games, the head . . . oh God, the list just went on and on – it was the fact that her classmates came from all over. And that was all over the world, not just all over the country.

Maybe Ashley knew someone who was holding a party they could go to – gatecrash if necessary. She could nick a bottle of fizz from the cellar so they wouldn't be empty-handed. Yeah, that was a plan. She'd work on it.

The next day dragged interminably. There wasn't even the distraction of avoiding sightseers visiting the house, so Tilly lounged around the sitting room, playing endless games of patience on her laptop and listening to various tracks she'd downloaded. After lunch she locked herself in the bathroom and used all the hot water as she exfoliated, pampered, shaved and beautified herself before emerging over an hour later in a cloud of steam and the scent of Diorissimo. She then spent the next hour doing her face and hair until she was sure she looked her absolute gorgeous best. Ashley would be knocked out, she thought, giving herself an appraising look in her mirror. Finally the hands on the clock managed to drag their weary way round to half past three, but by now the weather had taken a turn for the worse, and as well as being almost dark, the storm that had threatened for some time had broken.

Fucking typical, thought Tilly angrily as she threw on a coat and scarf and set off to the park on the other side of town.

Outside, the squall had struck with full force and rain was being driven almost horizontally by a full-on gale as Tilly battled her way down the long avenue, directly into the teeth of it. By the time she got to the bridge over the Hay, she was wet through, and she knew that far from the vision of beauty she'd wanted to present, she now resembled a soggy refugee from a disaster zone, with her hair plastered to her head, her mascara streaked down her face and her make-up ruined.

'Whose dumb idea was it to meet in the open?' she grumbled to herself as icy water trickled down the back of her neck. She considered texting Ashley to suggest another venue, but as the damage was already done she decided there wasn't any point. Doggedly she ploughed on, along streets empty of purchasers despite the proximity to Christmas; this weather was too much even for the most frantic and fraught shoppers. Finally she got to the place where the shops petered out and the turning to the rec joined the main drag. Only a few more minutes and she'd be with Ashley. Despite the numbing cold, despite the lashing rain, Tilly's heart beat faster and she could feel her face flushing with warmth at the thought. Her insides went all jittery as she approached the park.

And there he was. Oh God, her tummy went into free fall and her knees shook.

He had his back to her, he hadn't seen her, and then he turned. He broke into a run just as she did, and seconds later they were in each other's arms, the rain streaming down their faces as their lips met. Her dream *Wuthering Heights* encounter was actually taking place. She thought life couldn't get any better . . . ever.

Tilly had thought about being kissed by Ashley. She'd imagined it endlessly while she was supposed to be doing her prep at school, she'd fantasised about it, she'd dreamed about it at night, but she'd never thought that it would be such a moment of utter heart-stopping ecstasy, this total bliss of being enveloped by his arms, his warm lips pressed against hers, the clean, soapy smell of his skin . . . She felt his tongue flicker against her lips and she parted hers. Slowly, deliberately, he explored her mouth, and she responded. She felt herself melting against him, her breathing becoming ever more shallow and almost every sense electrically aware – taste, touch, smell, hearing. But not her sight. She'd shut her eyes to blot out the world. She just wanted the moment to be her and Ashley – not shared by the cars on the ring road, not the occasional passer-by, not any other living creature. Just them.

'Let's find somewhere dry,' murmured Ashley finally, pulling away from her.

Tilly opened her eyes and let reality reassert itself. She nodded. 'The coffee shop?'

It was Ashley's turn to nod. He threaded his fingers in amongst hers and slowly they left the park and headed back to town.

'How's the arm?' said Tilly.

Ashley flexed it. 'Fine. I'm back playing guitar again.'

'What about skateboarding?'

'Mug's game. Given that up.'

Tilly laughed. 'Just because you couldn't do it.'

'Maybe.' Ashley gave her a squeeze. 'It's so good to see you again, Till. The last weeks have been such a drag.'

'I know. I was going out of my mind waiting for term to end.'

'But you're back now. That's all that counts.'

'Back for nearly four weeks.'

'Four weeks! Blimey. You get well long holidays.'

'Oh, do I?'

'I should say. My school just allows us a crappy two weeks.'

'Well, maybe it's because my school's in another county – you know, different education authorities have different ways of doing things.'

'Do they? So why do you go to school so far away?'

Tilly shrugged. 'It's complicated.'

'Is it, like, because of your family? Is that why you're not back here very often, just access visits?'

Tilly nodded.

'Then we'll have to make the most of the time we get when you are here in Haybridge.'

If Ashley thought she came from a broken home it was OK, because she actually did – so she wasn't really lying to him, was she? And he didn't need to know her school was a swanky private one. Not telling him about it wasn't a lie either, was it?

'What were you thinking of, Miss Tilly, getting as wet and cold as this?' said Mrs Thompson as she stripped Tilly's coat off her and hung it on the clothes airer over the boiler in the kitchen.

'S-s-s-stop f-f-f-fussing, Mrs T-T-T.' But what Tilly said was almost unintelligible through her chattering teeth.

'You'll catch your death.' Mrs Thompson filled the kettle and switched it, then bustled out of the room. A few minutes later she came back with a towel and a hot-water bottle. Wordlessly she handed the towel, still warm from the airing cupboard, to Tilly, who began to dry her hair. The kettle clicked off and Mrs T filled the bottle and then made a cup of tea.

'Now take this and go and run a hot bath, and while you're waiting for it to fill, put the hotty down your bed. I'll bring you some supper later on. I don't want you catching a cold this close to Christmas, not with your father's party as well.'

'You j-j-j-just want me to stay f-f-f-fit so you don't have to c-c-c-cook the t-t-t-turkey,' said Tilly with a grin, despite her violent shivering.

Mrs T sent her a withering look. 'I've no doubt you'll need a hand, no matter what your dad says.'

Very likely, thought Tilly, wrapping her frozen hands around the warm mug. It was all very well everyone saying that you just had to follow the recipe, but she knew she could burn water, let alone a whole sodding turkey. She sneezed.

'There,' said Mrs T triumphantly. 'You're getting a cold. I knew it. Now get into a hot bath and then bed young lady.'

Normally Tilly would object to being sent to bed early, but the idea of being left on her own to relive her afternoon with Ashley was deeply enticing. No interruptions from her irritating sisters, no distractions from the radio or the TV; just herself and her thoughts and her wonderful, delicious memories of That Kiss. And the second one. And the longer, even more lingering one when they said goodbye.

She floated off to run her bath as directed, wondering if this state of extreme happiness and contentment could possibly last. It was just too good, too delicious to be true.

Next day Tilly woke without any further symptoms of the cold that Mrs T had blackly prophesied was bound to come her way. In fact she woke up feeling incredibly hale and chipper and still full of euphoria from her date with Ashley. Normally during school holidays she would lie in bed for as long as possible – generally until her father's nagging could no longer be ignored or she was gagging for a cup of tea – but today she sprang out of bed and almost danced into the kitchen to find tea and toast.

'Morning, Mrs T,' she chirped as she skipped across the tiled floor to the bread-bin. She extracted two slices of bread and stuffed them in the toaster, then moved to the kettle and flicked the switch.

Mrs T, taken by surprise by this happy, cheerful Tilly, looked at her with some suspicion. 'Morning, Miss Tilly. And how are you feeling today?'

'Fantastic!'

Mrs Thompson snorted. 'Well you've no right to, getting soaked through like that. Really.' Disapproval oozed from the housekeeper, though Tilly couldn't tell whether it was because she'd escaped ill health or because she'd actually courted it. 'So what was so urgent yesterday that you had to go out in that weather?'

'Just stuff.' Tilly didn't want to dilute her wonderful experience by confiding the details to others. One thing boarding school had taught her was the value of self-containment. Her sisters could share confidences with each other but Tilly had no one close – either in age or connectivity – who she wished to trust like that. And certainly not Mrs T, who was a renowned gossip, especially with the other staff required to run their huge decaying mansion.

Mrs T was well aware that pressing for details from Tilly was futile. She nodded and sniffed again. 'So are you going to be in for your lunch today, or dinner for that matter?'

'Dunno yet. I'll tell you later.'

'Just as long as you do. You know your father can't abide waste, and I need to know just how many chops to get out of the freezer.'

Tilly promised she would by crossing her heart and hoping to die as she made her tea and then carried her toast, slathered liberally with butter, back to her bedroom, where she could text Ashley in peace and privacy.

When shall we meet

Cant working 2day came his response.

Tilly's heart crashed. No! That was so unfair. It was Saturday and she'd banked on spending the day with him. Of course she remembered now that he'd told her, way back during half-term, that he'd got a Saturday job, but she'd managed to forget in the interim.

Where do u work

At greens the garage cleaning cars finish @ 5

Meet then

Sk8 park

Ok xx

Lol xx

She threw her phone back on her bed and stared at her cooling tea and the now soggy toast. She seemed to have lost her appetite. Five o'clock! That was hours away.

Ashley carefully hid all his school work under his bed, well out of the way of Kieran and Craig, and then checked his appearance in the mirror. Not that he needed to be particularly smart to valet cars, but it was company policy that he looked reasonable – at least at the start of the day; by the time he'd washed and polished fifteen to twenty cars, the way he looked by early evening was a whole other matter. He sighed. Normally he looked forward to his job: apart from anything else it got him out of the house all day and away from his stepfather, and secondly it put money in his pocket. Not that he spent much of what he earned. He gave a fiver to his mum and saved the rest; if he was going to go to uni in under a year, he needed to save every penny he could now to help pay his way then. He'd looked at numerous websites on the school computers, and although he knew it was feasible that he could earn enough to pay his tuition fees, his living costs, buy the books and manage all the other expenses, it was going to be a tough call. Anything he could do now to make it less hideous had to be a good plan.

And therein lay a huge dilemma: he so wanted to spend some of his hard-earned cash on Tilly, take her out, give her a good time, go to the cinema, buy her a drink, a meal perhaps. But his scare savings were terribly precious and represented his one hope of breaking out of this scummy council estate and making something of his life. He looked at people like his mum and step-dad and hated what they represented: scraping around on a hand-to-mouth existence, no prospects, no ambition, grinding routine and absolutely no chance of anything ever changing. Of course they always bought a lottery ticket, but Ashley had once added up all the money they'd spent on tickets over the years and had worked out that if they'd saved the money instead, they would be better off than they probably would be even if they got five numbers one weekend. Their only exit would be to get all six numbers, and at odds of millions to one . . . well, they really would be better off saving their pounds.

He gave his hair one last brush through, picked up his coat and made his way downstairs.

'Bye, Mum,' he called as he took two steps from the bottom of the stairs across the swirly carpet of the minuscule hall to the front door.

'Bye, Ashley,' she called back from the kitchen.

'Don't wait tea for me, I may be going out after work.'

'Hang on.' His mum came racing through from the kitchen. 'What do you mean, going out?'

Ashley frowned at her. 'Sorry, I don't get you.'

'You can't.'

'Why not?'

'Because Dave and I want you to babysit the little 'uns.'

'But I promised—'

'Never you mind what you promised. You'd better get your arse back here after work or Dave'll want to know the reason why.' Was there was a tic of fear beside her eye or was Ashley just imagining it? He couldn't let her down, not if it was going to send Dave into one of his moods. His mum returned to the kitchen leaving Ashley feeling totally despondent. Could he take the risk of pissing Dave off? But it wouldn't be him who'd be at risk, it would be his mum – or it might be. No, it was no good, he'd have to cry off their date. At least that solved his dilemma about his savings. He'd text Tilly later and tell her he couldn't make it. Maybe tomorrow.

It was tempting to spend the day finding excuses to keep texting Ashley, but Tilly knew that if he was on a pay-as-you-go phone he might run out of credit texting her back, and besides, she didn't know if his place of work might be cool about it or object madly. She really didn't want to jeopardise their relationship by pestering him. And it looked needy too. But it was aeons till he finished work.

She kicked around the house, getting under Mrs T's feet, annoying her sisters and exasperating hr father.

'For God's sake find something useful to do. Haven't you got any homework?'

'It's the holidays,' she snapped back. But she was wary of irritating her father any more so she retreated to her room, where she put on loud music, lay on the bed and planned to daydream about Ashley till lunchtime, thus wasting the entire morning.

A knock at her door roused her out of her reverie. Mrs T put her head into the room.

'Your father suggests you might like to do some cookery with me.'

And why on earth would I want to do that? thought Tilly. 'I'm busy,' she answered.

Mrs T stood her ground. 'Busy pressing your mattress. I'm going to make a quiche. You can learn how to make pastry, Miss Tilly.'

'Why would I want to?'

'Because one day you'll have a husband and kids and cooking's a useful skill. I won't always be around to do it for you.'

'Don't be silly, of course you will.'

Mrs T just shook her head. 'Have it your way, miss. Now, do you want to learn how to make pastry or not?'

Seeing as how she had nothing better to do to pass the time and the kitchen was guaranteed to be warm, Tilly hauled herself off her bed and followed the housekeeper. And although she wouldn't admit it, even to herself, she found the weighing, kneading and creating all strangely therapeutic. Besides, being surrounded by delicious cooking smells – frying onions, garlic and bacon – sharpened her appetite more than a brisk walk or some other rigorous exercise would ever have done, so when the quiche, golden, fluffy and glistening, emerged from the oven an hour later, she could hardly wait to tuck in once it was carried into the dining room along with a salad and some boiled potatoes.

'Blimey,' said Flora. 'Did you make this?'

Tilly nodded.

Daisy took a tentative bite. 'It's almost edible.'

Tilly narrowed her eyes.

'It's very good,' said her father, but Tilly thought she detected a faintly patronising tone in his voice, to say nothing of the possible note of surprise. She decided to give him the benefit of the doubt and ignore it.

'I had help from Mrs T,' she admitted.

'So she just made the pastry case and the filling while you did the rest,' said Flora, the epitome of innocence.

'Fuck off,' responded Tilly venomously. She was hurt that her sisters weren't raving and in awe over her creation.

'Tilly!' roared her father.

'Well she deserved it.'

'Quiet! I won't have this sort of behaviour.'

A sullen silence descended and Tilly's good mood at

her achievement with the quiche evaporated. She hoped it choked them all. She wished even greater evils on them when she got Ashley's text telling her he couldn't meet her after work as they'd planned. Life was shit and unfair, and her family was the personification of everything in existence that made it so. She hated everything and everyone – except Ashley.

His text promised her they'd meet on Sunday and in the evenings after school, but the time between trysts was endless and Tilly moped around the house miserably, snarling at her sisters, avoiding her father and being a pain in the backside. Her family tiptoed around her but Mrs T was having no truck with such behaviour and made it plain to Tilly that if she didn't put on a cheerful face when she was in the kitchen with her then she could spend her free time in her room being bored. On balance Tilly decided to comply with Mrs T's wishes.

As a result, between the blissful interludes when she escaped the house to meet Ashley, she spent quite a bit of time helping Mrs T in the run-up to Christmas: making mince pies and preserving tangerines, icing the Christmas cake and fashioning chocolate truffles. But she didn't just get lessons in creating festive goodies; Mrs T also showed her how to make a béchamel sauce, rub in fat and flour, bake a basic Victoria sponge and all sorts of other useful culinary techniques. She wasn't going to give anyone the satisfaction of admitting she found it all rather enjoyable, but Mrs T was nobody's fool and she saw the application and dedication Tilly put into her efforts.

As Christmas Day drew closer, the opportunities for escape became fewer and fewer, with family matters taking precedence over private outings to meet her illicit boyfriend. What with decorating the house, present-wrapping, a family shopping trip to stock up the larder that her father insisted all three children helped with, plus a big effort to clean the house – again a three-line whip – each day seemed to be quite full of things that Tilly just couldn't avoid. And it wasn't just Tilly who found it difficult to get away; for the first week Ashley had school each day, but once that was over, he had increasingly high obstacles placed in his way by his mother and step-dad, most of which seemed to involve him looking after his half-brothers while they went out boozing.

'I could come round to yours,' offered Tilly when they met again at their rendezvous point in the skate park one evening with less than a week to go to Christmas, but once again Ashley said no.

'Or I could come to yours,' he countered.

Which was a bit of a facer. Why couldn't he? What possible excuse could she come up with? She really didn't want him to know exactly who she was – which he would if he saw the house. And would it make a difference? Duh, of course it would. She hadn't got to the ripe old age of nearly eighteen without realising how people's attitudes changed when they discovered she lived at Haybridge Manor. Even people who had never been anywhere near Haybridge and had never even seen the place in the flesh knew about the house, and that it was one of the very few in the country that had been occupied by the same family in an unbroken line since it had first been recorded in Domesday Book. That was the trouble when you lived somewhere that had been designated a National Treasure; it tended to be on the radar of all sorts of people – not just the history fanatics, but people who watched heritage programmes on the TV and even those who just watched costume dramas, as it had featured in enough of them.

'It's tricky,' she said lamely. 'You know, family . . .'

'Do you want to talk about it?' said Ashley gently. He had his arm around her as they sat cuddled up on the cold metal bench. He rubbed the top of her arm with his hand – such a comforting action, Tilly thought.

She shook her head. 'It's not *that* bad. Just odd.' She

gave him what she hoped was a reassuring smile. She didn't want him to think there was anything pervy or creepy about her family. 'They're just really . . . odd and . . . well . . .' She screwed her face up as she tried to work out how she could explain her circumstances to him. 'It'd be tricky,' she repeated even more lamely.

'My home life's shit,' volunteered Ashley.

'So, worse than just being odd.' She tried to make a joke about her inability to reveal anything about her personal life.

He nodded gloomily. 'Comes of having a step-dad. And living on a council estate.'

So he did live on a council estate. She wondered just how grim it was. It wasn't an area of Haybridge she'd ever visited – or wanted to for that matter. But maybe that was about to change. 'At least I don't have a step-parent to contend with,' she said sympathetically, which she genuinely was, but she didn't say anything about the council estate; he'd know she didn't live on it and she was afraid that anything she said might be construed as patronising, so best not to mention anything about where she lived. 'My mum pushed off when I was eight, but Dad never remarried.' She decided to make a joke of it. 'So I've no wicked stepmother trying to lock me in the attic and make me do all the skivvying.'

'No ugly sisters?'

'Oh, I've got them. The twins are awful, complete pains in the arse.'

'But are they ugly?'

Tilly laughed. 'Not really, I suppose. In fact, for ten-year-olds they're quite cute. Pains, but cute.'

'Not like my half-brothers then, the escapees from *The Omen*.'

'They can't be that bad.'

Ashley told Tilly about the incident with his course-work.

'And they're still alive?'

'They didn't realise what they'd done.'

'Don't be ridiculous, of course they did. It might not have been malicious but they knew all right.'

'Well, water under the bridge now.'

God, he was so forgiving; that was one of the things Tilly loved about him. She didn't think she deserved such a lovely guy.

'But this doesn't solve the problem about meeting up,' said Ashley. 'I suppose you could come round to mine. The estate's a tip – a real shit-hole – but our house isn't too bad. I mean, not compared to some. It wouldn't be a good idea for you to be there when my folks are about. My step-dad . . . well, Dave's not really into welcoming visitors. And you'd best only walk around on the estate with me – no surprise visits. Some of the other residents . . . let's just say they're not the nicest of characters.'

Tilly wasn't sure if Ashley meant that Dave didn't want to meet Ashley's friends or Ashley didn't want his friends to meet his step-dad, but she suspected it might be the latter. And quite apart from the problem of Ashley's step-dad, there was no way she was going to risk hanging about on the estate on her own. She read stories about goings-on there in the *Haybridge Chronicle* – some of them quite hair-raising. Sycamore Drive – the main road that ran through the estate – was always featuring either as the place where some mugging or other had happened, or as the address of the criminal involved, or where the local police had lifted some crook or busted a drugs gang, so it certainly didn't appeal to Tilly as a destination of choice. She didn't fancy becoming the subject matter of another lurid crime report in the local rag.

A gust of chill wind blew through the skate park and penetrated Tilly's inadequate coat, and despite the shared warmth that seeped between her and Ashley, she shivered. 'Well, hanging out at your place would beat the crap out of freezing our arses off here.'

'I'll text you tomorrow to let you know when would be a good time.'

Tilly twisted her head round to smile at Ashley and he took the opportunity to kiss her. For all she cared the temperature could have plummeted to arctic levels; his kiss warmed her through and through as her pulse soared and her insides felt as if they were going into free fall.

Ashley shut the door to the room he shared with his half-brothers firmly. He'd promised them a chip supper if they left him and Tilly alone for an hour or so. Tilly sat on the edge of his bed while he perched on the hard wooden chair. Outside they could hear scuffling and sniggers, but after a less than a minute, when it became obvious that neither Ashley nor Tilly was going to react, the two younger boys got bored and thundered downstairs to watch TV – far more entertaining than eavesdropping or speculating about what their big brother and his 'friend' were getting up to.

Tilly looked about the room; opposite her was a bunk bed and to her right was a window with a table underneath. There was a built-in cupboard in one corner and a chest of drawers that meant the door into the room could only open halfway. A threadbare carpet covered the floor and tatty *Star Wars* curtains hung at the window. The room couldn't be described as spotless, but it was reasonably clean and tidy.

'It must be a squash for all three of you in here,' she said.

Ashley nodded. 'It's not easy. Do you have to share?'

Tilly shook her head. 'Although the twins do – but they like it that way.'

'So they don't have to.'

Tilly shrugged. 'Well, no. Don't you have a third

bedroom?' The house seemed plenty big enough to hold one, even if it was only small.

'We did, till Dave moved in. Well, we've still got it, but it's too jam-packed with his stuff to be used as a bedroom. Never mind the rest of us.'

'What stuff does he have in there?'

'He collects militaria.'

'What, like suits of armour and stuff?' Tilly knew quite a lot about militaria because of all the junk they had hanging around at the Manor – literally. In the great hall, in a tasteful arrangement on one of the walls, there was a large display of halberds, pikes, swords and bits of armour, to say nothing of quite a few muskets, a couple of blunderbusses and a cannon on the floor underneath.

'No.' Ashley laughed. 'Like anyone would want to collect old stuff like that.' Tilly kept quiet. 'No, he collects badges and buttons and military pamphlets and the like.'

'Weird.'

'He is, a bit. The weirdest thing is that a lot of it is German.'

'So?'

'From the last war. It's got swastikas all over it.'

'Yuck,' said Tilly. 'So is he into the BNP or anything nasty, or has he just got a thing about Hitler?'

'I don't know and I don't want to ask,' said Ashley.

Tilly shifted on Ashley's bed and her ankle connected with something hard stuffed under it. There was a muffled twanging. She bent forward to investigate what she'd kicked and pulled out Ashley's guitar. 'Play something,' she said, holding it out to him.'

Ashley looked sheepish. 'I'm not that good,' he said.

'I can't play at all so I'll be impressed anyway,' said Tilly reasonably, but Ashley still hesitated. 'Go on,' she encouraged.

Ashley reached forward and took the instrument. He slipped the strap over his shoulder and began to tune it, plucking at the strings and twisting the tuning pegs, making the notes he played change almost imperceptibly until he was satisfied. Then he began to strum some chords.

'What do you want to hear?' he asked.

'I don't know. Surprise me.'

And Ashley did, serenading her with a beautiful version of the Leonard Cohen classic, 'Hallelujah'. He followed it with something he said he'd written himself. Tilly was no judge of music but she thought it was beautiful.

'You must write some words to go with it,' she told him.

Ashley shrugged. 'Maybe. When I get an idea that'll fit the tune, maybe then.'

'Play it again, please.'

He began to strum the strings, and then he looked up from his guitar and into her eyes. 'I wrote this for you, you know. I wanted to create something specially for you.'

'Oh, Ashley, that's . . .' But Tilly couldn't go on. A lump formed in her throat and her eyes filled with tears of sheer happiness. No one had ever done anything like that for her before and she was completely overwhelmed.

'I love you, Tilly.'

'And I love you too. I love you so much.'

He pushed his guitar to one side and leaned forward to kiss her.

Tilly thought she would explode with happiness.

They met the next morning in the coffee shop in town to exchange gifts, and then, by previous mutual agreement, they parted until the festive shenanigans were over. There was too much going on at their respective homes to allow time for snatched visits to town and cups of coffee. However, as she walked home, her little present from Ashley, still unopened, clasped tightly in her hand, she received several texts from him all telling her how much he missed her and how he didn't know how he was going to survive till they could meet again. By the third one Tilly was giggling. Obviously Ashley was quite mad, but she loved him just the same. She loved him so much it was almost painful.

And what wasn't there to love about him? He was completely adorable, and so talented. His music was fantastic. As someone who couldn't hold a tune in a bucket – her music teacher at school had actually asked her *not* to join the choir – she was incredibly impressed by anyone who understood how music worked: all those funny little squiggles on lines and complicated chords, to say nothing of knowing just which finger had to go in what place at exactly the right moment to produce the correct note. Nope, far too complicated for Tilly, who at the age of eight had failed to master the recorder and whose interest in music had been on a downward slide ever since. She liked music that others produced well enough – she could appreciate a good tune – but the mysteries of how it was done eluded her completely.

She thought about how he'd serenaded her with the Leonard Cohen song – it was just so romantic. Even thinking about it made her feel quite emotional. No one had ever sung a song just for her before. It was sweet – although she hated anything that linked boys and the word 'sweet', in this case she couldn't think of any other way to describe it. If anyone else said that anything about Ashley was 'sweet', however, she'd probably have to kill them. And then there was that tune he'd written. She'd have to get him to play it again one day so she could learn it and hum it to herself in private. It was just so lovely.

The house was in chaos when she got back. The twins were both up stepladders trying to string evergreen garlands around the place as Mr Thompson dragged in the twenty-foot tree to erect in the great hall and Mrs T tried desperately to vacuum up the mess the three of them were creating, while her father was driving up his blood pressure trying to sort out the tangled strings of fairy lights that bore more resemblance to cat's cradles than usable decorations.

'Give me a hand here,' yelled Edward over the whine of the hoover.

Tilly had planned on going to her room to dream about Ashley, but she quickly realised there was a fat chance of that – not till after supper at any rate – judging by the amount of work that still had to be done on the house and with Christmas Eve only a day away. There was no escaping that deadline. Feeling grumpy about being denied her chance to fantasise privately about her new love, she rolled up her sleeves and got stuck in. One of the twins found an old CD of carols from King's and put it on the player in their room with the door propped open and the volume up loud, and after a while Mrs T stopped cleaning and disappeared, only to reappear a little while later with a plate of hot mince pies and a jug of cream. Tilly, despite her initial bad temper, caught herself singing along to the carols and realised that she was enjoying herself.

They ate supper on the go, and by nine o'clock the great hall, the stairs and their sitting room looked really festive.

'Just the boxes the decorations came in to tidy away,' said Edward, 'but we can do that in the morning. I'm bushed.'

'No, let's at least pile them into a corner so we can get the full effect and see how pretty we've made it,' said Flora.

The others reluctantly agreed and began picking up all the rubbish and cartons, stacking them out of the way.

'What's this?' said Daisy, finding Tilly's present on a windowsill where she'd put it for safe-keeping and then forgotten it. ' "To darling Tilly, with all my love Ashley",' she read on the label of the little package in her hand.

'Give me that,' snapped Tilly, lunging to get it, but Daisy was too quick and whirled it away out of reach.

'Tell us who Ashley is and I'll let you have it.'

'Give it to me right now,' said Tilly, sounding thoroughly menacing.

'Or what?'

'Or you'll regret it.'

'Come now, Daisy,' said Edward mildly. 'Give Tilly her present.'

'Aren't you curious as to who Ashley is?' said Daisy.

'I'm sure Tilly will introduce us to her friend in her own good time.'

In your dreams, thought Tilly. There's no way I'm going to inflict this bunch of losers on him.

But having seen where he lived, she knew her father would automatically disapprove of any hint of a relationship between her and a boy from the council estate. It wouldn't matter how nice and talented and kind Ashley was; as far as her stuck-up family was concerned, he was condemned to social exclusion because of his address.

'Here,' said Daisy, now bored with baiting her sister. She chucked the present at Tilly, who caught it and raced upstairs to hide it in her bedroom until Christmas morning, partly to keep it well away from her evil sisters and partly to remove the temptation to open it before the twenty-fifth. She had faithfully promised Ashley she'd wait till then so they could open their presents together, despite being separated by several miles.

Christmas passed as it always did, the only difference this year being that Tilly cooked lunch, which she managed fairly successfully, with only a little help from Mrs T. The housekeeper supervised the timings, oversaw Tilly stuffing the bird on Christmas Eve and came over to the Manor from her cottage just the other side of the gate-house to check that it was properly cooked when it was time to dish up. When Tilly protested over the telephone that if Mrs T just told her exactly what to look for she'd be fine, Mrs T was having none of it.

'It's only a step from my house to yours, and besides, we don't want your family going down with food poisoning, do we, Miss Tilly? That would be a sorry way to spend Boxing Day.'

The turkey might have been cooked to perfection, but the roast potatoes were tough on the outside and soggy on the inside, the sprouts were mushy and there was too much salt in the bread sauce. Tactfully, though, no one mentioned these short-comings, and Tilly felt justifiably triumphant at having managed the feast pretty much on her own.

'Pudding anyone?' she said as she surveyed the debris-laden table. It was littered with empty crackers, along with the (considerable) remains of the turkey, bowls of leftover vegetables, drips of gravy, a couple of wine rings left by the bottle Edward had consumed, with a little help from Tilly as a treat, and a puddle of orange juice courtesy of the twins.

'I'm stuffed,' said Daisy.

'Me too,' said Flora. 'Can we do presents now and have pudding later?'

As a rule, presents in the de Liege household weren't given out till the evening. Edward, generally a stickler for tradition, thought about it. 'Tell you what, if you two clear the table, I'll light the fire in the sitting room, and as soon as that's done we can open them.'

'But what's Tilly going to do? Why can't she help?'

'Tilly cooked the lunch, she's done quite enough. I think she should have a rest.'

The twins grumbled but didn't argue further.

Twenty minutes later there was a roaring fire of apple logs blazing in the grate, the table was clear, the dishwasher loaded and Edward had poured himself a glass of port.

'Come on, Daddy,' squealed the twins. 'Presents!'

For once the sitting room was really cosy, what with the fire and the lights flickering on the tree in the corner, the curtains drawn to keep out the already dark afternoon and Christmas songs playing on the ancient CD player. The great hall might have been decorated with a huge tree, evergreen garlands and matching colour co-ordinated decorations to impress any visitors to the house over the holiday and the guests at the party their father was planning to hold – and because it had always been a bit of a showcase at this time of year so they always did it that way – but their sitting room was where the baubles made by the children were displayed, the tatty paper lanterns hung and the fairy with one wing missing placed askew on the top of the small fat tree that filled the corner by the fireplace. There was something comforting and familiar about the elderly and rather dishevelled decorations that were only for private consumption.

'OK, Daisy, you can hand them round, and don't forget to keep track of who has sent you what so you can write intelligent thank-you letters later.'

'Yeah, yeah,' said Daisy, already rifling through the pile of brightly wrapped packages under the tree.

It didn't seem to take long for that pile to be distributed, unwrapped and the torn and crumpled wrapping paper pushed into a new mound.

Their mother had sent all the children the latest iPhones with a hundred-dollar note tucked into the box, together with a message that she loved them and would be thinking of them. Tilly doubted that last bit very much. Actually, she doubted the first bit too – if their mother loved them so much, why had she buggered off like that to the States? The excuse that it was for the sake of her film career didn't wash, no way. She could have come back; lots of actors criss-crossed the Atlantic so as to combine home life with their career. However, Tilly couldn't deny that she was pleased with her present – and the cash, which was always useful. It was a shame the banks were going to be closed the next day, otherwise she'd have changed the dollars into pounds and shoved a few quid on Electric Eel, which was a dead cert in the King George VI Chase at Kempton Park. But never mind.

She gathered up the rest of her presents into a tidy pile. Like her twin sisters, she'd been given mostly clothes, money and books – not stunningly imaginative, but welcome all the same. Edward had received similar gifts – without the cash, naturally – but he'd professed himself especially delighted with the case of Beaune his daughters had clubbed together to get him from the local wine merchant.

'So what did *Ashley* give you?' asked Daisy.

'Yeah,' said Flora. 'Tell us.'

'Never you mind,' said Tilly.

'I'd like to meet this Ashley,' said her father. He didn't

sound as though he would. In fact his tone of voice was quite ominous. 'You must invite him round some time.'

Which Tilly knew full well was code for 'I'd like to meet him to check he is suitable for my daughter.'

'Maybe,' she mumbled non-committally.

'Maybe after the party. Ask him to lunch one day before you go back to school.'

'Why after the party? Isn't he good enough to meet our friends?'

'I didn't say that,' said her father mildly. 'You did. Besides, if he's a local lad, it's doubtful he's got a DJ.'

How dare he! He didn't even know Ashley. Well that did it. She had been determined to keep Ashley a million miles from the party, but not now. It would serve her father right if he turned up in jeans and a hoody. And anyway, what was so good about owning a DJ, something you got out of the wardrobe once a year, if that? What a pointless waste of money, thought Tilly, hot with suppressed anger. She became absolutely and defiantly determined that Ashley should be there. She'd show them – bunch of stuck-up snobs.

'So you'll make sure he comes to lunch? You'll invite him?'

'I most certainly will invite him,' she said as she smiled sweetly at her dad.

The next morning, though, her father hadn't forgotten his invitation.

'Have you asked him yet?' he said as he bit into toast and marmalade, standing by the worktop in the kitchen while Tilly made a pot of coffee.

'Wha . . . ? Who . . . ?' In her pyjamas, having just crawled out of bed, she wasn't awake enough to be quizzed. Her father, on the other hand, was fully dressed and looked as if he'd been up for hours, which he probably had been, as he rarely slept in late.

'That young man of yours. Alfie? Angus?'

'Ashley.'

'Yes, Ashley.'

'What about him?' Tilly poured boiling water on to the coffee grounds in the pot and appreciatively sniffed the aroma that instantly wafted her way. Coffee, that was what she needed.

Her father sighed. 'Have you asked him?'

'It's Christmas, Fa.'

'But you message him all the time, don't you.'

'*Text*. It's text, Fa.'

'Does it matter?' her father sighed. 'The point is, have you?'

'Not yet.'

'What are you waiting for?'

'Maybe I don't want him to come to lunch,' Tilly said defiantly, pushing the plunger down in the cafetière.

'Don't be ridiculous.'

'What's ridiculous about not wanting my friends to have to eat a meal in this dump of a house?'

'That's enough. And don't be rude.'

'Why? You're the one who wants Ashley to come. It wasn't my idea.' She poured herself a cup of coffee and stormed back to her room.

But once she'd closed her door and sat on her dressing table stool, hands clasped round her coffee, she thought about her plan. It was all very well to invite Ashley to piss her father off. And it would mean that they'd be able to spend New Year's Eve together somewhere dry, warm and with lashings of food and drink. But what would Ashley think? He had no idea she wasn't just some ordinary girl from an ordinary house, and finding out who she really was might be – well, a bit of a shock. She wondered about spinning him a tale that she'd had an invitation to a party at the Manor with a 'plus partner' option. Could she pretend that she was just a visitor to the place, like him, and that it wasn't really her home? No, like that was going to work. There was no way her sisters would let her get away with any sort of subterfuge; even if she bribed them, they were bound to drop her in it, even if it was unintentional – although knowing them, they were far more likely to do it on purpose, just for the sheer devilry of it.

Maybe she should just be straight with him and tell him who she really was. If she phrased it right, maybe he'd be cool about who her parents were and where she came from. After all, it didn't change who she was – the girl he'd met at the skate park and who he seemed to like. No, he more than liked her; he'd told her he loved her. What they had going for them was *so* much deeper than 'like'. Way deeper. There were feelings between them that Tilly had never experienced about anyone before – not even her family. There was an intensity and depth there. She tingled every time she thought about him, she ached for him when he wasn't around, she dreamed about him, she was obsessed by him. It was true love, and they both felt the same way – she knew they did. Apart from the fact that he'd actually said 'I love you', there was that wonderful compilation CD he'd burned for her as a Christmas present. Didn't that prove what he felt for her? That it wasn't just words he'd uttered because he thought she'd like to hear them? That this was the real deal?

So if he loved her like she loved him, he'd be all right when she came clean about her background. All she had to do was pick her moment and use the right words.

'What the fuck do you mean, it doesn't change anything? It changes *everything*. I can't believe you lied to me, and so often.'

Tilly stared at the muscle twitching in Ashley's cheek. He was white with anger and his voice was so cold – almost as cold as the stiff breeze that was swirling around them in the skate park.

'I didn't lie,' said Tilly, her eyes watering as much from the icy wind as with hurt at his sudden change of attitude.

'You didn't lie?' Ashley's voice was so loaded with incredulity it went up half an octave in pitch. 'Sorry, I think everything you said to me about your family was a lie. You haven't a clue about being poor or living in a crap place. How can you, when you live in a vast great mansion that even has a moat to keep out the riff-raff.'

'But that's not true. The house I live in may be big, but it's damp and cold and falling to bits. And we never have any money, we're always skint—'

'Which is why you have to go to the local comp, I suppose,' interrupted Ashley with a sneer.

'I wouldn't mind if I had to,' protested Tilly. 'I didn't get much of a vote in where I was packed off to.'

'My heart bleeds. What I really don't understand is why you didn't tell me right at the outset where you lived.' Ashley stared at her coldly.

'I was embarrassed,' said Tilly. 'My family is rank, and

I don't want to be thought as some bit of posh totty, some sort of socialite who only thinks of parties and celebrities and getting her picture in *OK!*'

'Yeah, right.'

'But I don't!' Tilly was almost crying with frustration that Ashley didn't believe her.

'So this is why it was so difficult for me to come over to your place, because it certainly couldn't have been lack of space. How many bedrooms? I don't believe that you were embarrassed about where you lived at all; you were embarrassed about *me*. You didn't want your family to see you with a boy off the council estate.'

'No, no, it was nothing like that.'

'Oh no? How were you going to explain me to your lot? There was no way I was ever going to fit in, so you didn't even try.'

'No,' cried Tilly.

'Admit it, you couldn't invite me back to yours in case I made off with the family silver.'

'What family silver?' screamed Tilly. 'We sold all of that fucking years ago. We're skint, broke, on our uppers, poor as church mice . . . How many ways do I have to say it for you to believe me?'

'No you're not. You're not poor like I am. You're not poor like the people round us would understand. You might not have much cash, but you really don't know what poverty is like: to have scrimp to pay the bills, to have to eat endless crap food, to wonder how you can afford school shoes for the kids. You might not be as rich as your smart mates, but you're not poor. Try living on my estate.' Ashley suddenly laughed mirthlessly. 'Ha, that's good. It turns out we both live on estates. Funny how the same word can have two such different meanings. I bet you're looking forward to going back to your snobby school and telling all your toffee-nosed mates about how you slummed it when you visited a real live council estate.

How you went out with a proper bit of rough. I bet they'll be well impressed.' Ashley put on a falsetto voice, 'Oooh, Tilly, how brave. Fancy going to a place like that. Did you see any real low-lifes? Any alkies? Any dossers? And what was your bit of rough like? Catch any anti-social diseases?' He resumed his normal voice. 'I bet you and your friends will all be pissing yourselves when you tell them. That's why you want me to come to your crappy New Year's party. You want me there to give all your mates something to laugh at – I'm the entertainment, aren't I?'

Tilly was crying properly now. The tears that streamed down her face had nothing to do with the biting wind any more. 'No. I want you there because I want to be with you. I'd never make fun of you because of where you live. It's never been like that. I don't care, I never have. Why don't you believe me?'

'Once a liar, Tilly, always a liar.'

'But I didn't lie.'

'Huh. As far as I'm concerned you can call it what you like, but from where I'm standing, if it walks like a duck, quacks like a duck and looks like a duck, it's a duck. And frankly, what you led me to believe about your poverty-stricken, I'm-from-a-broken-home-too existence was a huge lie. Vast.' Ashley held his hands shoulder-width apart to underline his point. 'So forget it, Tilly.'

Looking weary and defeated, he turned away from her and headed off the skate park and across the ring road, back towards his estate.

'Ashley!' she cried after him, but his only response was to jerk two fingers at her. Tears streaming and feeling abjectly miserable and bereft, she made her way back to, as Ashley had so succinctly put it, her own estate.

'So what you planning on wearing?' Daisy asked Tilly, bouncing up and down on the edge of her big sister's bed with excitement. It was only a few days now till the big

New Year's Eve party, and she and Flora had talked of nothing else since Christmas.

'Nothing,' mumbled Tilly with a shrug. She sat at her dressing table staring at the twins' reflections in her mirror.

'Nothing?' said Flora. 'You'll be bloody cold in this house. Besides, Fa won't like that.'

Tilly didn't dignify the comment with a response. Instead she said, 'Why don't you two just fuck off and leave me alone?'

'What's rattled your cage?' said Flora. 'You're such a misery-guts at the moment. You're going to be a right laugh at the party.'

'You're mistaking me for someone who gives a fuck. Now sod off.'

Daisy got up off the bed. 'Come on, Flora, let's go and see how much Fa's giving us to spend on dresses. We can see if he'll split Tilly's money between us, as she obviously doesn't want to shop for a new one.'

The pair went out, slamming the door behind them. Tilly pressed the remote for her CD player and the words of Leonard Cohen filled the room as silent tears fell on to her hairbrushes and make-up bag and the other clutter on her dressing table.

She hadn't thought it possible to feel so much pain and yet not have any outward physical signs. Surely if you hurt as much as she did there should be a gaping wound somewhere, a great hole where her heart had been torn out, and the fact that there wasn't somehow seemed to make it worse.

All her life, when she'd hurt herself, Mrs T or the matron at school, or even her mother in the far distant past, had given her a cuddle, bathed the injury, administered tea and sympathy and a sticking plaster. But there was no sticking plaster big enough for the break in her heart, and with nothing outwardly to show for her inner pain, she couldn't expect any compassion or understanding. She had to weather this awful misery alone, and she wasn't sure she could. Morosely she dragged herself across her room and threw herself on her bed, tears still streaming as she listened to the music. She wished she could die.

Outside the rain lashed against the old leaky leaded casements of her room and the wind whistled through the gaps between the window and the frame, making her curtains twitch and rustle and creating a cold draught that swept over her. Her radiator badly needed bleeding and consequently the temperature in her room was low, which suited her bleak mood and her misery. Like some medieval sinner, she felt suffering and misery was all she deserved, her discomfort and unhappiness allowing her to wallow even deeper in the awfulness of life. And if she got pneumonia, so much the better. It would serve Ashley right if she died.

Mrs Thompson noticed Tilly's absence and was worried. Tilly could be difficult and moody – what teenagers weren't? – but this was something else. She tried to tempt her out of her room with the offer of making scones and other treats, but Tilly just turned her face to the wall. The twins tried to be nice to her briefly but gave up as soon as she was rude and shouted abuse at them, and her father, never brilliant with his children, decided that if she wanted to be a stroppy cow then the best place for her was her room. He didn't have the time or the inclination to try to work out why she was being so difficult, not with the party to organise, so he was relieved rather than worried when she didn't emerge from her room and he didn't have to cope with her hideous temper. And as he was so busy with the arrangements that he was taking his meals on the go, he didn't notice either that his eldest daughter had stopped eating.

Mrs T took in meals, which Tilly ignored, and after a couple of days of this the housekeeper took her concerns to Edward. All he said was that he thought it unlikely that Tilly'd willingly starve herself and that when she was sufficiently hungry she'd eat. Mrs T, although she had never had children of her own, wasn't so sure. By the third day she was beside herself with worry and refused to allow Edward to take such a laissez-faire attitude.

'Get in there and talk to her,' she snapped at her employer. Edward, stunned by Mrs Thompson's tone, meekly opened Tilly's bedroom door.

'What the blazes . . .' he blustered as he threw back the curtains in her stuffy, gloomy and cold room. As the light flooded in he saw the state of his daughter, and was horrified by her ashen, gaunt and red-eyed appearance.

His tone altered mid-sentence. 'Tilly, sweetie, are you ill?'

Tilly shook her head, but didn't trust herself to speak. Tears were so close to the surface they could spill over at any moment.

'You look awful,' said Edward.

His frankness made Tilly forget her misery for a split second. 'Thanks, Fa, you really know how to make a girl feel good,' she mumbled.

'We must get you something to eat.'

Tilly shook her head again. 'I'm not hungry.'

'Don't be ridiculous.' Edward knew that what Mrs T had told him about her not eating properly for days was the truth. 'I'll get you something.'

'Don't bother, honestly.'

Edward gave her a long stare and then disappeared out of the room.

'You didn't tell me she was *that* bad,' he said accusingly.

Mrs T was having none of it. 'I tried to tell you, sir,' she said, crossing her arms under her ample bosom and squaring her shoulders, 'but you said she'd eat when she was ready.'

'Well, I was wrong. Unless we get her better, she won't be able to attend the party.'

'That won't be the end of the world. If she's not better, she mustn't go. Her health comes before any junketing.' Mrs T bustled across the kitchen and began to rummage in the fridge. 'I'll make her a nice drop of soup.'

'Can't you think of something more nourishing than soup?'

'The poor girl needs tempting, not bullying.'

Edward left Mrs T to it. He knew from past experience that if he argued with her she'd only dig her heels in further. And he also knew that she loved Tilly quite as much as he did and that she probably knew better than he how to get her to take something, even if it was only a mouthful or two.

'What's wrong with your sister?' he asked the twins, who were lounging in the sitting room watching daytime TV. 'Why has she shut herself in her room like this?'

Flora shrugged. 'Dunno. She won't talk to us. But she'd been in a mood since she last saw Ashley. Maybe he dumped her.'

For some reason this infuriated Edward. What right had some dreadful oik to dump his daughter as if she wasn't good enough for him? Tilly? Not good enough? He could feel his blood pressure rising like mercury in a thermometer held over a flame.

'Do either of you know anything about this boy?'

Both twins shook their heads. 'She meets him somewhere in town,' offered Daisy.

Edward rolled his eyes. Yes, that was very helpful. 'Never mind,' he muttered. Frankly, if Ashley was off the scene, it might be something to be thankful for. At least it would be when Tilly was better. And although Edward would like to give the lad a proper dressing-down for making his daughter so miserable, the pleasure denied him of administering a tongue-lashing was counter-balanced by the pleasure that Ashley seemed to be history.

Which just proved to him that the sooner Tilly met up with Marcus, the son of Desmond Crosby, fellow board member, company director, entrepreneur and friend, the better it would be all round. Not that he had any particular wish to marry her off young, but he had a dreadful feeling that if he didn't, and knowing how independent and headstrong she was, she'd end up in some frightful misalliance that would finally bankrupt them all and cause Haybridge Manor to be lost to the family for ever.

No, he couldn't have that. He hadn't fought to keep the house afloat and in the family rather than handing it over to the National Trust just to have Tilly let it go through sheer thoughtlessness. She might not appreciate her heritage now, but she would in later years. He was sure of it.

Which was why he had to make sure she married well. It might be an old-fashioned concept, but she'd thank him later. And Marcus Crosby would be perfect. Desmond, his father, nouveau riche and horribly aware of the social limitations that went with it, was desperate for his son to gain the sort of respectability and gravitas that a connection with a family as old as the de Lieges would bestow. In return, Marcus would bring the money that the Manor so desperately needed. The fact that the de Lieges had no title had been a bit of a stumbling block as the two fathers had discussed the possibilities of the match over port and cigars at their club, but as Edward had pointed out, if Marcus played his cards right and made some substantial donations to a political party, he was bound to get a title of his own sooner or later. Desmond Crosby had seen the sense in this and the two men had shaken hands on the deal to do their very best to bring their two offspring together – even to the extent that Desmond was prepared to bankroll the New Year's party at Haybridge Manor. This was the 'investment' to which Edward had alluded.

So now he just had to make sure that Tilly was well enough to attend and looked a darn sight better than she did right now so as not to scare Marcus away completely. How the hell was he going to achieve that? He only had a couple of days.

E dward clucked around Tilly for the next forty-eight hours like a mother hen around her chicks.

'What's with Fa?' Tilly asked Mrs Thompson when she came in with yet another nourishing meal on a tray. 'He's always hovering, checking up on me.'

'He's just worried about you, my sweet.' Mrs T put the tray down on the dressing table stool before plumping up Tilly's pillows, straightening her bedcovers and helping her to sit up.

'He just wants me better so I can act as his hostess at his poxy party,' grumbled Tilly.

'Would that be so bad? It's a compliment that he thinks you're old enough and sophisticated enough. You're going to be eighteen soon; you'll be finishing school this summer and then you'll be off to university. I don't suppose you'll get the chance to go to many proper parties like this one once you've left home.'

'No, thank God,' said Tilly with feeling.

Mrs T put the tray of scrambled eggs and toast on Tilly's knees. 'Your father is really proud of you. He just wants an opportunity to show you off before you disappear.'

'My father just wants to make use of me while I'm still around,' countered Tilly.

'Well, if you can make snappy remarks like that, you must be feeling a bit better.'

Physically Tilly *was* much better. More than twenty-four hours of decent food and some proper sleep in a room with a working radiator and now additionally warmed with an extra fan heater had repaired the self-inflicted damage that three days of neglect had wrought. Mentally, though, she was still fragile. She still ached for Ashley, she still burst into tears intermittently and her sleep was troubled by nightmares; nightmares that she couldn't remember in the morning but which left her feeling upset and uneasy nonetheless.

She sighed as an unexpected wave of misery descended on her, and pushed her plate away from her.

'Come on, my sweet. Eat up for me. I can't bear to see you so miserable and suffering.'

Tilly looked away. She knew how much Mrs T cared for her, but the hurt she was feeling was too deep to be cured by comfort food.

'What is it, my sweet?' said Mrs Thompson. She settled herself down on the bed by Tilly's feet.

'Nothing.'

'Hmm. That would be the same nothing that stopped you from eating for three days, would it?'

'No.'

Mrs T raised her eyebrows and gave Tilly a long stare before she pulled the tray towards her and picked up the knife and fork.

'Yes,' admitted Tilly quietly as she watched the house-keeper cut up her scrambled egg on toast into bite-sized portions.

'Want to talk about it?' Mrs Thompson pushed the plate back towards Tilly and handed her the cutlery.

Without thinking, Tilly took a mouthful and considered her options – yes or no – while she chewed.

'You don't have to, but a problem shared is a problem halved.' Mrs T smoothed her apron over her lap and looked unconcerned and uninterested.

'Maybe,' said Tilly. She forked up another bit of toast and egg and then put it back on her plate.

'Now, now, Miss Tilly, one little bit of egg on toast isn't going to make you strong, is it? Believe me, whatever it is that's the matter won't seem so bad one day, but starving yourself won't do anyone any good. You can talk to me about whatever it is that's bothering you when you've got a full tummy.'

Tilly gave the housekeeper a wan smile and ate several squares of toast in silence. Then she said, 'I got dumped,' and pushed her plate away.

'Thought as much,' said Mrs T, pushing it back. 'It's not the end of the world, you know.

Tilly's eyes filled with tears.

'I know it feels like it. It feels like you'll never get over it. But you will.' She smiled at Tilly. 'I bet you're thinking "how does Mrs T know?" I'm right, aren't I?' Tilly snuffled and nodded, then absent-mindedly took another mouthful of egg. 'I haven't always been married to Greg – Mr T. And I haven't always been this old.' She was rewarded with a watery smile. 'I was once in love with a very handsome man – not,' she added hastily, 'that Greg isn't handsome, not that I haven't always loved him too. But James was my first love and there's never anything quite like that. He was gorgeous, a soldier; it was the fifties and he was just back from Suez, so he had the most wonderful tan. And handsome! He used to turn heads in the street in or out of uniform. I adored him totally, I was head over heels in love with him, so I know just how you feel.'

'Why didn't you marry him, then?' asked Tilly, her curiosity making her forget her own troubles.

'He died. Motorbike accident.' Mrs T shrugged. 'You didn't have to wear helmets back then and he just lost control, the police said. Came off on a bend on his way to see me. Killed instantly.'

Tilly was too stunned to say anything, and the house-keeper stared out of the window, lost in her memories of over fifty years earlier, when she'd been the same age as Tilly and deeply in love.

Tilly's heart went out to Mrs T. She was so shocked that this woman who had been so much a part of her life, who had been like a mother to her since her own had left almost a decade previously, who had always looked after her, whom she loved deeply, had suffered this awful tragedy and she hadn't known till now.

Mrs T's fiancé had been killed! How awful was that? So much worse than being dumped. At least Ashley was still alive, although what with the row and the way they'd parted, he might as well be dead. But he wasn't, a voice in her head reminded her, and as long as he was alive there was hope. Maybe she ought to stop feeling quite so self-pitying.

'Still,' said Mrs T, turning her attention back from her memories to Tilly, 'that's all in the past now. And although I thought I wouldn't, I did get over it. And then I met Greg and we've been married the best part of forty-five years and I've been very happy. There isn't just one Mr Right out there, you know.'

'Maybe not,' said Tilly, eating the last bit of toast and egg. She looked at her empty plate in surprise.

'Tiff, was it?' said Mrs T, getting up off the end of the bed and picking up the tray.

'Yes.'

'It's never too late to kiss and make up.'

'Maybe.'

'You get some rest. I'll wake you up at tea time. Maybe you'd like a hot bath.'

Tilly nodded. She rather thought she would. She yawned hugely. Now that she'd eaten, she was knackered. She'd have a snooze, just for a little while.

*

Ashley kicked about in town. He was wet and cold and it was growing dark, but he couldn't face Dave and the kids, especially as his mum had said she was going to a friend's house for the afternoon. Without his mum there to get between him and his step-dad, things could sometimes be very tricky indeed. He'd be thankful when the holiday was over and Dave would be back at work, because even with school taking up most of the day, there were usually a couple of hours before tea when he could find some space to himself; either the bedroom or the kitchen or the sitting room was free when it was just him and his half-brothers. With Dave home as well, there never seemed to be anywhere he could be on his own, and Dave would pick on him all the time; have a go at him about getting a job rather than wasting his time with school.

He pulled his jacket collar up and went and sat in the bus shelter. He was still cold as the wind whistled through the gap between the bottom of the bus shelter and the pavement and then found its way up his trouser legs, but the curved plastic roof kept the rain off him and the upper part of his body was pretty sheltered. The vile weather suited his mood. All the light had gone out of his life since he'd split up with Tilly. He thought about texting her and saying sorry for being such an arsehole; it wasn't as if she'd chosen to be born a toff, just like he hadn't chosen to be born on a sink estate. And he did miss her; she was so funny and lovely. He felt so right when she was around, like he could achieve anything, and now she was gone, there was just this awful black hole right in the middle of his life. Even mucking about on his guitar, which usually cheered him up, didn't make him feel better. In fact if anything it made him feel worse, because every time he picked it up, he remembered her face when he'd played her that Leonard Cohen song.

He got his phone out to text her and then put it away again. She wouldn't want to hear from him, not when he considered the way he'd spoken to her the last time. Every word he'd said had been aimed at causing the most hurt. She'd never want to have anything to do with him ever again.

Tilly woke up and stretched. It was dark, but that wasn't much of an indication of the time – not at this end of the year. She glanced at the illuminated display on the alarm clock on her bedside table. Just gone four. She switched on her bedside lamp and checked her phone to see if anyone – well, Ashley really – had texted her while she was asleep. Nothing. Oh well.

Despite the disappointment, she lay under the covers feeling cosy. She thought about the fact that Mrs T might be bringing her a little something for tea in a minute, and realised with a degree of surprise that she was feeling hungry and was looking forward to a scone or a slice of cake. She became aware that the deep hurt she'd felt about Ashley had deadened somewhat. She still missed him dreadfully, she still loved him, but the agony of their row, the awfulness of their parting wasn't as raw.

She thought about what Mrs T had said about it never being too late to kiss and make up. She ought to offer an olive branch, ask him to forgive her for not being completely up-front about her home life when they'd first got to know each other. What was the worst that could happen? If he didn't want to know, then she'd be no worse off than she was now. On the other hand, if he accepted her apology, they could be friends again. Either way she couldn't make matters worse.

Should she ring him to apologise? She agonised about this for several minutes, but eventually decided she couldn't bear it if he cut her off. That would be too painful. She decided to text, and then spent even more time working out exactly what she was going to say. She wasn't going to risk text-speak; she was going to write to him properly, using capital letters and punctuation. She didn't want to risk any sort of misunderstanding that a missing full stop or comma might incur.

Dear Ashley, I am so sorry. Please forgive me for the awful row but it's over stupid misunderstandings like ours that relationships go wrong. We mustn't fall out and I want you to know I love you. I really do. I miss you so much. Please please call me. Tilly xxx

She checked the message several times, worrying about the wording. Could he mistake how sorry she was? Should she tell him how she felt, or would that frighten him off? Was she coming on too heavy? He knew how much she loved him, but did this text really convey how devastated she'd been by their row? She wished she could see into the future and know what his reaction to it would be. But that wasn't a possibility, so was she or wasn't she going to send it? With sudden determination she pressed the send button.

There, gone. She put the phone back on her bedside table and waited for his response.

In the bus shelter Ashley felt his phone vibrate gently before the musical tone told him he had a message. He lifted up the sodden hem of his jacket and reached into his trouser pocket to retrieve it. His hand was wet and cold but he had nothing to wipe it on. He hoped his phone wouldn't object to the odd drip of water.

Around him were half a dozen middle-aged women and some young mothers, all in wet mackintoshes and jackets, laden with carrier bags as a result of a day spent at the post-Christmas sales, or encumbered by push-chairs and fractious cold, miserable small children as well as their shopping, and all of them impatient for the arrival of the C30 bus, which connected Haybridge with the surrounding villages and which was running late.

Just as Ashley's numb, wet, cold hand reached his

phone, the bus appeared from the side road and turned towards the bus stop. As one, the ladies began to gather their purchases and collect their children and fold their buggies and shuffle closer to the kerbside opening in the bus shelter, all intent on reaching the relative warmth of the bus as soon as possible, and all scrabbling around in their capacious handbags for the correct change or their return tickets. None of them was paying much attention to anyone else around them. Certainly none of them paid any attention to the soggy lad still sitting on one of the plastic seats fiddling with his phone.

Ashley flipped open his mobile. 1 new message, the screen told him. Tilly mob, it added helpfully. Oh thank God, he thought. She was talking to him. Maybe she wanted to see him again. His heart raced with pleasure and relief. He pressed the button to call up her text.

Dear Ashley, I am so sorry. Please forgive me for the awful row but it's over

He stared at the message in disbelief. No! She couldn't. Not by text. He was so shocked he just sat there, not moving, while the tide of shoppers surged forward to board the bus.

One woman turned to talk to an acquaintance and the corner of her handbag, slung over her shoulder, clipped Ashley's knuckles as he continued to stare at the screen. The phone slipped from his wet grip, shot a couple of feet to his left and clattered on to the paving slabs. Instantly the screen went blank. He lunged to rescue it, but another shopper, heading relentlessly for the bus, caught it with the toe of her thick winter boot and the mobile skittered over the pavement, under the side of the bus shelter and into the gutter between the front and back wheels of the bus.

Beside him the bus engine throbbed throatily, like some sort of giant purring cat, and the shoppers continued to climb aboard, oblivious to what had just happened. Ashley stared impotently at the puddle-filled gutter. There was nothing he could do till the bus drew away, but the one thing he was certain about was that his phone was fucked. It might survive a few raindrops, but a total immersion? No – that meant curtains. Still, he'd be able to rescue his SIM card. But he didn't care half as much about his phone as he did about Tilly's message. His phone was just a minor annoyance compared to the awful kick-in-the-guts feeling he'd had on reading her text.

As soon as he got his SIM card into a new phone, he'd ring her and beg her to reconsider. He didn't care that it was neither macho nor cool to beg – he couldn't bear the thought that she had given up on what they had going, and over such a stupid row.

The last of the passengers crammed themselves on to the now heaving bus, the windows misted with condensation from the steaming bodies packed inside. The regular throb of the idling engine changed to a dull roar as the driver pressed the accelerator, there was a hiss as the pneumatic door clunked shut, and the bus began to move. At once, Ashley dived forward to scour the section of gutter where his phone ought to be. But as the dirty, oily water settled after the huge tyres of the bus had moved through it, he could see that the puddle contained nothing more than a couple of cigarette butts and a few discarded bus tickets. He cast frantically along the road, and a couple of yards further on he saw a black shiny rectangle balancing on the edge of the metal grating of a drain. The bow-wave from the bus's tyres must have pushed it along the road. He moved to reach it, but too late: it plunged over the edge of the drain as the stream of water flowing along the gutter carried it into the Haybridge sewer system.

Ashley shut his eyes in anger, frustration and horror. Just how much worse could things get? Dumped by his girlfriend, soaked through, and now, to cap it all, minus his phone, which held all his mates' numbers, all his music downloads, his pictures, a couple of video clips . . . In fact his life – and Tilly's number – had been on that phone, and he'd lost it.

Fuck.

There'd been no mistake about Tilly's meaning, that much was sure, thought Ashley. The phrase Dear Ashley, I am so sorry. Please forgive me for the awful row but it's over was burned on to his brain like a song on to a CD.

Not that he blamed her. How could he? It was he who'd been at fault. He shouldn't have cared that she was a toff when he wasn't. What did background matter when you loved someone? It was just an accident of birth when all was said and done. She certainly hadn't cared that socially they weren't equals, so why should he? No wonder she hadn't told him about her family. She must have had him sussed from the start as the sort of loser who would react exactly like he had to the fact that she was just a bit different. No, Tilly was the innocent and injured party in this skanky business. It was down to him to put things right. The trouble was, he couldn't ring her direct, because her phone number was lost along with everything else that was on his mobile.

He tried ringing the number for Haybridge Manor that was in the Yellow Pages, but all he got was a recorded message saying that the Manor was closed for the winter season and would be reopening on the second of April. Like he gave a damn. And the de Lieges were ex-directory.

Which left him with no alternative but to go and see

her. Maybe if he explained that it was just the shock of finding out that she wasn't 'the girl next door' that caused him to react so badly, she might forgive him and give him a second chance. But the trouble was, when he went to the Manor the next day, the big gates across the entrance were closed and locked and he couldn't find any sort of speakerphone or bell to ring to inform anyone in the house that he was there and would like to see Tilly. He tried walking round the entire estate, and at one point his spirits rose when he found a side door in the huge wall that formed one side of the house itself, but this was locked and bolted too, and again no sign of a bell or knocker.

Having got back wearily to where he'd started from, Ashley leaned against the entrance and wondered what on earth he could do to get in. And then he remembered. In a couple of days the de Lieges were throwing a big New Year's Eve party. He reckoned there'd be a fair chance of being able to gatecrash it – in fact, it'd hardly be gatecrashing; Tilly had invited him when all was said and done – although given the row that had followed, she might have considered withdrawing the invite. He'd have to wait till then but he reckoned that was his best chance. And it was only a couple of days away. He could be patient. It would be tough, but he'd have to manage it.

Tilly prowled around the house. Why hadn't Ashley got in touch? she kept asking herself, even though she thought she knew the answer. She'd pissed him off too much to be easily forgiven. And he was punishing her by making her wait. She considered texting him again, but then decided that would look too needy, like some sort of stalker. No, she had to be patient and let him come back to her in his own time.

Unless he wasn't going to. A lurch of panic gripped her. Supposing he was never going to forgive her. Oh

God, that just didn't bear thinking about. And in only a week she'd be back at her awful school, with no chance of seeing him again for months. Tilly was beside herself, swinging between fits of doubts and despair interspersed with feelings that there had to be a rational explanation for Ashley's lack of response: his phone was out of credit, he'd forgotten to charge it, he'd misplaced it . . . Of course he wasn't blanking her, he wasn't that cruel. But what if she was wrong? Maybe he wanted nothing more to do with her.

She had to know, so she gave in and phoned him. She was sent straight to voicemail. Her heart plummeted. He *was* blanking her, but hoping she didn't sound too desperate, like some sort of bunny-boiler, she left him a message with her mobile number and the house phone number and asked him to ring her just as soon as he could. Then all she could do was wait.

She drove her family and Mrs T spare with her moodiness. All of the previous evening she'd jumped every time the phone rang, yelled at her sisters and father for receiving calls and gone ballistic when they'd wanted to make them. In the morning she'd been up first thing, getting under everyone's feet but not doing anything constructive or helpful, even though the rest of the family and Mrs T had more than enough to do with the party only a couple of days away.

'I wish she was still playing the drama queen in bed,' muttered Flora to Daisy as Tilly screamed at the pair of them in a fit of rage for the pathetic reason that they'd hogged the bathroom when in fact all the poor girls had been doing was cleaning their teeth. 'And why isn't she still in bed? She never gets up before ten in the holidays.'

'Search me,' said Daisy. 'You can bet she's not got up to help out with the party.'

Even Mrs Thompson was beginning to lose patience. 'If you're going to be like that, you needn't think you can help me in the kitchen today,' she'd snapped after Tilly had bitched about the freshness of the bread, complained about the temperature of her coffee and muttered that Mrs T had bought the wrong sort of marmalade, all in the space of about five minutes.

Tilly realised she had gone too far; upsetting her sisters was one thing, but Mrs T didn't deserve it. She apologised.

'For God's sake, Tilly, take this and go and get yourself a dress.' Edward held out a couple of twenty-pound notes towards his daughter. Anything was better than having her snarling and sniping and under their feet.

Tilly gaped at him. Forty quid! It was a pretty tempting offer. She couldn't remember the last time he'd been free with his cash like that. And if she did manage to make contact with Ashley and persuade him to come to the party, she'd now have the chance to knock him dead. She grabbed the notes, muttered her thanks and ran to get her coat before her father changed his mind.

As she made her way into town, her eyes were darting manically over the faces of her fellow pedestrians just in case Ashley was amongst them. There was a good chance that she'd spot him; Haybridge wasn't a big town after all. It was almost with reluctance that she made her way into one of the women's clothing shops that fronted on to the high street. A women's clothing store was about the last place Ashley was likely to be. However, if she was going to wow him at the party, she needed something sexy and seductive, and this shop seemed like a good place to start the hunt, especially as it had a reputation for providing value for money and her budget of forty quid was hardly going to allow her to buy a designer label.

After browsing through the stock of this shop and several others, numerous trips to various changing rooms and a great deal of agonising, she eventually settled on a strapless leopard-print dress with a wide black belt to cinch in her waist and a choker of faux tiger's-eye beads that picked out shades of tawny, amber and black in the dress. Even Tilly, admiring herself in the changing room mirror for a final time, had to admit she looked pretty hot. At home she had a pair of vertiginous black stilettos, which would provide the final touch. How would Ashley be able to resist her dressed like this?

Assuming he came to the party.

Which was a big assumption given that he still hadn't rung or texted back.

Even if Tilly was plagued by doubts as to where she stood with Ashley, she was sure of one thing – her father would heartily disapprove of her dress. But what did she care? She hadn't bought it for his benefit. When she got home she hung it carefully in her wardrobe and then resigned herself to helping to get the house ready for the big do. It had become apparent from the moment she'd returned after her shopping trip that her father was imposing a three-line whip on his children and there was no way she was going to be able to escape from lending a hand. In fact he'd caught her sneaking in her bags of shopping and demanded that she dump them immediately and help. She'd only managed to get to her room to hide the dress first by using the excuse that she was desperate to go to the loo.

The next couple of days were frantic with activity. Apart from getting all the best china off the dresser in the sixteenth-century kitchen and washing each individual piece by hand to ensure there were enough plates for their guests to eat off, the rest of the kitchen needed a thorough clean and to be cleared of all the kitsch wax-works so the caterers could set up and prepare food in a halfway hygienic environment. Then crates of wine and champagne had to be brought up from the cellars, to say nothing of gallons of soft drinks; plus dozens of glasses had to be unpacked, tablecloths washed and ironed, lights strung up around the hall, flowers arranged . . . The list of jobs went on and on.

It came as no surprise to any of them that in the mayhem and chaos accidents happened. Several of the antique plates got broken, as did a couple of bottles of wine, and Tilly dropped a two-litre bottle of lemonade on the cellar floor. The bottle, being plastic, didn't shatter, but the amount of pressure that built up from the violence of the fall was sufficient to break the seal made by the cap and let the fizzy drink leak out. Meaning to clear up the mess later – if she could be bothered – she shoved it in a corner at the bottom of the cellar steps and returned to the fray upstairs.

By four on the afternoon of New Year's Eve, everything had been done. The caterers had arrived and were busy taking over the kitchen, unpacking platters and trays and working out how the antique range worked. Luckily, thought Tilly, they had also brought a couple of microwaves and two portable gas hobs, as she didn't think that even professional cooks were going to get much joy out of the Victorian monster that had last seen active service at about the same time as the Light Brigade had ridden into the Valley of Death. As far as she knew, it just sat in the kitchen as a curiosity and not as a piece of working kit, but the caterers seemed to be determined to bring it to life. While they grafted in the kitchen, a four-piece band set up at one end of the great hall and a DJ set up a disco at the other. None of these people needed any help from the family, so Tilly grabbed the opportunity to shoot upstairs, bag the bathroom and run an enormous bath, not caring in the least that she'd used every last drop of hot water from the domestic system.

Once bathed, which took hours, she closeted herself in her room, painting her nails, plucking her eyebrows, moisturising and making up and making sure she wasn't available in any way for the last-minute errands her father wanted his children to run for him. She lurked in there until the top floor of the house went completely silent, a sure-fire indication that the rest of her family had gone downstairs to be ready to greet the first arrivals. She knew that if Ashley was going to turn up, he'd wait until there was a crowd of people about so that his presence was less likely to be noticed, so there was no need for her to be downstairs early for his sake. She was certain he would come. She'd left three messages on his voicemail imploring him to come along, telling him that she'd been so wrong in hiding her ancestry from him, telling him how much he meant to her. And she'd bought her dress with only him in mind. He had to see her in it, then how would he be able to resist her?

Of course Ashley's reaction to That Dress and her father's were going to be somewhat different, Tilly was sure of that. But Fa could yell at her as much as he liked later just as long as she wowed Ashley.

Buffed and polished and clad in her dressing gown, she lounged about on the sofa watching TV until she judged the moment to make her entrance had come.

It only took her minutes to slip on her new dress, cinch the belt up to its last buckle hole and push her feet into her towering stilettos. She checked her reflection, and even under her own critical eye she decided she looked utterly foxy. With careful nonchalance she sashayed down the stairs into the great hall, fully aware that jaws dropped and heads turned as she made her entrance. She scanned the upturned faces. No Ashley. Damn. But it was still quite early for a New Year's party, when the main event couldn't happen till midnight.

Her father looked daggers at her and she knew she'd get a row from him about her outfit when the guests had gone, but she didn't care. All she wanted was for Ashley to see her, and as long as he did, she was prepared for any sanctions her father decided to impose on her in the morning.

'You're late,' hissed her father out of the corner of his mouth as she swayed sinuously over to join him. Tilly just blew him a kiss and then smiled at the group of people around him.

She took them in. Boring City types with glossy wives and vacuous children was her assessment, but she smiled sweetly and allowed her father to introduce her to all of them. With the introductions she was able to fine-tune her assessment: the wives seemed to be brainless bimbos only interested in shopping and holidays, while the older children were arrogant and self-opinionated and the younger ones spoilt and badly behaved; some of them making it plain that they would rather be at home watching TV than enjoying the de Lieges' hospitality. Frankly she didn't care if they pushed off; she certainly didn't want to spend an evening with them either. All she wanted was for Ashley to turn up. But despite her views about her father's guests, she had had a sufficient sense of duty and good manners instilled in her (unlike some of the other offspring in the room, she noted) to know that she was a hostess and must behave like one.

A drink was offered, which she accepted, and she sipped and nodded as if she was interested in the self-satisfied, smug and banal conversation, while her eyes darted past the faces in the group around her and scanned the room for Ashley. She knew he hadn't answered her text, but surely he'd turn up tonight of all nights. Please God, she prayed silently. Please make him come. If he comes, I promise not to skip school assembly ever again, she bargained. Please.

But Ashley still didn't appear. Tilly grabbed another drink off a tray proffered by a passing waiter but eschewed the canapés and nibbles; her belt was so tight she couldn't bear the thought of eating anything. And anyway her longing for Ashley had taken away any appetite she might once have had. Maybe her pleading messages had fallen on stony ground. Maybe he wasn't going to come.

So if he wasn't going to spend New Year with her, where would he go? Maybe the skate park. She gazed around the room, wondering if she could escape to see if he was there. Perhaps if she waited until everyone – especially her father – had drunk a bit more, she might be able to get away with it. She'd slip out later and try to find him. And if he wasn't at the skate park, she resolved to go round to the council estate and find him there. She began to plan the best way, and time, to go.

14

'I say, you look jolly pretty,' said a yock-yock voice.
Tilly turned round to see who the twit with the cod
upper-class accent was. A mid-twenties chinless wonder
– no surprise there.

'You must be Tilly,' the chap continued. 'Let me
introduce myself. I'm Marcus.'

He seemed to say it so proudly, Tilly wondered briefly
if he wanted a prize for being able to remember it. She
restrained herself from retorting 'bully for you'.

'Hello, Marcus,' she replied, bestowing a smile on
him. After all, it wasn't the poor lad's fault he was such a
jerk he should've been drowned at birth.

'Can I get you a drink?' he offered.

Tilly glanced at her glass. It was empty again. How
had that happened? 'Go on then.'

Marcus found a waiter and grabbed a bottle of wine
and two glasses off him. 'Nothing like a bit of self-
sufficiency, I always say,' he said, pouring the wine.

Maybe he wasn't quite so dumb after all, thought Tilly,
taking a sip from her glass. She scanned the room again.

'Looking for someone?' asked Marcus.

'No, not really,' she lied.

'So what's it like living in a place like this?' Marcus
gestured at the vast room with its hammer-beam roof,
floor of ancient, worn flagstones and walls decorated with
arms and armour.

'Cold,' said Tilly laconically. 'Upstairs, where we live, isn't so bad, but I'd give my back teeth to live somewhere with proper plumbing, double glazing and a state-of-the-art kitchen.'

'But isn't the kitchen here renowned? Isn't it as amazing as the one at Hampton Court?'

Tilly snorted. 'You're kidding me? Have you seen it?'

Marcus shook his head, so Tilly grabbed his free hand and told him to follow her. She led him down the corridor and through the massive wooden door at the far end.

'There,' she said as they entered the huge space, with its gleaming copper pans, huge fire and now-empty dresser. Around them swirled the caterers and the waiters as the cooks prepared the canapés and arranged them on trays and platters ready to be offered to the guests. Other staff were preparing the cold buffet that was going to be served later that evening. There was an atmosphere of subdued tension, as the smooth service depended on careful timing and no mistakes or cock-ups.

'What's wrong with it?' said Marcus, perplexed.

Tilly's brow furrowed. 'So where's the dishwasher, the washing machine, the mixer . . .' She gestured to the huge pine table in the middle, nearly slopping the wine out of her glass in the process. 'And what about some surfaces that are easy to clean? Just wiped down and not scrubbed. And anything that might actually be called modern. Or functional, for that matter.' Her voice was raised as her diatribe against the state of the kitchen had to be held against the bustle of activity flowing around her. 'Of course this one is really only for show; we have another kitchen upstairs in the family apartment, but that is almost as bad. Just as decrepit in its own shabby way.'

'Excuse me.'

Tilly stopped her tirade and turned towards the

unknown voice addressing her. 'Yes?' She saw a young woman in chef's whites.

'Are you something to do with this place?'

Tilly nodded. 'I live here, yes.'

'Well we need some more mineral water. Do you know if there is any?'

Tilly thought. 'Isn't there some in the pantry – along with all the other drinks to be served?'

'Can't see any.'

They might have forgotten to bring up enough bottles from the cellar. Tilly couldn't remember whether they had or not. She was about to tell the girl where to find it, but she could see that she was up to her eyes already. 'I'll get some for you.'

'That'd be wonderful. Half a dozen big bottles should do the trick.'

'Come on,' Tilly said to Marcus. 'You can lend a hand.'

She led the way across the kitchen to the old wooden door in the corner. She opened it and went to the head of the stairs that wound down into the pitch-black depths. As she put her hand on the light switch, the door swung shut behind them. For a second they were plunged into silent darkness. Tilly flicked the switch, and as light flooded the place, an ear-piercing squeaking filled the air.

Tilly jumped. 'What the fuck . . .' she said. What the hell was making that ghastly noise? A mouse? A rat? She shuddered; mice she could cope with, but not rats. Nervously she crept down the steps, hugging the edge of the treads and ready to run if she caught so much as a glimpse of one.

'Is that a mouse?'

Tilly nodded and swallowed. 'I hope so.'

'Hope so?'

'Better that than a rat. And more likely, really, as the whole house is plagued by them and we regularly have to get the mouse man in to deal with them But he's very tidy and we rarely see the evidence of the cull. And generally we don't see much of the live ones either – we just smell them and see the droppings.'

'Yuck.'

'Yuck indeed.' She was now halfway down the steps and could see the floor of the cellar. Nothing. The squeaking was still carrying on, just as loud and just as awful, but whatever was making the racket was well hidden.

Tilly continued her descent. She was almost on the last step when she saw the mouse.

'Oh God,' she shrieked, jumping back up a step and cannoning into Marcus, who grabbed her to steady and reassure her.

'What is it?'

'It's awful,' she cried. 'You're going to have to do something.'

'Me?'

Tilly shot him a lethal look. 'Yes, you. You're a man, aren't you?'

Marcus quailed very slightly and then stiffened. 'Yes.' He moved down the remainder of the stairs and peered forward to see what was upsetting Tilly so much. In the now almost dry pool of lemonade at the bottom of the stairs was a mouse, stuck like a bluebottle to flypaper. Its paws, tail and belly were glued fast, while the upper parts of its body were trembling with violent shivers of fear, its little black eyes huge and staring, its whiskers quivering, while out of its mouth issued the constant stream of pathetic piercing squeaks.

'I'll kill it,' said Marcus. 'It'll be kinder.' He started to look around for a weapon.

'No,' said Tilly in horror. It was one thing knowing the mouse man put down humane traps which dispatched mice by the dozen. That way she didn't have to witness the deed being done. But this was different. Marcus was offering to slay this poor defenceless creature by stomping on it or bashing it on the head with a broom handle or something equally horrible, and in cold blood.

'Well, what *do* you want me to do?'

'Can't you rescue it?' asked Tilly pathetically.

'Rescue it?'

She nodded.

Marcus took a deep breath as he assessed the situation. 'I suppose I could try and unstick it. Maybe with some water.'

'Shit. The water!' Tilly leapt down the last two steps, tottered past him on her stilettos and grabbed several bottles of mineral water. 'Back in a minute.' She disappeared, while Marcus stared at the mouse.

'Why am I doing this?' he asked it. The mouse just looked at him, whiskers still quivering. He picked up another bottle of water from the stack on the cellar floor and unscrewed the cap. Slowly he poured some water around the mouse. He reckoned it ought to dissolve the sugar in the sticky lemonade pool, and once freed, the mouse would be able to escape and clean itself up. He thought it would only take a few seconds to take effect, but the mouse remained firmly stuck.

Marcus edged into the sticky patch to see if he could at least free part of the mouse. He tried unpicking the creature's tail from the floor. His efforts were rewarded with an even more heart-rending and piercing squeal.

'Careful!' shrieked Tilly, halfway down the steps, her cry adding to the din. 'You're hurting it.' Her previous revulsion to mice in general had been replaced by pity for this pathetic specimen in particular

'I'm doing my best,' grumped Marcus. 'This isn't easy, you know.'

Tilly reached the ground, grabbed another armload of bottles and ferried them upstairs. On her return, she brought with her a dustpan and a plate of vol-au-vents.

'Here,' she said, thrusting them at Marcus.

'Thanks,' he said, stuffing a pastry into his mouth.

'They're not for you,' she snapped. 'That poor little thing is probably starving. It could have been stuck fast for a couple of days.

Marcus meekly put a few crumbs of pastry in front of the mouse's nose. It ignored them, but he didn't dare snaffle another canapé himself, even if the mouse wasn't the least bit interested.

'What's this for?' He waved the dustpan at her.

'I thought you might be able to slide it under the mouse.'

Marcus looked at the dustpan, then at the mouse, and back to the dustpan. He bent down and pushed the edge against the tail of the poor trapped creature. The mouse shrieked but the tail moved. 'Maybe,' he said. He poured on more water. Perhaps it was having some effect.

Tillys at on the bottom step, her knees decorously clamped together in deference to the length of her skirt, and watched Marcus work. Water, then the edge of the dustpan, then the application of more water, then a gentle push with the pan . . . He was very patient, she'd give him that. And gentle. He might be a public-school twerp, but he was a kind one. She could forgive him for being a complete idiot because he was kind. That scored pretty highly in her book.

It took an age to sort out the mouse. Whether it was through exhaustion or whether the animal realised that the humans were trying to help it, the squeaks faded and stopped, although it was still quivering.

'Is it frightened or cold, do you think?' asked Tilly, noticing the juddering that seemed to rack the poor creature's body.

'Both, I imagine.' A couple of minutes later, Marcus managed to scoop the mouse into the dustpan, where it lay shivering and exhausted and completely bedraggled.

'The poor little thing,' said Tilly. 'We can't let it go outside in this state.'

Marcus looked at her. 'So what do you plan to do with it?' he asked patiently. 'Take it to A and E?'

Tilly ignored his comment. 'Haven't you got a hanky or something we could dry it with?'

Marcus sighed and extracted a pressed and monogrammed linen square from his jacket pocket. Tilly took it and shook it open, then gingerly put the hanky over the mouse and picked it up. The mouse squeaked once, pathetically, as Tilly cradled it in her hand with just its head and beady eyes poking clear of the material.

'Do you think it's got fleas?' she asked.

Marcus nodded. 'Probably.'

Tilly grimaced. 'We'd better hope all that mineral water drowned them, then.'

'What are you going to do with it now?'

'Once it's a bit drier, I think we should put it in the garden.'

'But it's a house mouse.'

'Then it's just going to have to start to love the outdoors. I can't let it go in the house. Dad would go mental if he found out. We spend a fortune on pest control every year.'

'Then you'd better make sure it's properly dry, otherwise it'll catch its death of cold. It's freezing out.'

Tilly nodded and looked at the little creature. Now that it had stopped its awful squealing and she could see it close up, she had to admit it was quite sweet, with its whiffly whiskers and bright little eyes. She could understand why kids liked having them as pets. It was really rather appealing. However, she wasn't so fond of it that she couldn't harden her heart to the fact that it was going to have to take its chances in the great outdoors.

15

Ashley stood in the shadow of the gatehouse and looked at the cars parked on the gravel forecourt of the Manor: Porsches, Mercs, BMWs, Jags, Lexuses – or should that be Lexi? Every top-of-the-range luxury car was represented, but no Corsas or Micras, he noticed wryly. Nothing cheap and cheerful parked here. Some of the lads from his estate would give their back teeth to get their hands on this lot. Although, he thought, they'd all have such high-end alarms and immobilisers that getting their hands on them would be about all they'd be able to do; they certainly wouldn't be able to sit in them or drive them away, with or without the owner's consent. And how much were the cars worth in total? One mill? Two? More? Ashley shook his head in bemused amazement. He couldn't imagine anyone knowing so many rich people. In fact he couldn't imagine what it would be like to know anyone rich. Most the people on his estate were just managing to scrape by if someone in the household had a job. If they didn't, they existed on benefits, which was about all benefits allowed you to do – exist. You couldn't call it living.

Of course, looking at the fabulous house that was Tilly's home, a casual observer would imagine that the occupants were as rich as Croesus, except that if what Tilly had told him was true, she and her family were flat broke. Ashley sighed. She'd been very insistent that she had been truthful, but it was hard to swallow looking at this car park. And Ashley imagined that the sort of people who swanned around in these sorts of cars weren't used to slumming it, so the party going on in the house had to be quite an event to get them to pitch up in the first place. Surely that stood to reason. Therefore it also stood to reason that the party had cost a great deal to put on. Which meant that Tilly's definition of 'poor' and his were still poles apart.

He slumped against the rough stonework and sighed again. Tilly was lush, a real babe, and he felt so much for her. He couldn't believe that she'd dumped him. Not over such a stupid row. Not when he considered how well they'd got on, right up to that point. Maybe, if he could just see her tonight, he'd be able to persuade her to change her mind. He didn't want their relationship to end. It had nothing to do with the fact that he now knew she had a vast house and an inheritance. He wouldn't have cared if she lived in a dump like he did. He didn't care about any of the material things he'd discovered she had; he just cared for her. She was so lovely and so beautiful and he hadn't been able to believe his luck that she had cared for him too. He couldn't lose her now.

He scanned the front of the house, now floodlit and looking stunning in the amber light that turned the grey stone to a beautiful honey colour. He remembered the last time he'd been to the place, when there had been no chance of getting in. That patently wasn't going to be a problem now: the gate to the forecourt was thrown back and the big double doors at the front were also standing wide. If there was any security or bouncers it was all very discreet. He had to hope there was no one checking invitations or a guest list inside; he didn't have anything to prove that Tilly had asked him along. Not that he'd accepted her invite anyway. He'd been such a stupid prat, yelling at her like that, but it was the shock of finding out that she wasn't the girl next door. In fact she wasn't even the girl from the other side of the tracks. It turned out she was the girl from a different planet. Was there ever going to be a possibility that he would fit in on her one? And thinking about fitting in, he wasn't even sure that his shirt and tie was going to fit the dress code. He had a feeling that it might be a black-tie do. He swallowed nervously. Talk about a fish out of water. Even looking the smartest he ever had, he was hardly going to blend in seamlessly.

Nervously Ashley began to make his way through the ranks of parked cars towards the front door. He spotted a movement ahead of him. Someone was coming out – no, two people were leaving. Or wanting a breath of fresh air. Or maybe they'd come out for a smoke. Ashley stared at the couple as they moved into the glare of one of the floodlights that shone up at the front of the house. Then he recognised the woman. Tilly! And she was with a bloke. In a black tie. They were very close, he noticed, feeling possessive. Then the pair of them bent down and a few seconds later straightened up again. Ashley didn't have a clue what they were up to – maybe the bloke was helping Tilly with her shoes or something – but they were laughing and joking, he could tell that from their body language. He watched, immobilised with anger and misery, as he saw Tilly lean towards the man and give him a light kiss on the cheek, and then they both returned inside, still sharing a joke, still very comfortable with each other.

She didn't waste much time, did she? As soon as she'd got rid of him, she'd moved on to someone else. Someone with a bigger wallet, no doubt. Someone who fitted better into her social circle of friends. Someone who hadn't come off the local council estate. Someone who wasn't a charity case. Ashley's anger ratcheted up a notch with every reason he came up with for being replaced by that . . . that . . . that bastard in a penguin suit. A part of him wondered which of these cars belonged to the bloke. He'd like to take his anger out on the car – key the paintwork, do something mindless and pointless.

And she'd kissed him. How could she kiss another bloke when she'd said she loved him?

Ashley felt rage, frustration and disappointment boil around inside him, and it was all made worse by the knowledge that it was entirely his own fault. If he hadn't gone off on one, just because she'd levelled with him, he and Tilly would still be together. He supposed he couldn't blame her for finding someone else, but it was the *speed* at which she'd done it that caused him so much pain. Bloody hell, she had probably had longer attachments to newspapers than she had had to him.

Which hurt. Deeply. Ashley could feel tears of self-pity welling up along with the eruption of rage.

Oh, what was the point? he thought, as he dashed the tears away. He'd never had a chance. He'd always been out of his league and he knew it. He'd known it deep down even before he'd found out who she really was. All that was happening now was that he was being shown just how right he was. Which made him feel used as well as stupid. He might as well face it: there'd never been a realistic chance for him and her. Just as well it had ended as swiftly as it had all begun – before he'd really fallen for her. Which, he told himself, he hadn't. But he knew that was blatant self-delusion.

He adored her. Still did. It'd be a long time before he'd forget the girl he'd met at the skate park.

Morosely he turned and left the Manor.

'So what do you think its chances of survival are?' Tilly said to Marcus as they returned to the warmth of the great hall and the buzz of the party.

'Fair to middling, I'd say. Given that you sent it on its way with a year's supply of puff pastry.'

'The poor thing has had a traumatic experience. It was the least I could do.' Tilly glanced at her watch.

'It's ages to go till midnight,' said Marcus.

'I wasn't . . .' Tilly halted what she was going to say – about working out if it was a good moment to bunk off the party to try to find Ashley. Not diplomatic, especially considering how she'd bullied poor Marcus into helping her with the mouse. 'Yes, ages.' Maybe she'd send Ashley yet another text to wish him a happy New Year. If he answered, perhaps she could arrange to meet him somewhere. That would be a better plan than just wandering around aimlessly on the off chance of running into him.

'Just need to pop upstairs for a minute,' she told Marcus as she headed towards the stairs. It didn't take her long to phrase a short message and press 'send', then she fiddled around for a few minutes while she waited for a reply. And waited and waited. Nothing. But she wasn't going to give up. If he wasn't going to reply to her text, then she had to see him in person.

She went to her wardrobe and swapped her stilettos for trainers, then pulled on a thick coat over her skimpy dress. At least she'd be warm, even if the wow factor was gone. She'd have to tell Ashley what he'd missed when she saw him. She hurried down the back stairs and along a labyrinth of passages until she was able to slip out via the tradesmen's entrance at the edge of the gravelled forecourt. She glanced at her watch. She had a little over two hours before midnight. And given the huge crush of guests in the great hall, she didn't think she'd be missed until then. She loped off down the avenue and towards the town and the skate park.

Ashley sat on the bench at the skate park thinking that this had to be the shittiest New Year's Eve ever. No girl, no party, no booze and all alone. He kicked his heels as he wondered what to do. His parents and the boys had gone out to a friend's house; Big Sal was from Glasgow and made it a point of honour to try to get the whole estate wasted every Hogmanay. But Ashley, hoping to spend the evening with Tilly, had declined the invitation, and pride now prevented him from admitting publicly that his 'better offer' was a bag of nails. He decided to go home. He might as well go to bed as do anything else. Wearily he left the bench and headed back to the estate. It was pretty quiet. Everyone else was round at Sal's, he concluded morosely as he let himself into the dark, silent house. He went up to his room, threw off his smart kit, climbed into bed and pulled the covers over his head.

The world could stuff itself.

He was woken by the doorbell ringing. Some stupid idiot first-footing, he imagined. Since Sal's arrival in the area there'd been a number of stupid Scots traditions she'd managed to import, first-footing being the dumbest. Who on earth wanted to be given a lump of coal, especially considering this was a smokeless zone and all the houses were on gas central heating? Well, he wasn't going to haul himself downstairs just for the pleasure of telling some fuckwit what they could do with it.

He pulled his covers tighter over his head and ignored the fact that whoever was on the doorstep wasn't taking no for an answer.

Tilly gave up. Ashley obviously wasn't in, and given that he hadn't been at the skate park and wasn't at home, she was now at a total loss as to where to start looking. She glanced at her watch. Only twenty minutes to midnight. She'd be pushed to get home before then. Maybe she'd catch sight of him on her way back through town. There was a chance – only a slight one – but everyone had to be somewhere.

She set off at a steady jog, back through the council

estate, back past the rowdy party that was spilling out of a house into the front garden and on to the grass verge by the road. She considered asking if anyone there knew Ashley, but the people seemed so pissed she didn't feel it was a sensible idea at all. She crept past the house on the other side of the street, keeping in the shadows. This wasn't an area that she felt was totally safe; plus she was a young girl on her own, late at night, on the one day in the year when it was almost guaranteed that almost every red-blooded male in the country was going to be totally tanked up. All in all, and given what she was (almost) wearing under her coat, the lowest profile she could get was the only option.

She slunk off the estate and made her way back through the town centre as fast as possible. Even the more crowded streets and the bright lights didn't allay her feelings of vulnerability. There were still a lot of drunken youths about and any number of dark side turnings, staff car parks and alleyways that might conceal threats and dangers. Her only consolation that as she was relatively sober and shod in running shoes, she had a better than even chance of getting away if anyone did try anything on.

She felt relief when she reached the bridge over the river. She was on home turf now and she felt almost safe again. She slowed her pace and allowed herself the luxury of glancing at her watch.

Shit. Five to. Suddenly she began to sympathise with Cinderella. The poor bitch must have been shitting herself if she felt anything like Tilly did right now. There'd be hell to pay if she wasn't around to see in the New Year with their guests. Her father would be livid. She broke into a run, up the hill, down the avenue and across the car park. Panting, she made it to the side door just as she heard the guests in the great hall start the countdown. She tore her coat off as she ran down the corridor and arrived, breathless, flushed and dishevelled, just as everyone threw themselves energetically and tunelessly into 'Auld Lang Syne'. In the melee and chaos, no one noticed her entrance, nor her state, and once the dancing and whirling had subsided, she wasn't the only person in the room flushed, panting and dishevelled.

'What happened to your shoes?' said Marcus with a faint slur.

Tilly jumped. Where the hell had he materialised from, and more importantly, had he noticed her absence? 'They were killing me,' she lied. 'I've just been upstairs changing out of them,' she added, hoping that he hadn't noticed she'd been gone well over an hour, rather than just a few minutes.

Marcus swallowed the fib. 'Shame. They made your legs look very sexy.'

Tilly smiled at him and pretended to be flattered. But now that she was home and safe, her anxiety subsided and allowed another, much rawer emotion to replace it. She felt completely bereft that she hadn't found Ashley, and while everyone around her was laughing and hugging and kissing, she was cracking up with misery that the only person in the world she wanted to be with right at this moment was nowhere to be found.

16

'I say, that's good news.' Her father looked up from the letter he was reading.

'What is?' asked Tilly as she buttered her toast. She didn't feel inclined to be cheerful or upbeat about anything. She still felt like crying every time she thought about Ashley, but he'd made his point – he didn't want her and she couldn't think of anything she could do to change his mind.

Edward waved a page at her. 'It seems you made quite a hit with young Marcus.'

'Marcus?'

'Marcus Crosby. You know. Nice chap. Came to our party.'

Tilly remembered. The twerp with the kind heart and the hanky. Well, whoop-de-do. The only man she cared about was Ashley, and she'd heard nothing from him for nearly two weeks. Nothing since the row. She knew she ought to accept that it was over between them, but it still hurt. The wound might heal, but there was always going to be a scar.

'Good,' she said, with no trace of enthusiasm.

'Anyway, the upshot is that the Crosbys want us to go skiing with them.'

'Skiing,' squealed Flora and Daisy in unison.

Tilly remained silent, but even she had to admit that the prospect of a skiing holiday held a certain appeal.

Actually, *any* holiday held a certain appeal, as they never had the cash to be able to afford to go off on jaunts. 'Abroad?' she asked dubiously. The idea of skiing was all right in theory, but only if it was to somewhere really lush. Which ruled out Scotland, as far as she was concerned. Freezing bloody cold and not the least bit glamorous.

And then there was the caveat that this was a skiing holiday with the Crosbys. Did she really want to spend a week with Marcus? Even if it was somewhere nicer than Scotland.

'Switzerland. They own a chalet. They wondered if we'd like to join them in February.'

Well, Switzerland wouldn't be so bad. At least there'd be chocolate.

'Can we?' pleaded Daisy.

'I'll have to think about it. Tilly's got her A levels in the summer and we haven't any kit.'

'Oh, Daddy,' wailed Flora, fearing her father had already made his mind up.

'Like I said, I'll have to think about it, but if the dates fit in with half-term, I might be persuaded.'

Tilly, who had no idea what was involved on a skiing holiday except . . . err . . . skiing, wasn't sure whether to be elated or worried. There were several drawbacks as far as she could tell. The first was that she didn't have a clue how to ski; the second was she'd have to spend time with Marcus; and the last was the prospect that if the weather was shitty (they'd be in the mountains in February so the chances were considerable) she'd also be closeted with her siblings. And as her father said, her A levels were coming up and she ought to be working, not gadding about. She really wasn't sure that the benefits outweighed the disadvantages.

Her father had returned his attention to the letter from his friend and his breakfast; the subject was now closed until he had made his decision. Breakfast stuttered on in near silence, the twins exchanging excited whispers about the possible holiday and Tilly lost in thoughts about Ashley.

When she'd finished her toast, she left the table and went to her bedroom. She knew she ought to revise for her mocks, which were imminent, but in fact all she did was lie on her bed and think about Ashley.

She was immersed in sad thoughts when she heard a soft knock at the door.

'Come in,' she called resentfully. She really didn't feel like being sociable.

Her father shuffled in, still clutching his letter. 'Desmond took a shine to you at New Year too,' he informed her.

Who the fuck was Desmond? 'Jolly good,' she replied flatly. 'But I thought you said at breakfast that it was Marcus who liked me.' Like she cared.

'Desmond Crosby. Marcus's father. He's only got the one child, and if Marcus likes someone then Desmond takes an interest.'

What?! Tilly's radar switched on. This sounded like there was a completely different agenda. What sort of interest? And why? This was all a bit creepy for her taste. She needed to pay attention.

'Anyway, it seems young Marcus has asked if it would be all right for him to come and visit you in your next exeat, maybe take you out for lunch. So I've just phoned his father to say that of course it would.'

'You did *what*?' asked Tilly.

'It'd be nice for you to have someone to come over and take you somewhere, someone nearer your own age, someone . . .' Edward stuttered to a stop as he saw the look of total horror on Tilly's face. 'Is that a problem?' he finished lamely.

'You said what to . . . ? What do you . . . ?' Tilly was

spluttering with indignation and was completely incoherent. 'Yes, it is a problem,' she managed finally.

'But he's a nice boy. And he likes you. And you've got lots in common.'

Tilly raised an eyebrow. What on earth would she have in common with that numpty?

'His parents are separated too.'

'So are the parents of half the girls at school, but I don't like most of them either.'

Edward sighed and tried a different tack. 'What's wrong with going out with him one Saturday? He's a nice bloke, he's got a good degree, a good job guaranteed for life in the family banking business and his father says he's got a decent car. You'd have a nice time.'

'Nice time?' Tilly snorted. 'No I wouldn't. And apart from the fact that I don't even like the guy particularly *and* he's a banker – I mean, puh-lease, that really *isn't* a recommendation – this is the twenty-first century and I'm British. Maybe it's passed you by, but we don't do arranged relationships in this country these days.'

'Don't exaggerate, Tilly. Who said anything about a relationship?'

'But it's what you and Desmond are plotting, isn't it? Otherwise why are the two of you trying to throw us together?'

'We're not.'

Tilly tossed her head. 'Oh no? The party? The skiing holiday, and now this exeat business? I'm not stupid, Dad. Marcus may be – in fact he *is* – as thick as shit; he's in banking, it's a given, but I'm not. I want to choose my own boyfriends.'

'Like that Ainsley—'

'Ashley!' Tilly yelled at her father in annoyance and frustration.

'Like that *Ashley* was such a winner,' her father yelled

back, angry at his daughter's defiance. 'He treated you so appallingly that he made you ill.'

'He didn't treat *me* badly. I treated *him* badly and now I can't make it up to him because I can't get in touch with him. It was my guilt that made me feel so awful.' The pair faced each other furiously.

'Then get over him. Move on.'

'Like you did with Mummy.'

Edward didn't reply. Silence fell.

'Sorry,' mumbled Tilly, fully aware she'd gone too far.

'I should think so too. And for your information, young lady, I loved your mother very much and I still do. We're still married and I still hope she'll come back one day,' and with that Edward turned and left the room.

Feeling shaky, Tilly sat on her bed. Once again she'd screwed up. Bugger. She wondered what retribution her father might exact. There were bound to be sanctions – like last time.

The feared sanctions didn't materialise, but Edward remained distant until Tilly departed for school a couple of days later.

'I'll be in touch with you about arrangements for your exeat,' was all he said on the subject as he dropped her at the school front door.

'Thanks for the lift,' said Tilly, purposely ignoring the reference to her weekend out.

Their farewell was cool and Tilly retreated to her study-bedroom to unpack and wallow in self-pity and memories of Ashley as she played, over and over, the CD he'd given her for Christmas. Not that her self-indulgence could last for long: the next morning started with breakfast, followed by the first of her mock A levels, and for the next few weeks she was in a whirl of exams and revision and panic about both.

In the evenings, when she sat in the sixth-form

common room with her peers, prep and revision done, she tried to ignore their mindless chat and gossip and used the time to listen to her music on her iPod and think about Ashley. It was impossible to ignore the other girls completely, although she did her best. She'd never really fitted in at school, as she'd always felt constrained by her family's lack of cash and the run-down state of their house – she was embarrassed by it, especially when she eavesdropped on the conversations about the jet-set lifestyles of many of the others: the places they went to, their holidays, their multiple houses in exotic locations.

And they all seemed so sophisticated. She felt like a complete country bumpkin when she heard them talking about the parties they'd been to, the people they'd met, the men they'd been with and the substances they'd tried. She wondered on several occasions if she was the only virgin left in the sixth form. But what chance did she have of rectifying the situation when the only boy she'd ever really loved had dumped her because of her family – and now that same family was trying to hitch her up with a brainless banker?

To escape from her miserable thoughts about Ashley, her family and Marcus, she threw herself into her school work, much to the approval of her house mistress, but it seemed no time at all before the mocks were over and the first dreaded exeat of the term arrived.

The subject of any planned activities for the long weekend was tiptoed around during the journey home as the conversation between Tilly and her father centred on Mrs T's health, the twins and the state of the guttering on the west wing. The subject of the skiing holiday was also avoided – or so it seemed to Tilly.

They were nearing Haybridge when Edward mentioned arrangements for the half-term holiday, albeit obliquely.

'I've made an appointment for you at the

photographer on East Street tomorrow, so don't make any plans for the morning, there's a good girl.'

'The photographer. Why on earth?'

'I need to get your passport organised.'

'Passport?' Tilly couldn't disguise her surprise. 'So does that mean we're going skiing?'

'It means we probably are,' said Edward guardedly.

'With the Crosbys?'

Edward nodded. 'As they're the people who have invited us, that would be the likely scenario.'

Tilly assimilated the information and tried to analyse how she felt. The prospect of a holiday, even if it was one that involved an activity she had never tried before, seemed fairly appealing, but a week with Marcus . . . hmmm, not so. Even if they weren't expected to spend time together on 'dates', she suspected that their every move was going to be closely watched by their respective fathers for any signs of friendship or affection. Frankly, thought Tilly, she'd be like a rat in a laboratory under such parental scrutiny, and probably just as miserable.

However, what were her options? She could refuse to go, pleading pressure of revision for her A levels (perfectly plausible), but was staying at home and fending for herself a better option? And that was supposing her father agreed. As she wouldn't be eighteen till April, she was pretty sure that if he demanded that she go with the rest of the family, she wouldn't be in much of a position to refuse.

'Do I gather it's not a done deal?' said Tilly.

'I just need to organise the flights. I'm waiting to hear back from the travel agent. A lot of people go skiing at that time of year, apparently.'

Most of her school friends – if the chat in the common rooms was to be believed. In the past Tilly had ignored all such conversations, knowing that the chances of her joining the après-ski set were negligible. This year, though, she'd paid rather more attention, trying to pick up the lingua franca of the ski slopes so she wouldn't sound quite such a novice. Not that she was going to be able to disguise the fact that she didn't have a clue about the whole skiing process as soon as she strapped those planks on her feet, but she'd cross that bridge when she came to it. The more she thought about it, the less able she was to work out if the flutterings in her stomach were nerves or excitement; the thought of going abroad for the first time in her life was quite exciting, but going abroad with Marcus – that was a different kettle of fish entirely. And there was the very real problem of how she might handle things if he got too friendly, egged on by his father. Yuck. Another bridge she'd have to cross.

But before the skiing holiday, if it materialised, there was the question of this long weekend. Were the Crosbys going to show up while she was home? Tilly wanted to find out without asking her father, partly because she didn't want to spark another row and partly because she didn't want him to think that her curiosity meant she was keen on Marcus. Just because he'd been quite sweet about that mouse didn't mean she saw him as a friend, or anything else for that matter. Blimey, thought Tilly, if having someone share an act of kindness with you meant they got singled out as your life partner, it was enough to turn most people into raving sociopaths – herself included.

As soon as she got home she wandered nonchalantly into the kitchen, ostensibly to say hello to Mrs T but really to find out what the catering arrangements were for the weekend.

'And can I give you a hand with any of that?' she asked casually, having discovered that it was steak and kidney pie for supper that evening, macaroni cheese for lunch the following day and roast pork on Sunday.

'You can help with any or all of it, my dear,' said Mrs

T cheerfully. 'But Saturday night your father's got people staying over. I expect he'd rather you helped him with entertaining them than gave me a hand in the kitchen.'

Tilly felt her heart sink. That was the answer she really *hadn't* wanted to hear. And she could guess who the guests were. Shit.

She kept herself busy with pointedly obvious revision and coursework all through Friday evening and Saturday, so that when her father suggested that she might like to change before dinner, her complaint that she had 'so much work to do' and her plea 'to have something in my room' seemed completely genuine.

'You can't,' said her father bluntly. 'It's the Crosbys.'

'You won't want me there, then. You'll want to chat to your friend in peace, won't you? Besides, I've got too much work to do to take a whole evening off.'

'We were going to make some plans for the skiing holiday.'

'And? What do I know about skiing? I can't possibly bring anything to the discussion. No, you'll be much better off without me there.' She knew she was being irritatingly reasonable. But she pushed her father too far.

'I don't care what you do or don't know about skiing, but you can put in an appearance at dinner, *looking as if you're made an effort*, and you *will* be pleasant.'

'Yes, Fa,' she agreed, backing down. OK, so she'd be there, but that was all she'd do. She wasn't going to help him out by being nice to Marcus, not one bit She didn't care what pact Desmond and her father had drawn up, she wasn't having any part of it and she certainly wasn't going to encourage him.

'So how are you, Tilly?' said Marcus when they met in the family drawing room before dinner.

'Fine thank you, Marcus.' She smiled sweetly.

'Oh, er, good. And your family?'

'Also fine.' Another smile.

'That's great. So, A levels this summer?'

'Yes indeed.'

'Right. You must be busy revising.'

'Hugely busy.'

'I'm surprised you're going to be able to spare the time to come skiing with us.'

'Yes, me too.'

'I'm really looking forward to it. How about you?'

'I can hardly wait.'

'Have you done any skiing before?'

'None.' Tilly could see Marcus was already starting to flounder. She wondered just how long it would be before he gave up and lapsed into silence or found an excuse to join in the conversation his father and Edward were having across the room. She made a mental bet with herself that it would be just ten minutes more, tops.

Across the room, Edward glowered at her, but Tilly just smiled at him too. You wanted me here, she thought, and I'm behaving perfectly. Put that in your pipe and smoke it. It was going to a long, long evening for Marcus, as she reckoned she could keep up her act for hours if necessary, not that it would be at this rate. She could tell she'd almost won, and Mrs T hadn't even come through with the canapés yet. She knew she was being bloody to Marcus, who hadn't done anything to deserve such treatment. In fact, thinking back, he deserved a great deal better, given the part he'd played in the mouse episode. She almost felt sorry for him. But she was determined not to allow either her father or Mr Crosby to push her in a direction she was pretty sure she didn't want to go. Just because they thought it would be convenient to get her and Marcus together didn't mean she had to go along with it like some swooning Victorian maiden straight out of the schoolroom.

At this point Mrs Thompson appeared with the

canapés and the twins bowled in, full of chat and
insatiable curiosity about skiing, the chalet the Crosbys
owned and the Alps, which provide Marcus with a
welcome distraction from the very one-way conversation
with Tilly.

By the end of the evening Tilly had managed to be
perfectly polite throughout but hadn't once batted back a
conversational ball to either Desmond or Marcus. She
reckoned it was quite an achievement. Perhaps not one to
be proud of, but she'd made a very obvious point to her
father. He might try to push her and Marcus together and
force some sort of magnetism between them, but she had
shown him quite clearly that unless you handled the
magnets correctly, they didn't attract each other but
repelled instead.

17

Despite Tilly's behaviour, the invitation to the skiing holiday didn't get withdrawn, and in February the de Lieges made their way to the airport and a flight to Geneva, where Marcus or his father, who had already been skiing there for a week, would meet them. The vague flutterings of anticipation that Tilly had felt about the holiday in the previous month were still there, and she still didn't know whether they were brought on by excitement at the prospect of her first foreign holiday or nerves at being forced together with Marcus again. By the time she alighted from the plane at Geneva, the flutterings had developed into agitated flappings, of a magnitude that might have been generated by a large bird, not some delicate little butterfly, although she was still just as unsure as to their cause

It was all right for the twins, thought Tilly as she watched them jump about with excitement. They'd been getting more and more hyper from the moment they got on the plane: exclaiming over the in-flight magazine, being thrilled by the catering, clamouring for their father to buy them a teddy with a sheepskin flight jacket and reaching fever pitch when they broke through the clouds and began to descend into Geneva, going into raptures over the snow-covered Alps and peering out of the tiny windows to catch sight of the city itself. The passengers in the surrounding seats had been amused to see such unbridled enthusiasm about flying, which was unusual in kids in an age when most children had flown away on at least one holiday a year since birth and had become blasé by the time they understood what the word meant.

Tilly, however, was careful to maintain an air of indifference. She realised that she'd look a total freak if it became obvious that this was her first flight too. Was she the only seventeen-year-old in the country who had never flown before? She certainly had to be the only girl in her sixth form who had never been abroad. Shit, the only virgin non-flyer, which made her even sadder. What a loser she was compared to her contemporaries. Of course, she reckoned that Ashley hadn't flown either – so maybe she wasn't the *only* person of her age who'd never done it. She wondered what he was doing. Revising for his A levels? Playing his guitar? Hanging out at the skate park? Suddenly she wished she wasn't on the plane and about to go skiing, but back in Haybridge with him. If only, if only . . .

She felt tears prick her eyes, so she turned to look out the window in case anyone noticed. Nearly two months had passed and the pain was still as intense.

She cheered up a little and smiled at her kid sisters indulgently as the wheels hit the tarmac and they gave little yelps of pleasure at being on foreign soil and about to go skiing, though she herself continued to pretend complete indifference – even boredom. Besides, feigning uninterest also covered her sadness, and the last thing she wanted was for anyone to notice that and ask awkward questions. She didn't think she'd cope if they did.

Even during the tedium of getting through the airport, Daisy and Flora found everything a thrill, from queuing for immigration to examining the posters for luxury watches and Swiss chocolate on the endless bland corridor walls they were herded down. Even the lengthy wait for the baggage – what had happened to the legendary Swiss efficiency? – seemed to have some sort of magical quality as far as the twins were concerned. They finally managed to retrieve their luggage and were free to make their way out on to the main concourse of the airport, which was, Tilly decided, disconcertingly like the one they'd just left in England.

Marcus was there to meet them. He shook Edward's hand with a 'Good to see you again, sir.'

Creep, thought Tilly. She wasn't going to refer to Mr Crosby as 'sir'.

Then Marcus turned to her. 'All set?' he asked. 'Ready to schuss down the slopes?'

Was he taking the piss? What hadn't he understood when she'd told him she'd never skied before? 'Maybe not schuss exactly,' she said cautiously. She'd gathered from overheard conversations at school that schussing was the proper word for sliding downhill at speed.

'Well I guarantee you will be by the end of the week. Dad's fixed for you to have some private lessons. I told him that it wouldn't be cool for you to get stuck in ski school with the younger kids. But I'm sure the twins won't mind that – ski school's a load of fun at their age.'

The twins were too excited about skiing to care what arrangements had been made for them, but Tilly was touched that he'd thought about her – especially after she'd been such a cow to him at their last meeting.

Marcus grabbed a couple of the family's cases and led the way out of the airport towards the short-stay car park, where a large Mercedes responded to his plip key.

'Here we are.' He opened the boot and helped them stow their cases. 'In some ways it's handy you don't have your own skis, as I don't have a ski rack.'

'So how do you get your skis to the chalet?' asked Tilly.

'We leave them there from one season to the next.'

Tilly felt a fool on hearing such an obvious answer.

'And we've got several sets that we keep for visitors

and heaps of spare clothing, so we'll probably only have to arrange to hire boots for you – or maybe skis for the twins. I don't think we've got much that would be right for them. Anyway, we can sort all that out later. Right now I imagine you just want to get to the chalet, freshen up and relax.'

They all got in the car, Tilly and her sisters in the back, Edward and Marcus in the front, and headed out of the car park and on to the road that led through the city of Geneva, down to the lake and its spectacular fountain, past some fabulous lakeside residences and finally into open country and towards the Alps. In the distance they could see snow-covered peaks, but down in the valley the fields were coloured by the drab tones of winter, the trees were bare and the sky was overcast. Disappointingly, it was not the winter wonderland Tilly had expected

Flora and Daisy found everything fascinating, however, and bombarded Marcus with endless questions, while Tilly sat silently absorbing the scenery, so totally different from anything she'd ever seen in England: the wooden farmhouses with balconies and ground-floor barns and very gently pitched roofs with wooden shingles, tidy wood piles stacked beside the walls; the grey-brown Swiss cows with black noses and adorable, patient faces; the immaculate neatness of every village and the differentness of everything from the shops to the buses to the general appearance of the countryside. It was the lack of hedges, thought Tilly as she looked at the acres of pasture and occasional square of ploughed earth.

In one village Marcus turned off the main road and instantly they began to climb. The new road twisted and turned, following, in the main, a stream that foamed and thundered beside them. Marcus had to engage a lower gear as they wound constantly upwards. The deciduous trees that had flanked them gave way to pines, and then occasional splodges of dirty snow became more and more numerous until the snow cover was continuous and the road had been carved from between the drifts by snowploughs. The hairpins became more frequent and more precipitous, the snow banks either side deeper, and finally the trees gave way altogether and they were driving though a vast snow field. And then, right on cue, the clouds began to clear and the sky that appeared was a deep cornflower blue.

'A cable car,' shrieked Daisy.

'And a chair lift,' yelled Flora.

'You won't be excited by the sight of them by the end of the week,' said Marcus with a laugh.

'And skiers, look,' said Flora.

On a slope on the other side of the valley, Tilly could see several people whizzing downhill, carving regular tidy turns in the snow.

'You're lucky,' said Marcus, changing gear again and negotiating yet another bend. 'We had a big dump of snow yesterday, so there's lots of lovely powder to play in. The conditions are perfect.'

Watching the skiers, Tilly decided that the flutterings she felt were excitement. Skiing did look fun. And she'd cope with Marcus if she could do what those people on the other side of the valley were doing. She couldn't wait to try it for herself.

A few minutes later they entered a village that Tilly decided was just like an illustration from *Heidi*. All it needed was a few goats and a little girl in a dirndl skirt, but instead the narrow street was thronged with skiers in multi-coloured jackets and salopettes, clumping along in heavy boots with boards or skis balanced on their shoulders.

'Here we are,' said Marcus as he swung the car through the double doors of what had once been the barn of an imposing farmhouse in the centre of the village. The ex-barn was now a spacious garage with ski racks along one wall and doors that led to further rooms.

The twins jumped out of the car with squeaks of excitement and Tilly and her father followed at a more sedate pace. Marcus closed and locked the garage doors, grabbed a couple of their cases and exhorted them to follow him. The family hauled the last of their luggage out of the boot and went after him, through one of the doors and up a flight of stairs to the first floor.

'Wow,' breathed Tilly to herself as she emerged into the main living room of the chalet. It was stunning: double height, with a galleried landing that ran around the entire first floor. The huge space was dominated by a massive picture window that looked across one of the pistes to the other side of the valley.

'You'd never know we're right in the centre of the village, would you?' said Marcus, cheerfully dropping the cases on the floor.

Tilly put down the bag she was carrying and wandered across to look at the view. Immediately outside the window was a balcony that ran the width of the house with expensive teak patio furniture on it, and below that was a stretch of perfect snow that ended in a boundary of wooden fencing. Beyond was the piste with skiers careering down it, and on the other side of the valley was a range of majestic mountains, silhouetted against a flawless blue sky. It was breathtaking.

'Like it?' asked Marcus.

Tilly spun round. 'It's the most beautiful view I've ever seen.'

Marcus looked pleased. 'Dad's out skiing. He should be back shortly. Meantime, I'll show you your rooms, find ski kit for all of you and if there's time before dinner we'll go to the hire shop and get boots and skis and anything else you need organised.'

The view was enough to convince Tilly that this was going to be a fabulous holiday – even if it meant spending a week with Marcus. Well, she reasoned, he wasn't so bad. He had a kind heart and both his eyes looked in the same direction, and he was only six years older than her so not completely ancient. But he was a bit . . . dull. Being dull wasn't an offence and he could have worse faults, so she reckoned she could cope with that for a week in exchange for just being here. It was worth it for the view alone.

However, the whole skiing holiday thing took a sharp downturn the next morning when first she got fitted for boots and then she had to put on her skis. She'd thought the boots were bad enough, heavy lumps of solid plastic that gripped her ankles in a vice and made normal walking impossible. It explained the extraordinary gait of all the visitors to the resort. No wonder they clumped along like robots. And then she was given her skis, and met her instructor Bernard – a man with skin the colour and texture of a leather armchair in a London club and who had to be sixty at least – who walked her to the nursery slope and made her clip the things to her boots. Whereupon she became totally paralysed.

She gazed at the skiers around her, feeling frustrated and helpless in equal measure. How could they possibly control these things? How could they even move in them? And how in the name of all that was holy could they swoop and race and skim over the snow like they were flying? It was impossible!

Bernard encouraged her and got her to point her skis down the slope, whereupon they took off and Tilly lost her balance and thumped heavily on to the packed snow of the piste.

'Ow,' she complained.

'Get up,' said Bernard, in impeccable English. 'Try again.'

Tilly floundered around on the snow. 'How?' she said petulantly. With her solid boots and two planks she couldn't kneel; she didn't have the strength to lever herself up using her arms, and when she pushed on her ski poles she just shot forward again on her bum.

Bernard leaned down and offered her his arm. With a total lack of grace Tilly managed to stand up, only to fall over again immediately.

Marcus swooped past, heading for a lift. 'How's it going?' he called to her as he kick-stopped, sending a pretty arc of snow drifting away behind him. Was he deliberately trying to make her look even more hopeless?

Tilly wasn't quite sure if she was closer to losing her temper or crying; those two falls had hurt.

'Too soon to say,' she responded carefully.

'I'll catch up with you at lunchtime. By then Bernard will have you whizzing along.'

'Goody,' said Tilly through clenched teeth. Fat chance, she added privately.

But to her surprise, Marcus was right. OK, she wasn't whizzing along by lunchtime, but she could cope with being pulled up the nursery slope on the debutantes' drag line and could make her way to the bottom doing a succession of careful snowplough turns before coming to a controlled stop back at the ski school meeting point where Marcus was waiting for her

'Well done,' he said, applauding her.

Tilly, who had been too busy concentrating on staying upright to notice him, blushed.

'Hardly,' she said.

'It's a start. All you need is some practice and some confidence. What do you say to a spot of lunch, and then I'll look after you this afternoon.'

As Bernard was only engaged to give Tilly private tuition in the mornings, she'd been wondering about how she'd spend the afternoon. She reckoned that being with Marcus had to be better than being on her own.

'Thanks, I'd like that.'

They had lunch in a little café beside the piste – an omelette and frites, a green salad, and a glass of wine for Marcus. Tilly decided to stick to water; she had enough of a problem staying on her feet stone-cold sober, so she didn't dare think what alcohol might do to her balance. When they had finished and paid, they collected their skis from the rack in front of the restaurant and Tilly began to head towards the little drag lift she'd been using all morning.

'Oh no,' said Marcus. 'I think you're ready for something a bit more grown-up.'

'What?' squeaked Tilly, a rush of nerves zinging through her.

'Follow me.' Marcus swung his skis on to his shoulder with an easy confidence and headed towards a chair lift.

'I can't go on that,' said Tilly, grappling with her skis. How come Marcus's stayed tidily on his shoulder and hers slipped all over the place so she ended up carrying them in her arms, which was difficult and exhausting?

Without a word, Marcus took her skis off her and swung them on to his other shoulder. 'But you're going to have to carry my sticks.'

Tilly mumbled her thanks, feeling once again that she was utterly useless. They arrived at the queue for the lift and clipped on their skis, then shuffled forward as each chair arrived and swept up its complement of passengers.

Suddenly it was their turn. Marcus held on to Tilly's arm tightly as she slithered through the automatic barrier and into position.

'Just relax and sit down,' instructed Marcus. The chair came round the huge driving wheel, smacked the backs of their legs, none too gently, and then she was airborne, being carried smoothly up the mountain.

'There, that wasn't so bad, was it?' said Marcus cheerfully.

'I suppose not,' she admitted. 'But how the hell do I get off?'

'Don't worry,' Marcus said blithely.

But Tilly did worry. Even the stunning view as they were carried up the slope couldn't alleviate her anxiety. Below them a stream meandered through the snow field and the tracks of some small but purposeful creature followed the line of the lift.

'Looking for food scraps dropped by people,' explained Marcus. And then he pointed out a deer hiding in the pine forest that covered part of the slope. Tilly was enchanted by the whole experience, but despite that, the worry of making a complete fool of herself when the moment came to alight gnawed inside.

When they got to the top, Marcus took her sticks and put his arm firmly around her waist. She wasn't sure she liked this close contact, but if she wanted to retain any dignity, she wasn't going to push him away. 'Now lift the tips of your skis so they don't jam in the snow and . . . stand up.'

She did, and found herself sliding down a gentle slope away from the chair, which was carried around another huge wheel on its perpetual journey.

Marcus let her go, just a second or two too late, thought Tilly. He really hadn't needed to hang on to her for quite as long as he had.

'Easy, wasn't it?'

'Only because you practically carried me off,' replied Tilly, slipping her poles over her wrists and putting a foot or two of distance between herself and Marcus. She turned her attention to her immediate surroundings and looked at the piste beside her. Oh . . . my . . . God. It was so much steeper than the piste she'd been on all morning. 'You expect me to ski down this?' she said, her panic level rising once again.

'You can do it. That nursery slope was getting far too easy. This is only one step up, I promise.'

'This is never *one step up*.'

'It is. Just follow me. I'll look after you. Ready?'

Tilly didn't think she ever would be ready, but standing looking at it wasn't going to get her to a place of safety – the bottom of the hill. She took a deep breath to steady her nerves, shot a smile at Marcus that she hoped made her look confident and said, 'Yes.'

Marcus set off, taking wide sweeping turns. Tilly followed in his tracks as Bernard had taught her to do. She noticed that Marcus was doing snowplough turns and not his usual parallel ones. She felt absurdly grateful for his thoughtfulness – which sort of made up for the way he'd grabbed her when they were getting off the lift. As she followed him in his slow, careful tracks, she decided that he really was kind. He'd been kind over the mouse, kind to suggest she ought to have private lessons and now he was being kind in giving up his own skiing time to take her down a slope at a speed that must bore him to death. She decided that she'd have to make an effort not to behave like a cow to him again.

Every now and then he would check over his shoulder that she was still with him before offering her a few words of encouragement and carrying on. After about five minutes he headed towards the edge of the piste and stopped. Tilly, almost falling over, managed to come to a halt beside him.

'OK?'

'Fine,' she said, panting.

'And just look what you've covered.'

Tilly looked back up the slope. 'But we've come miles.'

'Well, half a K, anyway. And you haven't fallen over once.'

'Oh don't tempt providence, please.'

'OK to continue?'

Tilly nodded enthusiastically. For the first time that day she 'got' skiing. She understood the exhilaration of sliding over the snow, of the clearness of the air, of the view, of the sheer fun of it. Of course her exhilaration was short-lived, as on her next turn she caught an edge and fell flat on her face, but this time she didn't feel anger or frustration; she just pushed herself up again and set off once more, determined to do better.

The pair of them completed the slope twice more before Tilly owned up to feeling knackered.

'And your legs are going to ache like crazy tomorrow. I suggest we stop, have a vin chaud and a slice of apple cake and then go back and see if we can't grab the sauna before your father and mine hog it.'

'You've got a sauna at the chalet?'

'Only a little one.'

Squashed in a *little* sauna with Marcus? Erm, no. Not an appealing idea even if it had been a big one. Tilly thought she'd rather eat her ski poles than share a sweaty cupboard with Marcus clad only in a towel. Or maybe even less. Which was a really disturbing thought, and disturbing in a very nasty way. Kind he might be, and she would fulfil her private promise to be nicer to him, but there were limits!

However, the vin chaud and cake sounded good, so they returned to the café where they'd eaten lunch. Although it was a relief to take her skis off, Tilly also felt a faint twinge of regret that the day was drawing to a close. They basked in the sun and watched the other skiers hurtling past, the snakes of small children following their instructors like ducklings and the general coming and going of activity at the edge of the piste.

Tilly could feel her eyes closing.

'Coo-ee! Tilleeeee!' She was roused by the dulcet tones of her sisters screeching across the snow. They were walking towards them, skis over their shoulders, looking as if they'd been at this lark all their lives.

They both began chattering to Tilly at once, and out of the gabbled sentences Tilly managed to gather that they totally loved skiing and that they'd been moved up a class already.

'Although only,' admitted Flora with admirable honesty, 'because Yvonne our instructor – she's really nice and speaks brilliant English – thinks we're a bit old to be in hers. But she said we'll cope in the next one.'

'I do hope so,' said Daisy. 'Don't want to make a prat of myself in front of a load of snotty French kids.'

Tilly could see that would be the ultimate in humiliating experiences. 'So you feel you've really started to crack it?' she said.

'We'll show you,' the twins offered. And without waiting for a reply, they slapped their skis on again and shot off to the nursery drag. Even Tilly could see that they'd progressed much further than she had in a day – despite the fact that she'd had a private lesson. She said as much to Marcus.

'But they're younger, lower centre of gravity, more flexible. It all makes a difference. You'll catch up. And when you do, you'll probably be much more stylish. Bernard won't let you get into bad habits, which the twins are bound to in a group class.'

Tilly liked the idea of being a stylish skier, although she had to admit that the twins did look pretty competent as they came zipping back down the slope; much better than she did – even if their arms and poles were all over the place and not neatly tucked in like Bernard had taught her.

She congratulated them on their progress, which she cheerfully admitted to them was pretty spectacular, making the girls blush with pleasure.

'We're going back to the chalet,' she added. 'You two can stay here if you want, but only on the nursery slope.'

The twins wrinkled their noses and looked as if they might disobey their big sister.

'Don't think of going further afield,' warned Marcus. 'All the lifts are going to close shortly and you don't want to get stranded on one overnight.'

The twins made noises of disbelief.

'It's happened before; it could happen again.'

'That shut them up,' said Tilly as they gathered their things and walked the short distance to their chalet. 'Has it?'

'What?'

'Happened before.'

'Oh yes. A woman and two kids got stranded on one overnight and nearly died of hypothermia. People forget that skiing can be bloody dangerous, and the weather here in the mountains can change in an instant, to say nothing of the avalanche risk. Just because we had wall-to-wall blue sky today doesn't mean that tomorrow will be nice. And if it starts nice, it could still change into blizzard conditions in a matter of minutes.'

Tilly made an appropriate comment about taking care but privately thought Marcus was being a bit of a drama queen. It couldn't get *that* bad.

They stacked their kit in the ski room and then sat on the benches to remove their boots. The relief of taking them off was heavenly, and Tilly felt as if she was suddenly almost weightless as she lost the heavy, inflexible lumps of plastic. Despite her tired and aching legs, she almost skipped upstairs to the living room. Mugs of tea and more cake waited for them, which the housekeeper – Antoinette – insisted she ate.

'But I've just had cake on the slopes,' protested Tilly.

'You must eat in zis cold,' said Antoinette, cutting her a huge slice of lemon drizzle cake. 'You need ze energy.'

'I'll need a larger size in clothes,' muttered Tilly.

As she ate her cake she saw Marcus watching her. She looked away. She didn't mind him helping her learn to ski, she didn't mind being friendly, but there was no way *ever* she wanted their relationship to progress beyond that.

Yes, he was kind and thoughtful; yes, he was patient; yes, his company wasn't unpleasant, but he was also a banker, for heaven's sake, and . . . boring. It was like he was middle-aged at twenty-four. Tilly couldn't imagine him going to a rave or clubbing. He wore slacks and polo-necks. Hadn't he heard of fashion?

But the trouble was that now she was here, skiing, they seemed to be *expected* to spend time in each other's company. Edward and Desmond skied together during the day, and the twins were in ski school – which left Marcus and Tilly as a couple. Only Tilly really didn't want anyone – least of all Marcus – to think of them in that way. No way.

She finished her cake and made for the stairs.

'You off?' asked Marcus.

'Thought I'd have a rest before dinner.'

'Oh. No sauna? It's really good for relaxing after a hard day on the slopes.'

Tilly shot him a smile. 'Don't let me stop you then.' She carried on across the huge floor of the living room.

'You really ought to think about having one. You'll be horribly stiff tomorrow.'

'I'll risk it.' She raced up the stairs to her room. No

way was she going to give him an ounce of encouragement. Besides, if her muscles needed therapeutic relaxation, she thought she could achieve it very well by means of a long soak in her en suite bath rather than by sharing a sauna with him. Yuck – Marcus semi-naked. The thought made her shudder.

She lay on her bed checking her mobile for missed calls and messages. She hadn't taken it on the slopes with her, afraid she'd fall on it and break it, or just lose it. Outside her door she heard the sound of voices as the others returned and fell ravenously on Antoinette's cake, chatting about their day.

A roar outside her window made her cross to it to look out. She saw a vast orange tracked bulldozer thunder past. When it had gone, leaving a fresh piste in its wake, the view was once again one of achingly beautiful tranquillity. The lifts had stopped, the skiers had all gone home for the evening and the sky was turning from lapis lazuli to apricot, pink and mauve. Worried that she wouldn't be able to imprint such beauty on her memory, Tilly took a picture on her mobile. When she was back at her poxy school next week, she'd be able to look at it and remind herself of a glorious day.

Tilly soaked in her bath till the water chilled and then lay on her bed wrapped in her bathrobe. She considered reading a book, but her thoughts turned to Ashley once again, and as always it left her feeling wretched. The pain and rawness of their break-up was just as bad as it had been back in December.

She wondered what he was doing, how he was getting on, if he still played his guitar . . . Did he still strum the strings as if he was caressing her face; did he still think about her like she thought about him? She rolled over and picked her iPod off her bedside table and popped in her headphones. She found the Leonard Cohen song and let it play. She remembered so vividly the day when he'd played it to her in his bedroom. He'd really sung it as if he'd meant it. She could feel a well inside her filling again with regrets and sadness at what she'd lost. She put the track on repeat and lay there listening to it, silent tears trickling every now and again down her cheeks, until she heard everyone assembling for supper.

She still felt weary when she got off her bed, although she wasn't sure if it was solely physical exhaustion from her day on the slopes, or whether her thoughts about Ashley had left her emotionally drained. She dressed but didn't bother with make-up – she didn't want Marcus deluding himself that she was making an effort for him – and made her way back to the living room. Antoinette had put a plate of amuse-bouches on the table and Desmond was standing by the bar in the corner playing the role of host. Her father was lounging on one of the huge leather sofas near the window, watching the lights of the piste bashers trundling up and down the slopes of the surrounding mountains, while her sisters were glued to some American soap on Sky on the massive TV in the corner.

'Tilly, m'dear,' boomed Desmond across the vast space. 'What's your poison?'

Oh for God's sake, what sort of prat used a phrase like that these days? 'Coke?' she asked, trying to hide her horror at the old duffer's attempts at being a host.

'I was thinking of making up some kir royale. Could I tempt you to a glass of that?'

Tilly shrugged. What the fuck was kir royale? Still, whatever it was, it might be fun to try it. If it were disgusting, she didn't have to drink it again. But it wasn't disgusting, she discovered. In fact she thought that the combination of champagne and cassis was one of the most blissful things she'd ever come across. Edward had taught her to sip her drinks, but it took all her self-control to behave as he would like and not just chug the whole glass down in one.

'Good day, Tilly?' Edward asked.

'Lovely,' she replied, crossing the floor to join him. She curled up at the other end of the sofa.

'I hear you did really well.'

Tilly shrugged. 'I think that's a bit of an exaggeration. But I've stopped falling over every two minutes. I've got that interval all the way up to at least every three minutes.'

'Not what Marcus said,' said Desmond, sitting opposite them on the other sofa.

'Well . . .' Tilly wasn't keen on talking about Marcus. She really didn't want anyone thinking that she cared about his opinion or thoughts in anyway whatsoever. 'The twins have got it, though,' she said brightly. 'They're zooming about like old hands.'

'The age to learn,' said her father.

'I don't think Marcus remembers actually learning,' said Desmond. 'I had him on skis not long after he could walk.'

Bully for him, thought Tilly.

'Talk of the devil.'

Marcus entered the room looking incredibly pink.

'Evening, all,' he said, going over to the bar to help himself to a drink. 'You should have had that sauna, Tilly. It's set me up for tomorrow, I can tell you.'

Well, whoop-de-do, thought Tilly. She loved the skiing, she loved the chalet, she loved almost everything about this holiday except being cooped up with the Crosbys and being forced into Marcus's company. Did they really imagine that she would ever think he was God's gift? It was almost as if they reckoned that, given sufficient exposure, she'd become immune to his dullness.

Her plans to keep Marcus at arm's length both physically and metaphorically were scuppered when they sat down to dinner by Desmond placing the pair of them next to each other. And there was nothing Tilly could do about it without being incredibly rude. Despite that, dinner was a fairly jolly affair – quite apart from anything else, Antoinette was the most superb cook and the food was heavenly. The twins were full of their day and chatted excitedly about their achievements between mouthfuls, their father listening indulgently and promising them a tenner each if they were able to negotiate the Roches Noires piste without falling over by the last day.

'But that's a black run,' said Desmond.

Edward shrugged. 'No point in setting the bar too low,' he said.

Tilly could see the twins were determined to get the

money. And they're welcome to it, she thought. She'd be amazed if she managed anything steeper than a blue.

The conversation and the banter went on as Antoinette brought out a succession of courses. Tilly, though, didn't join in, and concentrated on eating, not because she was especially hungry – not after two lots of cake at tea time – but because she was growing increasingly conscious of Marcus looking in her direction. She couldn't make up her mind whether he was just watching her in a faintly curious way or whether there was something deeper and, scarily, more significant in his glances. Please God, not the latter, she prayed. And she wasn't going to watch him to find out, because she was sure that if it *were* the latter, it would only make a sticky situation even stickier.

Still, at least she had a cast-iron excuse to plead exhaustion and disappear early.

'But it's only nine o'clock,' said Desmond.

'I know, pathetic, isn't it?' said Tilly. 'But I can't remember the last time I've had so much fresh air and exercise in one day.'

'Well,' said her father tentatively, 'I was planning to take you, Desmond and Marcus out for a drink in that nice-looking bar by the church. Do say you'll change your mind. Come on, Tilly,' he pleaded, 'après-ski is all part of the experience. Besides, you young things ought to get out and about a bit and have some fun.'

He looked at her meaningfully, but Tilly ignored his sub-text and his motives and made it plain that she was *far* too tired to contemplate such an idea.

'See you all in the morning,' she called as she made her way upstairs.

She thought she was probably going to see a lot of her room over the next week if she wanted to avoid Marcus in the chalet. Avoiding him on the slopes just wasn't going to be an option, though bundled up in a padded jacket and trousers, no one in their right mind would find her attractive. No, the danger lay in the evenings. She would have to retire to her room, which was dreary but safe.

She did ask herself if her imagination was being overactive. Were her father and Desmond Crosby really trying to push her and Marcus together? And was that what Marcus wanted too? If so, why, for heaven's sake? She was nice enough looking, she knew that, but no raving beauty, and who in their right mind would want to be saddled with her, because if they were, they'd also get the crumbling wreck that was Haybridge Manor. A complete money pit, a drain on resources and not even comfortable to live in. No, it just didn't add up, except that all the signs seemed to point that way.

The next day the weather was just as spectacularly beautiful as the previous one, and despite the protests from her aching calves and thighs, Tilly couldn't wait to get out on the slopes again. Bernard was impressed by the progress she had made through her assiduous practising the previous afternoon, and even more when she told him, rather proudly, that she'd already been on a chair lift and had managed it without accident. She skated over the details about quite how much Marcus had helped her, making it sound as though her achievement was all her own, and just hoped that her little white lie wouldn't get found out. Bernard pushed her on so that she progressed from snow ploughs to traversing the slope, to traversing the slope while lifting her uphill ski, to traversing the slope one ski lifted and her poles balanced on her outstretched forearms to keep her facing down the slope. And furthermore she had to negotiate several chair lifts, all of which she managed perfectly – to her considerable relief. Her confidence grew until she lost her concentration for just a second and ended up wiping out in a flurry of skis and poles. But, she thought as she retrieved her woolly hat and dusted the snow off her jacket, it was the first time she had fallen over that morning and she'd been skiing for over an hour.

When Marcus met her for lunch, part of her was hugely glad of the rest but the other part wanted to keep going, to show Marcus her new skills.

'Plenty of time for that,' he said, handing her the menu. 'Besides, I thought we'd go over there this afternoon.' He waved a hand at the other side of the valley.

'Uh?'

'There's a cable car that joins this resort to the one over there. And there's the most wonderful piste, down through the trees, which would be ideal for you. You'll love it.'

Tilly shrugged. Sounded good to her, and since Marcus's perfect choice of piste the previous afternoon, she trusted him. She picked tartiflette and a salad off the menu and settled back to wait for it to arrive.

Really, she thought, if Marcus were her cousin or some other close relative, life would be a great deal easier; she liked him, she did, but the idea that he wanted something rather more than friendship – and that their respective fathers also seemed to be engineering things that way – was rather scary. If he were a relation she could still like him but that other possibility wouldn't be in the equation.

Or if he were truly horrible it would all be much simpler, but the trouble was that he was basically nice . . . decent . . . kind. And dull. There was no denying the fact that Marcus was beige.

After lunch, Marcus led her carefully down the piste to the cable car. Tilly had been expecting a slightly larger version of the little gondolas that swung over the pistes carrying about a half-dozen passengers at a time. She certainly wasn't expecting to see the type of cable car that greeted her now. It was a metal box about the size of a small warehouse, and it carried around two hundred people at a time across the valley to the adjoining resort. She found she was strangely apprehensive as their turn came to board, and she couldn't believe that the thin cables that hung across the gap between the stations could possibly support the weight of all the people as well as the car.

Skis off, she and Marcus shuffled forward, up the metal steps, through the barriers and finally into the cable car. They weren't lucky enough to be near a window and were trapped in the middle of the huge press of fellow travellers and skis. Tilly wasn't sure if it was better not being able to see quite how much fresh air there was between her and the ground, or if the slight sense of claustrophobia was worse. With a lurch the car moved off and she felt a small surge of panic kick in.

'All right?' said Marcus.

'Fine,' she lied.

She gazed at the sky and the peaks of the mountains, which was all she could see between the press of people around her. She tried desperately not to think that there was only a thin sheet of metal between the soles of her boots and the ground hundreds of feet below.

The next sickening lurch sent her heart rate soaring again, and then she felt slightly foolish, because the bump didn't presage a fatal plummet to the valley floor but was caused by them docking at the other side.

A few minutes later they were off the car and clipping on their skis.

'Ready?' asked Marcus.

Tilly nodded, and Marcus set off across the piste towards a small cluster of houses near the trees at the edge. He skied between them and led Tilly down a narrow but relatively shallow slope, stopping to check she was following him OK.

'This track is a road in the summer,' he explained, 'and it takes us down through the forest to the next village. It's really pretty and mostly dead easy.'

Mostly?

'When we get to the bottom, we'll take the chair up and then go back over on the cable car.'

Tilly thought that sounded OK, and just the one run wouldn't be too exhausting. The light suddenly changed, making her look up. A little puffy cloud had blotted out the sun.

'Push off, cloud,' she said, and obligingly it did.

They set off down the track. Once they entered the trees, the silence that fell was absolute; no clanks and thuds of the chair lifts being carried over the pylons, no yells and shrieks from other skiers, no music blaring from the outdoor speakers of piste-side restaurants. It was delightful, and the run was easy. Tilly began to relax and look about her.

Because the track went almost straight and the gradient was gentle, all they had to do was stand on their skis and let gravity pull them down the slope; no turns, no avoiding other skiers hurtling across their paths, nothing. Marcus was right, thought Tilly, this was wonderful. The only sound was the quiet swish of their skis over the snow and occasionally the sound of a bird calling. Other than that, the silence continued Every now and again they came to a hairpin bend, and Marcus would pause to give Tilly a breather before they carried on again.

'Right,' he said at another bend. 'This is the tricky bit.'

Tilly's heart sank. She'd known it was too good to last. 'How tricky?' she asked warily.

'Not very. You just have to believe in yourself and have confidence.'

Tilly swallowed. 'Believe that I can do what exactly?'

'The next bit is a bit steeper.'

Tilly peered round the corner – Marcus wasn't joking.

'But you need to go down it as fast as you can, because around that slight bend the track goes uphill. If you get up a good head of steam you'll make it to the top of the hill, which'll save you having to herringbone for miles.'

Tilly, who hated herringboning, liked the logic, but she didn't think that hurtling along such a narrow track at breakneck speed was going to be quite as easy – or doable – as Marcus suggested. She was considering this when the sun went in again. The light went completely flat as all the shadow disappeared, obliterating the slight ruts and bumps on the piste. Tilly glanced up and saw that a sheet of thin cloud now covered the sun completely.

'Let's do it,' she said, with fake bravado.

Marcus set off, his skis pointing straight down the track, crouched down to reduce wind resistance to the absolute minimum. In seconds he was streaking away towards the slight bend he'd pointed out earlier. Feeling jittery with apprehension, Tilly followed. Her jitters gave way to exhilaration as her speed increased. She was flying down the slope, the wind making her cheeks tingle even more, then ooops, she was going so fast her hat was in danger of blowing off her head.

She reached up a hand to grab it, but that small action made her wobble. She panicked and tried to slow down but only succeeded in crossing the tips of her skis. A second later she was face down in the snow, sliding forward on her nose, skis and poles all over the place and heading for a tree. She shut her eyes and waited for the impact. Her shoulder connected with a numbing crunch.

She lay there, panting slightly, scared, shaken and wondering how much damage she'd done. She opened her eyes and looked down the track. Marcus obviously hadn't worked out that she'd fallen, because there was no sign of him. Suddenly the silence, which before had seemed so peaceful, was scary. She was alone, abandoned.

Warily, tentatively, she began to disentangle herself from the big pine tree and her skis. Her shoulder ached horribly, but when she touched it, the pain didn't increase noticeably, which made her think it was probably just bruised rather than anything more serious. The thick clothes she had on obviously didn't just protect against the cold.

She staggered to her feet and began to sort out her skis and poles. She was almost ready to set off again when Marcus, his own skis off, came running towards her, or as close to running as he could get in ski boots.

'There you are,' he shouted at her. 'I was worried. What happened?'

Tilly shrugged. Ouch! Big mistake; she wouldn't do that again in a hurry. 'Took a tumble. I was doing fine and then I just lost it. Wiped out.'

'But you're OK?'

'I don't think anything is broken,' said Tilly. 'I hit a tree with my shoulder so it aches a bit, but I'm going to live.'

'Sure?'

'Sure I'm going to live?'

'No, silly, sure you're all right.'

'I think so. It was a bit of a shock and all that, but hey, look, I'm standing.'

A snowflake floated down and settled on the dark fabric of Tilly's jacket. She glanced up at the sky again. In the last few minutes the thin veil of cloud had coalesced into something much thicker. Marcus looked at it too. A frown crossed his face momentarily.

'Let's get going, then. The sooner we get to the bottom, the sooner we can get back.'

They set off but had to walk the uphill stretch. Marcus had left his skis at the top of the slope when he'd returned to look for Tilly, so he carried hers for her as they trudged up the snowy hill. Once at the top, they both clipped their skis on again and set off.

It was starting to snow more heavily now, and the lack of definition on the piste due to the flat light made it very tricky to see any stray ruts or bumps. Tilly, sore from her last fall and with her confidence dented, was finding it more and more difficult. She tried to keep up with Marcus, but at every bend he seemed to have to wait for her for increasingly long periods of time. And she was tiring, so when she reached him she needed a breather before setting off again.

'Is it much further?' she said.

'Almost there,' replied Marcus cheerfully. But Tilly spotted a village through a gap in the trees and it seemed miles away, and if it was the one they were heading for, Marcus was lying through his teeth. Not that there was any choice but to soldier on.

The snow fell more heavily and Tilly was aware that the wind was picking up. In amongst the trees they were pretty sheltered, but she could see that the tops of the pines were bending and thrashing about. She didn't fancy emerging from the trees and into the teeth of the snow-storm. She reckoned it was going to be a cold journey back up the hill on the exposed chair lift. At least once they got in that flying garage it would be sheltered – scary but sheltered.

The weather was distinctly dodgy by the time they finally emerged from the track through the forest and skied across the lower slopes of a piste to the chair lift. There were very few other skiers about.

Given up and gone home, thought Tilly, wishing she could too. Then she noticed that the lift was stationary.

Marcus had a conversation with the attendant. There was an exchange of rapid French and some gesturing from Marcus followed by a shrug from the Swiss. Marcus, shaking his head in disbelief, turned to Tilly.

'They've shut this lift and the cable car. The conditions are too dangerous – high winds, apparently.'

Tilly was numb with disbelief. 'So . . . how . . . what about us?' she managed to stammer out.

'We'll have to get a taxi from the village.'

'Oh.' Well that wouldn't be too bad.

'Let's go and get a drink, thaw out and then see about ordering one.'

Which sounded good to Tilly. She was tired, cold and sore and the thought of hanging around in this blizzard held no appeal.

They skied across to a small bar that was belting out pop music and was obviously packed with happy après-skiers warming up before they returned to their apartments and chalets. They kicked off their skis and squeezed in through the door. Tilly didn't think she'd ever been so grateful to be in the warm and dry. She pulled off her snow-caked hat with almost numb fingers.

'I must phone Dad and tell him I'm safe,' she said to Marcus.

'You do that. What would you like to drink? Vin chaud? Hot chocolate?'

Tilly thought her nerves needed a restorative after

what she'd just been through. 'Vin chaud, please.' Her fingers were starting to ache almost as much as her shoulder as the circulation began to return to them. With difficulty she unzipped her sodden jacket and fished in her inside pocket for her mobile. She pressed the buttons to get her father's number and then hit 'dial'. Nothing. She looked at the screen. No signal. Shit. They'd have to find a public phone before her father called out the search parties.

Marcus returned with their drinks, and Tilly explained about the lack of signal.

'What's your father's number?' he asked. Tilly found it on her phone and handed it to him. Marcus left his vin chaud on the table and went and had a word with the barman. She saw some Swiss francs change hands and Marcus disappeared into a back room.

Tilly clasped her cold hands around her hot drink, savouring the smell of orange peel, cinnamon and wine that wafted up in the steam. She shut her eyes, grateful for the warmth, grateful for being safe. She didn't want to think about quite how scared she'd been; it didn't help knowing that people *did* die on mountains in lousy weather – experienced, competent skiers. And there was no way either of those adjectives could be applied to her. Crap summed up her skiing. She wasn't sure whether she ought to be angry with Marcus or not. The piste hadn't been that difficult and it was only the weather turning so bad that had made it dodgy. So should he have checked what the forecast was? Or should she treat it as a case of 'all's well that ends well'? There was no denying he'd done his best to look after her and to keep her as safe as he could given the awful conditions.

'All done,' he said when he got back to their table.

'You got through?'

'No problem. I said we were just having a drink to warm up and then we'd get a taxi back. Home in time for supper. Your dad didn't sound too worried about us but he's glad we phoned. I said we'd keep him posted and let him know when we're on our way. He told us not to hurry.'

He's hoping we're getting friendly, thought Tilly.

'Fancy another?' offered Marcus.

Tilly shook her head. 'I think I'd just like to get back now. Where can we get a taxi?'

'The barman said the numbers for the local firms are all by the Office de Tourisme, near the church. And there's a public phone there too.'

Tilly gathered up her still sodden hat and gloves. 'Then let's go and find it.' She thrust her hand into her cold wet glove and felt she couldn't wait to get home and really warm and dry.

They went out into the bitter cold, stamped their feet into their ski bindings again and, buffeted by the increasingly wild wind, laden with fat, soggy flakes that stung against their faces, slid off down the piste that led on to the main street through the village. There was no traffic, so they skied along the packed snow in the middle of the road, past the usual array of ski resort shops: a pharmacy, a couple of ski hire outlets, a bakery, a small supermarket, a dress shop selling ladies' designer fashions, a bank and a couple of bars. Soaring above them though the falling snow, they could see a needle-shaped spire covered in green copper piercing the gloomy sky. And beside it, as promised, the tourist office. They took a note of the number of one of the cab firms and then found the phone.

Marcus pulled a handful of small change out of his pocket and began dialling. There was a brief conversation in rapid French and then Marcus went to the notice-board, took down another number and repeated the exercise.

'What's the matter?' asked Tilly, shaking with cold and impatient to get home.

Marcus ignored her. Again another conversation that Tilly didn't understand – or only the odd word – and again Marcus replaced the handset.

'So?' said Tilly.

'It appears there's been an avalanche and it's closed the main road to our resort. The taxis can't get through.'

Tilly was dumbfounded. 'You're joking.'

'No. I did wonder if the first company I phoned just used it as an excuse – you know, like London cabbies not wanting to go south of the river.'

Tilly shrugged. No, she didn't know, and she didn't know what it had to do with their predicament.

'That's why I checked with another firm. But it was the same story. I don't think they'd both lie.'

'So we're stuck here,' said Tilly. She was cold, she was exhausted, she was hungry, her shoulder was hurting beyond belief and she wanted to be at home. She felt tears well up. 'What are we going to do?'

'We're going to find a hotel.'

'Oh.'

'Don't worry, we'll be fine.'

But by the time the third establishement had told them they were *complet*, Tilly doubted that they would be. Marcus's suggestion to one hotelier that maybe it was possible for them to sleep on the sofas in the salon had met with such a snort of derision that it wasn't a proposal they felt inclined to make again. Eventually they found a little boutique hotel down a back street that had a room. Just the one, a double room with a double bed.

'Take it,' Tilly told Marcus, spurred on by desperation. A bed was a bed; they'd work out the logistics once they got into the room. There was bound to be a way both of them could get a decent night's sleep without having to snuggle up. Perish the thought.

The landlady showed them to their room, having first made them remove their ski boots, and Tilly felt the tears well up again in her eyes. Box room was the term that sprang to her mind. It wasn't even a full-sized double bed. The only saving grace was that the ensuite had a proper bath in it as well as a shower, and was kitted out truly sumptuously. It seemed a bit of an odd choice to spend more money on the ablutions than on the bedroom, but whatever Tilly thought, the situation wasn't going to alter. The bedroom was a cubbyhole, the bed was minute and she was going to be sharing it with Marcus. Shit.

She sat on the bed feeling wrung out. How much worse could things get?

'You'll feel better when you've had a hot bath and something to eat,' suggested Marcus, judging her mood.

'How can we go and eat?' said Tilly bleakly. 'We've only got ski boots to put on our feet. My clothes are damp and sweaty. We can't go to a restaurant like this.'

'Leave it with me,' said Marcus. He left Tilly sitting on the bed looking miserable and went in search of their landlady. He returned a few minutes later bearing a towelling bathrobe.

'I managed to borrow this. Hang your ski kit over the radiator to dry, and go and have a hot bath. While you're doing that, I'll see what I can sort out.' He smiled at her; she looked very vulnerable and young. 'OK?' he asked encouragingly.

Tilly managed to summon up a smile and nodded. 'OK,' she affirmed.

'Good girl.'

Marcus left her to get ready for her bath and slipped down the hotel stairs to the boot room, where he shoved his feet back into his ski boots. He thought for a second about Tilly relaxing in a bath of piping-hot water and felt a twinge of envy – he could kill for a nice soak in a warm bath – but as he'd got them into this predicament, it was up to him to get them out of it.

*

Tilly lay in her bath and thought about Marcus and the fact that she was going to have to share a bed with him. If only it were Ashley she'd been stranded with, she thought, revelling in the fantasy that such a possibility conjured up.

But Marcus? She couldn't dislike him; there was nothing to dislike. He was kind, polite, well-heeled, reasonably intelligent and not unattractive. He wasn't a stunner – no one would sign him up as a model – but he was . . . OK. He was nice. He was fine. But he was *dull*. No, there was nothing really wrong with Marcus; the trouble was, she couldn't find anything that was really attractive either, nothing that was right. Except that he had been wonderful about that mouse – she could like him for that.

She sloshed the hot bath water about as she washed in a desultory way and wondered why she'd found Ashley instantly irresistible and why, despite everything, Marcus left her pretty cold. Well, maybe lukewarm, given his positive attributes. She raised a foot out of the water, pushed the hot tap on to bring the temperature of the water back up to near-scalding and let her mind drift to the prospect of having to share a bed with a man for the first time in her life, and all the possibilities that were thrown up as a consequence.

If she were honest, she admitted to herself, there was only one possibility that was really in her mind, and that was would she finally find out about sex, because if she were totally honest with herself, even with all Marcus's shortcomings, his undiluted dullness, this was an opportunity that most girls her age didn't get handed on a plate every day. And she really, *really* did want to find out about sex.

It wasn't that she wanted to do it with Marcus, certainly not – but he was what was available and this was her chance to have her curiosity assuaged first hand.

Eavesdropping the conversations of the other girls at school on the subject of their sexual encounters, she'd managed to gather really quite a lot of information. One thing she had certainly learnt was that an awful lot of their first experiences had been dreadful, fumbled, unsatisfactory affairs because neither party had known what to do or what to expect, with the result that it had hardly been a rapturous introduction to lovemaking – far from it. Despite that, Tilly was a teenage girl with teenage raging hormones and her body was hard-wired genetically to want to propagate the species. But she was also a hopeless romantic, and unlike her fellow sixth-formers she wanted perfect sex from the outset with her true love, not some sweaty, panting, fumbled travesty.

But sex with her true love wasn't going to be an option now, so Marcus would just have to do.

Tilly wasn't desperate to lose her virginity for the sake of it, but she was desperate to find out what all the hoopla was about. Was it, as some of her peers reported when they'd apparently found a bloke who knew what he was at, the most fantastic experience ever, or were they exaggerating? Could anything done between two consenting human beings possibly be so amazing?

Of course she wanted to believe that with Ashley it would be a wonderful, life-enhancing moment that would transport their relationship to a higher level. That is, she conceded with a sigh, if they ever got their relationship back on track. If they did – and she so wished and longed that that might happen – would their lovemaking take them to some wondrously magical place where she'd be filled with bliss and then be left feeling like a goddess? She could only dream that it would be like that. But if neither of them had done it before, it wasn't very likely; not if the rest of the sixth form was to be believed. The one thing that her fellow sixth-formers seemed to be unanimous about was that it was a waste of time expecting sex to be good if both of you were virgins. No, they all agreed, you needed a man with a bit of experience for that first, precious time.

And, thought Tilly, pulling out the plug with her toes, with six more years of life under his belt, even if he was dull, surely Marcus should have managed to accumulate a bit of know-how. All she had to do was to get him to share it. She felt quite nervous at the prospect of what she had planned, but how difficult could it be to seduce a man when you had to share a bed with him?

Zipping up his coat, Marcus braced himself before braving the elements again. If it were possible, he thought, the temperature had plummeted even further and the snow was falling even more thickly. Not an evening to be out and about. He pulled his collar up around his face and headed along the street to the dress shop. Despite the weather, there was a fair scattering of people on the streets, trudging head down through the snow, heading for homes or bars. There didn't seem to be many out intent on retail therapy – which suited Marcus down to the ground. He wanted to get this over and done with a quickly as possible. Like most men, shopping was not his pastime of choice.

He reached his destination and pushed open the door to the shop before kicking as much snow as possible off his boots on the big doormat. He was greeted by a waft of warm, expensively scented air and a beautifully coifed woman.

'*Bon soir, monsieur*. Can I help you?'

Marcus explained his requirements and told the assistant that he didn't know the lady's size but he knew her height and weight because he'd overheard her tell the ski technician those details when she'd had her bindings adjusted in the hire shop. Madame assured him that with that information she could pick out an ensemble that would be perfect, and she would ensure that she included everything the mademoiselle would need for the next twenty-four hours, including, she smiled coyly, any necessary lingerie.

Marcus left the shop assistant to her task and whisked along to the supermarket to pick up a hairbrush for Tilly and some toiletries for the pair of them, and then went to the ski shop to see if he could find some casual clothes for himself. He was in luck. They had a fairly decent selection of menswear including, to his surprise, a rack in the corner with a range of undergarments and socks. Having kitted himself out and bought a rucksack to shove all his purchases in, he then moved on to a shoe shop a couple of doors down where he bought two pairs of cheap moon boots.

When he returned to the dress shop, Madame had a large carrier bag and an even larger bill waiting for him.

'If there is a problem with anything, we can exchange it.'

'I'm sure it will all be perfect,' replied Marcus, trying not to look too shocked about the number of Swiss francs he'd just dropped. He gathered up all his purchases and made his way back to the hotel.

Tilly was sitting up on the bed, wrapped in her robe with her hair in a towel.

'Where have you been? I was worried.'

'Just out,' said Marcus, dropping his shopping on the bed.

'Shopping?' There was an accusatory note in Tilly's voice.

'Don't you want something other than ski kit to wear out to dinner tonight?'

Tilly nodded. She eyed the bags warily.

'I hope that whatever the lady in the dress shop chose is OK. I left her to it, thinking her taste was probably going to be a better bet than mine. I suggest you try it all on, and if it's dreadful or doesn't fit, we'll go back and you can pick something else. And while you're seeing what delights – or otherwise – are in the bags to surprise you, I'm going to pop into the bathroom, have a bath to warm up and get into the clothes I bought for myself.'

Marcus picked up his new clothes and the toiletries and left Tilly to see what had been chosen for her.

When he emerged some twenty minutes later, clean, warm, dry and shaved, Tilly was sitting on the bed flicking through the satellite channels on the TV. She was wearing a pale pink cashmere sweater and a pair of dark grey trousers. She looked very elegant and pretty.

'Wow,' said Marcus.

'You like it?'

'It's very nice. It, er, fits.'

'It's perfect. You look OK too,' said Tilly.

'This old thing,' he said with a grin. 'And I bought us some moon boots so we've got something to put on our feet.'

'You thought of everything. Just one thing, though.'

'Yes.'

'Exactly what did you tell the woman in the dress shop?'

'I told her we were stranded here overnight and you'd need stuff for twenty-four hours.'

'So she doesn't think we're on our honeymoon or anything.'

'Lord, no.' Marcus was quite stunned. 'Why on earth . . .'

Tilly produced from the carrier bag a negligee that seemed to consist of a few wisps of sheer chiffon and some strategically placed tufts of ostrich down.

Marcus stared and it and swallowed. 'Crikey,' he said after a couple of seconds. 'I hope you don't think I . . . I mean, I never said . . .'

'No, well,' said Tilly, replacing it in the bag with a

smile. 'But it might come in handy,' she said with a raised eyebrow, trying to sound sophisticated.

'We'll take it back to the shop. Change it for something more . . . suitable.'

'Spoilsport,' said Tilly lightly, to hide her disappointment at his reaction.

Marcus felt his face flare and he swallowed. 'It's just . . . under the circumstances . . .' Tonight was going to be tough enough as it stood without the bloody woman in the dress shop providing a nightie more suited to a porn movie, and Tilly trying to be provocative.

He changed the subject – firmly. 'I don't know about you, but I'm famished. Let's go and find somewhere to eat.'

'Let's.'

The nightie was forgotten as they grabbed their still-damp ski jackets and headed out of the room.

Tilly looked at her watch for about the tenth time. 'How much longer before we get to eat?' she complained, rolling her eyes. She took another sip of her vin chaud, her third.

'The waiter said he'd find us a table as soon as possible.'

'But that was an hour ago. I'm famished.'

Marcus looked around the packed restaurant. 'There's a group there who seem to be finishing.' He watched a harassed waiter clearing their pudding plates and then groaned as the same waiter, having dumped the plates in the kitchen, returned with his notebook and took a further order. Tilly saw where he was looking and understood the reason for his groan. What on earth could they want? Coffee and liqueurs? Why couldn't they just bugger off and find those in a bar somewhere else? she thought grumpily.

She downed the rest of her mulled wine and then

sucked on the piece of orange that she fished out of the bottom of the glass. 'Is it worth trying somewhere else?'

Marcus shook his head. 'I expect everywhere is busy, and if we move, we'll only wind up at the back of a new queue. We could have another drink.'

Tilly was torn. Part of her didn't think that was a good idea, although the other part of her would have liked one very much indeed. She was taut with jitters over what she had planned for later, but equally she didn't want Marcus getting pissed and not being able to perform. God, if only they'd hurry up and feed them – then they could go to the hotel and . . . Oh fuck it.

'Yes please, I'll have another vin chaud.' She just had to hope Marcus could hold his liquor.

When the waiter finally informed them that their table was ready, Tilly was feeling quite a lot calmer. Possibly down to the effect of the mulled wine, she admitted to herself. Maybe she'd better take it steady. Too much Dutch courage might be a mistake. But although she was feeling calmer, she was still absolutely ravenous and barely glanced at the menu before deciding on the steak frites and a green salad. Marcus chose the same and ordered a *demi litre de vin rouge*.

'*D'accord*,' said the waiter and whizzed off to the kitchens

'And make it snappy,' muttered Tilly to his retreating back, her stomach rumbling loudly. She tucked into the sliced baguette and butter on the table to try to appease it – she didn't think that a few mouthfuls of bread were going to spoil the monumental appetite she'd built up.

Luckily, it was now so late that the rush in the kitchens was almost over and they only had to wait for the time it took the chef to cook two medium steaks before they were served. Even Tilly admitted, not very clearly through her full mouth, that it had been worth waiting for.

'Pudding?' offered Marcus when she laid down her knife and fork on a cleared plate.

Tilly shook her head. 'I'm stuffed.' She hiccoughed quietly. It had been a really big plateful and she'd wolfed it with astounding speed, which explained why she now had mild indigestion. She could hear Mrs T tutting about not chewing each mouthful properly and bolting her food.

'In which case, I think I'll order us both some coffee and then we can think about getting back to our hotel.'

'I don't want any coffee.' Her jitters about her plans for the night were back with her with a vengeance, and now all she wanted to do was get back to their room before she got cold feet and bottled it.

'Well even if you don't, I do.'

Tilly sighed. God, she just wanted to get the next bit over and done with. The delay was agonising.

It was snowing again when they left the restaurant, but the wind had dropped, which was the important thing; it was the gale, not the snow, that had closed the cable car, and if conditions remained the same till morning, they'd be able to return to their own chalet first thing. In the meantime there was just the tricky matter of getting through the drifts back to their hotel. Even though Marcus had had the foresight to buy them sensible footwear, it still wasn't easy as they slipped and slithered on the ice concealed beneath the calf-deep snow. At one point Tilly nearly went arse-over-tit and Marcus grabbed her elbow to stop her from falling flat on her face. Having just managed to keep her upright, he hooked his arm round her waist to stop her going over again; apart from anything else, it was easier for both of them to walk with the shared support of the other.

'This is nice,' said Tilly, resting her head on his shoulder. She was hugely conscious of what she had planned once they got back, and she thought that a bit of preparation, a little light flirting, could only be a help. The fact that Marcus was actually holding her against him right now was something she knew she had to make use of, to capitalise on, if she was going to get him to teach her about sex in the next few hours. That thought – being taught about sex! – hit her with more of a shock than she expected, and she nearly lost her footing again. God, if she was this worried about it here in public with all her clothes on, she was going to be a basket case by the time she was in the privacy of their shared room and was taking her clothes off.

Sadly, Marcus hadn't seemed to notice the way she was snuggling up to him. Or maybe he was concentrating on staying upright.

She decided to come on a bit stronger. 'I'm so glad I've got you to look after me,' she purred.

'That's all right,' said Marcus automatically, busy concentrating.

'But you've been so kind,' she insisted, giving him a bit of a squeeze as she said it.

'Only done what anyone would do under the circumstances.'

'No.' She added another squeeze for emphasis. 'What you did was really special. I appreciate it. Truly I do.' She looked up at him and batted her eyelashes. She saw his Adam's apple bob as he swallowed.

He shrugged diffidently. 'Nah. Honest. After all, I got you into this mess, didn't I?'

'It's not so much of a mess. Not now. I mean, at least we've got somewhere to stay.'

'Yes, but . . .'

Tilly looked up at him again from under her lashes. 'I don't think there's going to be a problem.' A significant pause. 'Do you?'

It was Marcus's turn to almost lose his footing. He let go of her to flail his arms around in a desperate attempt to stay vertical. Eventually he got control of his feet and stopped thrashing around.

'No.' His voice wasn't entirely steady. Tilly saw his Adam's apple bob again, and smiled to herself.

When they reached the front door of their hotel,

Marcus extracted his key and let them both in. Tilly suddenly got another burst of the jitters.

'Shall we have a nightcap?' she suggested.

Marcus shook his head. 'I'd rather not. Do you mind frightfully?'

Tilly chewed her lip momentarily. 'No, of course not. Tell you what, if you're tired, why don't you go up and use the bathroom first? I'll come up in ten minutes or so.'

Marcus looked a bit surprised.

'It's just,' continued Tilly, 'I ought to phone Fa, and there's a pay phone here so I don't have to worry about my credit or the signal or anything.'

'Oh, OK.' Marcus bundled off towards the stairs, leaving Tilly in the lobby.

She thought for a few seconds about having a brandy to help stiffen her resolve but decided against it. If she was going to learn properly from the lesson she really hoped Marcus was going to give her, she wanted to be able to remember it in the morning. Any more to drink and there was a real danger she might find crucial gaps in her memory. Instead she did as she'd promised and rang her father's mobile.

He seemed remarkably sanguine about his daughter being stranded and didn't ask anything about the hotel – and nothing at all, thankfully, about their sleeping arrangements – beyond wanting to know if it was comfortable. Tilly was able to reassure him truthfully and to tell him that her bathroom was really nice. She promised they'd try to get the first cable car back over in the morning and she'd ring him to let him know if there was going to be a problem.

'If there is, can you find Bernard and explain why I'm late?' she asked. 'Tell him I'll ring him when I do get over the valley and we can arrange where to meet.'

'That's fine. Your sisters tell me they managed a red

run today. They're certain they're going to manage the Roches Noires by the end of the week.'

'Bully for them,' said Tilly, trying not to show how jealous she was of their rapid progress.

She wished her father good night and hung up, then checked her watch. She reckoned Marcus had had more than enough time to change into his pyjamas – or whatever he'd elected to wear in bed – clean his teeth and get under the duvet.

This is it, girl, she told herself as she followed his path to the stairs.

She reached their room and quietly knocked on the door.

'Come in,' called Marcus. 'It isn't locked.'

Tilly took a deep, steadying breath and opened the door. 'Hi,' she said, hoping that her voice didn't sound as shaky as she felt. She didn't want to give Marcus any indication that she was horribly nervous; more nervous than it was natural to be if she was just going to *sleep* with a man.

'How's your dad?' asked Marcus. He was propped up against the pillows idly flicking through the satellite channels on the TV. He didn't turn his head to look at her.

'Oh, fine.' She scuttled past the foot of the bed to the stash of goodies that Marcus had bought her earlier. She grabbed the hairbrush and a few other bits and pieces and then whizzed back, past the telly and into the bathroom. She shut the door and put her things on the counter. She noticed her hands were shaking like crazy.

She put the seat down on the loo and plonked herself down. Get a grip, she told herself sternly. For a few minutes she considered whether or not she really wanted to carry out her plan. It's not compulsory, she told herself. There won't be any loss of face. It doesn't matter to anyone at all, except yourself.

But, argued her other half, this is a golden

opportunity. You won't get another one like this coming along in a hurry.

But does it matter? So what if your first experience of sex isn't perfect? You don't know that sex with Marcus is going to be anything other than mediocre.

It's a risk I'm prepared to take, she thought determinedly.

In which case . . .

She looked at the minuscule nightie that the lady in the dress shop had picked out for her. Shame to waste it. Besides, wearing that, he wouldn't be able to resist her, surely.

She looked at her reflection in the mirror and saw that a nervous smile was playing across her lips.

Tart! she told her reflection.

She got undressed, cleaned her teeth, brushed her hair and then slipped the nightie on. It was unbelievably seductive. He would be in her power. He'd be her slave. Her sex slave. She felt that smile breaking out again. She knew she was being naughty – no, *wicked* – but she really needed to find out about sex, and Marcus had the answers, she was sure. She opened the door to the bedroom and stepped out.

Marcus felt a bolt of unadulterated lust jar him before he clamped down on his instinctive, and very male, reaction. 'For God's sake, Tilly. What are you playing at?'

'I'm not playing at anything. Yet.' She leaned against the door jamb and batted her eyelashes at him seductively.

Marcus leapt out of bed and over to the tiny wardrobe, where he found the bathrobe he'd borrowed for Tilly earlier that evening. He spun her round and bundled her into it, and tied the belt as tight as he could.

'Now get into bed and stop fooling around,' he ordered angrily.

'What?' She was flabbergasted. This wasn't in the scenario she'd rehearsed in her head. 'Why . . . why are you cross with me?'

'Because you're behaving badly and you know it.'

Tilly looked stunned, which left Marcus completely bemused. What on earth had the silly girl expected? That he'd throw her to the bed and take her there and then? She was still at school, for heaven's sake. And their fathers were friends. How the hell would he be able to look Edward in the eye ever again if he allowed himself to . . . ? Stop it, he told himself. Don't even think about making love to Tilly.

'Don't you like me?' she asked. Her lower lip seemed to be quivering.

'I like you fine,' he growled, trying to blot out of his mind the image of her in that tiny nightie. 'But what on earth are you doing dressed like that? For God's sake, Tilly, it's so inappropriate.'

Tilly's eyes welled up with tears. 'But I thought it was pretty. And you bought it for me.' A tear spilled over her lower lashes. Marcus wasn't entirely convinced it was genuine. He kept his distance. He wasn't going to offer a sympathetic cuddle. Christ, if he got close to her, knowing what was under the bathrobe, he might lose control.

'It is pretty,' he conceded cautiously, 'but I didn't choose it and you know that. Besides, I thought we decided earlier that what with you and me having to share a room . . . Well, it's hardly suitable, under the circumstances.'

'You don't fancy me, that's it, isn't it? You think I'm fat and ugly. That's why you covered me up.' She sat down on the edge of the bed.

'Tilly, don't be such a little fool.' Oh shit, that wasn't the right thing to say. He could tell by the way the tears spilled even faster from Tilly's eyes that she was feeling very vulnerable, and telling her she was a fool hadn't helped one jot. 'I don't think anything of the sort,' he added much more gently. He pulled a tissue from the box on the bedside table and handed it to her, then sat beside her. 'You're a very attractive girl and I like you very much. I really don't know why you thought it would be a good idea to wear that silly nightie. I don't think your father would like it.'

Tilly pushed her shoulders backwards. 'This has nothing to do with Fa. This is about me.'

'Well, yes, obviously.'

'No, you don't understand.'

'What don't I understand?'

Tilly turned an impressive shade of red. 'I want . . .' She stopped and stared at Marcus helplessly. 'I need you,' she stammered.

'Need me for what?'

'For . . . for . . .' She stopped again, her eyes wide and worried. 'I want you to make love to me,' she finished in a tiny whisper.

Her voice was so quiet, Marcus misheard what she'd said. 'You want me to love you?' he yelped. Crikey, the girl hadn't gone and fallen for him, had she? Oh Lord, oh no, it was all too sudden. His mind whirled in a panic. His dad would like it, obviously, but he wasn't ready for commitment, not yet . . . 'Don't be silly, Tilly,' he blurted out. 'What on earth are you on about? I mean, I like you, of course . . .'

'Please, Marcus, please do it. Show me how.'

Do what? Show her how to do what? Then the penny began to drop. Of course . . . the nightie, her embarrassment . . . Double shit. She hadn't said 'love me', she'd said 'make love to me'! He swallowed involuntarily. What the fuck was he supposed to do now? If he told her no, she'd cry. If he did anything else, he'd have his conscience to deal with – to say nothing of Tilly's father.

'Tilly . . .' he began.

'Please, Marcus.'

'Tilly, it's just not . . . I mean, I appreciate the offer.' No, this wasn't right. He sounded as if he was turning down a cup of coffee, not her mind-boggling present of her virginity. Or at least he assumed that was what this was all about; he couldn't imagine that she was going through this charade with this amount of nervousness and embarrassment if she was used to jumping into bed with men. No, given her present demeanour, there was no way she'd done this before. He swallowed again. 'Tilly, sweetheart, I'm not the person you want. Honestly.'

'But you are. This isn't a spur-of-the-moment thing.'

Marcus raised his eyebrows. 'Oh, so you planned the cable car service being halted and then the avalanche to get us trapped here.'

Tilly shook her head impatiently. 'No, don't be stupid. But we *were* trapped here and, well, I did some thinking.'

'About what, exactly?'

Tilly, regaining some of her poise and composure, blew her nose, then turned to look him straight in the eye. 'You know exactly what,' she said quietly.

'But why? Why now?' He thought of adding 'why me?' but thought that it would sound ungrateful and even rude.

'It's just I think I'm about the only girl in the sixth form who's never done it.'

'I'm sorry?' said Marcus.

'You know.' She paused. '*It*.' He could hear the embarrassment in her voice.

'Having sex isn't something to be proud of. And not having done it isn't something to be ashamed of either,' he said gently. Oh God, he was having to act as an agony uncle now. Could the night get any more surreal – or worse? 'It'll happen to you when the time is right.'

'Isn't the time right now?' she said in a small voice.

'No, sweetheart, it's not. For a start, we don't love each other.'

'You mean you don't fancy me.'

Marcus, remembering what Tilly had looked like in that nightie, felt easily able to contradict that with utter conviction. 'Tilly, you're young and very gorgeous, but it's absolutely wrong for you and me to have sex. Just because you're in this really bizarre situation of having to share a bed with a strange man doesn't mean that you need to do anything other than sleep. Honest. You're feeling vulnerable because of our situation, you're worried by what the girls in your class are saying, though I bet half of them are lying, and if I overheard your sisters correctly, you recently got dumped by your boyfriend.'

'What . . .! Bloody twins, I'll kill them,' she muttered.

Marcus ignored this outburst. 'But,' he stressed the word again, '*but* this is totally the wrong moment for you to find out about sex first hand.'

'I don't think so,' she insisted.

'Tell me, truthfully, why me? Why now? Is it just because we've been put into this weird situation? I mean, don't get me wrong, it's a very flattering offer. I'm touched, but it seems a serious decision that has been made by you in a pretty short space of time.'

Tilly looked at the soggy tissue squashed up in her fist. 'I don't want some hopeless boy who doesn't know what he's doing either to be my first experience. I've heard the girls at school talk and know how awful most of their first times were.' She gave a nervous little laugh. 'Bad enough to put you off ever doing it again, to listen to some of them. Wouldn't it be better if you went with someone who knew what they were doing for your first time?'

'And you probably will,' said Marcus. He turned her face with his hand so she had to look at him. 'But that someone ought to be someone you have real feelings for. Not someone who just happens, in your opinion, to be a bloke who might be able to teach you what goes where without making too much of a cock-up of it.'

'Well, I do like you, Marcus. You were really sweet about rescuing that mouse and you were brilliant about getting me down the mountain today.'

Marcus sighed. 'Listen, Tilly, thinking that someone is quite nice because they've done their Boy Scout good deed for the day isn't enough of a criterion to decide that this is the right bloke to go to bed with for the first time.' Shit, he thought, the restraint he was exercising ought to earn him a bloody medal. He reckoned any other bloke would have probably had Tilly on the bed and given her a darn good seeing-to the instant she'd walked out of the bathroom dressed like a porn star. So why did he feel obliged to act like a saint? She was virtually offering herself to him on a plate, they were sharing a double bed, he knew exactly what she had on under the rather frumpy bathrobe . . . and here he was trying to say no. If only she knew what a struggle it was. Or maybe it was much better that she didn't. Marcus wasn't sure how much longer he could hold out if she really came on to him.

Tilly flopped back on the bed and stared at the ceiling, feeling defeated. Angry, *embarrassed* and defeated. So much for Plan A. He obviously didn't fancy her, no matter how he dressed it up with kind words. And she could hardly force him to have his wicked way with her. Which left her looking like some sort of desperate, needy loser. How humiliating. And it wasn't as if there was anywhere she could run to, to hide her burning shame.

She felt tears leaking out of the sides of her eyes again. What was wrong with her? Just when she thought things couldn't get any worse, here she was crying again. Like that was going to help matters. And it would make her look all red-eyed and snotty. Annoyed and scowling, she dashed the tears away with the palms of her hands.

'Don't be like that, Tilly,' said Marcus.

'Like what?' she snapped. Like he cared about her. If he did, he'd do as she asked.

'I'm doing it for your own good.'

'Yeah, right.'

'You'll thank me one day.'

Tilly gave him a vile look. 'Like when I do find Mr Right.' She sneered the last two words.

'Well . . . yes.'

'And we go to bed, get it together and it's a complete disaster. He's embarrassed and I'm fed up because all I get to do is look at the ceiling, while he pants and puffs and squashes me flat.' She was quoting a remark she'd heard in the common room, but it seemed quite descriptive and summed up just how bad she feared things could be, just how unromantic and unfulfilling. 'Then we part, very acrimoniously, because we both know that it's been a complete disaster, so I never see Mr Right again. Yup, I'll be sure to thank you then.'

'Now you're exaggerating.'

'Don't.' She rounded on him, her temper finally getting the upper hand, beating shame into second place. 'Don't you *dare* patronise me. Just because you're a few years older, you think you know everything. You think you have the right to tell me what I ought to do and think.'

'I wasn't—'

'Don't interrupt,' she shouted. 'I'm a grown-up, I'm almost eighteen. In a few months I'll have left home and I'll be at uni and no one will be able to tell me what I can and can't do.'

'I wasn't—'

'No? Aren't you, right now, trying to tell me how to lead my life?'

'No, I'm not. And if you stop to think about anything for a second, what you proposed involved me too. Remember?'

'Yes, but—'

'Yes but nothing. Have you any idea what you did to me, standing in the doorway in that ridiculous nightie? And have you any idea what a terrible effort it's been for me to behave with any sort of honour?'

'But I don't want you to. That's the point.'

Marcus released a long groan. 'I can't cope with this and I'm not going to argue any more. Just get into bed and go to sleep.' Tilly began to untie the belt of the bathrobe. 'Hang on,' he ordered, stopping her in her tracks, her hands still fumbling with the knot he'd tied so tightly. He reached into one of the carrier bags that littered the dressing table and pulled out a T-shirt, the one he'd planned to wear tomorrow. 'Put this on instead of that bloody nightie.' He shoved it into her hands and pushed her, none too gently, back towards the bathroom.

Tilly, still feeling humiliated and rejected, slammed the door behind her before slumping once again on to the loo to think.

How could he turn her down like that? How could he! Bastard. She really hadn't expected this reaction, which was why it had come as such a shock. From the stuff she'd gleaned at school, it seemed as though a girl only had to make the vaguest of offers to find herself getting rogered senseless. What had she done wrong?

It all proved, she thought morosely as she pulled the nightie over her head and dragged on the T-shirt, that she needed even more help than she'd thought. She obviously didn't have a clue about blokes, not the first idea about how their minds worked or which buttons you had to press to get them to respond. In fact, she thought, she might as well forget the whole sorry business of wanting to form a relationship with a man and just sign up for Holy Orders right now.

She shoved the nightie into a corner of the bathroom and went back into the bedroom, tugging down the short hem of the T-shirt rather self-consciously. She didn't want to give Marcus another reason to disapprove of her. Even though she knew the T-shirt to be his idea, it covered very little more than the nightie and she didn't think he'd be thrilled at the amount of leg she was displaying.

Only the bedside light was shining when she got into the bedroom, and Marcus was lying on his back on his side of the bed, his hands clasped together on his chest, which reminded Tilly of some of the stone knights on their tombs in the family chapel. She glanced at him as she crept round the end of the bed and was relieved to see his eyes were firmly shut. Slowly and carefully she drew back a corner of the duvet and crept under the covers.

'Night, night,' she whispered, still raw with humiliation.

'Night, Tilly,' he responded.

Being very careful to stay on her half of the bed and not wishing to touch him and get accused of breaking some sort of code, she turned on her side to face the wall and curled up, willing sleep to overwhelm her. By rights it should do: she was exhausted physically from skiing and emotionally from her set-to with Marcus, and on top of that she'd had a certain amount to drink and it was late.

But sleep didn't come and she lay awake, hideously aware of Marcus lying next to her. Every slight movement he made reverberated through the mattress; she could hear the sound of his breathing, and the occasional gurgle from his stomach, but was he asleep? Or was he as alert as she was and just faking too? Tilly felt that once she was certain he was out for the count, she'd be able to relax, maybe even fall asleep, though at the moment, she thought glumly as she stared at the curtain, there seemed precious little hope of that.

And then suddenly there was an almighty grunting and harrumphing and Marcus turned over and threw his arm across her and snuggled up next to her, his body pressing against hers, which was naked from the waist down, her T-shirt having ridden up when she'd slid under the covers. Tilly lay paralysed. Apart from the fact that he was crushing the breath out of her, she felt, given his earlier rejection, that this proximity was wholly out of place. What on earth should she do? Wake him up? It wasn't as if she could move away: firstly, he had her pinned, and secondly, where could she move to? She was already right on the edge of the mattress.

Then, horrors, she could feel something stirring. She

knew exactly where Marcus's right arm was – across her shoulders – and she reckoned his left arm had to be pinned under him somewhere, so there was only one possibility left for what was moving gently against her bare buttocks. She went rigid with tension and embarrassment and that slight movement must have penetrated Marcus's subconscious, for in the next couple of seconds he worked out for himself exactly what she had found so disturbing.

He was awake in an instant and threw himself away from her and over to the other side of the bed, almost taking all the covers with him.

'God, I'm sorry,' he said groggily.

'Don't be,' said Tilly, still facing the curtains, thankful he couldn't see how red her face was.

'No, after what I said to you – how preachy I was earlier – what just happened was unforgivable. But will you? Forgive me, that is?'

Tilly turned over and was surprised at how close their faces were. His was just a few inches from hers. 'It doesn't matter,' she said dully. But it did. His reaction when he'd realised how close he had been to her spoke volumes as to how he felt – which was that she repelled him. He couldn't get away fast enough.

'Look, Tilly. I'm really sorry, but I'm a bloke and my body has a mind of its own sometimes.'

'I understand. You really don't want to have anything to do with me, but you can't be held answerable for your hormones, which aren't obeying the party line. Is that it?'

'No, it's nothing like that.' Tilly could see him smiling at her in the dim light that came through the curtains. 'If circumstances were different, if our fathers weren't such friends, if I didn't feel so responsible and if you weren't still at school, I would feel very differently about spending a night in the same bed as you. But I can't change the circumstances. And yes, you're right, my body doesn't give a toss about behaving properly.'

'But you do.'

'If I'm honest, I wish I didn't have to.'

'Yeah, right.' The way he'd leapt away from her when he realised he was touching her wasn't going to be an image she'd be able to dismiss lightly.

'Seriously.'

Did she believe him? His actions had sent out one message but his words were sending out another. And he sounded genuine, so maybe he didn't think she was a total dog. She decided to push it. Maybe there was just a chance that she could get her way after all.

'So if you feel like that, couldn't we just ignore the circumstances? Pretend they don't exist.'

'It wouldn't be right.'

'Who's to know? I won't tell if you don't.' She could tell he was weakening. 'Go on, you know you want to,' she said, taking a gamble that he really did.

'You're a very naughty girl. Do you know that?'

She nodded. 'Incorrigible is what my house mistress calls me.'

'I'm not surprised. And no, I can't just ignore the circumstances.'

'But only we would know,' she insisted.

'Tilly, it wouldn't be right.'

Tilly leaned towards him fractionally so her nose was now just inches from his. 'But you'd be doing me such a huge service. Would it be so terrible?' She saw Marcus shut his eyes as if he were struggling. 'And I'm on the pill,' she lied. His eyes snapped open.

'What?'

'You heard. I was in the school Guide troop – a patrol leader. "Be Prepared" and all that.'

'Shit, Tilly, you certainly know how to make it hard for a bloke.'

Tilly giggled and raised an eyebrow archly. 'Do I really?'

'And you being on the pill isn't really good enough. For all you know I might have some awful disease.'

'Have you?'

'No, but that's not the point, is it? Unprotected sex is a really, *really* bad idea.'

'I know, but you're all right and so am I, so what's the problem?'

Marcus groaned. 'This just isn't fair.' He shook his head. 'I tried so hard, I really did. I'm sorry.'

'Don't apologise,' said Tilly. She shut her eyes, leaned a little further forward and kissed him on the lips. 'Just be gentle.'

'I promise,' said Marcus, kissing her back.

Yessss, rejoiced Tilly silently.

'So,' said Marcus softly, 'how was it for you?'

Tilly opened her eyes. 'Blissful,' she said with a small sigh. 'And thank you.' She wouldn't ever tell him that all the time he'd been making love to her, kissing her, running his fingers over her, exploring her body and encouraging her to explore his, she'd kept her eyes shut and pretended to herself that it had been Ashley doing all those wonderful and arousing things to her. She knew it was unfair of her, but she felt that if she couldn't have Ashley in real life then at least she could have him in her fantasies. And was it so very wrong? As long as Marcus never knew, what harm would it do?

Marcus kissed her on the tip of her nose. 'Now then, it's very late and we both need some sleep. Turn over.'

Tilly did as she was told and Marcus snuggled up against her, wrapping his arms around her. It did feel nice, she thought, as warm fuzziness swept over her. And now she could see why such a big deal was made about sex; it had been wonderful. Well, it had hurt for a second and then it had been wonderful, and Marcus had been very gentle and patient. She wondered if it would be better with Ashley if she ever got back together with him. She really hoped she'd find out.

Which made her think about Marcus again. He was really kind, she had to concede that, but try as she might, she couldn't see him as anything more than a friend, no matter what had just happened. She might meet him for a drink now and again, they'd always be mates and she'd always be hugely grateful to him, but did she want him as a boyfriend? No. And she was sure of that because she didn't think about him when he wasn't around, she didn't feel fluttery and breathless when he was, she didn't feel that *connection* that she did with Ashley. She hoped, she thought sleepily, that Marcus felt the same way and wouldn't see this as anything more than a one-night stand. She didn't think about the consequences if he didn't as she yawned and snuggled deeper down the bed. She was asleep in minutes.

A stupid tune penetrated her consciousness.

'Wha . . . ?' she mumbled, trying to make sense of her surroundings. The stupid tune continued until she felt a movement and it abruptly ceased. Shit! She wasn't alone. Then the memory of the previous night came piling back. Her and Marcus . . .

She felt a little pinprick of shame that she'd thrown herself at him so shamelessly. Quite the hussy, she thought. But, she justified to herself, finding out about sex had been important, and a girl had to grab the opportunities as they arose. And hearing the lame tune that he'd chosen as his alarm call made her even more certain that Marcus could never be more than just a friend.

She lay quietly on her side of the bed recalling exactly what had happened about eight hours earlier. She hadn't lied when she'd told him the sex had been blissful and she would always be grateful for such a comprehensive and wonderful introduction to it. And now she knew what was what, she felt confident that when the occasion arose again – please God with Ashley – she and he would be able to reach similar heights of ecstasy together.

So, she thought, that was it: virginity gone, kaput,

never to be regained. And did she feel any different? She pondered for a few seconds. There was no doubt that she did feel a bit older, more grown-up, and certainly a touch more sophisticated. After all, she was a woman of the world now. She'd been around the block and all that, even if it was only the once. She just had to hope it didn't show. The last thing she wanted when she got back to the chalet was her father giving her the third degree about how she and Marcus had spent the night. She'd have to have a careful look at her reflection when she got up. Not that she expected to see a big 'H' for 'hussy' or 'harlot' on her forehead, but she'd want to be sure.

She stretched luxuriously.

'Morning,' said Marcus. 'How are you this morning?'

She rolled over. 'Fine.'

He searched her face. 'No regrets.'

Tilly shook her head. 'None at all,' she said as lightly as she could. She didn't want him to think that just because he'd slept with her, this gave him some sort of hold, a *droit de seigneur*. 'How about you?'

'Don't be silly. I feel incredibly flattered and privileged – if that doesn't sound OTT.'

'A bit,' she admitted.

'And I'm still worried I won't be able to look your father in the eye.'

'Why on earth? I'm not going to tell him and there's no reason for you to, is there?'

'No. I'm just being paranoid. Deflowering the eldest daughter of a family like yours ... Surely there were gruesome penalties for such miscreants in the past.'

'Maybe, but I can tell you that some of my female ancestors were right old slappers. Committed adultery with kings and all sorts, one or two of them. Probably where I get it from,' she added with a grin.

'I don't think you're a slapper.'

'Good. That's something, I suppose.' Tilly glanced at

her watch. 'I think we'd better get up.' She leapt out of bed and pulled back the curtains. The sky was overcast but it wasn't snowing and the trees in the hotel garden were hardly moving. 'Looks like the cable car should be running.'

'Well, that's a good thing. It isn't that I don't want to be stranded with you here any longer,' explained Marcus, 'but you've got lessons booked and my phone is going to run out of charge any minute now and I like the creature comforts of my own place.'

'Then we'd best get washed and dressed and back there.' Tilly was determined, now she'd got what she'd wanted from Marcus, to get things back to normal as quickly as possible. She knew she was being selfish and unfair but she reckoned Marcus was big enough to handle it. And besides, she'd never promised him anything in return for her sex-education lesson, so she wasn't being *that* tough.

The end of the holiday came around with startling speed. For the rest of the week, Tilly had gone out of her way to make sure that the family always met up for lunch, and that she and Marcus spent very little time together by insisting that she wanted to practise her turns on her own, or go on the slopes with her sisters so that Marcus could ski with the two older men.

'You'll have so much more fun,' she'd told him, in front of Desmond and Edward, 'and you've already been too good to me. Besides, I'd like to ski with Flora and Daisy.'

And Flora and Daisy, longing to show off their skills to their older sister, had jumped around with excitement in such a way that Marcus couldn't refuse.

In the evenings she'd have supper with everyone before insisting she needed an early night and disappearing as soon as she could to her room.

'It's the mountain air,' she explained. 'It knocks me out. And all this exercise. Phew!'

Edward and Desmond took her explanations at face value and her sisters didn't care. Which just left Marcus, who would give her a long, disappointed look. But he said nothing.

On the last day all six of them went together on a long ski, with Tilly surprising everyone by attempting almost all the slopes. The twins raced around showing off their skills and challenging each other to short cuts through the trees or jumps that other skiers had made out of hillocks of snow. Desmond and Edward skied very competently but wanted frequent stops for refreshments on the grounds that they were too old to be tearing about like teenagers. These stops were useful, as the twins went up the chair lifts and down the pistes again whenever the grown-ups had a break, while Marcus shepherded Tilly like a border collie till she caught up. But there was no chance for them to chat on the slopes, as Tilly was too busy concentrating on her skiing, and she made sure they always rode up on full chair lifts so that any sort of intimate conversation while they were being swept upwards was equally out of the question. At the end of the day they were all knackered. The twins were triumphant that they'd finally managed the Roches Noires piste, although they hadn't won the bet as they'd both wiped out.

'But we got down it,' they crowed, terribly proud of their achievement, dusting snow off their jackets, trousers and hats from spectacular tumbles.

'More fool you,' said Tilly, who'd thought they'd been mad in the extreme to even contemplate the idea, let alone have a go.

Back at the chalet, the last day of skiing over, Tilly found she was suffering from conflicting emotions. She was thrilled to be getting out of her ski boots for the final time – they were hideously uncomfortable, despite the fact that she was now used to them – and the thought that she'd never have to cram her feet into them again was a definite bonus, but she was really sad to be packing to go home. Despite everything, and her misgivings about having to spend a whole week with Marcus, she'd enjoyed herself. The skiing had been fun, and she could now completely understand why people got hooked on winter sports. She'd had a total blast, and of course she had had the added, and unexpected, bonus of That Night.

Finding out about sex was definitely a plus, even if it had been with Marcus and not Ashley – an experienced Ashley – as it had been in her dreams. The mystery had been removed; she knew what to do. But despite her hard-nosed determination to keep her relationship with Marcus on a very practical and unemotional footing, she was left with residual guilt. He'd been such a gentleman about the entire business, but since that Monday he'd been looking at her with puppy-dog eyes, while she'd been using every strategy in her arsenal to avoid him. She knew she was being unfair, but she felt that Marcus still hoped for something else, something more, and she couldn't bear the thought of him getting heavy. If he did, then she'd have really to reject him. What she wanted to happen was that her indifference would drive him away, a bit like turning away an unwanted puppy; there was only so long it would whine at a closed door before it finally moved away to look for a more welcoming home. Easier to avoid than confront was the way her reasoning worked.

So when, after their last dinner together – a sumptuous feast prepared by Antoinette – he suggested they ought to go for a drink together, Tilly cast desperately around for some excuse not to but could come up with nothing plausible. Their flight the next day wasn't until mid-afternoon, she didn't have to get up early, so there was no reason why she shouldn't go out. Trying to feign pleasure, she agreed.

She noticed their fathers exchanging a meaningful look. Well, they could make all the conjectures they liked, but she was going to use the opportunity to make sure that Marcus knew where he stood with her: she liked him as a friend, she would always be hugely grateful to him for everything, but that was all. She didn't, she couldn't love him. Illogical as it was, given how Ashley had rejected her attempt at apologising to him, he was the one she still wanted, still ached for, dreamt about and longed for, and Marcus was never going to be the cure.

As she left the chalet, the two fathers were already having a chat on the sofa in low voices, and she wondered if they were discussing their offspring. Significant glances were being cast in her and Marcus's direction. She wasn't stupid; she could guess what they were cooking up. The de Liege name and the Crosby money. What a merger and acquisition that would be.

Well let them, she thought, and the devil in her almost turned back to tell them what had really gone on the other night. Would they rejoice, slap each other on the back and break out the cigars at the thought that it was almost a done deal, or be horrified – especially when they subsequently found out that the brief relationship between their children wasn't anything more than a one-night stand. But she wasn't going to tell them and neither was Marcus. Not if he knew what was good for him.

'What do you fancy?' said Marcus, as they sat at a table in a cosy bar in the heart of the village.

'Do you think they've got WKD?'

'I can ask. You don't fancy anything more sophisticated – a kir, for example?'

Tilly remembered the delicious drink she'd had the first night. 'Ooh, yes. Lovely.'

When the waiter came, Marcus ordered the drinks and then gazed at Tilly across the table. 'So,' he said.

'This sounds serious,' joked Tilly. She knew what was coming – the elephant in the room that she'd been avoiding all week.

Marcus shrugged. 'I suppose it is. It's just, since Monday we haven't really had a chance to talk.'

'No.'

'And I think we ought to.'

'Must we?'

'Yes, I think we should.'

Tilly shrugged but didn't meet his eye.

Marcus reached across the table and put his hand over hers. 'Come on, Tilly, you know as well as I do what this is about. Where do I stand?'

'Cut to the chase, why don't you?' she quipped. But Marcus didn't respond; he just looked at her. Shit, this was going to be tough. She had a horrible feeling that Marcus might have thought that what happened on Monday wasn't just the sex education lesson she'd told him she'd wanted (and which bore no resemblance to *anything* she'd ever done in GCSE biology). Did he really, despite the way she'd treated him since, think it might lead to something else? That how she'd behaved since was just a ruse to get him to make another move because she was too embarrassed to tell him she secretly fancied him? Oh no! How did you tell a bloke you really *had* only wanted him for his body? That he was the lab rat in your experiment? Was there a tactful way of doing this? Suddenly Tilly didn't feel the least bit sophisticated and worldly-wise; instead she felt like a very awkward and gauche schoolgirl.

'Well . . . er . . . it's tricky.' The waiter arrived with their drinks, which gave her a few seconds to try to rally her thoughts.

'Is it?'

Tilly nodded. Bugger, her thoughts had stayed resolutely shambolic and she knew she was blushing. Nothing for it now but honesty. 'Look, Marcus . . . you're really kind and I *do* like you, honest.'

'But.'

'But . . . Well, for a start you're a lot older than me.'

'Six years isn't a great deal. It's not like I belong to another generation or anything.'

'Maybe, but it seems quite a lot to me. And then . . .' What she really wanted to say was that she found him dull, but that would be so hurtful, even if it was honest. And whatever else she said or did, she mustn't hurt his feelings. She had been brought up to be mindful of other people's sensibilities, and meanness wasn't something she could bring herself to show. But she could avoid that truth and tell him another . . .

'And then . . .' prompted Marcus.

'And then there's the complication that I'm still in love with someone else.' Which *was* honest, even though she knew it was a hopeless excuse.

'The mystery boyfriend who dumped you.'

Tilly nodded sadly, still staring hard at the tabletop in front of her rather than look Marcus in the eye.

'He's a fool,' said Marcus. 'He must have been special, but he's mad.'

Tilly shrugged. 'He was special. I think he's wrong too but I can't force him to take me back.'

'You could have me in the interim,' Marcus said quietly.

Tilly looked up and sighed, hopelessly. 'You are kind, really you are, and I don't deserve to have you as a friend, never mind anything else. I can't imagine how you manage at work.'

'I'm not kind when I'm working. Money is a serious business and there's no room for sentiment when you're dealing in huge sums.'

'I suppose.'

'So I need to make up for my all-round general nastiness at work when I'm with people like you.'

Tilly smiled sheepishly. 'I can't imagine you being nasty, but thanks.'

'But it's not going to alter my chances, eh?'

Tilly shook her head.

'Heigh-ho. But perhaps it's for the best. To be honest, I didn't think I really wanted a proper relationship until I was at least thirty, and then you came crashing into my life. I thought I could contemplate seeing a lot more of you; in fact it seemed rather a tempting idea. But we're both still young, there's no rush and we'll still be mates, yes?'

So he wasn't going to get heavy. He just sat there quietly and sipped his drink, which left Tilly feeling surprised – and relieved. Maybe he'd already known in his heart – how could he not, given the way she'd been behaving – what she was likely to say. Somehow, because he was being so nice and decent, she felt even more of a cow. Relieved, but a cow.

Marcus took another sip of his wine. 'One other thing.'

Uh-oh, here comes the recrimination, thought Tilly.

'I just want you to remember something: that if ever you need someone, I'm here. OK?'

He really meant it, too. He really was too nice for his own good, and it made Tilly feel even more of a selfish bitch.

'Oh Marcus.' She shook her head. 'I'm so horrible. I can't think why you're like this.' She wanted to tell him that she'd feel better about everything if he was vile to her, but as this was the punishment she deserved, she had to take it on the chin. 'I don't deserve your kindness. I'm really not worth it.'

'Yes you are. Or you are to me.'

'Now you're making me feel like a shit.'

'Good,' he said with a rueful laugh. 'Although that wasn't the object of the exercise. I just wanted to be sure that you were OK about Monday and that there was no residual misunderstanding between us.'

Tilly shook her head.

'Good. Now let's stop worrying about you and me and just enjoy the evening.'

Tilly felt a rush of relief that the ordeal was over. Not that it had been much of one as ordeals went, although there was a little part of her that wished Marcus hadn't been so bloody reasonable about the whole matter. If he'd shouted at her or told her she was a heartless bitch, it would have been no more than she deserved and it might have made her feel a bit less of a cow. She just hoped that one day he'd find a lovely woman to make him a great wife – someone who wouldn't mind that he was a bit, well, beige.

25

Ashley stared at his mother and stepfather, wondering if he'd heard correctly.

'Moving?' he repeated. 'You can't be serious.'

'I've been offered a job in Newcastle,' said Dave. 'The cost of living is much cheaper up there and I'm going to be paid a relocation allowance. Besides, it's promotion; I'll be in charge of a whole team of gas fitters, which is a big step up from where I am now. It's a no-brainer, Ashley. We're going.'

'But when?'

'Easter holidays.'

'What!' Ashley was horrified. This made it even worse – which was difficult, but it had. 'But I'm doing my A levels in the summer. I can't move then.'

Dave shrugged. 'Not my problem. Those exams are a waste of fucking time anyway. I keep telling you to go and get a decent job, a skill or a trade, try contributing to the family for once instead of being a fucking leech, but no. Well, now you won't have any option, will you?'

Ashley looked at his mum for support. 'Can't I stay here? Join you later?'

'But Newcastle's a nice place, Ash,' said his mum brightly. 'Much more going on.'

'But my A levels, Mum.'

'You could get a job, like Dave has always said you should.'

'I don't want a job, I want to go to uni. I've got to stay here.'

But she looked away, guilty that she couldn't support him against Dave.

'What, and have us pay rent on two places?' said Dave. 'I don't think so.'

'We could ask the council to put the house in my name for a month or two. I'd pay the rent. I've got money saved from my weekend job.'

'No,' said Dave bluntly. 'We're all going, you included. No arguing. Besides, the council's never going to let you stay on your own, you're not old enough.'

'They needn't know if we didn't tell them. They won't care as long as the rent's up to date.'

'No. Which bit of that word don't you understand, thicko?'

Ashley flung himself out of the room, grabbed a coat and took off out of the house into the dark evening. He headed for the skate park. He had to get away from Dave and his smug, self-satisfied face before he hit him. There was no arguing with him, and his mum wasn't going to stand up to him, that much was blindingly obvious. It was hopeless.

He kicked about the skate park until he was chilled to the bone, reluctant to return home until it was absolutely necessary. He found a couple of quid in change in his pocket and went to a local chippy, where he bought chips that he ate in the shop, as slowly as he could, trying to defrost from the wicked February wind that had been cutting through him all evening. It was late when he returned home, and the house was in darkness. He let himself silently in and crept upstairs. He undressed in the dark so as not to disturb his half-brothers and set his alarm for six in the morning. He wanted to be out of the house before the family got up. He didn't trust himself not to do something he'd regret if he ran into any of them.

*

'What are you doing at school this early?' said Miss Edwards, catching sight of him in the sixth-form locker room as she made her way past to the staff room at the end of the corridor.

'Nothing, miss,' said Ashley. He felt he could ask her the same question, because as far as he knew, teachers rarely rolled up till after eight o'clock, and it was not quite half past seven. But he didn't as it would only make him look cheeky, and he liked and respected Miss Edwards and didn't want to get on the wrong side of her.

'Nothing. I see.' She looked completely unconvinced. 'Have you had any breakfast?' she suddenly shot at him.

Ashley shook his head. 'No, miss.'

'Stay there,' she ordered. She returned a few minutes later bearing a mug of tea and a saucer piled with digestives. 'This hardly meets with government guidelines on your healthy diet at school, but it's got to be better than starting the day with nothing inside you.'

'Thanks, miss.'

'I didn't know if you took sugar but I made a guess that a lad of your age would. Was I right?'

Ashley nodded as he took a scalding sip. 'Thanks, miss. You didn't have to, though.'

'I want you paying attention in English, not falling asleep because you're weak with hunger.' She looked at him, her arms folded across her chest. 'So why the early start?'

'Dunno,' he lied.

Miss Edwards leaned towards him. 'Don't bullshit me, Ashley. I've been around a long time, and kids don't come to school this early unless there's a reason. So what is it? Trouble at home?'

'Not really.'

'Not really,' she repeated. 'Which I shall translate as "yes, miss".'

Ashley shrugged and drank some more of his tea.

'Your half-brothers making life hell for you?'

'No. Not this time.' Ashley had had to tell Miss Edwards about how difficult it was for him to study at home, to say nothing of the couple of occasions when Craig and Kieran had spoilt his work or wrecked school textbooks.

'Well that makes a change.' She moved over to a row of chairs and sat down. 'Might as well make myself comfortable,' she said half to herself. 'I've got a feeling it's going to take me a while to get to the bottom of this. Or we could just get on with it so I don't have to feel like I'm pulling teeth. Up to you.'

Ashley sat opposite her and sighed. He put his tea down on the chair next to him and then took a biscuit off the saucer and bit half of it off in one go. Miss Edwards waited patiently till he was ready.

'It's my step-dad.'

'And?' she prompted.

'I mean,' said Ashley, 'he's done nothing really bad. Not that he does,' he added hastily, just in case Miss Edwards thought about getting social services in. 'It's just he's got a new job.'

'Well that's all right.' Then Miss Edwards saw the look on Ashley's face. 'No, I can see it isn't. Why not? I mean, a job's a job and they're not that common around here at the moment.'

'It's in Newcastle.'

'Newcastle!' Her horrified reaction mirrored his own. 'And we're moving up there so he can take it.'

'When?' asked Miss Edwards quietly.

'Easter.'

'Ah.'

Ashley nodded.

'Your father—'

'Stepfather.'

'Your stepfather does know you're taking A levels and that you have an excellent chance of going to university?'

Ashley snorted and explained Dave's attitude to his education.

Miss Edwards rolled her eyes in disbelief. 'But doesn't he have the first idea how important this is?'

'Oh yeah, but he still doesn't care. He wants me to be a gas fitter or a plumber, have some sort of trade. Like his trade has got him anywhere much. We live on a crappy council estate here and we'll be moving to another crappy one up north.'

She sighed. 'There has to be a way around this, Ashley. It's only a matter of a couple of months between your parents moving and your exams finishing. Have you got any other relations that live in this area?'

Ashley shook his head.

'Or do you know anyone with a house big enough to take in a lodger for a little while?'

Yes he did, someone with a huge house, the biggest in town, but he wouldn't be welcome. Anything but, in fact. He shook his head again.

'Friends?'

'Don't think I haven't thought about it, but most of me mates at school don't have the space to take me in, not for weeks and weeks anyway. It's a lot to ask, miss.'

Miss Edwards nodded, acknowledging the truth of it. One thing to have a strange kid to stay for a few days, but two months! And there was the responsibility.

She stood up. 'I'm not going to let this defeat me, Ashley. I'm going to come up with something. Just leave it with me for a day or two, OK? And try not to worry. I'm going to make sure you can take your A levels if it's the last thing I do.'

Ashley drained the last of his tea and passed the mug and the now empty saucer back to her. 'Thanks, miss.' Maybe life wasn't completely shit after all. As long as people like Miss Edwards were on his side, there was a glimmer of hope.

The day at school dragged and Ashley only half concentrated in class, the rest of his mind preoccupied with what he would do if Miss Edwards couldn't fulfil her promise. Maybe he could find a college in the north-east that would let him sit his exams with them. Or maybe he could come back down to Haybridge and take them here as planned. He wondered if he could obtain a tent and camp. Or could he persuade one of his mates to lend him a spare room? There had to be something he could do or someone who could help.

He was packing his bag at the end of his last lesson when Miss Edwards caught up with him again.

'Well,' she said, 'there's good news and bad news. The good news is I've found someone who is willing to take you in as a lodger.'

Ashley felt his heart lift. Yesss.

'And it's a really generous offer. All your host will want is a contribution towards your food. He won't charge you for the room as long as you help around the house, that sort of thing.'

'That sounds more than fair,' said Ashley. 'I'm quite handy with an iron,' he added with a grin, 'and I know where the on-off button is on a hoover.'

'Goodness, a veritable domestic god. But the bad news is . . .' Miss Edwards paused. 'The bad news is that it's the Head who's made the offer.'

'Ah.' Ashley considered this. Would it be so bad living with Mr Higgins? Could he manage it and not end up going mental? Shit, what would it be like living with the Head? He knew the guy by sight, had even spoken to him a few times, and he seemed a decent sort. Not creepy or anything. But – well, it was the Head.

'Mr Higgins says their spare room has its own

bathroom, so you'll have quite a lot of space to call your own. What do you think?'

'Well, it's very kind of him,' said Ashley hesitantly. He was terrified of sounding rude or ungrateful – pissing off the Head wasn't a good idea – but on the other hand, this was going to take a bit of thinking about.

'You want to think about it, I imagine,' said Miss Edwards.

Ashley nodded, grateful for her insight.

'There's no hurry with giving an answer. You'll have to discuss it with your parents; we'll need a letter from them agreeing to this – that is, if you want to go ahead,' she continued.

Ashley thought Dave would be only too happy to send his stepson packing. He was always banging on at Ashley about being a leech, so he was likely to jump at the chance. If Ashley wasn't living with them, eating Dave's food, using Dave's electricity, Dave was going to be well chuffed. And if Dave agreed, then he thought his mum probably would. She wouldn't like it, but he couldn't see her putting up a fight.

'Fine,' he said with a sudden sense of optimism.

'So if you can let me or Mr Higgins know your decision with in a week or so . . . Would that be enough time? By the way, Mr and Mrs Higgins live locally, so there'll be no problem about getting to school. Mr Higgins didn't think you'd want to be seen arriving and leaving with him, so if you'd rather not, it'd be easy for you to walk.'

That made a big difference. Ashley could just imagine the comments from some of the kids if he seemed to be too friendly with the Head. If he thought life was bad because he lived with his step-dad, he could only begin to imagine how bad it might be if some of the kids at school got wind of the fact that he lived with Mr Higgins.

Tilly sat in her bedroom at home, ignoring the beautiful spring day outside her window while she stared at her English coursework and tried to revise for her impending A levels. But however hard she tried, nothing was going in. She knew perfectly well why she was having so little success: she felt horrible. Really shitty. Vile. She wondered if maybe she'd eaten something that was making her feel so shabby, but no one else seemed to be suffering, which made it unlikely. She remembered the one time at her school when there'd been a case of food poisoning and no one had been spared. The illness had struck with spectacular speed and effects. Tilly shuddered as she remembered the stench of vomit – and worse – that had pervaded the entire school for days.

No, she was fairly certain it wasn't food poisoning, so maybe it was just a bug. Thinking about it, she'd been feeling fairly ropy on and off for about a week now. Not really ill, just not well. Under the weather, she supposed was how Mrs T would describe it. But now, this afternoon, she'd gone beyond that and she felt crap. Over and above the waves of nausea that kept attacking her, she felt totally exhausted. Still, she thought a tad more cheerily, if it was a bug she had, she wouldn't be able to oversee the visitors when the house opened to the public for the Easter weekend. It was almost worth feeling so awful if she was spared that.

She gave up with her revision and wandered into the kitchen in search of a cup of tea and a biscuit. She hadn't managed much lunch and now she was famished, but there wasn't a great deal that she actually fancied. In fact most things she'd normally want as a snack – hot buttered toast, one of Mrs T's scones with jam and cream, or even just a handful of peanuts out of the storage jar – made her feel even more nauseous. She pulled out a chair from under the kitchen table and flopped down on it. The walk from her bedroom had left her feeling wrung out.

'You're looking peaky, miss,' said Mrs T.

'I'm fine. Could murder a cuppa, though.' Tilly shot Mrs Thompson a winning smile.

'Just as well I'm about to put the kettle on, then, isn't it?' Mrs T filled it at the tap and plugged it in, then took a tin down from the shelf above, opened it and pushed it on to the table in front of Tilly.

Tilly gazed at the butterfly cakes with their pink buttercream icing and felt her stomach lurch. She gave a wan smile and pushed the tin back towards Mrs T. 'Actually I'm not that hungry. But thanks.'

'But they're your favourites.'

Tilly shrugged to conceal the wave of nausea that engulfed her.

'You're not being silly and not eating again like you did at Christmas?'

Tilly shook her head. 'No, nothing like that, honest.'

Mrs T gave her a long stare with narrowed eyes before turning back to get the mugs and tea bags out. 'Hmm,' was all she said.

Tilly sighed. And now how was she going to find a way to ask for a plain biscuit without getting the third degree about how she really felt? Mrs T would insist on taking her temperature or sending her to bed or making a fuss. No, best she just shut up and drink her tea, and try to sneak something really plain to eat later.

Wordlessly Mrs T made the tea and passed a mug to Tilly, who decided to take it to her room rather than risk a full-on interrogation in the kitchen. Maybe the tea would make her feel less rough.

But it didn't, and ten minutes after she'd finished sipping it, she had to rush to the loo, where she lost the lot.

Feeling shaky and with her head spinning, she sank back on her heels, wiping her mouth on the back of her hand. Not good, she decided, not good at all.

She went to the basin and rinsed her mouth out with cold water, then filled a glass and took a few tentative sips. She decided she felt a whole lot better for actually being sick rather than just feeling it. Maybe some fresh air would help. Besides, her revising wasn't going well, it was a lovely day, and a stroll might sort her out. She needn't go far after all.

She dragged on a coat, told Mrs T she was off out for a bit and would be back for supper and made her way out of the house, where the soft spring sunshine, acid-green leaves just breaking on the trees, carpets of daffodils on the grass either side of the long drive and flawless blue sky all instantly lifted her spirits. The air felt fresh and clean and there was a real hope of summer being just around the corner. She strolled aimlessly along the avenue, enjoying the peace and the song of a blackbird and thinking about nothing much in particular, just letting her feet take her where they led. The fresh air did clear her head as she'd hoped, and she felt her energy levels increase. She decided to walk into town.

As she took the familiar route, she found herself thinking about Ashley yet again. She wondered what he was up to, where he might be. She assumed he'd be on holiday too as it was so nearly Easter; surely the state schools had also broken up. Maybe, as she was feeling so much better, she would take a turn up to the skate park.

As she made the decision, she was filled equally with hope and fear; she felt there was a very real chance she might run into him at the park, as it was quite close to where he lived, but she also dreaded the encounter. What if he cut her dead? What if he refused to listen to her? What if he told her he never wanted to see her again? Could she bear it? She trudged on, wondering if she wasn't making a dreadful mistake. Perhaps he wouldn't be there at all. She so longed to see him, the disappointment of that would also be terrible. Was it worth it? Was it worth the angst and the heartache?

It had been around three months since she'd been back in Haybridge for any length of time. After their row, and her abortive attempt at an apology, she'd had to go back to school, and in the half-term she'd been in Switzerland, so this was her first real opportunity to try to get to see him. Might he think she'd deliberately kept out of the way? Deliberately avoided him?

She wished she knew what it was she'd done that had been so terribly wrong, so utterly unforgivable. Surely this couldn't just be about her background. It wasn't her fault she'd been born who she was. Was it really such a crime to belong to a family that got a billing in Domesday Book? Going back over their relationship, she wished she'd been straight with him from the start, but she'd thought that just as she didn't care about his background, he wouldn't care about hers. *He* was what mattered to her, not who he was, and she'd just assumed he'd feel the same. She snorted as she thought that. How wrong could you get? It wasn't a mistake she'd make again if ever she found someone else she could love as much as she loved him, which she felt was unlikely. She didn't believe you could feel so strongly about two people – no matter what Mrs T had told her about losing James and then finding Greg. Just because Mrs T was desperate enough to take second best didn't mean that Tilly was ever going to.

And what made everything about the whole sorry affair so much worse was the fact that she couldn't really confide in anyone. Yes, Marcus knew a little – well, he knew she'd been dumped by a boy she'd met in Haybridge – but there was no one whose shoulder she could really cry on, no one at school she was close enough to who would understand and not make snide comments about a boy off a council estate. She couldn't tell her father, her sisters were too young to be any use to anyone, Mrs T wouldn't approve and her mum was in the States. Sometimes she felt so lonely she could almost cry.

She hadn't been lonely when she'd been with Ashley. She'd known she was the centre of his universe and he'd been hers. Which made his absence even worse and more painful now.

The skate park, when she got there, was packed with kids enjoying the Easter holidays and the good weather. She scanned the faces and saw immediately that Ashley wasn't there. The blow of disappointment twisted her insides. She felt devastated. She'd so hoped he'd be there.

Wearily, her energy evaporating along with her spirits, she slumped on to one of the benches at the side of the park. It had been a mistake to walk so far, and now she was going to have to walk back. She'd have to rest before she attempted that, because right now she felt too knackered to walk even one more step, let alone to the other side of town.

After half an hour or so, despite the sunshine, Tilly was getting cold. Sitting still on a cold metal bench in April, even with the sunshine, and especially considering that she was feeling under the weather, wasn't perhaps the wisest thing to do. Tired or not, it was time to go, she decided.

She stood up and made her way to the crossing over the ring road. As she waited for the lights to change, she saw the roofs of the houses on the council estate. She stared at them, wondering about the wisdom of going there to see if she could find Ashley. She remembered her last foray there, at New Year, and how uneasy she'd felt, but that had been in the dark, and there'd been quite a few people about who'd been drinking. But this was an April afternoon. She'd be fine. It was the Haybridge council estate she was planning on going to, not some desperate African township or a tinpot country in the throes of a civil war.

Her mind made up, she strode purposefully over the road and made her way to the street that led to Ashley's house. No one took the least bit of notice of her as she walked along the pavement, past gardens that seemed to be either immaculate and full of bright bedding plants or complete tips with broken toys lying on unkempt patches of grass – no way could you call them lawns. She rounded the corner and there was Ashley's house. But it looked different. She checked the road name and the house number, and yes, this was the right house, but something didn't look right. She went up to the wooden fence that divided the front garden from the road.

The house was empty, that was what was different about it: no curtains at the windows, no car in the drive, no sign of life. But it couldn't be. Where had they gone? It didn't make sense; this was Ashley's home, he had to be here somewhere. She gazed about at the other houses, as if she was expecting his family to pop up from somewhere and tell her it had all been an elaborate April Fool's joke. This couldn't be right, she told herself. There had to be a mistake. They couldn't have just *gone*.

'Do you want the Drivers?'

Tilly whirled round to see who was talking to her.

A woman in jeans and a sweater with slippers on her feet was putting rubbish into a wheelie bin on the other side of the road.

Tilly realised that she hadn't a clue what Ashley's surname was. Was it Driver?

'I thought Ashley lived here,' she said.

'He did, but they moved out a month or so back. His dad got a job up north.'

'Up *north*?' Tilly felt horrified

The woman nodded. 'Don't know where exactly. They didn't leave an address.'

'Oh.' Tilly was so stunned by this news she had no idea what to say. She felt numb and her mind seemed to be incapable of coherent thought. But what else was there to say? Ashley and his family had gone to God only knew where, and there was no forwarding address. So that was it. He'd effectively disappeared completely and there was no way to contact him. He had vanished so comprehensively he might as well have died. And the grief Tilly felt at this total absence of hope of ever seeing him again overwhelmed her.

It took all her energy and willpower to drag herself back through the town to her home. She was too stunned and shocked to cry. She felt completely empty. Drained. When she got in, she went straight to her room and collapsed on her bed.

'What's the matter with you?' said Mrs T from the door.

'Nothing,' said Tilly, wishing she'd go away. She couldn't cope with other people right now.

'You're as white as a sheet and you've hardly eaten anything. Are you sickening for something?'

Tilly shook her head. 'I'm fine.'

'And I'm the Queen of Sheba. You ought to see the doc.'

Tilly shook her head more vehemently. 'Honestly, I'm fine. Just stressed about my A levels.'

There was a sigh from the doorway. 'Well they're not worth making yourself ill for.'

Tilly shrugged but was thankful that Mrs Thompson had accepted her excuse at face value. She simply didn't have the physical resources left to enter into an argument or discussion.

At suppertime she dragged herself from her bed and made an attempt to eat her meal, although inside she felt so numb and dead that she didn't notice a thing about the food she picked at. She escaped back to her room as soon as she could and left the twins and her father speculating about what was wrong with her, till Mrs T informed them that she was worried about her exams. Tilly, overhearing this exchange just before she shut her bedroom door, was, for once, grateful for the looming exams. They were going to serve as a perfect shield for the real misery in her life; a misery she couldn't explain to anyone and which she would have to cope with by herself.

The next morning, just when she thought things had got as bad as they could, she woke up feeling worse than ever, so bad that while she was waiting for the hot water to work its way through the decrepit plumbing system so that her shower was on the right side of lukewarm, she found herself once again bent double over the loo retching her guts up. The trouble was, she had nothing to bring up, and all she produced was vile greenish-yellow bile. Feeling weak and wobbly, she flushed away the evidence and then sat on the edge of the bath.

She was being sick. In the morning. She sat there paralysed with fear at the awful implications of what she'd just concluded, while her mind whirled and her stomach churned. How could she have been so dumb as to think she wouldn't get pregnant? She'd lied to Marcus about being on the pill, and now that lie had turned right round and bitten her, hard! How could she have been so mind-bogglingly stupid? And now what? What the hell was she going to do?

Eventually she was brought out of her catatonic trance by hammering on the door.

'Come on, Tilly,' yelled her sisters. 'Are you going to be all day?'

'Just shut up and push off,' she snarled at them, but the hammering continued.

Wearily Tilly turned off the unused shower, hauled her dressing gown round her and unlocked the door.

'Blimey,' said Flora. 'You look like death warmed over.'

'Piss off,' sniped Tilly as she dragged her way along the corridor and slammed her bedroom door. She flopped on to her bed while she went over the implications of her situation once more. She tried to think if she'd missed a period, but she couldn't be sure. Since they'd started when she was twelve they'd always been hideously irregular, but she was pretty certain she hadn't had one since she'd been back from the skiing holiday. If that was the case, then there was every possibility that she really was pregnant. Bugger.

Firstly, she decided, she had to be absolutely sure. She'd have to nick some money from her father's wallet and get herself a pregnancy testing kit. Till she knew for certain, there was no point in panicking. And if she was . . . If she was, she'd have to work out what to do next.

No doubt about it then: a blue line told her all she needed to know. She was up the duff, in the family way, expecting, pregnant, with child or any other way anyone might care to put it. At least it explained why she was feeling so rubbish. She stared at the wand, willing the line to go away, but it didn't. The leaflet that came with the kit, which had given her detailed instructions about how to use it, had also suggested that in the event of a positive test, she ought to make an appointment with her doctor. Like she was going to do that. For a start he was a mate of her dad's and she couldn't be sure he wouldn't tell – especially as she still had a week to go before she turned eighteen. And even if he didn't tell, he'd send his bill to Fa, who would then be bound to ask her what was wrong. Why, oh why, couldn't they be like other families, she thought, and use the NHS?

After a few minutes of dejected thought, she gathered all the bits and pieces together, stuffed them back into the carrier bag she'd brought the kit home in and hid it in her wardrobe. She needed space to think and she didn't want Mrs T coming across the box and asking awkward questions. Having hidden the evidence, she sat at her desk pretending to revise while she tried to come to terms with her situation. Obviously Marcus was the father, but he was the last person she wanted to involve in this sorry business. It wasn't his fault that she'd got him to make love to her, nor that she'd lied though her teeth about being on the pill. No, the last thing he deserved was to be made to feel guilty or responsible. This mess was entirely of her own making and it was up to her to sort it out, and without telling her father. She could just imagine the row and the recriminations. That was to be avoided at all costs. It would just make life even shittier than it was right now, if that were possible. She had A levels looming, her ex-boyfriend had moved away completely just to make sure they never met again, and to cap it all, she was pregnant.

Tilly groaned. Life was the pits. Any one of those three and she'd have bloody good reason to be totally stressed out, but she had to get all three. The jackpot. The line of cherries on the fucking fruit machine.

She pulled a pad of file paper towards her and doodled on it as she began to look at her options. For a start, she reckoned that someone in the sixth form might be able to help or advise her. She could also trawl the web for information. The great thing was that there was no desperate hurry. She knew exactly when she'd got pregnant and it was only about six weeks previously, so she did have the luxury of time being on her side. Obviously she'd have to get rid of the baby; there was no question of being an unmarried mother, not if she was going to go to uni in September, but she didn't have to worry about having an abortion immediately. She knew enough from her general knowledge to understand that she could be quite a few months pregnant and still get it done.

A plan began to form in her mind. She'd go back to school, sit her A levels and use the time between finishing her exams and the end of term to get everything sorted out. If she dressed carefully she didn't think anyone would notice her weight gain, so she could probably get away with it – and the last thing she wanted was to have her exams buggered up on top of everything else.

Of course, she thought with a sigh, there was the tricky issue of how she was going to fund this. It didn't cross her mind that she might be able to get it done on the NHS for free – the de Lieges always paid for their health care, like they did their education. Asking her father for the cash was out of the question, but maybe her mother would help. She could tell her she needed the money to see her through university. It was an idea. Or maybe she just ought to tell her the truth, swear her to secrecy and ask her to pay for everything. That was it. Her mother would understand. Tilly bet that Susie Hutton had put the odd foot wrong in her life, so she'd understand and bail out her eldest daughter, surely she would.

'You're what?' Even across the whole of America and the Atlantic Ocean, Tilly could hear that her news had not gone down well with her mother.

'You heard,' she mumbled sulkily.

'You stupid, *stupid* child.' But there was more disappointment in her mother's tone than reproof.

'I know, Mum. You don't have to rub it in. It was a really dumb thing to do and now I'm paying the price.'

There was a pause. 'So who's the father?'

'No one you know.'

'Does that mean you don't either?' asked Susie in a voice laden with suspicion.

'For God's sake, Mum, what do you think I am? Some sort of tramp?'

'Well, given your circumstances, I think we've established that.'

Tilly felt tears welling up. That was such an unfair comment. 'No,' she said, trying to keep the tremble out of her voice. She was not going to give her mother the satisfaction of knowing her jibe had hit home. 'No, I went to bed with one man, once. I'm just unlucky.'

'Unlucky and careless.'

'Yes,' admitted Tilly. 'But it was only once. One man, once,' she repeated. The silence down the line told her that her mother didn't believe her.

'Tilly, I can't say that I'm not angry and upset. And this news has come as a shock to me, it really has. I blame myself for not being there for you, for not being a better mother, but I thought that school we chose for you would at least have managed to teach you some common sense.'

'It's nothing to do with the school. This is entirely my fault.'

Her mother's sigh came whistling down the line. 'Your fault and the father's. I blame him just as much as I blame you. When did it happen?'

'When we were skiing with the Crosbys.'

'So this is Desmond's son's child?'

'You know them?' Tilly couldn't hide her surprise. Her mother had been in the States for years and she didn't think she and her father had many friends in common any more. Susie Hutton lived amongst Hollywood celebs and film stars and her father moved in the stuffy circles of the British Establishment and commerce. As far as Tilly could see there were absolutely no crossover points.

'Darling, everyone knows them.'

'In Hollywood?'

'They back films.'

Tilly rolled her eyes. Were there no pies in the world that Desmond and Marcus hadn't got their fingers stuck in? Apparently not.

'You didn't answer my question,' said Susie.

'Yes, it's Marcus Crosby's.'

'Well that makes things easier.'

'You're not to tell him,' yelled Tilly. 'I forbid it.' There was silence. 'Please.' She paused. 'Look, Mummy,' she pleaded, 'I just want rid of it and I was hoping you'd pay. I don't want Daddy to know, or Marcus, or anyone. This is my mess and I want to get myself out of it, and I would have done it by myself if I had any money, but I don't. In fact if I'd had the money, no one would have known anything about this but me. But I need you, Mummy. I'm going to have the abortion as soon as I've done my exams, and then I can go to uni as I planned and everything will be just as if it never happened. But I need the cash. Please.'

'I see. You do know you can have an abortion on the NHS? For free.'

'What?' Tilly's shrill response told Susan that she didn't.

Susan sighed again. 'Well I suppose I have to be grateful that you didn't know – otherwise you'd never have told me.'

Tilly now felt doubly stupid, firstly for getting pregnant at all and secondly for involving her mother when she could have sorted everything out quietly by herself. Well, too late now. There was no way to stuff this particular moggy back in the bag.

'Of course I'm glad you have, although I won't say it hasn't come as a bit of a shock,' continued her mother.

'Sorry, Mummy.'

'Look, I need to think about this, but while I do, don't you go and do anything rash. I'll see what I can organise that would be best for you. I understand your feelings about your future being in jeopardy, but this isn't something you ought to rush into headlong. I'll call you tomorrow, is that OK?'

It was going to have to be. What pressure could she put on her mother from over five thousand miles away?

Tilly was lying on the sofa in their shabby sitting room, trying to memorise a list of facts about various linguistic rules that applied to the English language, when she heard the crunch of car tyres on the gravel in the courtyard below.

Eager for any interruption, she shoved her file on the table beside her and got to her feet to look out of the window. From where the dormer window was set in the ancient moss-covered roof it was impossible to see the whole of the courtyard, but she could just glimpse the boot of a shiny black saloon that had been parked near the front door.

They weren't expecting visitors, so who on earth was this? Probably someone for her father, she concluded. Some boring businessman or one of his fellow club members. She sighed. No excuse to quit revising, then. She returned to the sofa, picked up her file and immersed herself in the differences between Saxon, Norman and Latinate English. She worked solidly for another hour or so until her brain was reeling from facts forced into every nook and cranny, then flung the file down again and wandered back over to the window. The car was still there. She was considering going in search of a cup of tea when Mrs T came in.

'Your father wants you downstairs, miss,' she said.

'Why?' No doubt some errand needed running.

Mrs T looked shifty but all she said in reply was, 'I think you'd just better do as he asks.'

Which sounded a bit ominous. Actually, it sounded more than a bit ominous; it sounded really horribly serious, and the way Mrs T wouldn't meet her eyes just underlined it. Tilly's insides lurched as her guilty conscience kicked in. Could her father have found out? Had Mrs T discovered the pregnancy testing kit at the back of her wardrobe? But Mrs T never snooped in her room. Even so, Tilly had a premonition that she was in the shit. Big time. It couldn't be that her mother had spilled the beans, because since that call, Tilly had been so desperate to hear what Susan had decided that every time the phone rang she grabbed it first. No one had called except a couple of her father's friends and a company offering them double glazing at a bargain price.

Well, she thought as she squared her shoulders and made her way down to her father's office on the ground floor, there was only one way to find out.

She rapped on the door, trying hard to feel brave but inwardly bricking it.

'Come,' called her father.

She opened the door and saw Fa seated behind his desk, looking stern. Then she became aware that there was someone else in the room. Oh my God!

'Mummy!' She ran forward to hug her and felt the bliss of being enveloped by her mother's arms and a cloud of her scent. It should have been the most wonderful, glorious surprise, but Tilly knew exactly why she'd come. The feeling of trepidation quadrupled. But over and above her fear she also felt betrayed. She'd pleaded and begged with her mother not to tell her father; to help her sort out her predicament quietly and privately. But no. And now there was going to be an awful row and everything was going to be horrible. Even worse than it was already.

As she was released from the embrace, she sat down in the chair next to her mother's before her knees gave way.

Her father stared at her in silence. After an interminable and agonising pause he finally said, 'You'll know why your mother felt it necessary to travel all this way.'

Tilly nodded, not daring to speak.

'Susan tells me this happened when we went skiing.'

She nodded again.

'That night you got stranded by the avalanche, I suppose.'

She nodded a third time.

'So Marcus took advantage of you.'

'No.'

Her father looked taken aback. 'I'm sorry.'

'No.' She wasn't having Marcus take the rap for this, no way. His kindness and reluctance didn't deserve to be repaid by a lie to get her out of a hot spot. 'It wasn't like that. In fact it was entirely my idea.'

Edward's eyes narrowed. 'You mean to tell me that a daughter of mine behaved . . .' He grew red in the face as he tried to find the words to sufficiently express his disgust and disbelief.

Tilly suddenly felt defiant and bold. So what if she was pregnant? It wasn't the worst thing someone of her age had ever done, and to judge by the family tree, she wasn't the first de Liege to have a child out of wedlock. Their ancestors had left bastards all over the place and civilisation hadn't come to a grinding halt back then. She wasn't a criminal and she was blowed if she was going to be made to feel like one. 'Yes, Fa, that's exactly what I'm saying. Yes, I behaved like a tramp, as Mummy put it so delicately when I told her. So what?'

'So what do you plan to do about it?'

'I plan to get rid of it, that's what.'

'Yes, that's what your mother said you'd do.'

Tilly shrugged. 'It seems the sensible solution. I'll sit my exams, have the op, and go to university as planned in the autumn. I can't see there's going to be a problem.'

'The Crosbys might feel differently,' said her father.

Tilly looked at him aghast. 'What the hell has this got to do with them? She knew her voice was strident and shrill, but she was completely bewildered.

'I think this has got a lot to do with them. Marcus is the father after all.'

'So we don't tell him. So what? What he doesn't know won't hurt him. Besides, I can't imagine he'll be overjoyed at the idea of being a father. He won't want the responsibility, and anyway it's not his fault. I told him I was on the pill and he believed me.'

It was her father's turn to be shocked. 'You did what?'

'I lied about being on the pill.'

'What on earth did you do that for, Tilly?' said her mother, her perfect brow marred by a frown of disbelief.

Despite her earlier bravado, Tilly couldn't bring herself to admit to her parents that she'd gone all out to seduce Marcus because she'd been desperate to find out about sex.

She shrugged her shoulders again. 'Dunno,' she lied. 'It seemed like a good idea at the time and I suppose I thought I'd be all right. I didn't really think.'

Her mother sniffed. 'I suppose drink was involved. All that money we've spent on your education for nothing. Haven't you learned anything?'

Tilly nearly retorted that she'd learned not to trust her mother, but bit it back. She might hate what her mother had done, but a comment like that would be a step too far, and for all Susie's faults – disappearing off to the States, telling her father about the pregnancy – Tilly still loved her beautiful, ethereal mother.

'Well,' said her father, 'I understand how you are thinking, but I am of the old-fashioned opinion that

Marcus needs to be told. After all, half of this child is his. I think it would be only fair to involve him in any decision we make.'

'But this isn't his decision, it's *mine*. What – although I think it's totally unlikely – but what if he wants to keep it? It won't be him going through nine months of pregnancy and giving birth to the kid, it won't be him having to give up going to uni because he's seven months pregnant, it won't be him having his life wrecked. This has nothing to do with him and everything to do with me.'

'This child is the heir to the Crosby fortune.'

'Only if I don't abort it. If I do, it's heir to diddly-squat.'

'Which is why we consult them,' said her father coldly, looking extremely angry.

Tilly stood up to leave. She'd heard enough. Her parents weren't supporting her, this was a farce and she wanted out of it.

'Sit down,' thundered her father.

Shocked, she did as she was told.

'Tilly,' said her mother more gently, 'I think you need to understand some facts of life.'

'A bit late for that,' she said ruefully.

'Not that sort – the financial sort. Do you have any idea what this house costs to run?'

'A lot?' hazarded Tilly.

'A heck of a lot. And over the years I've done my best to contribute to this from my earnings. But I'm not getting any younger, and with Dames Helen and Judi on the scene I don't seem to be able to pick up decent parts for older women, while I'm getting too old for the younger ones. My income isn't what it was.'

'I'm sorry.'

'I'll survive,' said Susie lightly. 'But the money I send back to your father isn't what it used to be and the upkeep of this place doesn't get any less. The reverse, if the truth be told.'

'So?'

'So either your father sells the Gainsborough to raise enough cash to buy somewhere else and gives this place to the National Trust, or he turns the house into some sort of theme park, with events every weekend – jousts, medieval fayres, Tudor banquets in the great hall – or he finds someone to invest millions to keep it standing for another few hundred years.'

Tilly grabbed the least hideous option. 'Daddy knows lots of businessmen. Surely some of them might invest.'

'But what,' her father said, 'would be in it for them? Businessmen want a return for their investment. Businessmen don't, on the whole, run charities. If they put money into a project they want something to show for it.'

'Your father and I have been discussing this and we've come up with an ideal solution.'

Something about her mother's tone made Tilly think this didn't sound good. 'And . . . ?' she said warily.

'As you know, Desmond Crosby is a self-made man.'

Tilly looked at Edward blankly. What had this to do with the running costs of the house? 'So?'

'So, he doesn't have the right social connections. He doesn't get invited to the sort of events he feels he ought to be. That's why he invests in Hollywood movies, because no one cares about his background out in Tinsel Town, but he wants the same acceptance here.'

Tilly felt completely at sea. One minute they were discussing her baby and now they were on to the Crosbys' circle of friends.

'However, while we don't have two ha'pennies to rub together, we do know everyone.'

'You might,' said Tilly. 'I can't remember us ever going to a big society do.'

'We don't these days because we can't afford it,' said her father. 'Those sort of functions cost money to attend by the time you've dressed correctly and hired the right sort of car to arrive in. But if we had the cash we would. And even though we're not very visible socially, you'd be amazed at how many people, *important* people, we know. The name de Liege can still open more doors than you can shake a stick at.'

Jolly good, thought Tilly, although the only door she wanted opened was the one to the abortion clinic. 'I still don't follow you, though.'

'If they had our name . . .' said Susan.

'And we had their money . . .' added Edward.

'Their fortune is estimated at forty million pounds,' interjected her mother helpfully.

'. . . everyone would be happy.'

'But how . . . ?' Nope – it still didn't seem to add up. Tilly just didn't see how that could happen.

'If you married Marcus,' said her father.

Tilly was awfully glad she was sitting down, because as it was, she nearly fell off the chair.

29

'No!' she shouted. 'No! I won't and you can't make me.' She stared wildly around. How could they even think of it as a solution? She wasn't some commodity who could be bought and sold. This was Britain, for fuck's sake, and girls like her weren't shoved into arranged marriages.

'But Tilly,' pleaded her mother.

'No,' she shouted again and made a dash for the door. She had it open and, taking the old shallow treads of the stairs two at a time, was at the top of the first flight before her parents had got to their feet. She charged up the other two flights and fled into her room, slamming the door with an almighty crash behind her. How could they? How could they even think it? Shocked, stunned and bewildered, she lay on her bed as she thought about her parents' suggestion.

Marrying for money – that was what it came down to. That was what they wanted her to do. How could they? It was like something out of a Victorian novel. Well, she wouldn't do it. They couldn't make her and she'd find some other way to sort this wretched pregnancy out. If her parents wouldn't help her, she'd find someone who would, she thought defiantly.

She curled up on her side and chewed at a nail. Her mother was behaving like Mrs Bloody Bennet. Just because Marcus was in possession of a fortune it didn't follow that he wanted a wife, and it certainly didn't follow that she was going to be that wife. Tilly punched the pillow in frustration. How could her parents even contemplate such an idea? And all because he was loaded. Minted.

But then she wondered what it would be like to have forty million pounds. Actually, it would be nice just to have forty pounds. Right now, she wouldn't bitch at four quid. Being broke all the time sucked, but she wasn't so desperate for money that she'd consider tying the knot with Marcus, she told herself, putting the idea out of her head. It was gross, really rank.

There was a gentle tapping at her door.

'Go away,' she yelled.

But the door opened and her mother put her head around it. Tilly pointedly rolled over so that she faced the wall.

'Tilly,' started her mother tentatively.

'I've got *nothing* to say to you,' Tilly mumbled crossly into her pillow.

'Tilly, sweetie, I'm sorry.'

Tilly turned her head. 'What for? Dobbing me in it with Fa or trying to sell me like a slave to the Crosbys?'

'Don't exaggerate,' said her mother mildly.

Tilly raised an eyebrow. 'Oh? So what would you call it?' She rolled back to face her mother.

'It isn't like that.'

Tilly snorted. 'It looks bloody like it from my perspective.'

'Don't you want to lead a comfortable life and have nice things?'

'Not if it means being shackled to a man I don't love.'

'But you like him.' Susie sat on the edge of her bed.

'I like lots of people but it doesn't mean I want to

spend the rest of my life with them. I like Mrs T but that doesn't mean she's my soulmate. He's a nice guy, but . . .' She shrugged.

'You could do a lot worse.'

'And I could do a lot better too,' she snapped. 'Did you marry Fa just because he was "nice"?'

Susie tilted her head. 'Yes.'

Tilly felt quite shocked. 'But you loved him too. You must have done.'

'I did, later.'

Tilly frowned. What was her mother telling her – that she and her father had married for business reasons? How rank was that! No wonder the marriage hadn't lasted. 'Which explains a lot,' she said sourly. 'Look where it got you. I bet you were counting the days till you could pack your suitcase and run away.'

'It wasn't like that.'

Tilly's expression said exactly what she thought about that denial. 'Just because you were happy with a marriage of convenience doesn't mean that I fancy one.' She thought for a moment. 'I can't believe you're telling me this. Do you think that the example you've just shown me is anything but gross?'

'It really wasn't like that. Honest.'

'Really.' Tilly was impressed by the amount of sarcasm she managed to lard onto that one word. And she saw from her mother's face that she'd hit home.

Susan sighed and paused before she spoke again. 'Your father and I really believed we could make things work, and we tried, we totally did, but I had to be in the States for work and he wouldn't leave his home. This place is his life, you know that. It's more than that, it's in his DNA. I was just a Johnny-come-lately. I knew I couldn't compete in a straight race.' She said it lightly, but Tilly could see that it still hurt.

'I don't see why you couldn't have stayed here. Other

actresses manage to live in the UK and pick up roles in American films.'

'Of course they do when they're household names. But when you're breaking into films, when you're only known on the West End stage and then barely, you have to be over there. The minute you're not around, you become completely invisible, off the radar, gone. And even though you may not believe me . . .'

No, I probably won't, thought Tilly.

'. . . I went to America to try to earn enough money to hold this place together.'

'But you didn't come back.'

'No, sweetie. It all got very complicated.'

'I overheard a phone call between you and Daddy once.'

'Yes?'

'I heard you tell him that the money was more important to you than we were.'

'No.' Susie's brow furrowed again.

If she carried on like that, thought Tilly she'd need Botox. 'I heard you. You told Daddy that the nanny looked after us fine, we didn't miss you and the money was important.'

'All of which is true. But I was sending a lot of my money back to your father. I wanted you to have a nice warm house, for your inheritance to be safe, and I could only do that if I kept getting film roles.'

'So why were you and Daddy talking about divorce?'

'Because I didn't think it was fair for him to be married to someone who wasn't a proper wife. I offered him a divorce and his lawyers wrote back telling me he didn't want one. He didn't want our marriage to end. At the time I was cross, really angry. I thought he was making the wrong decision, but as there wasn't anyone else in my life, I let it go. Your father knows he can have his freedom any time he asks for it, and he says he doesn't mind what *I* do as long as it doesn't make the papers – unless it's to do with my acting, of course.' She gave her daughter an embarrassed smile. 'Our marriage may not be conventional, but we still love each other – in our own way.'

'I didn't think you did.'

'No, well . . . we don't tell everyone everything.'

'So why did you never come to see us?'

'Your father and I thought it would be better to make a clean break. Less disruptive. If I came and went you wouldn't know what was going on, and besides, you were going off to school and the twins were too young to understand. It seemed the right thing to do. Or it did at the time, anyway.'

'Oh.' All those years Tilly had felt abandoned by her mother and maybe things hadn't been quite as she'd perceived them to be. But it wasn't her fault. If someone had just bothered to explain to her, to tell her what was going on. Really, she thought, her father could be useless as a parent sometimes.

'So you see,' said her mother, 'our marriage does work. Maybe not brilliantly and not conventionally, and perhaps we made some wrong decisions where you and the twins were concerned, but we did what we thought was best at the time. The trouble with being a parent is there's no blueprint to follow. Every family is different and you just have to muddle along as best you can. Maybe with hindsight our best doesn't look as good as we thought it did at the time, but we did try our hardest. Honest.'

She sounded so convincing Tilly almost believed her – then she remembered her mother was an actress. Or was she being too cynical?

'Anyway, what I'm trying to tell you is that marrying *just* for love isn't necessarily the only way. My association with Edward kick-started my career and his with me made a huge difference to visitor numbers here for a bit, while my financial contribution kept this place just about tottering on. At least it meant that the sale of the Gainsborough could be postponed.'

Tilly had never really thought about the Gainsborough. It was just a nice picture of the countryside that hung in the long gallery. Judith always took pains to point it out to the visitors and it generated quite a few sales of prints, posters and postcards in the shop.

'Fa likes the Gainsborough, doesn't he?'

'He'd do anything to save it.'

Including marrying me off to Marcus Crosby, Tilly thought. 'It's worth a mint, isn't it?'

Susie nodded. 'One like it went for about five million pounds a few years ago at Christie's.'

Tilly whistled. 'That's a lot of roof repairs.'

'I don't think it would go on those. If your father had to sell it, it would be the final straw. It's the last thing of any significant value left in the house, so he'd want to use the money to make sure that you girls had a secure future. He always said that if the Gainsborough went, that would be the moment the National Trust got the house. And can you imagine how he'd feel if, after the best part of one thousand years, he was the member of the family who had to let this place go. Can you think what sort of failure he'd feel? The guilt? Your ancestors held this estate together through wars, pestilence and famine and then – when there's nothing really terrible threatening the place – he runs out of money and that's it. Gone.'

Gone? For ever? Much as Tilly loathed the crap heating system, the useless plumbing, their shabby apartment, this was her home. She couldn't imagine living anywhere else, not looking out on the familiar views, not walking in the grounds, not being surrounded by all those bits and pieces of family history . . . It was as if the fabric of the house and her flesh and blood were intertwined. As she thought about it, she realised it was in her DNA too. The thought that she and her family might have to leave it, go and live somewhere else – which was a *real* possibility – was a facer. And her mum was telling her that she had it in her power to stop it happening. Shit. She felt weak with the responsibility, but could she just shrug it off?

'So the Crosbys' millions would save more than just the roof,' she said lightly to cover her anxiety.

Susie nodded.

'I see.' But of course, she realised, it wasn't just her in this equation. Marcus would have an opinion, and all things considered, given the way she'd treated him, he was hardly likely to agree to this idea. Tilly felt quite light-headed with relief at this thought. If he turned her down – which he almost certainly would – then she was off the hook. If the house couldn't be saved, it wouldn't be her fault; she'd be guilt-free. No one would blame her. 'I don't think Marcus is going to go along with this, though,' she told Susan carefully.

'But . . . I mean . . . you and he . . . Surely you must have been quite close.'

Tilly decided to ease her mother's bewilderment at just what had gone on between her daughter and Marcus in Switzerland. 'Mummy, it was just a one-night stand. Sorry, but there it is, and I made it plain to him that I wasn't interested in our relationship going any further. I'm not proud of what I did and I *really* don't want to go into details, so can we drop the subject now?'

Susie nodded. 'I don't think I've been enough of a mother to you to expect that you might wish to confide in me.'

'No, well . . . Anyway, I can't really see Marcus wanting me for anything serious – certainly not marriage, anyway.'

'Don't you believe it,' said Susie. 'If he's his father's son, he'll recognise a good deal when he sees one.'

'Come off it, Mummy, he's got squillions of pounds, he can live anywhere he likes, he could have any woman in the world as his wife.'

'Yes, he could, but I can tell you something for certain: he wants a wife whose name will give him instant respectability in the sort of toffee-nosed circles that shun him now.'

Tilly shrugged. She didn't see that being connected with the de Lieges was that much of a big deal.

'OK,' said Susie. 'Let's put this into a context you will understand. Remember the film *Pretty Woman*?' Tilly nodded. 'Remember when Julia Roberts goes into the dress shop looking like a hooker and the shop assistants sneer at her and throw her out?' Tilly nodded again. 'And then she goes back with Richard Gere and those same shop assistants can't fawn over her enough?' Tilly nodded a third time. 'The shop assistants still didn't care a toss for Julia Roberts but they did care about the company she was keeping – that's human nature for you. At the moment the clubs in London, the social circles that Desmond and Marcus want to join, just blackball them. But once they're a part of our family, those same snobs will be forming an orderly queue to get them to sign up.'

Tilly wrinkled her nose. 'Seems daft to me. If people treated me like that, I wouldn't want to have anything to do with them if they suddenly changed their minds. I'd still think them bastards.'

'But you're not a businessman where access to people, getting their confidence, is important. Darling, the one really important thing in life is it's not *what* you know but *who*. And the de Lieges are definitely people to know.'

'Even me?'

Susie nodded.

'I still don't get it, but if that's what floats their boat – well, good luck to them.'

'It does. And it probably floats it enough to make

any past behaviour of yours something that can be overlooked.'

'Even the fact that I'm pregnant?'

'Just means there's going to be no problem at all producing heirs.'

Forty million, thought Tilly. Could she sell herself and her birthright for that? If nothing else, she could comfort herself with the thought that she hadn't come cheap.

Edward and Desmond sat in the comfortable bar of Edward's club, which was just off St James's Street. With its deep claret-coloured carpet, oak panelling, brass and leather bum-warmer in front of a cheery log fire and oil paintings of bewigged gentlemen round the walls it could have been a room in a stately home somewhere in the shires. Even though the room they were sitting in was called the bar, it did not boast one. The members of this establishment had never seen the need for one, and indeed, very many of them felt that such an amenity should only be found in hotels and the homes of people who favoured electronic gates, basement swimming pools with dolphin mosaics and green pantiles on the roof – not the sort of people who were encouraged to join an establishment such as this. A waiter stood discreetly by the door; when a drink was required, the member in question caught his eye, and he took the order and returned promptly with it on a silver salver. It was a system that had worked for centuries and would probably continue to do so for a few more.

Edward leaned forward in his large leather armchair, which had the patina and colour that only came with age and prolonged use, and placed his whisky and soda on the low table in front of him.

'Jolly good holiday we had with you. First rate.'

'Glad you enjoyed it. Must say, I was impressed by the

way your girls took to it – Flora and Daisy are naturals.'

'Thanks.' Edward accepted the compliment casually but was pleased Desmond had recognised their ability. 'Anyway, dinner here tonight is just a bit of a thank-you for all your hospitality back in February. I'd have done this sooner but it's been a bugger trying to find an evening when we've both been available.'

Desmond took a swig of his gin and tonic before saying, 'I've been frantic since our return. That's the trouble with taking any sort of holiday. Had to go to the States three times last month. Anyway, here now.' He raised his glass to Edward. 'And how's that eldest girl of yours? Pretty little thing, I thought.'

'Tilly's fine. Up to her neck in schoolwork. Her A levels are due to start any minute now, so you can imagine.'

Desmond nodded. 'Thank God Marcus has got that all behind him.' He sipped his drink again. 'So what do you think about Tilly and Marcus? We've introduced them, they know each other pretty well, they seem to be getting along. Do you think there's been any progress on that front?'

Better than you could ever imagine, thought Edward, but he remained silent while he tried to think exactly what to say in reply.

In the pause, Desmond continued. 'I'd like to think there were signs of a romance. I know Marcus is keen, but your girl . . . can't make her out.'

Edward reached forward for his drink. 'Ah,' he said as he took a sip. If Desmond was going to bring up the matter of how their children felt about each other, maybe this was the moment to come clean about Tilly's condition. Although as a subject, he'd been hoping to avoid it till they got to port, cigars, coffee and brandy, when Desmond would be mellow and fed and possibly more relaxed.

A waiter materialised silently at his elbow. 'Your table is ready for you, Mr de Liege.'

Edward grasped this interruption with alacrity. That particular conversation could wait a while. Maybe a couple of hours if he was lucky. 'Shall we go through, Desmond? Bring your drink.

To Edward's relief, the small details the waiters needed them to deal with as they arrived at the table – did they want water? Still, sparkling or tap? Bread? Butter? – occupied the next few minutes, and he had every hope that Desmond would have forgotten his conversational thread by the time the waiters got round to bringing them their first course.

'So,' said Desmond, getting stuck into his foie gras, 'you were telling me whether you thought there was any hope for something between our kids.'

Edward took a time-wasting mouthful of grilled chicken livers and chewed before answering. 'We'll need to get the two of them together before I can speak with any certainty, but I think you may be wrong in your assumption that Tilly's not so keen. Of course,' he added quickly, 'she is still very young. Still a schoolgirl in reality.'

Desmond raised an eyebrow and smeared another large dollop of pâté on to some toast. 'There's no need for any hurry, though, is there? If we can be sure that they are are friends, can't we let events take their own course?' He took a bite of his toast and pâté and chewed before adding. 'They both know the advantages of a link between the two families, they're both sensible kids; they'll do the right thing. After all, Tilly can't be hankering after a career, surely. Her future is almost as clearly mapped out as Prince William's.'

Edward nodded. 'I agree, although she's keen to go to university and get a degree. Something to do with the hospitality industry or event management. She says you can't afford to assume to know how to run a place just because you've been doing it for centuries. Sounds like claptrap to me and an excuse for her to waste another three years, but she insists my idea are all way out of date and she will be able to do better once she's got the skills. Given how things stand with the Manor at the moment, I've got nothing to lose if I let her have her head. However, as regards Tilly and Marcus . . . events might have moved on already. I think things went a great deal further in France than we were privy to.'

'Capital news. How much further?'

Edward looked at Desmond thoughtfully and wondered how he'd take it when he found out things had gone about as far as they could have. He shovelled up some more liver to give himself some thinking time. Not that it did him any good; there was really only one way to tell Desmond the news. 'The thing is, despite the fact that she's still at school . . . Well . . . look, there's only one way of saying this, Desmond.' He took a quick glance around the dining room to see if anyone was within earshot and then lowered his voice. 'Tilly's got herself knocked up, and your Marcus is the father.'

Desmond had been in the process of raising another pâté-laden slab of toast to his mouth but now lowered it slowly as he gazed slack-jawed at his host. 'Bloody hell, Edward, are you sure?'

'For God's sake, Desmond, of course we are. Remember that night the two of them got stuck the far side of the valley?' Desmond nodded. 'Well, do I need to spell it out to you?'

'No, no, not at all.' Desmond's food lay forgotten on his plate. 'Has Tilly told Marcus?'

Edward shook his head. 'No, and she doesn't know I'm meeting you tonight. She's going to tell him, of course, but she's worried about how he'll take it. Just because she's having his child doesn't mean it's all sweetness and light between them.'

'But they seemed to be on good terms. Heck, they went out for a drink together on the last night.'

Edward nodded and shrugged. 'Desmond, I'd be lying if I told you I understood how the minds of the young work.'

'True.' Desmond sighed. 'So what do you suggest?'

Edward finished his chicken livers before he spoke. 'The problem is that Tilly isn't keen on going ahead with this baby.' Desmond's eyes widened in shock. 'To be honest with you, she wants an abortion.'

'Bloody hell.'

'I know. But you've got to look at it from her point of view. She's only young, and what sort of life would she have going off to university dragging a kid behind her?'

'I'd pay for a nanny. I'd set her up in a nice house, all mod cons, anything. This is my grandchild we're talking about here.'

'And mine,' Edward reminded him.

'Yeah. Sorry. But this is important to me.' Desmond looked across the table to Edward. 'When I made my first million, I thought I'd have the world at my feet. I thought I could buy anything I wanted – and so I could, up to a point. But then I realised I couldn't buy acceptance, or respect. I thought it would be different for Marcus, because I made sure he went to the right school and spoke with the right accent, but that didn't work either. He's had almost as much trouble as me when it comes to being welcome in some circles. I tell you, if the guests at your New Year's party had known I'd bankrolled it, half of them wouldn't have come. And don't you deny it, because you know as well as I do I'm speaking the truth. Well, I'm not having that sort of discrimination for a third generation. No grandchild of mine is going to have to put up with the sort of crap I have, and if he or she is related to the de Lieges, that won't happen. Which will make everything I've done, all the crap I've had to deal with, worthwhile. Classless society? My arse!' He spread the last of his foie gras on some toast and shoved it in his mouth. 'I sometimes wonder why you bother with me, Edward. You've got more class than most of the rest of the flaming aristocracy yet you don't care I was born the son of a coal miner.'

'That sort of thing has never been important to me,' said Edward. He didn't add that when you were as broke as he was, serious money – whoever owned it – was always quite attractive. Not that money was his sole reason for liking Desmond; he respected the man because he was the most honest businessman he'd come across. There was no side to Desmond, just straight talking and even straighter dealing.

'So you'll talk to Tilly, tell her she can have whatever she wants, within reason, if she keeps my grandchild?'

Edward nodded. 'And Marcus?'

'Leave him to me. He'll see sense. But one thing I would like.'

'What's that?'

'I'd really like this kid born in wedlock.'

Edward shrugged. 'Look, Desmond, we've got dozens of bastards in our family. To be honest, some of the highest in the land come from bastard stock. It really doesn't matter, you know.'

'Well that might be all well and good for the aristocracy, but it doesn't do in my family. Understood?'

Tilly stood still, gazing into space, her mind miles away and certainly not listening to the voice that was droning on at her just a couple of feet away. She was wondering what Ashley was doing. Had he passed his A levels? The results had come out just a few days earlier, so was he now celebrating that he was off to university as he'd dreamed? Or had his parents finally scotched that idea? And how was he coping, living up north?

The voice stopped and Tilly became aware of a pregnant silence. Blimey, she thought, suppressing a giggle, pregnancy must be catching. Then, fuck, she realised the silence was because everyone was waiting for her to say something. Shit, what was it? Oh yes, she remembered.

'I will.'

She could hear the sigh of relief of the tiny congregation behind her. Had they really thought she'd bottle it at the last minute? Maybe they were worried that she'd changed her mind about exchanging her vows in such a low-key setting. This wasn't the wedding she'd once dreamed about; not that she'd wanted the sort of extravaganza some girls fantasised about. No, she'd never been keen on the whole meringue, dozens of bridesmaids and a splash in *OK!* bit, but something a tad bigger than this would have been nice.

However, she supposed that her father probably didn't want to advertise to the entire world the fact that his daughter was six months up the spout, and given the size she now was, there was no way of hiding the bump – not even with the lovely bouquet of white freesias and cream roses that her mother had organised for her. She had a nice dress for the occasion – Empire line (to try to disguise her pregnancy) in pale yellow silk. 'I can't wear white, people'll laugh,' she'd told the dress-maker that Desmond paid for, bless him. And getting married in the family chapel as opposed to the cathedral wasn't so bad. But this was a bit quieter than even she would have liked. She felt that there'd been more of a fuss and almost more people present when she'd signed the pre-nup. Oh well, did it matter?

The vicar asked who was giving her in matrimony. Tilly was tempted to interrupt that there was no giving about it. She was actually being sold for forty million pounds. Time was when stuff like that cost forty pieces of silver, but that was inflation for you. The service continued, and Tilly paid attention rather better than she had at the start, making her responses clearly and promptly. She was surprised at her lack of emotion when Marcus actually slipped the ring on her finger.

'Whom therefore God has joined together, let no one put asunder,' said dear old Dr Holroyd, their vicar, looking delighted and joyful.

Well I'm glad one of us feels like that, thought Tilly. She herself felt a definite sense of unease. She looked about her at the effigies on the family tombs – the knights in armour with dogs at their feet and their legs crossed at their ankles or knees to signify how many crusades they'd been on – and felt that they disapproved. The atmosphere should have been joyous, but that wasn't the vibe she was getting. But too late now, she thought.

The signing of the register and the congratulations of the members of their families who accompanied them into the tiny vestry all passed in a haze, and then Tilly was waddling back down the aisle and wishing her back didn't ache quite so much from all that standing about at the altar.

'Mrs Tilly Crosby de Liege,' whispered Marcus to her.

'Mr Marcus Crosby de Liege,' she whispered back at him. 'How do you feel about the new name?'

'Thrilled,' he said. 'It's got so much more class than my old one.'

''Spose.' Tilly had to admit he did look chuffed to bits. In fact he'd been like a kid looking forward to a birthday ever since Tilly had told him about the baby and he'd suggested that it might be an idea to make it legitimate. She'd been surprised about that; she'd thought he was going to kick up a stink about it, refuse to have anything to do with the kid or her, but quite the reverse. He'd been so focused on his own impending parenthood, the wedding and everything that he'd almost failed to notice the lack of excitement that Tilly had displayed – and on the rare occasions when he had been surprised at her demeanour, he'd justified it to himself as her being tired and hormonal because of the pregnancy. His enthusiasm had actually been quite endearing, and he'd been terribly thoughtful about consulting her as to what her dream of a honeymoon would be.

And as for his assurances about the pre-nup, which she'd thought tacky and American, not to say unnecessary. 'But we've both got stuff that, well, should stay with the original owner.'

'So you're saying this marriage is doomed before we start,' countered Tilly.

'No, but things happen and, if it does, I don't want to spend money on lawyers if I don't have to.'

'So you're spending it now. And it isn't as if there's going to be a problem in the long run, as the kids will get everything eventually – even if we split up it'll all go to them when we pop our clogs.'

'Kids? This isn't twins, is it?' he'd said, putting a proprietorial hand on her enlarged stomach.

Tilly shook her head, irritated that he was distracted from the real issue. 'No, of course no, but now that I've started a family I might as well make sure we have the standard two point four. So, as I was saying, why the pre-nup?'

But Marcus wasn't going to be swayed on the issue, and Edward had surprised her by telling her he thought it was a good idea too, so in the end she'd signed the pages and pages that it consisted of, skimming the endless convoluted paragraphs and initialling each interminable sheet in the presence of both fathers, several lawyers and a couple of witnesses.

So now the pre-nup was filed, the church register signed and she was Mrs Crosby de Liege, about to embark on a life of wedded ... well, not bliss, but wedded OK-ness perhaps.

Mrs T, who had been sniffing loudly at the back of the church, slipped away as the pictures were being taken to get the food ready for the little reception that was planned back at the house. It wasn't long before the rest of the wedding guests followed in her wake – it didn't take a great deal to organise such a small group into producing a number of very reasonable shots, although the photographer had had to work at getting Daisy and Flora to smile, as they were still cross at being denied their chance to be bridesmaids.

Everyone made an effort to make the reception a jolly affair, but for all the attempts at back-slapping and the toasts and smiles, no one could forget that it had only been a matter of a few months earlier that they'd been celebrating Tilly's eighteenth. To see her getting married so soon afterwards seemed somehow inappropriate and unduly hasty – which it was, there was no denying that.

After a couple of hours, Tilly went to change, and then she and Marcus were whisked away on their honeymoon – a fortnight on a luxury yacht in the Mediterranean. As they drove away in their chauffeured limousine, Tilly felt Marcus's eyes on her. She returned his gaze.

'Happy?' he asked.

Tilly knew what the expected answer was. 'Of course,' she lied with a smile as the car swept along the ring road and she caught a glimpse of a lone figure in the skate park. For a second, her heart lurched. Ashley! But it couldn't be – he'd moved away and she was never going to see him again. Besides, she was a married woman and shouldn't even be thinking about him – except that she did, all the time.

The honeymoon on the private yacht that Marcus had chartered in the Med was glorious. The crew of two fed them with fabulous food, looked after their every need, took them to beautiful locations and made each and every day a real treat. Tilly lounged around, basking in the sun in a voluminous maternity swimsuit, getting tanned and larger than ever and pretending she was idyllically happy. Not that she was unhappy – given her circumstances, it would be tough to be miserable – but she was aware of an emptiness, a nothingness inside her. Where there should have been a bright coal of love and fulfilment burning, there were just the ashes of her feelings for Ashley. She tried to feel something, *anything*, for Marcus, but she just couldn't. She liked him well enough; there was nothing to dislike, but that was hardly a solid footing for a marriage. She hid her feelings behind a bright smile and dark glasses and wondered how she'd cope when they returned to Haybridge and began life proper as Mr and Mrs Crosby de Liege. On the bright side, Marcus would be off to work in London each day, doing whatever it was he did, and it wouldn't be long before she had a baby to look after. She supposed, in a desultory way, she'd find enough to do to fill the days.

And there would be the work on the house that she could help her father oversee. That was one definite advantage of being married to a multi-millionaire: Marcus was used to having efficient plumbing and a heating system that actually warmed the house. As soon as he realised just how bad things were at the Manor, he'd thrown all manner of resources at the place to start the process of bringing it up to an acceptable standard. And furthermore, he'd also decided that the old stable block would make a perfect apartment for him and Tilly to live in till they eventually inherited the main house. While they were soaking up the summer sun in the Med, his architects were drawing up plans and getting all the permissions necessary from English Heritage to start work on the ancient building.

While the boat rocked gently in Kyrenia harbour in northern Cyprus, Tilly found herself musing on the novel idea of spending winter in a warm house. Her thoughts were interrupted by Marcus pottering along and plumping himself down on the sunlounger beside her.

'Hello, gorgeous,' he said gazing at her with his puppy-dog eyes.

'Hello,' she responded, flashing him a smile.

'And how's junior?' He put his hand on her rotund belly.

Tilly resisted the urge to slap it off. 'Fine. Wriggly.'

'What do you fancy doing today?'

'Nothing much. Lazing around is fine. I'm getting too big to think about much else.'

'But surely there must be something you'd like to do?'

Yeah, have my old life back, be off to uni, not be married to you but to Ashley. Tilly shook her head. 'No, honest.'

'Well, if you're sure you're happy . . .' He gazed at her,

unable to believe that anyone would be content just loafing in the sunshine, flicking through fashion magazines, being brought cold drinks when she fancied them and great food if she decided she was peckish. 'If you're *sure*, I'm going to go for a run ashore.'

Tilly bit back a snarky comment that just because he'd hired a boat it didn't make him Sir Francis Fucking Drake and he could drop the nautical chit-chat. 'You do that, darling. Enjoy.'

She watched him disappear down the gangplank and on to the bustling quay and went back to flicking through her copy of *Vogue*. Wonderful smells from the nearby tavernas wafted across to her, the boat rocked incredibly slowly and gently and the hot sun bounced off the tiny ripples in the port, making the water sparkle like a Swarovski window display. She put her magazine down and watched the people strolling along the quay. They all looked so happy and contented – just like she ought to be. She had no right to feel so out of sorts. She had pots of money, she was lounging on the biggest yacht she'd ever clapped eyes on, she was expecting a baby, she was on her honeymoon – there were millions of people in the world who would give their back teeth to be in her position. There were millions of people who would be insanely glad for just one of the items on her list of advantages. And the fact that she didn't feel ecstatic just made her a moody spoilt bitch.

But this wasn't what she'd planned for her life. None of the things she had were the things she'd wanted. What she'd wanted was to leave school, go to university for three years, maybe have a bit of fun, find out what it was like to be independent, go back home, run Haybridge Manor for a few years, marry someone she really loved and maybe, when she was around thirty and had grown up a bit, maybe start a family then. University was pointless now, even though she'd got the grades she'd needed to take her to Brighton. In fact she'd got grades that would have made her acceptable to almost any university in the country, but now there was no reason for her to get a degree in event management or tourism or any damn subject – except maybe childcare, she thought wryly. And although she was sure she'd want kids one day, she was still hardly more than one herself. She hadn't had time to discover what it was like to be a grown-up, or be independent, or to live a little, sow a wild oat or two, and here she was married and pregnant. When was she going to get the chance to go a little off the rails, do all the things her friends were going to experience, go travelling, try illegal substances, get into scrapes, get out of them? That was the way to grow up. She sighed, and remembered a saying of Miss Cunliffe's: 'Good judgement comes from experience, and most of that comes from bad judgement.' At this rate she wasn't going to be the judge of anything, good or bad, because she wasn't going to get the chance to learn *anything* from experience.

Tilly shut her eyes against the glare and wondered what Ashley was up to. She made a bet with herself that whatever it was, it was going to be more fulfilling than what she was doing.

Ashley sat at Mrs Higgins's kitchen table and stared at the local paper in disbelief. Tilly? Married? Shit a fucking brick! He pushed the paper away from him and shook his head. He just couldn't believe it. She was so young. And why? She was going to go to uni, she had her future mapped out; she'd told him all her plans and marriage certainly hadn't figured in them, or not at this age. He sat there staring at the little paragraph, feeling slightly sick. This final total rejection of him and their brief love affair was hurting more than he thought possible. So that was that. There was no way they would ever get back together again now. He shook his head sadly at the thought of what he'd lost.

'Something up?' asked Irene Higgins, who was standing on the other side of the table, slicing up some ham.

'Not really,' lied Ashley. 'Just there's a bit in the paper saying someone I used to know got married last week, and she's about my age.'

'Crikey, that's quite young.' Irene paused in her slicing. 'Still, your friend actually *got* married; so many of your generation think it's OK to live together and not bother with the formalities.'

Ashley didn't feel like getting into a discussion about the morality of co-habiting, so he just smiled. Mrs Higgins was nice enough and it was cool that she and Mr

Higgins had let him stay on since he'd officially left school. Although now he was paying them rent for his room as well as paying for his food, as he'd got a job waiting on tables in a local restaurant and it was only fair to stop freeloading. His pay wasn't fantastic, but the tips helped, and as he had precious few overheads beyond his board and lodging, he was able to save a bit towards his university fund. He now reckoned he had enough to tide him over the first couple of terms, and he hoped to find another job when he got there to help him through the rest of the three years.

'Talking of families,' said Mrs Higgins, which Ashley didn't think they had been but it would have been rude to contradict, 'have you heard from your mum recently?'

'I phoned her last week to tell her about my results.'

'I bet she was thrilled. Three As, Ashley – just fantastic.'

Thrilled? No, but she had said well done and asked if three As was good, to which he'd replied that it was.

'So why don't you get a proper job if your results are that good?' she'd said. 'Why waste another three years of your life at uni? What good is a degree in sociology? You won't ever earn a decent wage without a trade. Look at Dave.'

Yeah, just look at him, thought Ashley. Some role model he was. But he didn't contradict his mum. If she thought Dave was worth staying with, who was he to argue?

'So, off to Southampton in the autumn,' said Mrs Higgins, putting the carving knife down. 'The house will seem empty without you.'

'I'll be sorry to go,' said Ashley, with truth this time. Although it had been odd living with the Head at the beginning, he'd loved the calm and order of this house from the start: no rows, no slanging matches, no minging kid brothers wrecking things, decent food on the table, not junk out of packets or fry-ups, and peace and quiet almost all the time. And the area was nice – all detached houses with lovely gardens, a grass verge and trees either side of the avenue the house was on, lots of birdsong and almost no traffic; so different from the scabby estate where, if it wasn't cars burning rubber that ruined the silence, it was people shouting, kids screaming or music blaring. No, this place was such worlds apart it was hard to believe that the Higginses' house was only about a mile from where he'd lived before.

When he'd first moved in, he'd really worried about disturbing everyone when he played his guitar, but Mr Higgins had insisted that he liked hearing him strum away.

'You've got talent, Ashley, and I think you've the application to do really well with that instrument of yours. Have you ever considered trying to earn some money through playing?'

'Nah. I just do it for fun.'

'Well you should have a go. Maybe when you get to uni you'll be able to play in the student union. Or maybe you'll find some other musicians and get a band together.'

Ashley had laughed. 'I can't see that happening.'

'Why not? And you ought to compose your own stuff. That's where the money is if you ever crack any sort of success. I've heard you sing; you've got a good voice. Well, I'd be lying if I said you were the next Pavarotti, but you can hold a tune.'

Ashley had felt bashful. He wasn't used to compliments – he'd certainly never had them from his mum and step-dad – so he wasn't sure how to handle this. And he didn't tell Mr Higgins that he'd already had a go at writing a few tunes, as he was afraid that he'd ask to hear them. He wouldn't be able to refuse the request and he was terrified that the Head might think them rubbish. He'd plucked up the courage to play one to Tilly once, but that was different – or it felt so to him. But the other idea that Mr Higgins had offered – playing for money . . . why not? Maybe he ought to see if he could get a gig in a pub or somewhere. Even if he only earned a couple of free beers it would make it a cheap evening out and he'd get to spend more time playing. And maybe he would have another go at writing a song or two. Why not?

'So,' said Irene Higgins, bringing Ashley back to the present, 'what do you think you'll do in the vacations?'

'Go up to Newcastle, I suppose, or stay in Southampton,' said Ashley, without enthusiasm.

'Newcastle'll be a trek, won't it?'

Ashley nodded.

'And not much fun when you get there. All your friends are here, aren't they?'

'I know. Still, I suppose we'll all move away from here eventually. I'll just be the one to go first.' Besides, he thought, with Tilly married there was never going to be a chance of them being reconciled – ever – so there was no point in hanging around this town any longer. No family, no girl and no home – definitely time to move on. 'I think I'll probably try and find digs in Southampton as soon as I have to move out of hall. I'm going to have to get a decent job while I'm there. I can't afford to pay for everything if I just do a standard part-time student job, so I'll have to find something that isn't just for evenings or holidays or seasonal.'

'Will you be able to cope with that and your degree?'

'I'm going to have to, aren't I?' He had no option, he knew that. There was no way his mum was going to be able to slip him the odd extra bit of cash for food, pay for books or help out if he got into a mess financially. And to think that his step-dad might was just laughable. No, if Ashley was going to get a degree and a decent job and wind up living in a lovely house like this one, he was going to have to work his bollocks off, and it was going to start as soon as he got to Southampton. As long as he managed to get a job. Fuck knew what he'd do if he didn't – apart from starve. But the place he was working at in Haybridge had promised him a good reference when he left in September, and Mr Higgins would also give him one. He'd be as well placed as any student arriving in the city, although he might be amongst the most desperate.

When Tilly and Marcus arrived back at the Manor after their honeymoon, the builders were already in. Edward and the twins had moved into a cottage in the grounds that had been lying empty since the family had done away with the post of chauffeur thirty years previously. It was weatherproof and just about habitable, but beyond that it had nothing to recommend it. Even so, the twins reckoned it was a step up from their shabby apartment in the Manor. However, because Marcus was able to throw almost unlimited amounts of money at the renovations, no one expected that they'd have to camp there for more than a month or so. There might be residual work going on, but the family flat in the Manor would soon be habitable again, with a modern kitchen and reliable central heating.

The stable block was going to take a lot longer to fix, so it was decided that Tilly and Marcus would move into the Crosbys' London flat until their new home was ready. Tilly found this quite an exciting prospect. The idea of having money to spend and thousands of shops to spend it in was still such a novelty that it held a terrific appeal. And then there were all the plays and musicals that she'd be able to go to. Yes, living in London would be fun for a bit. Living with Marcus . . . well, she could tolerate that. She'd have to. And was it such a big price to pay for financial security for her and all her family?

She was in her room, packing up a few of her possessions – books, CDs and a few photos – ready to take to the flat, when the twins sidled in, closed the door and sat down on her bed. They watched her for a minute or two.

'Are you here for a reason, or do you just want to get under my feet?' asked Tilly after a minute or two of silence. Outside her room there was anything but, as the builders were in the process of ripping out the antiquated kitchen, and the sound of units crashing to the floor was almost masked by the blare of Radio One and the high-pitched shriek of a power tool.

Flora sniffed. 'Are you going to be away for long?' she asked.

Tilly shrugged. 'How do I know? The plan is we'll be back for Christmas, but that depends on the builders finishing the conversion of the stables. As they're concentrating on getting this place sorted out for you as fast as they can, things may slip and I might be in London for a while.'

'Oh,' her sisters said in unison.

'Why do you want to know?'

'We were wondering if we'd be allowed to come and visit you,' said Daisy.

'We thought you might like to take us shopping,' said Flora hopefully. Adding, 'It's all right for you, you've got lots of new clothes, but we're still in hand-me-downs and stuff we've almost grown out of.'

So that was it. Well, she couldn't blame them, although they hadn't realised that with the pressure of having to maintain the family seat taken off Edward's shoulders and his wallet, there was going to be a lot more in the way of creature comforts at Haybridge Manor even without the help of the Crosby millions – possibly even new wardrobes for the twins. Yes, it all just confirmed that her marriage to Marcus had done the whole family a favour – except she was the one who had Marcus as well as the money.

Not that being married to him was all bad, it really wasn't. She had to admit that not having to think about the price of anything was both novel and wonderful, although she'd discovered whilst on honeymoon that she'd had to be a bit careful about admiring anything in a shop window, as the next thing she knew, Marcus had bought it for her. While it was rather sweet of him, she also found it a bit over the top and rather irritating. Just because she liked something didn't mean she had to possess it. But that seemed to be how Marcus worked. If he liked and wanted something, he bought it – and, thought Tilly, that sometimes seemed to be the way he thought about her. She, along with her unborn baby and her family connection, now belonged to Marcus. She felt that she'd lost her identity, lost everything that had made her *her*.

Tilly thought she'd be happy in London, but the reality didn't live up to the dream. The reality was that she was lonely and bored. She didn't know anyone in the bit of Chelsea where Marcus's flat was. When she was out and about, she sometimes waddled past smart restaurants and saw groups of women all chatting and laughing – the Ladies Who Lunched, she supposed. But she had no idea how to become a part of this set, how to make friends, how to meet new people. She didn't have work colleagues, she was too pregnant to belong to a gym, her school friends had mostly buggered off on gap years to the other side of the planet and the ones who'd gone straight to university were busy making loads of new friends, while she was suffering from an aching back, swollen ankles and almost permanent heartburn, which didn't help matters one jot. And Marcus didn't help either. He didn't seem to have a circle of friends in London, or if he did, he kept them to himself. He and his father were very keen to tag on to the people the de

Lieges knew in the country, but that was a fat lot of good to Tilly up in London.

So with no social life to speak of and no one to have girlie lunches or trips to the flicks with, shopping was her sole pastime, and there was only so much of that she wanted to do – even with an unlimited budget. The twins came up to see her on a couple of occasions and made being dragged round the shops a fun day out, and she enjoyed buying stuff for the baby, but when all was said and done it was only going to need one cot, one buggy and one colour scheme for its nursery. Besides, autumn had decided to start off with a bang and the weather was glorious and very warm, which would have been fine under normal circumstances, but Tilly found that the combination of being seven months pregnant and living in the middle of a city was deeply uncomfortable, especially at night, when she found sleep difficult to come by anyway.

Then there was the fact that there was a Filipina housekeeper who cooked and cleaned and generally fussed over her and who wouldn't let Tilly lift a finger for herself, which reduced her to watching daytime TV, flicking through fashion magazines and reading endless novels. Marcus worked long and hard in the City, making more millions she supposed, and rarely got back home before eight at night, and then when he was home he was so knackered he was hardly any company at all.

It was, thought Tilly, enough to drive her to drink, only she couldn't even do that because of the baby.

She should have been so happy: newly married to a wealthy, generous man, living in a beautiful flat in a lovely, vibrant city, waited on hand and foot . . . She had everything, didn't she? But she couldn't shift the overpowering feeling of dissatisfaction. Was it just because she was bored? Was it her hormones? Would this feeling go away when the baby arrived and they moved back to Haybridge? Tilly was scared that it might not – and then what? Could she face years and years of being married to Marcus and feeling as if life was just passing her by? Of having nothing to do but pointless shopping, lounging around on foreign shores, polishing her nails and wasting her days. And to think it had only been a year previously that she'd been pinching fivers from her dad's wallet and longing for riches.

Be careful what you wish for, she told herself; it might come true.

33

The baby arrived a fortnight early, a little girl they decided to call Charlotte Susan. The birth was relatively straightforward, Tilly was told, although it had seemed anything like it to her at the time. She'd been to her antenatal classes, she'd been told what to expect, but the bone-wrenching, mind-boggling pain that went on and on still left her gasping, frightened and utterly exhausted. And Marcus was no help. He flapped around her, patting her hand and dabbing her forehead, until she yelled at him to fuck off.

'Lots of mums are like this in the latter stages of labour,' said the midwife placatingly to the startled Marcus.

Because lots of mums have fuckwits for husbands, thought Tilly angrily, her teeth clenched around the mouthpiece of the gas and air tube. Husbands who haven't a clue what to do to help and who think their wives give a toss that they're there in the delivery suite when in reality all they can think about is that it was their husband's fault they're now having to shit a watermelon. The man has a few minutes of pleasure and all the wife gets is nine months of looking like a barrage balloon followed by . . . Another contraction ripped through her, putting a stop to any sort of lucid thinking.

And just when she thought that labour couldn't possibly get any worse, her body suddenly insisted on trying to push a huge object out of a tiny little orifice.

Every couple of minutes she was overwhelmed by this horrific urge that left her knackered, breathless, panting and aching. And then suddenly . . . suddenly . . . it was over and the pain just ceased like a magic wand had been waved. A small bundle was put in her arms and a little screwed-up face looked up at her, and Tilly knew she would go through it all again just for this moment.

When Lottie was six weeks old and a week before Christmas, they moved back to Haybridge. For most families a move with a baby at such a time of year would have been impossibly stressful, but once again cash was thrown at the problem and all Tilly had to do was make sure she and Lottie had everything they needed for the hour-long car journey from London to the country. She walked out of the London flat and into her new home without having to lift a finger, while around her the staff Marcus had hired for their country property dealt with everything.

Although Tilly was ecstatic to be back in Haybridge and thrilled to have such a perfect and pretty daughter as well as Christmas to look forward to, her sense of dissatisfaction was still there, a feeling that got worse when the nanny arrived and swept little Lottie off so Tilly could 'rest'. Tilly had told Marcus that a nanny was completely unnecessary, but he was adamant. The old Tilly, the one who'd hung about in the skate park smoking nicked fags, would have thrown a strop, but the new one, the one that was married to Marcus, gave in. So what if the nanny took control of Lottie? She'd lost control of her life when she'd agreed to marry Marcus – what was the point of trying to retain control of her daughter? Besides, the nanny was awfully efficient, and Lottie seemed to prefer her capable hands to Tilly's fumblings.

She wandered round the house and gardens watching the renovations take place. It was extraordinary the transformation that was occurring; the house positively glowed with the attention that was being lavished on it. All the wood shone, the paint was fresh and chip-free, the flagstones in the ancient kitchens and the great hall – still worn, still ancient with the patina of age – now gleamed brightly having been scrubbed properly by teams of specialist stonemasons, the soft furnishings had been cleaned professionally and, where necessary, mended, the ancient drapes had had the same treatment and picture restorers were working on removing cracked and yellowing varnish from the most important oils around the house, including the Gainsborough, revealing lustrous, bright colours that transformed the once-dull paintings. Outside, the gardens were getting similar treatment, with prize-winning landscapers revamping the herbaceous borders, replanting the parterres, reseeding the neglected lawns and pruning the overgrown arbours.

Lottie grew, spring arrived and Tilly still felt bored and fed up. She was impatient and snappy, and the fact that the weather refused to buck up and remained dank and wet didn't help matters. Life with Marcus staggered on. He went to work early and returned late, their paths hardly seemed to cross and even when they did he was often preoccupied. At the weekends, when he should have been free to enjoy family life, he often shut himself in his study or spent hours on his BlackBerry. What, Tilly often wondered, was so desperate that he couldn't lighten up and relax?

She kept telling herself that she was incredibly lucky: she had a beautiful daughter, their new house was stunning, she had everything she'd ever dreamed about, but she felt as if she'd been utterly cast adrift from real life. Even cast adrift from her family, as her sisters were occupied with school, getting into the sports teams, learning lines for the school play and enjoying the novelty of being allowed to take extras like music and riding lessons because there was now the money to pay for them. Her father too had been given a new lease of life and seemed nearly as rejuvenated as the house, as he bounced around overseeing the builders and specialists, organising a website, designing new brochures, planning events to take place in the grounds, while she . . . she had nothing to do except drift about her perfect house, buffing her already perfect nails, having her perfect hair arranged even more perfectly and playing – when Nanny Emma allowed it – with her perfect daughter. And the more bored she became, the harder she found it to motivate herself to do anything; even getting out of bed in the morning was a trial.

In an effort to find something to occupy herself, she offered to help her father with the house and the building project, but he refused her.

'Sweetie, you mustn't even think about it. You should be spending all your time with my darling granddaughter. I don't need your help – I've got staff and contractors for all of that. No, don't you worry yourself with the house. Plenty of time for that when you inherit the place.'

So with nothing available for her to do and with Marcus racing off to his office in London at around six o'clock to be there for when the markets opened, it was often after nine before Tilly could drag herself into the shower and face the day. What reason had she to get up, she wondered – just to sit around looking at yet more pictures in glossy magazines, or read another book, or watch daytime TV or play endless games of patience on the computer? What was the point?

The days and weeks drifted on. Lottie began to crawl and needed a whole new wardrobe as she grew steadily. The daffodils in the grounds faded and were replaced by the late-flowering cherries and the peonies, and then the roses bloomed. Most of the restoration work on the house was finished and the visitors came in droves to see what had been done, and for everyone except Tilly, life seemed to be on a roll.

In fact for Tilly, life was anything but roses, despite the ones that filled and perfumed the new gardens. It really didn't help matters that Marcus was working longer and longer hours in London – staying overnight occasionally – leaving her feeling more petulant and more bored than ever. When he was home he seemed exhausted and snappy – no wonder, with the hours he worked – and any spare energy he did have was saved for playing with his darling Lottie. Tilly tried to make a big effort to take an interest in whatever it was he did in the City, but he seemed reluctant to answer any of her questions, and when she pressed him he just got even more irritated. She gave up the struggle but ended up feeling yet more isolated and resentful.

She simmered, he sulked; the honeymoon was most definitely over.

Throughout the summer, things staggered from bad to worse, Marcus getting more tense and shirty, Tilly suffering ever-increasing feelings of despair and redundancy. Even Lottie seemed to want to spend more time with Nanny Emma than she did with her mother, and Marcus seemed to avoid her at all costs. There were some days when Tilly wondered if anyone would notice if she just buggered off out of their lives and left them to it.

Ashley was almost at the end of his first year. He'd had a fantastic time, made friends, worked hard and got good initial marks, and was predicted to be on course for a 2:1. Best of all, he had a job in a furniture showroom where the sympathetic manager allowed him to work his shifts around his lectures and tutorials, so the fact that he had to earn his tuition fees didn't actually affect his tuition. Twice a week he performed at the Three Crowns in the city centre in return for a couple of pints of beer and twenty quid in his pocket, and he'd found a tiny bedsit to move into as soon as the university term finished in June, so he didn't have to go to Newcastle for the vacation and risk losing either of his jobs. All in all, thought Ashley, life could be a lot worse.

It was a Tuesday night towards the middle of June and he was performing as usual at the Three Crowns. He was paid to do three sets of forty minutes each with a break of a quarter of an hour between them, when he got a free pint. For the crowd in the pub he was little more than background noise, and he was used to the fact that most people didn't come to listen to him but to drink and chat. He didn't mind; he got his beer and his money and two hours of playing to an audience, which gave him the feeling of being a professional even though he knew he was really only an amateur. And because he knew that no one was really listening to him, every now and again he'd slip in a song he'd written himself. He had no idea if they were any good or not, but the landlord hadn't told him to stop and no one had booed him off, so he carried on. He now had half a dozen songs in his repertoire that he'd composed himself, and the rest of the music he performed was covers of old favourites. He reckoned, though, that by the time he'd finished his degree he might be able to play for an entire evening using just his own stuff – assuming the customers let him.

The last chord of the song he'd been singing died away and he glanced at his watch – break time. A smattering of applause rippled over the sound of chatter. Ashley analysed it. No, not ironic; quite genuine in fact. Well, that was nice. He flashed a quick smile at the punters to acknowledge his gratitude for the support, then propped his guitar on its stand and made his way to the bar to collect his pint.

He was taking a welcome gulp of the chilled lager

when a voice by his shoulder said, 'I enjoyed that. You're good.'

Ashley swung round to see who was talking to him. It was a twenty-something man wearing scruffy jeans and a stripy sweater that judging by its shape had seen too many trips through the washing machine. His hair was in need of a decent cut – and a wash for that matter.

'Thanks,' said Ashley diffidently, still unused to handling compliments.

'Some of your songs . . .'

'Yeah?'

'I've not heard them before. Your stuff?'

Ashley nodded and shrugged. 'Yeah, well . . . I just mess around a bit, try things out.'

'You should do more of it.'

'Really?' But then what did this guy know? Probably nothing. Ashley wondered what his game was.

'Do you always perform solo?'

'Yes.' Ashley took another slurp from his pint. It wasn't that he didn't want to chat, but this was his break and he just wanted to chill, relax, and making small talk with a stranger didn't tick those boxes.

'If you got the chance, would you play with a band?'

Ashley put his drink down on the bar. 'Can I ask, pal, why the interest?'

'Just curious. Would you?'

'What?'

'Play in a band if you had the chance.'

'If REM or the Arctic Monkeys gave me a call and said they needed a guitarist, what do you think?'

'What if the band was a bit less famous?'

'Then I'd have to think about it. Now if you'll excuse me, I've got another set to perform.' Ashley took his drink over to his stool and began to tune his instrument again, taking occasional sips of his drink while watching his interrogator over the rim of his glass.

He played his second set, although being watched so closely made him disinclined to perform any of his own songs. The scruffy bloke was still there, waiting for him at the bar, when he finished.

'Have you thought about it?'

'Thought about what?' said Ashley, getting impatient with the constant questioning and taking his free pint off the barman as he spoke.

'Joining a band.'

'No. Why should I?'

'Because I know a band – well, it's my band really – that's got a vacancy, and I think you could fill it perfectly.'

Ashley leant on the bar and eyed the guy up. 'Do you now?'

'Yeah, and we've got a slot at the Rock Festival.'

'Congratulations. Lucky you,' he said laconically, trying to keep the fact that he was pretty impressed from showing on his face. The Rock – wow! After Glasto, Reading and the Isle of Wight, it was one of the biggest.

'Yeah, but we'll look right dipsticks if we show up without a lead guitarist. This is our big break, and unless we find a new guitarist bloody soon, it ain't going to happen.'

Ashley sipped his drink as he considered the implications of what he was being told. 'So why,' he said after a few moments' thought, 'why the vacancy?'

'Rob, our guitarist, got an offer he couldn't refuse.'

'Poached by another group?'

'No, a job. He's a geology graduate and BP offered him a job on the rigs with masses of perks, a huge pension plan and a salary to make your eyes water.'

'So he chose a secure future over the dream of being a rock star.'

'That's about it.'

Ashley nodded. Maybe this Rob had done the right

thing. He stuck his hand out. 'Well, thanks . . .' He paused and looked expectant.

'Mike.'

'Thanks, Mike, for the vote of confidence, but I don't know I can afford to take the time off the day job.' He sighed. 'And I'd have to learn your material before the concert – that's a mission in itself. What have I got? A month? Six weeks?'

'You could do it. We'd help you; we'd rehearse as much as you wanted, that sort of thing.'

'I need to think about it.'

Mike handed him a card. 'Don't take too long, please. Ring me as soon as you've made your mind up.'

'OK. By the way, what's the band called?'

'Hash Tag.'

Ashley considered the name. It was OK, he reckoned. He wondered what the other band members were like.

He found out the next night when they met for their first rehearsal. From then until the day of the festival he spent every spare moment with them, learning the words, learning the music and the harmonies. University term had ended, so he was able to spend even more time practising, so much so that the tips of his fingers became raw and sore, and then slowly hardened off with tough calluses. The sign of a real guitarist, he told himself, not some amateur like he had been

In late August they had their final rehearsal before the event. Ashley didn't know whether the dreadful sick feeling in the pit of his stomach was caused by nerves or excitement. But one thing he did know: Hash Tag was the best thing that had happened to him since he'd broken up with Tilly. The only thing that worried him now was whether the public would have an equally high opinion of the band.

Tilly drifted around the gardens of the Manor, pushing Lottie in her buggy. It was early evening, the visitors had all gone for the day and peace reigned. She looked about her at the immaculate lawns, the perfect, weed-free flower beds, the raked gravel paths and thought how different it was from just a couple of years before, when the whole place had been dying on its feet, signs of neglect as obvious as the molehills and potholes. This gold-standard tourist attraction was what could be achieved with staff and money. She sighed and wished she could feel more grateful

It was going to be her first wedding anniversary in just a few days, and the way she felt right now, she was beginning to wonder if it was going to be the only one she'd celebrate. Not that she planned to do much celebrating – drown her sorrows, more like. She wondered if her family had guessed quite what a disaster area the whole marriage was; she was pretty certain she was covering up quite well, so she thought on balance they didn't.

It helped that her father had never been very good at spotting the moods of his children, and anyway, he was now completely immersed in the house, now that it had turned from being a rancid, decaying albatross hung around his neck into a going concern. He seemed to have little time for anything outside of the business of running the place.

Susan, of course, was back in the States, working on another film. Since her emergency dash to sort out the matter of Tilly's unplanned pregnancy, relations with her husband and children had taken a whole new turn, but Tilly was very careful about the façade she exhibited when her mum was around. Susan was still beating herself up about abandoning her kids, and she didn't need the guilt of having engineered Tilly's dud marriage to cope with on top. Tilly had discovered that despite everything, she and her mother still had a fairly good relationship, and they now chatted frequently on the phone when Susan was abroad or on location. Of course, the gap left by the years when she hadn't been around wasn't ever going to be closed completely, but on balance the two of them got along pretty well. The fact that Susan now had a room at the Manor where she kept a wardrobe full of clothes and was always around for birthdays and other celebrations meant that at last Tilly felt as though she had two parents rather than just one.

Had the twins worked out that her marriage was a sham? Unlikely, thought Tilly. They were too self-centred to notice anything that didn't directly concern themselves. The only other person who might spot something untoward was Desmond Crosby, but Tilly didn't think he paid any attention to anything that didn't have a profit and loss account attached.

She heaved a sigh and carried on with her walk through the knot garden. Was it so bad being a bird in a gilded cage when the cage was so comfy; trading emotional happiness for financial security – was that such a raw deal? Maybe she should just suck it up and get on with it. She pushed the buggy along the gravel path towards the gate to the kitchen garden and the back of the Manor, passing the window of the office, open to the warm summer evening.

'What do you mean, everything?' It was her father's voice, loud, angry and unmistakably worried.

Tilly glanced down at Lottie to check she was still dozing, and paused to listen.

'Everything, Edward. Every last fucking penny.' That voice belonged to her father-in-law, who sounded just as angry as Edward.

What was this all about?

'But didn't you have any control over him? Didn't you monitor what the hell he was up to?'

'Marcus is my son, Edward. I trusted him. He's not someone just plucked off the street, someone I know nothing about. It never occurred to me he would do something like this.'

There was a silence. What had Marcus done? Whatever it was, it wasn't good, that much was crystal clear.

'So what's to be done?' said her father.

'It's in the hands of the police now.'

The *police*? Tilly felt her heart jolt with shock. Shit, what on earth had he done? She crept closer to the window.

'But there's no clue to his whereabouts?'

There was a sigh from Desmond Crosby so heavy that Tilly could hear it in the garden. 'I think the saying goes – he can run but he can't hide.'

Tilly shivered. This was getting worse and worse. Making her mind up, she turned the buggy through one hundred and eighty degrees and raced back to the door into the Manor. A minute later she burst into the office, causing the two men to turn their ashen faces towards her.

'What's going on? What's Marcus done?'

'Tilly! What . . . ? How . . . ? How do you know?'

Tilly stared at her father. 'What do you mean, how do I know? I don't know anything. But I want some answers now.'

The two men exchanged a look. 'I'm sorry,' said her father after a pause. 'I thought perhaps Marcus had been in contact.'

She shook her head. 'I was in the garden, under the window. I heard you talking.'

'So there's been nothing on the news?'

'The news!' screeched Tilly. 'The *news*?' she repeated, going a few semitones higher still.

Again that look between the two men. Lottie stirred restlessly. As well she might, thought Tilly. Something was making everyone very uncomfortable and she was going to find out . . . right now.

'What is it? What's happened?'

Desmond sighed. 'She's going to find out very soon.'

Edward nodded.

'What is *she* going to find out?' demanded Tilly.

'It seems Marcus has made an error of judgement,' said Desmond.

Tilly's eyes arrowed. Error of judgement – just what did that mean? He'd bounced a cheque? He'd run a red light? She thought not, not if the tension in this room was anything to go by. 'Go on,' she said.

'He's lost some money,' said Desmond.

'What, a few quid, down the back of the sofa?'

'Don't be flippant, Tilly,' snapped her father. 'This is no laughing matter.'

'He's lost it all,' said Desmond.

'All?' repeated Tilly stupidly. Then she remembered what she'd heard in the garden. *Every last fucking penny.* 'Forty million,' she whispered.

Desmond nodded, his face pinched, his lips white. 'Actually, rather more. All of our money and a lot of our investors'. More like one hundred and forty million.'

Jeez . . . 'How?'

'Bad judgement, bad investments, the credit crunch, stupidity . . . I could go on, but what's the point?'

Tilly's knees suddenly felt weak. She groped for a chair and sat down. 'A hundred and forty million,' she repeated.

There was silence, only broken by a faint whimper from Lottie. Tilly felt like whimpering too.

Ashley's mouth was dry, his knees were wobbling, his hands were shaking and he couldn't hear anything because of the racket going on just yards from where he was standing: shrieking, whistles, yells, clapping, air horns blasting . . . Why, he wondered, had he agreed to this? It was madness. He wasn't ready, the rehearsals hadn't prepared him for this, he'd never realised quite how awful stage fright could be. It was one thing playing for a few punters in a pub – this was something else. And he wasn't sure he was going to cope.

'Come on, Ashley,' said Mike, shouting directly into his ear and giving him a punch in the ribs. 'We're on.'

Feeling sicker than ever, Ashley began to move towards the lights ahead. Banks and banks of lights hung from a rig thirty feet above his head, a wall of amps to his right and then . . . he glanced to his left . . . oh, shit. Big mistake. Huge. There was the audience. Thousands and thousands of kids. He stumbled but forced his legs to keep going till he reached his allotted mic on the far side of the stage. He plugged his guitar in with trembling fingers

'Hi,' roared Mike to the crowd.

'Hi,' ten thousand voices roared back.

'Hi, we're Hash Tag,' roared Mike again. 'And you're . . .' He paused. 'You're a fantastic audience!'

The crowd cheered. Easily pleased, thought Ashley. He wondered if they'd be so pleased at the end of their set. The cheering continued as the group members strummed a couple of chords and made sure the set-up was OK. The noise and power coming from the crowd was awesome. Ashley wondered if being in the middle of a hurricane was like this.

Mike glanced left and right to make sure his band members were looking at him, paying attention. The crowd sensed the set was about to kick off; the cheering died down. Ashley felt dizzy. Come on, Mike, he thought. Let's get this over with.

'One, two three, four,' Mike called and Ashley's hands moved automatically to the strings and frets and the first chord of the song blared out, then muscle memory took over and despite the fact that his brain was still frozen with fear, his fingers performed.

By the third song he was beginning to thaw out and actually take in just what was going on around him. In front of him was a sea of faces, all staring at them; above them vast, tall flags reached skywards, fluttering in the light evening breeze; scaffolding towers were dotted around with cameras positioned to get the best view of the stage so as to project their image – *his* image – on to the giant screens around the field and at the back and sides of the stage.

The band weren't supposed to be here, not on this stage at any rate. This wasn't what they'd been signed up for. Hash Tag's gig was supposed to be later tonight on a side stage with a possible audience of a few hundred if they were lucky. But there'd been a monster problem and the band doing this slot, the band that had attracted this vast audience, was still somewhere over the Atlantic, having been delayed at Chicago airport by a faulty aircraft for over for four hours. As the organisers were running around trying to reorganise the programme, Hash Tag had rolled up in their beaten-up minibus.

'Would you,' asked a fraught-looking rock chick, 'be prepared to hold the fort on the main stage for thirty minutes? No money, and this would be as well as, not instead of, your other performance.'

'Would we? Of course,' responded Mike, without even asking the other three members of the band.

'What the fuck are you thinking of?' Ashley had yelled at him as they'd walked away. 'We can't perform to a crowd that size. They're expecting Def Leppard and they're getting us. They'll kill us. We're going to get lynched.'

'Get real, Ashley. This is the biggest break we're ever going to get.'

'But we're not ready for it.'

'Why aren't we?'

'Because . . .'

'Because we haven't rehearsed enough? Our songs aren't good enough? Bollocks.'

'Supposing we're shit?'

'Supposing we aren't.'

And as Ashley looked at the kids swaying to their music, dancing to their beat, enjoying the songs, he knew they weren't shit. Mike had been right. And fuck the money – or lack of it. If he'd had to, he'd have sold some of his own body parts to pay for this experience, and here he was getting it for nothing. Fucking ace.

Desmond, Edward and Tilly sat at the dining room table in Tilly's beautiful stable conversion and stared at each other glumly. Lottie was with the nanny and for once Tilly was glad to be able to hand her over. Given the events of the past week since Marcus had gone missing, she felt she couldn't cope with being a mother as well as the wife of a wanted criminal.

'So, have the police crawled all over your place too?' said Tilly to Desmond.

'Took the whole house to pieces. Carted away computers, files, personal papers, the works.'

'Same here,' said Edward.

'So it's definitely more than just bad judgement,' said Tilly.

'The Serious Fraud Office think there may be more to it than that – possibly because he's fucked off and no one has a clue where he is.' Desmond jerked a look in Tilly's direction. 'You haven't heard anything, have you?'

Tilly shook her head. 'No, not a word. Nothing.' And although she didn't want to admit it, she was getting increasingly worried about the silence. Her marriage, what there was of it, hadn't been ideal, but she didn't like to think that Marcus had come to some sort of harm. He might have bored her, he mightn't have been her ideal man, but she would never forget the fact that he'd been kind to her. He'd been ... nice. He didn't deserve anything horrid to happen to him. She couldn't believe that he would have knowingly done anything criminal or malign. Stupid – she could believe that he'd been stupid – but not fraudulent.

The lack of communication was becoming a real matter for concern. What if he'd done something drastic: thrown himself off a cliff or jumped off a cross-Channel ferry? The fact that the police hadn't come knocking at her door asking her to identify a body didn't mean that it wasn't a very real possibility. People who'd chucked themselves into the sea had been known to just disappear. Had Marcus done that? She didn't dare say anything, because she felt that if she voiced her worries they might become reality. She could tell from the tension in Desmond's face that he felt the same way and was keeping quiet for the same reason. Their unvoiced thoughts made the atmosphere heavy and uncomfortable, like the minutes before a thunderstorm broke.

There was another worry she didn't like to voice, too. What about the house? The whole place had been renovated with Crosby money, but given that there were now creditors around the world baying for the return of funds they'd given to the Crosbys to invest, did that mean that Marcus had jeopardised Haybridge Manor on top of everything else? Was this the sort of situation where the bailiffs would come knocking? Could they flog the Manor to recoup some of the funds? She didn't care a jot about the jewels Marcus had bought her, the designer clothes, the shoes, the bags, the trappings every trophy wife should have – the lot could go to pay the debt as far as Tilly was concerned.

But the Manor?

The Manor was everything, and if he'd jeopardised it she'd . . . she'd . . . Gah, she didn't have a clue what she'd do, apart from fight to her last breath to keep it. She could only hope that the pre-nup that Marcus had insisted on to protect his assets was going to protect hers instead.

35

Tilly sat in the estate office and tapped a pen impatiently on the blotter.

'Listen,' she said into the telephone receiver, 'I don't care if you've got problems. You promised me one hundred mobile lavatories and now you're telling you can only produce fifty.' She listened to the frantic voice for a few seconds before interrupting. 'I don't want problems, I want solutions. I don't care how you find the other loos, but I suggest you do . . . Well sub-contract then . . . No, I don't care if you do make a loss. I can't be expected to bankroll your inefficiency, can I? . . . Yes, and the same to you.' She slammed the receiver on to its rest and sighed. 'Wanker,' she muttered.

'Tilly,' remonstrated her father from another desk in the office.

'Sorry, Fa, but he was.'

'That's as may be, but . . .' He was interrupted by the phone ringing again and had to wait until Tilly had finished dealing with an enquiry about media access.

'So,' he continued when she'd ended the call, 'how's it going?'

'Fine,' she said. 'If we make a proper success of this, next year we might try for a two-day festival. I know it'd be more work, but it isn't as if we haven't got the land. We've got acres of space to create campsites, and frankly, I can't believe that organising a two-day concert is twice the effort of putting on a one-day one. In fact I should think it's almost exactly the same amount of work but for twice the revenue.'

'If you say so,' said her father.

'I do, but until I do it I've no idea. If I'd gone to uni and done event management, as I'd planned, I wouldn't be running about like a headless chicken like I seem to be doing most days. I know there's a whole team with me in organising this, but they're professionals and I'm not – and it shows.'

'It doesn't,' said her father mildly. 'Besides, we never imagined we'd have to resort to this sort of thing to keep the place afloat.'

Tilly stared at him. 'What?' Was her father mad, or had Alzheimer's finally caught up with him? Didn't he remember quite how skint they'd been only a few years ago? 'Fa,' she explained, slowly and carefully, 'before Marcus's money we were *always* going to have to do this. All I can say is, thank God we got the place properly done up before he lost the lot.'

'Yes, I suppose we've got that to be grateful for.'

'Let's face it, we've got a good ten years before we need to think about any further work on the house. If we make a success of running events in that time, we'll be able to stash enough cash to keep the place in tip-top condition for another generation.'

Right on cue the next generation burst into the office, raced across the thick carpet and threw herself into her grandfather's lap.

'And how was playschool?' he said indulgently, twiddling Lottie's blonde plaits.

'Fun,' she said. 'We made sandcastles.'

'Did you?'

'And I got all sandy.'

Tilly stared at her daughter, now almost four, and wondered where the years had gone. It seemed only a few weeks since she'd brought a tiny baby home, and in a little over a year, Lottie would be going to school. And Marcus had missed it all: Lottie's first words, first steps, first day at playschool . . . All of that had been accomplished while he'd been . . .

Been where, exactly? Somewhere in Brazil, the police said, which hardly narrowed things down much, given the size of the place. Not that the authorities were inclined to look for him either, since there was precious little chance of getting him back to face charges if he didn't want to return. And, given the length of time he'd been gone, it seemed increasingly likely that he didn't. If he hadn't missed his wife and daughter sufficiently to come home after the first few months, what were the chances he'd have a change of heart after nearly three years?

Was it all her fault? wondered Tilly. If she hadn't seduced him, hadn't got pregnant, if she had been a better wife . . . If, if, if . . . Maybe he'd have made a mess of his father's business anyway, but maybe if his home life had been better he wouldn't now be skulking in some foreign backwater.

She wondered vaguely what he was up to. Had he found another partner? Was he happy? Healthy? A father again? She kind of hoped he was. Despite everything, she still had fond memories of him. It amazed her, given Marcus's total lack of spirit, his almost complete dullness, his beigeness, that he could have brought a major financial institution to its knees and, having done so, fled the country leaving barely a trace. It showed he did have a bit of a spark about him after all.

The police had said that he'd known for several months, perhaps at Easter that year, that the financial mess he'd got into was unsolvable and so had planned an escape route. It had, thought Tilly, explained why he never wanted to talk about work, why he was always so tense and shirty – who wouldn't be, knowing they'd lost over one hundred million pounds and the only way out was to sack everything: friends, family, his home – the lot.

Only it hadn't had to be like that. He wasn't the first banker, she discovered, to have made such a monumental cock-up of everything, and none of them, apparently, had got anything much worse than a slap on the wrist, a few years in an open prison at the very worst. So why had he chosen a lifetime of exile in a foreign country over a stint in nick and then a return to his family?

Which brought Tilly back to the uncomfortable feeling that it wasn't just punishment he was trying to escape from. Maybe he'd felt as trapped as she had. Maybe, if she hadn't been such a rubbish wife, Desmond would still have a son he could see once in a while.

The family had staggered on, coming to terms with their own sense of guilt, their feelings of abandonment, the scandal and the press interest. As far as the latter was concerned, the de Lieges had been relatively all right: Tilly had had a sufficiently low profile before the even lower-profile wedding as to be almost a nonentity as far as Fleet Street was concerned, and the rest of her family had nothing whatsoever to do with the matter. Also, they'd been able to withdraw into the confines of their ancestral home and pull up a metaphorical drawbridge.

Poor old Desmond Crosby hadn't been so lucky. He'd been left with the task of trying to salvage what he could from the train wreck of the financial mismanagement his son had left behind. Naturally the police and the Serious Fraud Office had crawled all over every aspect of the two families' lives, but they had concentrated most of their attention on Desmond. It had been intrusive and scary for all of them but especially bruising for him. Then there had been the press, who had been particularly cruel to him, as long before the police had finished their investigations they had decided he had to be guilty by association. When he'd arrived at work each morning, trying to limit the damage as much as possible, they'd been waiting there to pounce. Or they had been till another, bigger news story took over.

Out of the mess, however, some good had arisen: the fact that they had all gone through the same hideous experience had brought the two families closer. They shared the same sense of loss and the same bewilderment that someone they thought they knew had acted in such a way.

Once the worst of it had been sorted out, administrators brought in and the police had wound up their investigations, Desmond had moved quietly out of his London flat and into the now-refurbished chauffeur's cottage in the grounds of the Manor.

One good thing about having him as a neighbour was that he was able to bring his considerable business brain and weight of experience to bear on the matter of running Haybridge Manor as a profitable enterprise. His son might have been incompetent financially, but Desmond was made of different material. He was a true entrepreneur who understood about maximising profit, minimising expenses and grabbing every money-making opportunity with both hands, and with his help the Manor was starting to earn its keep.

For starters, the live-in Norland nanny was an unsustainable luxury, so she went and was replaced by a childminder from town at about a tenth of the cost. With no nanny to accommodate, it was possible for Tilly and Lottie to move out of the huge new apartment in the stable block and back into the newly refurbished Manor, and the flat was let, at vast expense, to some hotshot executive and his family. Mrs T had been replaced as housekeeper but she was now employed – at an increased salary – in the great kitchen giving cookery demonstrations and lessons on a replica (but working) range. In addition, they'd turned the lake into a coarse fishing venue and all film and TV production companies had been reminded of the availability of Haybridge Manor as a location – and now that the gardens had been sorted and tidied, it was in even greater demand. All in all there was enough money coming in to keep the staff employed, the garden neat and the house warm and dry.

Tilly suspected that Desmond's enthusiasm for turning the Manor into a going concern had a lot more to do with finding an activity that took his mind off his worry over his missing son than a desire to see the de Lieges stay solvent, but whatever the reason, it was working for them all.

Now, the latest, biggest and most ambitious of his money-spinning enterprises was just a week away from happening, and Tilly was feeling completely stressed, despite the fact that she was just a small cog in a big wheel of professional event managers. As far as she was concerned this was her venue, her name on contracts, her responsibility, and the buck, when it stopped, would stop on her desk. But although she was frantically busy, she was also aware that she was getting a great buzz from being part of something so immense. And that amazing kick she was getting was one of the reasons she was keen that, assuming it ran at a profit this year, they should repeat the exercise next year but for a whole weekend, not just one day.

The phone on her desk rang again.

'Hello, Tilly de Liege.'

'This is Jim Thompson, arts desk at the *Gazette*. Have you got the final line-up for the festival yet?'

Tilly, now unfazed by daily phone calls from the media correspondents of some of the country's biggest papers, tucked her phone under her ear and scrabbled about in the pile of papers to the side of her. 'Just about,' she said, fishing out the piece she was looking for.

'Can you tell me who they are?' the journalist asked.

'I can fax the list to you, if that'd be easier.'

'Perfect.' The reporter reeled off the number and Tilly jotted it down. 'Are you pleased with it?'

Tilly glanced at the list as she took it over to the fax in the corner of the office and began to feed it in. 'Yes,' she lied. 'Thrilled.' She'd been told by agents and managers that the bands were all in demand, that they'd been lucky to get most of them, but if she was totally honest, there were quite a few she'd never heard of. Of course there were some names on the list whose fame was so stellar that she would have come across them even if she'd been living on Mars, but some of the others? The Legion, Millie Bee, Hash Tag – who the hell were they? These days, she simply didn't have time to listen to the radio, to read gossip mags, to spend hours downloading music on to her iPod. When she'd been at school and during her first and only year of marriage, she'd always had music as a background track to her life, so she was up to speed with the latest hits, but now . . . By the time she got Lottie to bed at the end of the day, she was too knackered to do much more than eat her supper, watch something mindless on TV and then hit the hay. She couldn't remember the last time she'd been clubbing. She realised with a nasty jolt that her youth was whizzing past and if she wasn't careful she was going to dip out on being young altogether and segue straight into middle age without breaking step.

The machine bleeped and blipped and the fax was transmitted. She could hear simultaneous bleeps and blips at the other end of the phone line as the reporter received it.

'I agree,' said Thompson after a pause as he scanned the document. 'Fantastic. And you've got some new talent there. Great.'

Tilly took the paper from the machine and stared at it.

Did they? She'd have to make sure she spent some time at the festival and caught up with the real world. After all, what was the point of being in charge of something like this unless you completely abused the all-areas VIP pass she'd already issued herself with?

Tilly didn't need to make use of her pass to hear the music at the festival. Half of Haybridge would be able to hear it, given the volume at which the amplifiers were pumping it out. In fact, although she was outside the arena itself and, in theory, well away from the action, she was hard pressed to hear the voice at the other end of her radio. She clamped it to her ear, trying to block out the thumping, insistent beat and the blare of the music. She managed to interpret the message and realised it wasn't anything she had to deal with. She had minions who could cope with the problem – but it seemed to be a good one in some respects. They were running out of space in the car park allocated for people who hadn't pre-booked their tickets. Which meant the festival was going to be a sell-out.

Flashing her pass as she made her way to the arena, Tilly felt almost light-headed with relief. The outlay for a gig like this beggared belief. Of course, they'd known for a while that the event would run at a profit, what with the sale of pitches to stalls and food concessions plus the number of advance tickets they'd shifted, but the size of the profit was dependent on the final gate money on the day. Now it looked as if it was going to be better than they'd dared hope. She swiped her pass through yet another security turnstile and pushed her way through to the backstage area.

Here, behind the amplifiers, the noise was less

mind-blowing. She made her way to the giant marquee that had been erected for the comfort of the bands and singers. Inside there were plasma screens relaying pictures from the TV cameras filming the festival for a satellite music channel; there were waitresses circulating with refreshments, armchairs and tables scattered around, and off to one side a canvas corridor that led to the dressing rooms. A girl with a clipboard was keeping track of timings, making sure that the act due on next was ready, checking that those on stage later were en route, organising transport to take away those who had already performed and generally keeping the wheels oiled. As far as Tilly could see, it was all running like clockwork. Maybe she could allow herself ten minutes of relaxation time.

She sank into a deep armchair and put her radio on the table in front of her. Instantly a waitress appeared.

'Coffee,' she ordered, 'milk, no sugar.' The waitress, a local girl awed to be working amongst some of her rock heroes, sped away, eager to please the woman who'd given her the job. Tilly smiled. The promise of a job next year to anyone who did well today had obviously been a good move if this girl's turnout, deportment and general air of efficiency were anything to go by. The coffee arrived and Tilly took it with a grateful smile; she'd been up since five and she needed all the caffeine she could get to keep her going till ten that evening; adrenalin alone wasn't going to cut it. About ten feet away from her was a screen showing the current performers – not a band she recognised, but then that was the case with more than half the acts. There was something in her subconscious, however, that was telling her that she'd heard the music before. She racked her brains – on the radio? Had her sisters played it when they'd come home from school? No, that wasn't it. She stared at the screen and let her mind drift while the music made connections in her brain, and suddenly she wasn't sitting on a sofa in a swanky marquee in the VIP area of a rock concert but in a scruffy, cramped bedroom on a council estate at the other end of town. And it wasn't a band playing, with keyboards and drums and amps to enhance their Stratocasters, but a boy – her age – and his battered guitar. This was the song Ashley had played her, the song with no words. The song he'd played the day she'd known she'd fallen completely in love with him.

So how had this band got hold of it? She stared at the screen and began to listen to the lyrics.

> She is the girl with the money and power,
> She's the girl up there in the tower
> She's the princess, the one in the myth
> She's the girl who doesn't know I exist.

The words resonated within her, and for an inexplicable reason she felt tears springing to her eyes. Whoever had written this song might have been writing about her and Ashley. And it was Ashley's tune.

But the singer wasn't Ashley. She didn't have a clue who he was, nor who the other band members were, not that the camera was focusing on them; it was just the face of the lead singer that filled the screen.

The girl with the clipboard shot past, watch in hand. Tilly caught her as she passed. 'Who's this?' she asked.

'Hash Tag.' And she gave Tilly the sort of look that implied that Tilly must have either been in a coma for a few months or off the planet. Tilly was none the wiser but she nodded, sagely, and the girl, on a mission, raced off. Maybe, thought Tilly, Ashley had sold his song to them. She hoped he'd got a good deal and hadn't been ripped off. He deserved some luck and a decent life. Despite the messy way their relationship had ended, she often wondered – when she drove around the ring road that skirted the council estate – what had happened to him: whether he'd managed to make it to university, how he'd coped with living up north. Whether he ever thought about her like she thought about him. She still missed him, she acknowledged. Maybe a part of her still loved him.

She watched the band on the screen for a few more seconds before finishing her coffee. She couldn't sit around here all day enjoying herself; she had things to do. She had to check the catering arrangements for the acts arriving later that evening, and one of the female American singers had insisted on some ridiculous riders in her contract, so she had to make sure that her Oreos, her green Smarties and her lilies (stamens removed) had been delivered, along with the rest of her ridiculous demands.

As she exited the marquee and headed across the trampled grass towards the path back to the Manor, the band on stage finished their set. The applause was rapturous. Tilly made a mental note to buy their album – if nothing else, she wanted to see who was credited with writing that song she'd just heard.

'Did you see Hash Tag? Weren't they awesome?' said Daisy at breakfast the next morning. 'Just ace,' she added, answering her own question with a dreamy look on her face.

'Uh huh,' answered Tilly, her mouth full of toast. She was poring over a review of their festival in the *Gazette*. Five stars – just what they needed. She knew they'd sent the audience away happy, but to get critical acclaim in a national paper was the icing on the cake. Jim Thompson was especially lyrical about Hash Tag – 'the band most likely to get the Best Newcomer award at the next round of the Brits'. Well, good for them. And they obviously appealed to teenagers as well as ancient crones like herself, which was even better.

'Ace,' echoed Flora, looking equally soppy.

'And to think they were here.'

The girls sighed in unison.

'I got Mike Adams to sign my CD,' said Daisy

'I saw, you jammy cow. I didn't think to bring mine home from school.'

'More fool you.'

Tilly hastily swallowed another chunk of toast. 'You've got their CD?'

Daisy and Flora looked at their elder sister as if she was in need of care in the community. 'Everyone's got it,' they said in unison.

'Can I borrow it?'

'Suppose,' agreed Daisy grudgingly. 'But if you muck it up . . .'

'I don't want to play it, I just want to look at it.'

Both twins stared at her as if she'd lost it completely – now less care in the community, more in need of sectioning.

'I just want to see who wrote one of their songs.'

'Which one?' asked Flora.

Tilly shrugged.

'It was probably Ashley,' said Daisy with the authority of an aficionado.

Tilly's world shifted on its axis. She clutched the edge of the table to stop herself falling. 'Ashley?'

'Yeah, Ashley Driver. He's really fit – but not as fit as Mike Adams.'

'Ashley Driver?'

Daisy nodded.

'Ashley Driver?'

'God, sis, have you got a problem or something? Yes, *Ashley Driver*, their guitarist, who also writes most of their material.'

Tilly felt her world tip again. Ashley had been here, on the stage, just yards from her, playing at her gig at her house.

And he hadn't made an effort to say hello to her.

Had he come here to gloat, to show her how successful he'd become, to show her that he didn't need her? Was he still so angry with her he couldn't bring himself even to speak to her? For a second Tilly felt her eyes prick. The memory of what they'd had together and was now lost still smarted. She swallowed and regained control of herself.

Why did it still hurt so much? It had been years ago. She'd got married, had a kid, been through a scandal, come out the other side . . . And yet she still remembered her feelings for him, how much she'd adored him, and she never drove past the skate park without wondering what might have been if only she'd levelled with him right from the start. If only . . .

Water under the bridge, she told herself briskly. She made herself regain control. It was over; she had to move on. She had her life now, which was centred around Lottie and the Manor, and he had his. And he wanted nothing to do with her. In fact, that he wanted nothing to do with her couldn't have been more obvious if he'd hired a plane to trail a message across the sky to that effect. He might lower himself to play at her venue, but he hadn't tried to see her. He'd come, he'd played, he'd left. End of.

The new housekeeper, Anna, came to the door of the breakfast room carrying a huge bunch of flowers.

The twins and Tilly looked at her in surprise.

'Blimey,' said Daisy eventually as Anna hovered on the threshold.

'Who are they for?' asked Tilly – rather expecting the answer to be herself. A thank-you from a grateful band or fan.

'I don't rightly know,' said Anna, a frown on her brow. 'In fact I'm not sure they've sent them to the right place.'

'Tricky to mistake an address like Haybridge Manor in a place the size of Haybridge,' said Tilly reasonably.

'I know, but the name on the card is Rapunzel.'

'Rapunzel?' shrieked all three de Liege girls together.

Anna nodded. 'I know. Mad, isn't it? It isn't as if any of you live at the top of a tower, or have ridiculously long hair.'

'Well bung them in a bucket of water for the time being and ring the florist to check they've been sent to the right address,' suggested Tilly.

She finished her breakfast, forgot about the odd bouquet and went downstairs to the estate office. She had a million things to do; for a start, all the contractors who were coming to clear up the grounds following the festival were due in very shortly and some of them would need quite specific instructions. She began to work, telephoning staff, issuing orders, sending emails, but her heart wasn't in it. Her mind was elsewhere – in the past in Ashley's bedroom, and he was playing for her. A memory that became even more vivid when through the open door she heard Hash Tag's music drifting down-stairs from the twins' room. It was that tune again – that one Ashley had serenaded her with all those years ago. She stopped work and listened to the words again.

> She is the girl with the money and power,
> She's the girl up there in tower . . .

Once again she felt that sense of connection with the song.

No, don't be stupid, you're just indulging in wishful thinking, she told herself sharply. Of course Ashley hadn't written the song about her. He'd made it perfectly plain that Christmas that he wanted nothing more to do with her. The blanked phone calls, the unanswered texts – and then yesterday, when he hadn't even come to see her, when he must have known she'd have been there. How much clearer could it be?

She walked across the office and slammed the door, shutting the music out, and made herself concentrate on her work. By lunchtime she'd done most of what needed doing. The contractors were beavering away, the grounds were slowly being cleared, she'd written a dozen thank-you letters, made up even more invoices and there wasn't much more she could do for the time being. She threw her pencil on her desk and flexed her shoulders. Now what?

Lottie was in the care of her childminder, the twins were happy in their bedroom dreaming about their recent encounters with rock stars and God only knew what her father was up to, but he was old enough and ugly enough not to need his daughter to look after him. She was free to do whatever she liked; besides, she'd worked quite hard enough over the last few weeks to earn some free time.

She stood up and stretched. A walk would be good. A glance out of the window confirmed that the weather was glorious, so why not? She made her way through to the back door and grabbed a floppy straw hat, which she crammed on her head, bunging on a pair of sunglasses for good measure. Since the scandal involving Marcus she'd found herself frequently recognised by locals and visitors to the Manor – being incognito was something she now had to actively work at.

She let herself out of the house and allowed her feet take her down the main avenue. Maybe she'd have a look at the river. But she crossed it without even being aware of it, and then almost before she knew it she was past the bookie's shop and at the end of the high street. If she took the road to the left she'd find herself at the rec sooner or later. She hadn't been there for years – the closest she'd been had been whizzing past it in her car as she'd travelled round the ring road. She wondered if the old place was the same.

She drifted down the street, past the rows of terraced houses, until she came to the point where it joined the ring road, and there was the crossing to the park. She waited for the traffic to stop and took herself across. To all intents and purposes nothing had changed since she'd met Ashley there the day he'd broken his arm. The day she'd known there was something special about this boy who was crap at skateboarding.

She sat on the bare metal bench in front of the skate ramp and stared at the scene. Nearby a gang of boys on skateboards and BMX bikes dared each other to try increasingly dodgy and dangerous tricks. Over by the swings a new batch of mothers were pushing another crop of toddlers back and forth. In the corner of the rec a bunch of girls were trying to look cool and sophisticated by puffing on a shared ciggie. No, the rec was the same; it was just everything else in her world that had changed.

The last time she'd sat here she'd still been a smoker – well, that had gone out of the window long ago. Then she'd been a teenager, a sixth-former; now she was married, abandoned and mother of Lottie. Ashley had been the kid from the council estate with a lousy sense of balance, a worse sense of self-preservation and a gift for playing the guitar; now he was a key member of a famous band and very possibly rich.

Back then they'd loved each other.

And now he hated her.

Tilly felt tears welling up again. Tears at the waste of it. At the loss. Tears of self-pity. Tears for what might have been.

She swiped her hand across her cheeks and sharply told herself to grow up. It was over. She'd made her bed, and although she knew it wasn't a bed of roses, it was still full of nasty prickly thorns. And she had no one to blame but herself.

'You came.'

Tilly's insides lurched. Ashley? No, she'd imagined it. It was just a case of wish fulfilment. But she didn't dare look up and really ruin the illusion. She stared at the ramps until she felt the bench rock slightly.

'You got my message.'

This wasn't in her head. This time Tilly turned and looked. Ashley, recognisable despite the baseball cap and dark glasses, was smiling at her. 'What message?' she said softly.

'The flowers. For Rapunzel.'

'Rapunzel?'

'You're the girl in the tower.'

'Me?'

'Who else?'

'But you hate me.'

'I'm not the person who married someone else,' Ashley responded quietly.

Tilly felt a stab of pain. Did he really think she'd chosen Marcus over him? But why wouldn't he? 'We need to talk. You need to know how it was.'

'Where? Neither of us is exactly anonymous these days.'

She stood up. 'We could go back to mine.' She remembered the last time she'd invited Ashley to her place, and his reaction. 'If you don't mind.'

'I'd love to.'

Not that either of them waited until they reached the Manor before they began swapping their own personal perspectives on the past: the misunderstood text and the lost phone being the first issues to be cleared up.

'Surely you didn't think I'd dump you by text?' said Tilly, horrified.

'Frankly, by then, having discovered the girl I was dating wasn't from next door but from some other planet, I wasn't sure that I knew the real you. I just thought I'd got you all wrong and you really were capable of such a thing. I mean, how else do you interpret a text that says that you were sorry but it was over.'

'No, I didn't.'

'I know what I read, Tilly. Before my phone disappeared into the Haybridge sewage system I read "I'm sorry, Ashley, but it's over".'

'You couldn't have done; that wasn't what I wrote. Honest. The message I sent you was quite long, because I wanted you to be sure of exactly how I felt about you.' Ashley looked puzzled. 'Listen,' she said, 'I read it over and over after I'd sent it to try to work out why you didn't reply, to see if there was something in it that might have upset you even more. But there couldn't have been, because what I sent was "I'm sorry, Ashley, but it's over stupid rows like ours that people fall out".' She stopped. 'Oh shit.'

'Oh shit what?'

'Oh Ashley, you only read the first bit of the first sentence.'

'Shit, no.'

'Shit, *yes*.' Tilly shook her head ruefully and sighed. 'Well that explains quite a lot. And then in the Easter holidays I went to your house, but you'd moved.'

'And I went to yours and I couldn't find a way in.'

They both started to laugh.

'Jeez,' said Tilly after a little while. 'Were we just dumb or unlucky?'

'Both, I guess.' Ashley got serious. 'I read about your wedding.' He shook his head. 'Why, Tilly? You were only eighteen, for God's sake.'

'It was a disaster – almost from the start. I did it for all the wrong reasons, and love certainly didn't enter into it. You know, even while I was standing at the altar I was thinking about you. I knew it was a mistake, I knew I didn't really love Marcus. I knew I loved someone else.' She let the last sentence hang in the air for a second or two, staring into Ashley's eyes

'So why on earth . . . ?' His bewilderment was plain.

'I was pregnant and Marcus was the father. It was a stupid one-night stand and an even stupider idea to marry him.' She sighed and decided to come completely clean. Look what had happened before when she'd indulged in half-truths. 'And I married him for money.'

Ashley stopped dead in his tracks. 'You're kidding.'

'No. I suppose you really despise me now. But – and I know you don't believe me – my family was totally skint and Marcus wanted to be connected with a family who had a bit of a lineage. I wanted an abortion but his dad and my parents persuaded me there was a better way.' She shrugged. 'Yeah, well . . . You read the rest of the story about Marcus in the papers, so we're back to square one – well, almost; at least we got a load of repairs done before it all went tits up – which is why we have to think of ways to make money, like running a pop festival.'

They had crossed the bridge over the Hay and were almost at the big gates at the end of the avenue.

'In a way, I'm glad. If that hadn't all happened I wouldn't have got a chance to play the gig here and meet you. Although I thought I'd see you yesterday. I thought you'd search me out. When you didn't, I left as soon as I could because I thought you still hadn't forgiven me for what I said all those years ago. Luckily the people I'm staying with here – a couple I owe almost everything to – told me to make a proper effort to make contact. I guess I owe them even more now.'

Tilly shook her head in embarrassment as she admitted her ignorance about the rock scene. 'I had no idea that you were a part of Hash Tag. But my sisters are mad about you. They've both bought the album.'

'Thank God I've got at least two fans! So what made you come here today?'

Tilly confessed to feeling a connection with the song. 'And then, I guess, fate just took over. Perhaps it decided to give us a break, having done so many crappy things to us all those years ago.'

'Tilly, I know this sounds corny, but I don't think a day has passed when I haven't thought about you, wondered if you were happy. I worried so much about you when there was that problem with your husband, but then you and your family just disappeared off the radar again. I nearly got in touch, but I thought if you still hated me for all those awful things I said to you then I'd just be adding to your troubles.'

'I never hated you, Ashley,' she said quietly. 'I blamed myself for not levelling with you at the start. I could never hate you. All I've ever felt for you is love.'

They'd reached the gatehouse. Tilly reached into the ivy and parted it to reveal a keypad. She punched in a number and then opened the lychgate in the huge wooden doors. As she did so she felt a huge sense of rightness, as though the house approved of the person she was bringing home. Maybe her ancestors, those stone knights in the chapel, were watching over her and trying to tell her something.

She was about to step over the sill when Ashley stopped her. 'Just a minute,' he said and pulled her into his arms. 'I've been dreaming about doing this again for five years.'

Then he kissed her. And Tilly fell totally in love all over again.

Pick up a *little black dress* – it's a girl thing.

I DO, I DO, I DO
Samantha Scott-Jeffries
£5.99

Izzy Mistry has a boss from hell and a boyfriend so elusive he's almost non-existent – life's looking pretty drab. What's a girl to do? Six months as a wedding planner in Majorca could be the answer. But when love is in the air, things don't always go the way you plan . . .

978 0 7553 5282 1

ABOUT TIME
Niamh Shaw
£5.99

Why is Lara so nervous about moving to New York with boyfriend Barry? Of course, there *is* the small matter of forgetting about socially inept super-geek Conn, who has an annoying habit of making repeat appearances in her love life. It's about time she put the past behind her. Although that's easier said than done . . .

978 0 7553 4857 2

You can buy any of these other
Little Black Dress titles from your
bookshop or *direct from the publisher*.

FREE P&P AND UK DELIVERY
(Overseas and Ireland £3.50 per book)

Nina Jones and the Temple of Gloom	Julie Cohen	£5.99
Improper Relations	Janet Mullany	£5.99
Bittersweet	Sarah Monk	£5.99
The Death of Bridezilla	Laurie Brown	£5.99
Crystal Clear	Nell Dixon	£5.99
Talk of the Town	Suzanne Macpherson	£5.99
A Date in Your Diary	Jules Stanbridge	£5.99
The Hen Night Prophecies: Eastern Promise	Jessica Fox	£5.99
The Bachelor and Spinster Ball	Janet Gover	£5.99
A Romantic Getaway	Sarah Monk	£5.99
Trick or Treat	Sally Anne Morris	£5.99
Blue Remembered Heels	Nell Dixon	£5.99
Handbags and Homicide	Dorothy Howell	£5.99
Heartless	Alison Gaylin	£5.99
Animal Instincts	Nell Dixon	£5.99
I Do, I Do, I Do	Samantha Scott-Jeffries	£5.99
A Most Lamentable Comedy	Janet Mullany	£5.99
Shoulder Bags and Shootings	Dorothy Howell	£5.99
Perfect Image	Marisa Heath	£5.99
Girl From Mars	Julie Cohen	£5.99

TO ORDER SIMPLY CALL THIS NUMBER

01235 400 414

or visit our website: www.headline.co.uk

Prices and availability subject to change without notice.